HIDDEN SECRETS

WENDY CHARLTON

HIDDEN SECRETS

This book is a work of fiction. Names, characters, places, and incidents are either the product of the authors imagination, or are used fictitiously. Any resemblance to actual persons, living or dead, events or locales is entirely coincidental.

For more information, email
wendy@wendycharlton.co.uk

This paperback edition October 2022
ISBN: 9798356595059

In loving memory of Ada Cottrell (Nee Hale)

The funniest and fiercest women I ever drank with.

Table of Contents

Acknowledgements

With thanks to David Turner for the background on serving in Ireland during the troubles and (the amazing) Graham Cadd, for his backgammon knowledge.
As always, grateful thanks to Andrew Garcarz for his contributions.

Prologue:

5th October 1968 – 3.30pm
Londonderry

Colm Devey was just thirteen the day his father died. He was angry that his mother had forbidden him to go to the rally, after all, he was not a little kid any more. So he left the house anyway, and watched from the end of Spencer Street as the conflict erupted.

The road was soon littered with the detritus of a running battle. Bricks, bottles, and bits of wood were strewn across the road and lined the gutters. Men in their working clothes throwing stones were no match for the uniformed officers of the Royal Ulster Constabulary, armed with batons and riot shields. They outnumbered the protesters three to one. Colm stood terrified and helpless as the uniforms formed a cordon and charged into the protesters. As the smoke from the tear gas cleared, he saw his father: A Police officer was attacking him. The first blow dropped him to his knees, two others joined in, beating him around the head. His Da collapsed to the ground, not moving. The attack was over in seconds, but to Colm it seemed to last forever.

In shock, Colm ran towards him, he had to get to him, to get help. He saw their priest Father Gibbons and his Da's best friend Jon Jo Callaghan on the edge of the crowd and shouted to them. The panic in his voice cut through the racket as they both looked at him, sensing his distress. They rushed to his father, picking him up and carrying him to the relative safety of a side alley. The priest was frantically waving a white handkerchief, hoping it would be enough to ward off another onslaught. Colm had felt like a coward, just standing, watching, unable to go to his fathers' aid. Now, as he cradled his Da's battered head, all he felt was the warm, sticky blood on his hands.

It seemed like an eternity until the ambulance got to them. It had bravely battled its way through the chaos, those still fighting were completely oblivious to the urgency of the blue flashing lights. The medics seemed strangely unaffected by his father's condition as they loaded him onto a stretcher, they were concerned for their own safety. Someone had fetched his mother, who, it seemed to Colm, had aged a great deal in the thirty minutes since he'd last seen her. She climbed into the back of the ambulance with his Da, but before they closed the doors, she said,

"Colm, go home and look after Sinead, she's next door at Aunty Eileen's. I'll be home as soon as I can."

He watched the ambulance navigate the chaos until it disappeared. Jon Jo placed his hand on Colm's shoulder.

"Let's go home and see what Sinead's been up to. Your Da will be fine, don't worry." But he didn't sound very convincing. His Da wasn't fine. He never recovered consciousness and died less than a month later.

Guilt overwhelmed Colm's soul. He'd done nothing to prevent his father's murder. The sense of injustice was crushing him. He vowed that never again would he be so powerless, and that he would seek revenge on those who did this terrible thing, they would pay! He would become someone who set the rules rather than just followed them. And although he didn't realise it then, on that tragic day he became the head of the family. That was just the beginning for Colm Devey.

Chapter 1:

Friday 19th July 2019 – 2.30pm
Somewhere over the Atlantic Ocean

CIA Special Agent Phil Santos relaxed into the comfortable cream leather seat that was wider and infinitely more comfortable than those on charter flights. He took a sip of hot black coffee, served to him on this occasion by the perky Zoe, an in-flight attendant with a fizzing personality and a playful sparkle in her jade green eyes. Santos was medium height, slim build with short cropped, fair hair and an olive complexion. Not conventionally handsome, but with a degree of personal confidence that rendered him attractive to women.

He was heading to London in a CIA operated Gulfstream G650 jet to meet with the newly appointed

Director General of the British Secret Service, Daniel Grant. A man whose company he'd enjoyed on the missions they'd worked. Phil was eagerly awaiting to catch up with Daniel over a bottle of Jack Daniel's and perhaps some hot barbecued ribs.

He had spent the last thirty-six hours travelling; a flight back from Bogotá where he had led a taskforce investigating the murder of five US citizens in a bombing that had also killed the Colombian President, then straight on to Langley to discuss the disturbing link to the UK they had uncovered, now he was on his way to London.

Santos had worked with the Brits on several missions during his career and had spent some time in the late nineties in Northern Ireland when his President, Bill Clinton, made a state visit to help broker the peace agreement. That seemed like a lifetime ago and yet here he was, focused on the dossier in front of him, re-familiarising himself with the background, names, and current whereabouts of people he had almost forgotten. His boss Bruno Gomes had given it to him as a refresher on the Good Friday Agreement. It had been compiled by State and the CIA's political research team and would probably tell him stuff he already knew. As he read it, he thought he could have done a more thorough job just from memory, but that was not what he was going to London for.

He turned the first page and read:

EYES ONLY: RESTRICTED CONFIDENTIAL

1: EXECUTIVE SUMMARY

There are four things that are important to understand about the Good Friday Agreement:

1. *The IRA and later Sinn Féin, were mainly funded through a US-based organisation called NORAID, (later used by Clinton to apply financial pressure on Sinn Féin).*
2. *The population of Ireland (North and South) voted overwhelmingly in favour of the creation of a United Ireland.*
3. *The Irish Assembly was established in Northern Ireland (Stormont), where some former ex-IRA members, now Sinn Féin politicians sat as Ministers*
4. *Approximately 100 IRA fugitives, believed to be responsible for up to 300 deaths were given "letters of comfort" from the UK government stating they were no longer wanted for past crimes.*

2: HISTORICAL PERSPECTIVE

In February 1972, horrific bombing campaigns took place in Northern Ireland in retaliation to Bloody Sunday, after Royal Ulster Constabulary officers killed 28 unarmed civilian protesters in the Bogside area of Derry. The campaign then turned to mainland Britain, with attacks on military targets and high-profile locations, such

as the Houses of Parliament, 10 Downing Street, Oxford Street, Harrod's, Hyde Park and Regent's Park.
The Provisional IRA (PIRA) and the Irish National Liberation Army (INLA) assassinated prominent British figures, most notably Lord Louis Mountbatten; Former MI9 commanding officer and shadow Secretary of State for Northern Ireland, Airey Neave, and Tory MP Ian Gow.

They also attempted to kill Prime Minister Margaret Thatcher and her cabinet at the Conservative Party conference in the infamous Brighton Hotel Bombing. Thatcher narrowly escaped the blast, but five people were killed, including a Conservative Member of Parliament Sir Anthony Berry, 31 others were injured.

In total, the Provisional IRA's mainland campaign claimed the lives of 175 people, injured more than 10,000 and caused property damage exceeding one billion pounds.

3: US INVOLVEMENT

NORAID, officially the Irish Northern Aid Committee, was founded in 1969. Their purpose was to aid in the creation of a United Ireland and support the Northern Ireland Peace process. NORAID was known for raising funds for the Provisional Irish Republican Army and other Nationalist community groups.

> *In 1994, Under the Clinton administration, Sinn Féin was delisted as a terrorist organisation by the US State Department and NORAID became openly supportive of the peace process and the subsequent Good Friday Agreement.*
> *President Clinton was keen to support the UK Government to affect a Peace Agreement and appointed George Mitchell as Special Envoy for Northern Ireland to support the Northern Ireland Peace Process.*
>
> *In 1995, President Clinton visited Northern Ireland, holding personal meetings with leaders from Sinn Féin to encourage participation in the ceasefire and disarmament of the IRA brigades.*

Phil remembered that trip vividly. He was assigned to the President's security detail and recalled the lengths the British Government took to distance themselves from this formal acknowledgement. He smiled when he remembered the endless phone calls, trying to dissuade Clinton from a public meeting, and the customary handshake with those present. At the request of his President, Phil had surreptitiously engaged an independent photographer and a video camera operator to record the momentous event just in case the British tried to block the publication of the images. It was a great success.

He returned to the summary:

On 10 April 1998, a deal was reached, bringing to an end the Northern Ireland 'Troubles', with a Multi-Party Agreement known as the Good Friday Agreement.

The peace process sought to reconcile two different traditions in Ireland establishing a lasting end to hostilities, provide pardons for some key players and construct of a path to a safe, devolved, self-governing Island of Ireland, when the time was right.

4: LEGACY

The legacy of the Agreement was that elections to the Assembly in Northern Ireland took place and the Assembly sat. The Commission on Policing transferred all IRA members detained in British prisons back to Ireland.

In a secret scheme negotiated as part of the process, the UK government gave nearly 100 IRA fugitives "letters of comfort", stating they were no longer wanted for past crimes. They were suspects in nearly 300 murder cases. This immediately angered Unionists, calling the 'Comfort letters' the "get-out-of-jail free" scheme. The key people on the negotiating team responsible for drawing up the list were Colm Devey, Peter Adams, and Martin Downey.

The details of the comfort letters were only exposed during the collapse of the prosecution relating to the 1982 Marble Arch bomb, which killed five

> *British soldiers, when the suspect's legal team produced such a letter from 2007, which suggested he would not be prosecuted.*

Phil closed the folder and reflected on the critical success factors that those compiling the dossier had not been party to. It had been the categoric ultimatum delivered by the US that their funding would stop within a month unless Sinn Féin agreed to attend and see the negotiations through. They would not survive without that money, so had no choice but to agree. The political solution would be one that delivered peace, and leaders of Sinn Féin would have to ensure that the IRA complied. Phil was sad that the nature of the special relationship between the two great nations was not fully appreciated by the general public. America had yet again, come to the rescue.

If he was honest, he thought that that would be the end of it, but the Colombia assassination had thrown a spanner into the works.

The CIA had uncovered hard evidence that the explosives used in the assassination of the President were from an undisclosed IRA weapons cache, and that a key republican figure might be implicated. To add to the problem, he had heard on the grapevine that the Brits were about to bring in a high-ranking IRA Supergrass, someone who knew where the bodies were buried.

He felt caught on the horns of a dilemma. He hoped that Daniel could shed some light on his case, but his orders were to keep the information he had close to his chest and find out exactly what the British already knew about his target.

Zoe appeared as if by magic, “Can I get you more coffee Sir, or perhaps you’d like something more… stimulating?” she purred and raised her eyebrows quizzically.

Phil held out his mug, “er, sorry, just coffee this time I’m afraid”, and wondered how long before they landed at London City airport.

Chapter 2:

Saturday 20th July 2019 – 8pm

Thames House, London

The Director General of British Security Services Daniel Grant breathed a sigh of relief as the Secretary of State for Northern Ireland left his office. This was the aspect of his job that he disliked the most. He understood the politics even if he didn't necessarily agree with them, but it was his job to ensure that policy was implemented into practice. Though, if he was honest, he struggled to come to terms with the endless procession of politicians who saw the world as just black and white, a two-dimensional space where their decisions had no lasting consequence. In Daniel's experience, policy was when you know everything, but nothing works, and practice was when everything works, but no one is quite sure why.

The end of the Cold War had set in motion a profound re-examination of the clandestine nature of national security methods. The very idea that the details of what they did in secret was a subject for public discussion, robbed it of a high degree of its effectiveness. The domestic and international arenas that his people operated in were now the source of constant public debate and media scrutiny, which made information sharing and collaboration with counterparts across the world profoundly difficult. It simply didn't work unless everyone played by the same rules, and Daniel knew that nothing could be further from the truth. The reality was that when politicians decided to turn enemies into allies overnight, it never ended well. They didn't invest the time or resources to bring people on board with their thinking. And Daniel knew from experience that hearts and minds drove religious conflicts, bombs, and bullets were merely the tools of the trade. The people he wanted to catch held an overwhelming sense of injustice and a deep passion that drove them to commit their acts of terrorism. Organised crime was driven by money, a transitory motivator, but ideology was much more dangerous, it was an intense and lasting motivator.

His conversation with the Minister had centred around the critical nature of the Good Friday Agreement and how nothing could be allowed to put it at risk. What the Minister and his predecessors had failed to appreciate was that the intelligence community had spent the last twenty years managing the fallout from that watershed agreement. It was solely down to the activities of his teams that the troubles had not been reactivated by the disenfranchised and disgruntled players that the Agreement had left behind. The political figures had won the public battle one press conference at a time, but the guerilla war still smouldered just beneath the surface and could be ignited by the smallest spark.

The recent news that they had been approached by an ex-IRA hitman who wanted to share what he knew, was about as welcome as a hole in a lifeboat. Daniel had given the Minister his assurance that the intel' this man could provide would bring down one of the biggest and most vicious crime cartels operating in Europe. The Minister had been less than impressed. Whilst agreeing in principle about the value of such an asset, he had emphasised caution regarding any information that might surface relating to historic IRA crimes. He had been quite emphatic that any such information must be bought to his attention immediately, before any action was taken by the security services. The irony was that for decades, Daniel had run an agent close to the top of the IRA and later within Sinn Féin without the knowledge or permission of politicians. The 'intel' he received from him had prevented numerous bombings and saved countless lives. This minister, whose exposure to fear was limited to being grilled on BBC's Question Time, was lecturing Daniel on the sensitivity of intelligence. It really was laughable.

He imagined the look on the Minister's face if he'd told him that the safe house they intended to hold their Supergrass at was actually a retirement home for ex MI5 and MI6 agents, called Shady Fields.

Most of the residents were elderly, some had memory problems, a few struggled with the ravages of Dementia and Alzheimer's that made them aggressive, and sometimes dangerous. The staff there were all highly trained operatives who dealt with difficult and sensitive situations every day. Their work required tact, diplomacy, and often, unarmed combat skills. In fact, only last week when he was at Shady Fields making preparations for his 'guest', he'd observed a 'personal care assistant' in action, speaking soothingly to an agitated resident,

"How about a nice cup of tea and some cake? But we will need to leave your crossbow here with Jonny, they don't allow weapons in the restaurant."

Shady Fields was not the most notable achievement of Daniel's long career, but strangely, it was the one he was most proud of.

There was a knock on his office door, it opened, and a familiar face appeared in the gap.

"OK to come in, or will I need a hard hat?" Mitch Bennett was forty-one, tall and powerfully built. He had wide-set piercingly blue eyes, a strong mouth, a nose that had been broken more than once and a scar that ran across his chin giving him a horizontal dimple. He had not been recruited through the Oxbridge universities like so many of his contemporaries, he had worked his way up through the service solely due to his intelligence and capability. Not only that but harboured a nagging feeling that others thought he was too young to be the Head of MI5, but Daniel had been clear, Mitchell was ready for this. The two men had history that went back a long way. Mitch had saved Daniel's life on his last mission, and the respect was professional, not sentimental. He took the glass of Jack Daniel's offered and sat down.

"I remembered: no ice. How are the preparations for 'Ragair' going?"

Mitch raised the cut-crystal glass to his lips and drained the single measure in one. "Everything's on track; we're lifting him tomorrow morning in Dublin, shipping him back on a charter flight into RAF Northolt then onto a holding pen for the initial debrief. Because we can't be a hundred percent sure, there's no leak, we've decided to bring him directly to London, but we won't move him to Shady Fields until later in the week. I've got Marina Kinskey running point on the interviews, her psychology background and profiling skills will be invaluable."

"Could you do with an extra pair of hands?" Mitch's interest was piqued.

"Who do you have in mind?"

"I've had an offer from the CIA. Phil Santos, their US/Irish expert. He's an excellent agent and well aware of the history."

Mitch nodded in agreement. "They say never look a gift horse in the mouth, although it's unlike the Americans to be so helpful. What's in it for them?"

"Not sure, but I'm not asking too many questions at this stage, it's a good offer of help, so I've already accepted on your behalf. I've worked with Santos a couple of times in the past. He's just back from Colombia, the CIA have been assisting with the investigation into the Assassination of the Colombian President."

Daniel raised his glass to see if he could tempt Mitch to another, but Mitch declined the offer.

"How's Marina shaping up, Mitch?"

"She's taken to us like the proverbial duck to water. Exceptionally bright, but quite understated, with a very cool head and good profiling skills. I like her!" Mitch placed his empty glass on the edge of Daniel's desk.

There was a pause in conversation as Daniel stood and stretched. "The ripples of this are spreading, Mitch, and it is making some people very nervous. We're under strict instruction not to overstretch the brief. We have to focus solely on 'Ragair's' organised crime links, we can't stray into historical incidents or missions. His deal is based on the intelligence he can give us on the Albanians, in particular, Yilmaz and his trafficking, drugs and arms operations. I want you to report any intelligence he might offer up, which is outside that remit, directly and only to me. Keep documentation to a bare minimum, this needs to be done on an eyes-only basis."

"Yes, I understand, Daniel. But what happens if he does give us something that's a game changer?"

Daniel was obviously irritated, "We'll cross that bridge when we come to it. There are people he was involved with who've had their pasts cleansed by the agreement. It's remarkable how a terrorist turned politician can become very judgmental about the illegal activities of others. The difficulty is that when you open closet doors, skeletons have a nasty habit of falling out, and as George Bernard Shaw said, if you can't stop them falling out, you better teach them to dance."

Mitch smiled as a thought struck him. "You know we've received a request from the Northern Ireland Executive wanting to be kept up to date with any information he provides. They were insisting that Special Branch should handle the interrogation, but we think that's because they have an insider in the department, maybe more than one. We certainly ruffled feathers when we refused their demands and took over the operation directly. Some of them are close to the Deputy First minister, Colm Devey, and the Executive leadership. They were seriously pissed-off when we took control of the extraction and debrief, so now they're being pedantic about procedure and pressuring us to be as cooperative as possible."

Daniel smiled, "Oh dear, what a shame, never mind. Do I need to have a word?"

Mitch shrugged, "I can handle it. I'll feed them enough to keep them pacified, but I don't trust the relationship with Stormont. It is almost certain that Ragair's colourful past will be directly linked to several sitting representatives, and we don't know what lengths they might go to, to prevent him from sharing information. It's possible that some of them could be implicated, and under the terms of the Good Friday Agreement, they only receive immunity from prosecution on existing evidence. If new information were to come to light, it might prove very difficult for some."

Daniel remembered the time he spent in Northern Ireland in the eighties, he knew how ruthless the key figures had been.

"The problem we have, Mitch, is the system we work with is seriously flawed. The political solution turned domestic terrorists into politicians overnight. They may not have been directly involved in bombings or punishment beatings, but their nearest and dearest were, so they will want to do everything in their power to keep their activities hidden, we are going to have to tread very lightly, is that understood?"

Mitch stood up to leave the room. He grinned, "Of course. I can be subtle when I need to be."

"Yeah. About as subtle as a hippopotamus in a fish-pond." But he said it to a closing door

Chapter 3:

Friday 19th July 2019.
Ingleby, Derbyshire

Hilary Geddes felt guilty about being away from her job. Her position as the CEO of Shady Fields carried a lot of responsibility, but in fairness, she did have good reason. She had recently organised her mother's funeral, which had gone off without a hitch last week. This week, her focus was her Aunt Ada, whose health was deteriorating fast. Ada was currently in St. Mary's hospital and would be transferred to Shady Fields by private ambulance early next week. She wanted Hilary to pick up a few things from her cottage. Hilary now realised that it was infinitely more difficult to complete her aunt's request than attending her mother's

funeral. This would probably be one of the last things she could do for her.
So now, on Friday, just a couple of days after the funeral, Hilary was heading north out of London. She felt the tension of the last few weeks start to ease, but she knew a different sort of emotion would soon replace it.

Ingleby, in the Derbyshire Dales, was mentioned in the Doomsday Book. Although not much more than a hamlet, it was famous for providing shelter for the Anchorites in the 12th Century. When Hilary was a little girl, her aunt would take her to look at the Anchorite dwellings at least once during their holidays. They often had lively discussions about what it would be like to give up all contact with society and live a life completely devoted to worship. Hilary had a strange fascination for the stories, but Ada was very disparaging about their way of life. She insisted that if the devil did indeed make work for idle hands, he would have been rushed off his feet with the Anchorites!

Growing up, Hilary had known nothing of Ada's history. Ada had always been there for her in a way that her mother had not. Hilary smiled to herself and turned on the radio. Smooth FM, the automobile equivalent of elevator muzak, oozed from the cars' speakers.

Ada's cottage was located at the end of a quiet country lane, surrounded by long-established trees and mature shrubs. Hilary drove through the open gate and parked in front of the garage. She got out and took a deep breath. By comparison to London, the air here was clean and fresh, with an earthy smell that was somehow reassuring. A familiar calm descended. She always experienced that when she came here.

The ‘cottage’ was actually a sturdy Georgian building that she’d lived in for more than forty years. It had been modernised to make it practical and comfortable. The wooden panelled front door was painted heritage green and decorated with a huge wreath-shaped wrought-iron door knocker. A spare key was hidden in a key-safe disguised as a rounded stone, concealed in the rockery to the left of the house. Hilary retrieved the key, let herself in, and picked up the mail from the door mat.

There was a strong sense of continuity for her in this place. Her Mother’s house didn’t have as much as an echo of Hilary in any of the rooms. It was all her mother, the decor, the history, the money.

Ada’s home was entirely different. There were signs everywhere that Hilary had lived here. Her walking boots were still under the coat stand where her green wax-jacket hung.

She walked along the hall and into the kitchen. Bright sunshine flooded through the windows, washing the tiled floor with comforting warm light. But today there were no familiar baking smells, just a neat and tidy work area with the collection of old recipe books, painted jugs and of course, a well-stocked wine rack under the counter.

It had been a long drive, so Hilary switched on the coffee maker while she fished the list of Ada's requirements from her handbag. As she climbed the steep stairs to Ada's bedroom, her mind filled with memories and reflections from the past. She crossed the polished floorboards and opened the burr walnut veneer doors of the armoire. Her aunt's familiar fragrance wafted out. She had worn Phenalgin's 'Artemisia' for as long as Hilary could remember. The subtle under notes of vanilla and peaches were ever present.

She swallowed hard, took the small, wheeled, overnight case down from the top of the wardrobe and began to fill it with her aunt's things, clothes, some lingerie, and toiletries, a couple of books from her bedside table, her small leather jewellery box from the linen press in the corner and her writing case from the table under the window.

Hilary suddenly felt overwhelmed by the finality of it all. She sat down heavily on the chintz nursing chair, as though the wind had suddenly been knocked out of her. She had begun to notice small but telltale signs of the illness when she visited Ada at Christmas, but had deluded herself into thinking that it was simply Ada taking a little longer to recover from her surgery. The breathlessness, the reduced appetite, the extra cushions on her chair in the living room. She couldn't understand why Ada hadn't said something about it then.

Hilary felt a pang of guilt. She should have insisted, made her have a rest in the afternoon……. Unexpectedly, she burst into a peal of laughter, imagining Ada's response if she'd even dared to suggest that she take it easy!

Hilary took her mobile phone out of her pocket and pressed the speed dial for Ada.

Ada picked up after the second ring. Her familiar telephone voice was there, but softer.

"You're at the cottage, then?"

Hilary opened her mouth to speak, but all that came out was a gut-wrenching sob.

"Come on Hils. Let's have none of that!"

Hilary took a deep breath and composed herself. "I got here about half an hour ago. Why didn't you tell me how bad things were? You never said anything. I could have helped, done something."

"You did" said Ada. "Didn't we have a lovely Christmas? Binge-watching the Thin Man films, the Fortnum and Masons hamper, the excellent Tanqueray Gin, and the walk by the river on Boxing Day". There was a slight pause as these memories flickered through Hilary's mind. Ada spoke again. "How did the funeral go? I was sorry I couldn't be there. She was my little sister, even if we didn't always see eye to eye."

Hilary thought she heard a catch in Ada's voice but couldn't be certain.

"It was fine as funerals go. Uncle Aubrey was great and virtually hosted the wake. He sends his best wishes by the way. The car is picking you up on Tuesday, about 2.30pm. Will that be OK?"

"Yes that's fine. I'm really looking forward to seeing you, and please Hilary, no special treatment. You have a job to do, and I do not expect you to spend all of your time with me!"

Hilary jumped in, "Yes, I get it, but I've arranged to stay at Shady Fields for a few nights just while you settle in. We can have dinner and breakfast together if you like?" She quickly changed the subject to prevent Ada from protesting. "Are you OK there? What's the food like?"

Ada replied with her customary dry wit, "It's terrible! You know, on reflection, I think I would rather be shot than poisoned."

Hilary smiled, "You asked for your silver pen and spare reading glasses, but I can't see them in the bedroom, any ideas where they might be?"

"Yes, they will be in the library. Can you also bring my grey case with you, the square one with the Bahrain label on the side"? It's in the window seat. Ada sounded breathless.

"Are you OK?" Hilary felt her concern rising.

"Yes I'm fine. Don't fuss, I'll see you next week, Hils. Thanks for doing this for me." And with that, she was gone.

Hilary ended the call and tears began to flow. She didn't think it strange that she felt more grief for Ada than for her mother's passing. The thought of losing Ada was devastating. She had been her rock, her confidante, her confessor, and her best friend.

It was Ada that had helped to develop her intellect, her values, and her principles. Hilary's desire to have a meaningful career based more on altruism than commercial gain came directly from Ada. It was she that had encouraged her to apply for a place at Newnham College. Not because Germaine Greer had studied there (though her mother had been thrilled), but because they taught women how to be trouble in the most productive way. It even said so in their literature!

When Hilary gained her Degree, Ada had questioned her choice of a Civil Service career. She had come up with something about wanting to give something back and talked about taking on the Government machine. The young idealist in her envisaged how she would be the grit in the system, bringing about real change and genuinely improving people's lives. Ada had smiled knowingly and urged caution, but her warnings fell on deaf ears. With hindsight, Ada had been right as usual. She had been too small a fish in too big a pond to make change happen. It wasn't until she came to Shady Fields that she genuinely felt she was making a difference.

She went back down to the kitchen with Ada's things and poured strong black coffee into the hand-painted Emma Bridgewater mug that bore the legend 'Little Star' that Ada had bought her as a stocking filler.

She took it through to the library with her. The cottage wasn't huge, but it did have a library. During the renovations, Ada had paid a local craftsman to line the old parlour walls with floor-to-ceiling bookshelves of honeyed oak. This was the room of a book lover. The distinctive smell of smokiness, old paper, and leather. Some of Hilary's childhood books and trinkets were in a glass fronted cabinet to the side of the fireplace. The two well-used classic Eames chairs in caramel coloured leather with matching footstools did not look out of place.

She quickly spotted Ada's glasses and pen, then moved across to the window seat. She removed the worn seat cushion, noticing that the piping on the edge was just beginning to fray. The hinged wooden lid of the seat concealed the case in the space below. Hilary took it out, closed the lid and replaced the cushion.

It was strange, but in all the years she had visited Ada, she could not remember seeing this case before. Hilary tried the catch, but it was locked.

A wave of loneliness and grief hit her again, she knew that she faced a future without her best friend, and she felt desolate. Obviously, Ada had known of her illness for a long time but hadn't said anything. She recalled one of their final conversations here in this room. They had talked about death. They had discussed whether people should have the right to decide the timing of their own death. When Ada had asked her to be her

Lasting Power of Attorney, Hilary had tried to dismiss it with the usual platitude

"You will outlive us all. There's plenty of time for that.'

But Ada had been adamant. "We never know what fate has in store for us. I have never been a burden to anyone, and I would rather not start now!"

A living will had been drawn up and registered. It stipulated that a non-resuscitation order was to be put in place. It was clear that Ada wanted the same level of control over her death that she had exercised all her life, and Hilary respected that, although she had not expected that it might be used this soon. Ada might be a frail eighty-seven, but her mental faculties were still as sharp as a pin.

Hilary cleaned the coffee filter and washed her mug under the tap. She took Ada's things and put them in the boot of her car. With a last look around the hall, she closed the door behind her. She had no idea when she would return. She replaced the key in the stone fake and placed it back in the rockery. Then, Hilary did what she always did. She took a deep breath, pushed her emotions deep down inside, and focused on the practical to-do list that was forming in her head.

On the drive back, she reflected on the conversation she'd had yesterday with her boss Daniel Grant in his office overlooking Vauxhall Bridge. She enjoyed the privileged position of reporting directly to him. They hadn't known each other that long, but the events of the last year meant they had gained a healthy respect for each other professionally, and an unspoken personal chemistry was slowly developing. Daniel was physically attractive and appeared younger than his forty-nine years. He radiated integrity and a passion that made you want to be in his presence. Hilary also knew that he was unmarried and that the woman he loved had been killed on a mission some years ago. That same mission resulted in him being shot and removed from active field work. He never spoke about it; she had gleaned those sparse details from Mitch.

Whilst discussing the status of her latest project with him, she noticed Daniel studying her with his intense blue eyes.

"This is the first time we will have used Shady Fields as a safe house, Hilary. Are you confident that everything is ready?"

"Yes. I've been working closely with Mitch and Marina on security. We have agreed that our 'guest's' presence will be on a need-to-know basis, meaning that the only contact he will have while he's with us will be with MI5 staff. They will be responsible for everything from serving his food to vetting visitors to Shady Fields. Even I don't know his real identity."

Daniel had nodded thoughtfully. "I can understand Mitch's caution. It will be safer for all concerned if no one knows where this asset is."

It sounded so straightforward as they discussed the details, but Hilary was well aware that it wasn't going to be quite that easy. Her other residents may be getting on in years and some of them were now experiencing memory problems, but they had been some of the best secret agents in their day. Many of them had a sixth sense for deception and an appetite for intrigue. Their training in surveillance and observation would tell them that something out-of-the-ordinary was happening. Her staff would need to take extra measures to ensure their guest retained his anonymity.

Chapter 4:

September 15th, 1993
Belfast

Colm had been a quick study. He knew what the effects of a kneecapping could be on those considering becoming a tout *(an informer)*, he also knew what the strategic results of a mainland car bombing would be. He understood that gratuitous violence was more for the pleasure of the perpetrator than justice for the guilty party, and he firmly believed that the end justified the means. It was these qualities which had propelled him through the ranks of the IRA. His success had been achieved because he was always two steps ahead of everyone else.

When he reflected on the pain and suffering, he had asked himself, “what was it all for?” Nothing had really changed. With his Da gone and his mother concentrating on making ends meet, he assumed responsibility for the family. The weight of that responsibility had made Colm a pragmatist.

On the face of it, he was the archetypal freedom fighter; an angry man flipping between revenge and revolution. Colm had willingly played a part in it, and yet deep down he knew it was not a lasting solution.

After his Da’s death, JJ Callaghan had become a father figure to him and his younger sister, Sinead. He was also his brigade commander and had protected Colm when needed because he understood his value to the cause. He recognised that Colm offered him an edge because they thought differently. In turn, Colm Had come to see JJ for what he really was, a common thug; he tolerated him because of the powerful position he held, but he was clear that he represented the past.

From their heated debates, Colm could see that JJ believed the bombing campaigns, punishment beatings and random murders would eventually work, and they would win independence for Ireland, but Colm understood the limitations of that approach.

It stood to reason that if true power lay with the political classes, then that's where a solution could be found. Many believed a peaceful solution was impossible, but he knew that given enough time, the British establishment (particularly their Labour sympathisers) would be anxious to repair the damage done and seek a peaceful way forward. It was a waiting game. In the end, it was about two things: power and being on the winning side.

He had wrestled with his conscience. Was it worth the risk he would be taking? It would be dangerous, maybe even life-threatening and to many he would be seen as the ultimate traitor if he were to be discovered, and yet he believed it was the only thing that made sense; it would be worth it if it produced a peaceful transition. The decision to become an MI5 informant was one he had struggled with briefly, but ultimately, there would be a winning side when a united Ireland was achieved, and he wanted to be on it!

It wasn't an ideal arrangement, the British paid very well, but they thought they owned him. He was the jewel in their crown, near to the top, close to the leadership and above reproach. He found it easy to manipulate those around him, and they were so wedded to the cause that they only saw what he wanted them to see.

He had been very detailed in his demands; a single handler that knew his identity, only ever referred to by a code-name (Ryder). He had negotiated regular payments into a numbered account in a private New York Bank. That was his escape route to the States if he was discovered. His contact had promised him that much.

So far, he had led a charmed existence. He was a year into the arrangement, and they had allowed him a couple of small victories that kept his cover firmly in place. He had developed a grudging respect for his handler, who had been true to his word and delivered everything in their agreement.

Obviously, MI5 agents didn't use their real names, they had a series of legends they used on assignments, but he knew that his handler's real name was Danny. It was the price he'd demanded to reassure him that both sides had skin in the game.

This latest development was a real concern. His secret and therefore his safety could be under threat. His sister Sinead was the problem. She wasn't wired like ordinary people. She had a passion for their cause and a hatred of the British that made her unquestioningly loyal but hugely unstable. She knew nothing of his double-life, and he needed it to stay that way. Earlier in the day, she had called him about Theresa Farrell, Dessie McFee's girlfriend. Dessie was their 'hit-man' and she hero-worshipped him. She was devastated when he started seeing Theresa. Her jealousy was palpable. She told him that one of their foot patrols had spotted Theresa coming out of a house that was known to be used by the British

Secret Service. It was a lodging house on the other side of the city, and there was no obvious explanation for her being there. For Sinead this was personal, she was stirring up bad feeling wherever she could, spouting conspiracy everywhere. Colm suspected there was more to it than that. Sinead felt that Theresa wasn't good enough for the great Dessie McFee and couldn't understand what he saw in her. Her feelings for him bordered on an adolescent crush. She had gone over Colm's head in taking her information straight to JJ because she knew he would also jump to the same conclusions that she had.

Colm parked his car on the hardcore at the back of the disused scout hut. It was shielded by a thicket of young trees that offered protection to anyone approaching the building or the playing fields. With some trepidation, he pushed open the door and stepped into the shadows to wait for Callaghan.

The autumn nights were drawing in, and it was still relatively mild, though rain was forecast, so he hoped Callaghan wouldn't keep him waiting too long. Within minutes, he heard the noise of car tires crunching along the uneven track.

Colm knew he had to tread carefully. JJ loved Dessie like a son, but if Theresa was collaborating with the British, he would order her execution without a second thought.

He heard the car door close and the sound of footsteps on the wooden deck outside. He opened the door, allowing Callaghan to enter.

"Evening Colm, what's going on with the girl?" Callaghan said abruptly.

There were to be no pleasantries then.

"I've got people out there confirming the story, but honestly I think there will be a simple explanation. I can't see Dessie not knowing his girlfriend's a tout, can you?"

Callaghan shook his head and replied,
"If you'd said that a year ago, I might have agreed with you, but something's changed with him. I think he might be losing his taste for the fight." He looked around for a seat, but the hut was empty, he continued, "Theresa's young, she comes from British stock, and we know that sympathisers are never as passionate about the cause as us. I also know that she's questioned Dessie's methods at times, but I thought he'd handled her, then out of the blue Sinead calls me and tells me what's happened, and you must admit, if they could turn her and put a tout at the heart of Belfast's most effective brigade it would be a hell of a feather in their cap. I need to know that it isn't just Sinead stirring up bad feeling, she looks up to Dessie, and she's jealous of Theresa. Honestly Colm, I don't have time for this. I need to find out the truth and take swift action."

Colm knew he had to nip this in the bud. "I'm really sorry about Sinead; you know what a hot head she can be sometimes. She should have come to me with this first rather than getting everyone riled up about it. Let me check it out, and I'll get back to you tomorrow."

Callaghan's brow furrowed and he shook his head. "No Colm, I don't want it to look like I'm going soft about this just because it's Dessie's girlfriend. I want you to pick her up and question her… tonight. Get to the bottom of it. I'll keep Dessie out of the way and if you find there's nothing to it, it will calm down soon enough. But if she's working with the British……. Then we need to make an example out of her. You'll have to get rid of her. I can't trust Dessie with this, I need someone objective. Sinead even asked me if she could do it, but I want this to be cut and dried, can you handle that?"

Colm paused for a few seconds then said, "Yes, no problem" and waited for his belief to catch up with his bravado.

Callaghan turned and left the building leaving Colm alone in the hut. He knew that he had to find Sinead. She was as mad as a wet cat and twice as unpredictable, had a vindictive streak a mile wide and always acted without thinking of the consequences. When her temper flared white-hot she was uncontrollable. Her viciousness deeply troubled Colm. True, it had served the cause well in the past, but it had also been a liability. When she was in a rage he was the only one who could reason with her, but sometimes even he failed.

She was probably out looking for Theresa right now and she wouldn't wait to be told what the plan was. Luckily she was a creature of habit so if she did find Theresa, she would definitely bring her here. All he had to do was wait.

Colm had put a message out to Danny to see if this was true; was Theresa working with them? He knew that Danny would never disclose the details of another agent to him. Who was he kidding, especially not to him! But he'd reasoned that the message itself might be enough for them to pull her out if she was working for them. He couldn't risk an interrogation in case she was MI5. She may even know about him, though his gut reaction was that she didn't have that much deception in her. He broke free from his thoughts and chastised himself, those sorts of assumptions were dangerous. The British might work with him but they sure as hell didn't trust him, and with good reason, he was playing both sides. It was the most dangerous game in town and every situation had to be weighed up on its merits. Predictable actions ended up with someone dying and Colm was adamant that it wasn't going to be him.

He waited almost an hour and was beginning to think that Sinead wasn't coming. Perhaps she hadn't found Theresa, or perhaps she had already found her and was conducting her own interrogation. What if she had decided Theresa was guilty and had taken things into her own hands, dishing out swift justice? It wouldn't be the first time. He decided to give her another five minutes and if she didn't appear he would have to find Theresa himself.

Then he heard the distinct noise of her van's engine labouring along the lane parallel to the field. He moved further back into the shadows to wait for his sister.

The van stopped outside the hut. The light was fading fast now, the encroaching darkness providing enough cover to ensure that no one would see any comings and goings. He heard Sinead open the van's rear doors and a scuffle follow. Sinead was swearing and cursing under her breath. Colm could make out a pitiful, whimpering sound. She had obviously found Theresa.

The hut door was flung wide open, and a shape stumbled and fell into the room. He couldn't recognise who it was, but he could not mistake that distinctive smell. His nostrils were filled with it, almost making him wretch; pitch-black, dark, and bitter. That acrid, smoky, oily scent, cloying at the back of his throat. His heart was racing.

"My God Sinead, what have you done?"

In the beam of moonlight that shone through the opening he saw a single white feather float silently to the floor.

Chapter 5:

Friday 19th July 2019 11.30am
Belfast

Where the hell is he then, Seamus?"

Jon Jo Callaghan was used to being in control and disliked this feeling of playing catch up. His patience was wearing thin. He stared straight ahead through the windscreen, a muscle in his jaw rippled as he ground his teeth.

The stationary Jaguar XJ6 they were sitting in should have felt comfortable. The air conditioning masked the humidity outside, but to Seamus Meehan it felt cold and threatening. He could feel the leather detailing of the seat through the thin fabric of his tracksuit pants. He didn't know whether it was this or being questioned by his boss that was making him feel so uncomfortable.

Why was he always the one that had to break the bad news? He felt the familiar wave of anxiety in the pit of his stomach. He was a solidly built man, a shade under six feet tall and a very dangerous man who could look after himself with his fists or a weapon and was feared by all. Yet, that didn't stop him feeling weak in Callaghan's presence. The first time he'd done Callaghan's bidding and killed someone was indelibly etched on his memory. There was a matter-of-factness about the way he had been ordered to murder a man who had wronged his boss. Mr. Callaghan was cold, calculating and without any empathy; all wrapped up in his signature camel coat. What Mr. Callaghan wanted, he got! Seamus was acutely aware of the cost of failure. He had personally buried three men who had disappointed Callaghan, he wanted to avoid being number four.

Seamus felt his heartbeat quicken at the thought of their quarry. Dessie McFee had originally been the one who administered the ultimate punishment when people needed to disappear. He was an Irish republican who had been with Callaghan for three decades. Throughout the troubles they had been together. Callaghan had been the Brigade Commander and McFee had been his Lieutenant. These men were still a powerful pair even though the troubles had ended nearly twenty years ago. Callaghan had created a criminal enterprise that was known across Europe and McFee was the 'security'.

Seamus had known them both all his life. He knew what they were capable of, so he did as he was told and asked no questions.

He suddenly realised his boss was still waiting for his answer. “Er, I’m sorry, Mr. Callaghan, he was last seen in Antrim on Tuesday, but we lost him in the orange parade.” He watched the vein pulse in Callaghan’s temple.

Seamus shifted uncomfortably in his seat, making the leather squeak. His boss turned to look at him. Callaghan was also a large man, solidly built with sandy, thinning hair and a white beard that was impeccably groomed. He was wearing an immaculate Irish linen suit under his camel overcoat. It suddenly struck Seamus that regardless of the weather or how many layers he wore, this man never perspired.

Jon Jo spoke through clenched teeth, “Christ Seamus, how difficult can it be? I want him found! We’re not the only ones looking for him! There’s a lot at stake, but I have the most to lose, so I want to know exactly what he told the journalist. I don’t care how you do it. If there’s collateral damage that’s fine, but I need to know in the next forty-eight hours! Do you understand me Seamus?”

"Yes Mr. Callaghan”. Seamus heard the tremor in his voice. He swallowed hard. He knew this conversation was over, so he opened the car door and stepped out on to the pavement. He was grateful to be in the warm July drizzle. The car roared away towards Belfast city centre.

Seamus was left wondering how he was going to track down a retired IRA hitman when he clearly didn't want to be found.

He set off along Connisbrook Avenue and into Larkin's public bar. As he opened the heavy wooden door he expertly scanned the room. There were a few familiar faces that nodded in recognition at him. He walked up to the bar where a short, scrawny man was polishing a pint glass. Everything about the place exuded Irishness, it was almost a cliché. There was the distinctive smell of draught beer, the wooden floor was slightly sticky from spilled Guinness and then there was the clientele.

Seamus leant on the wooden bar, "Hi Neilly. Pint of Smithicks please". The barman reached out to the old-fashioned beer pull and began to fill the glass.

"Has McGinty been in today?"

Neilly passed the pint across the bar. "He's in the jacks. That'll be £4.75."

Seamus reached into his pocket for a note. "Jesus Neilly, I came in for a drink not to be mugged!"

The barman took the note and crackled it between his thick, stubby fingers. "I don't steal, I don't lie, and I don't cheat! The government hates the competition." He turned to deposit the money in the till and took out some coins. Handing the change to Seamus he said,

"What'll you be wanting with McGinty then?"

Seamus looked towards the door leading to the toilets. “I’ve a message for him. His wife’s won the lottery, and she said to tell him that she loves him. She’ll miss him, but she still loves him!”

The barman took the hint and went back to polishing another glass.

McGinty came back into the bar and sat down at a table where a solitary half-filled glass of beer stood. He sat on the bench seat looking out into the bar and nodded in recognition to Seamus. He walked over to him and sat down.

“Can I join you McGinty?”

The man didn’t look up. “It’s a free world. I was just finishing a quiet lunchtime drink.”

He stood up to leave and Seamus pushed him back into his seat. “No need to rush off. Let’s chat for a bit.”

McGinty was in his forties with jet-black curly hair and hooded dark eyes. He was lean and he bristled with tension. He had an open friendly face and when he spoke, there was a gentleness to his voice that was surprising.

“What do you want to chat about Seamus? I really should be getting back to work?”

Seamus took a long drink from his glass. “I needed that. Can I get you another?”

“No, honestly, I have to get back. My lunchtime’s over”. McGinty looked uncomfortable. His eyes darted around the bar.

OK" said Seamus. "I won't keep you long. Mr. Callaghan wants to know if you've seen Dessie McFee recently?"

The reaction to the name had quite an effect on McGinty. He gave a visible shudder. He hunched his shoulders in a bid to become smaller, wishing himself invisible and said quickly

"No, haven't seen him for months." His hand shook slightly as he lifted his empty glass, then realising, set it back down again on the beer mat.

"Well that's strange because you were seen with him at the march on Tuesday in Antrim. Immediately before he went to ground."

"Oh yes, I forgot. I did nod to him, but we didn't have a chance to chat. It was a bit crowded."

Seamus emptied his glass and banged it down on the table. "Don't piss me about McGinty! We know you were with him on Tuesday. We have photos, so cut the crap and tell me where he is, now!"

The man began to squirm. "Honestly Seamus. I don't know where he is now. I do know he's been on edge since he spoke to the journo. Rumour has it he was going to disappear for a while till things cooled off. The problem is, if he wants to avoid being found he has the experience to drop off the grid, doesn't he?"

Seamus lent in and whispered into the now shaking man's ear. "Mr. Callaghan was very grateful when you helped Dessie out last time. He needed to lie low for a month or two, and you were very accommodating. So, you can forgive us for thinking that that's why he found you at the march. To repeat the favour."

McGinty knew the dangerous line he was walking with this conversation. His wife Mary was Dessie's cousin, and he had helped him out in the past. He felt his forehead prickle with moisture, and he ran a finger around his collar. They had all been close in their youth, until Theresa, Dessie's girlfriend was killed. Her death had done something to Dessie; to his brain. He was never the same after that. McGinty had distanced them from Dessie to protect Mary more than anything.

Dessie had changed, he had lost his lovable roguishness, and it had been replaced with something darker and much more sinister. When he'd helped him to disappear before they used an old farm building to hole up in. One night over a bottle of whiskey he had told McGinty about losing her. With dead eyes, he explained that since her death, the missions he completed in the name of the cause gave him momentary relief, but the loss always came back with a vengeance.

It disturbed McGinty, he had never seen a man so utterly lost or tormented. At that moment, he had felt truly sorry for Dessie McFee.

McGinty shook himself to rid him of the memories. "No, honest Seamus. It wasn't like that at all.

He didn't ask me for anything. When he left me, he was looking for his uncle. That's all I know".

The shake in McGinty's hand suddenly got worse, he clasped them together under the table, still unable to meet Seamus's gaze. "Mr. Callaghan said I should ask how your family are doing now, particularly Mary. I passed her new shop in the high street on the way here today. Very nice.... I do admire her starting her own business. Keeping things going isn't easy in this climate. Insurance premiums alone can be crippling, and it only takes one claim to make the payments rocket. It can be enough to finish off a small salon before it gets properly established. Are you sure you won't have another?" The veiled threat hit home.

"Please Seamus," he pleaded "Not Mary's shop! She's worked hard to get that together."
Seamus sat back in the chair. "All we want is an address, that's it. Nothing else."

McGinty looked beaten. "I really don't know where he is Seamus. When I saw him, he was looking for his uncle Tommy. You know, Tommy Ryan the car dealer. I told him he wasn't at the parade because he was in Limerick for the races. I couldn't help him."

Seamus considered his empty glass. "Is Uncle Tommy a regular race goer then?"

"Yes, he does a little bookmaking on the side too." He offered this little tidbit as a way of placating Seamus. He felt sure that Mr. Callaghan didn't know that Tommy Ryan had gone into competition against him. McGinty owed no allegiance to Tommy Ryan. He'd sold him a Ford Focus last year that turned out to be a ringer. The police had confiscated the car without compensation and Tommy had walked away with just a caution.

Seamus was looking at him with an intent that was disturbing. "You know Dessie has turned tout, don't you? He spoke to that journalist, no doubt looking for cash in turn for information. Only scum turn on their own, McGinty. You can see why we need to find him quickly can't you?"

His shoulders slumped a little further. He looked beaten. "If you want to speak to Tommy, there's a big race meet at Cork tomorrow. He'll definitely be there.

"Thanks McGinty. He'd better be….. Otherwise, I'll be back."

Chapter 6:

Saturday 20th July 2019
Tottenham Hale, London

Lynsey Parry was surprised how quickly the novelty of winning a BAFTA had worn off. '*Cold Comfort; The NI Connection*', was the documentary that had won her the prestigious award.

It had not been a journey without bumps in the road. She had gained a first at Cambridge then secured herself a series of reporter jobs at provincial newspapers churning out stories about local fêtes, baby competitions, flower shows and election results for parish councils. She had written about the mundane until 2002, when she got a significant promotion as a senior reporter for a Fleet Street broad sheet. She was proud that she'd done this on her own and not used her family connections to 'grease the wheels'.

Her family were of aristocratic stock, but coming from money made her more determined that it should not define her professional life. Lynsey adopted a pseudonym, never using her family name or connections in her work. Her mother had never tired of telling her that she could have been a features' editor at 'Tatler' or society reporter for 'Horse and Hound'. Instead, the catalyst for her career had been attending a talk by the journalist Julian Manyon. He had led a team of reporters that made the highly controversial 'Death on the Rock ' documentary in 1988 for Thames Television.

On a damp night in 2003 at Waterstones in Piccadilly at his book launch, he had spoken of the repercussions that he and his producers had experienced after the programme had aired. It had sparked her passion for hard-hitting reporting. Subsequently, her career had gone in an upwards direction and her personal life had gone the opposite way.

Her mother had despaired! She could have had an easier life, nice clothes, a moneyed fiancé, and a decent expense account. Lynsey had other ideas. She had decided that there was no place for intimate relationships in her life, her career came first. Instead, she chased stories in dangerous settings, living on fast-food snatched at ridiculous hours, supplemented by twenty cigarettes a day. She was on the scrawny side of slim and disguised her 5'6" frame with baggy tops, jeans, and a Burberry trench coat that had seen better days.

Her mother had died ten years ago, and Lynsey thought it was probably a good job she wasn't here to see her now. Her complexion looked washed out and the dark circles under her eyes were due to the meagre five hours sleep a night she allowed herself. The heavy drinking she was partial to didn't help either. She couldn't remember the last time she'd bought new clothes or had a proper haircut. In truth, she may have been a good journalist, but she was a bit of a mess.

Finally, after years of hard graft her break had come. Sky Television had commissioned her to make a film about the Northern Ireland Peace Agreement now nearly twenty years on. This period of history intrigued her. Her mother's family had banking and property interests in Ireland, and she remembered visiting a large house in Ireland during school holidays when she was a young girl. Her mother never talked about her grandfather and a family scandal that happened all those years ago. The mystery surrounding those events had sharpened her curiosity and fine-tuned her nose for a story.

For this project, her angle was to look at how the agreement had been reached. Currently, there was a lot of noise in the system about how British soldiers that had served during the troubles were being prosecuted now for the actions they had taken back then. As part of the agreement both sides had secured an undertaking to issue 'comfort letters' to known republican and loyalist terrorists. Receiving one of the letters virtually meant freedom from prosecution for historical crimes. Some recipients had live arrest warrants for their involvement in punishment beatings, arms smuggling and in some cases, even bombings.

These letters had been highly controversial, as it was unclear how the lists had been arrived at. There was a suspicion that senior people on both sides had helped to compile them to protect the favoured and to pay back old debts. The honeymoon period that followed the peace agreement had given some members of the Provisional IRA a clean bill of health in the transition and had drawn clear distinctions between the terrorist group and the political party.

The media had played their part by being helpful when it reported on former members who had adopted exclusively political or community roles. Their crimes were never publicly mentioned again. It was clear that a line had been drawn in the sand. They had manufactured a past to move to a new future.

It fascinated Lynsey that terrible crimes committed by the IRA could be so easily glossed over in the name of a political solution. The shocking nature of some of the punishments were almost worse than the killings, no one had been safe. She had interviewed one woman who had been accused of having an affair with a British soldier, she had been tarred and feathered by her neighbours. Until this interview, Lynsey had believed that it was done with road tar and that because of the heat, the victim died. However, the woman explained that the victim would be stripped naked, or just to the waist then molten wood-tar poured onto them while they were restrained. It was used because of its stickiness, it burned slowly because it had a lower melting point than road tar but was much harder to remove. The victim would then be rolled in chicken feathers that stuck to the tar. The removal of the tar involved peeling it away often taking layers of burnt skin with it, leaving open wounds. The punishment was intended to inflict the greatest pain and leave the victim alive and with permanent scars as a reminder of their crime.

Her research had shown that nothing was as it first seemed. People had talked to their sworn enemies. Traitors were accepted back into the fold. Those guilty of the worst crimes were no longer being prosecuted. History had been rewritten.

Power and tactical advantages had been surrendered inch by bloody inch to achieve the Peace Agreement. It was a masterclass in political manipulation and propaganda or a stroke of altruistic genius, depending on which side you were on.

She knew her project had come to the attention of the security services when she uncovered the extent of President Bill Clinton's involvement in the negotiations. One of the staffers involved in his visit had described how Clinton had personally intervened, threatening to stop American funds getting through unless Sinn Féin came to the table and took the negotiations seriously. Shortly after that conversation, she spotted a black SUV with US diplomatic plates which trailed her for two weeks, until they lost interest. Her journalists' sixth sense had raised the hairs on the back of her neck. She had definitely drawn attention, even if she didn't always know who the interested party was.

She had become intrigued with the story of what happened to those that were left behind. Her interviews with IRA brigade commanders and activists who had been left out in the cold were telling. They were understandably very bitter. They had never been part of the political establishment and were not legitimised with a comfort letter. Instead, they were simply frozen out. For her, this was the real story.

Angered by their treatment and in an attempt to make ends meet many of them had moved into organised crime. This fed her cynical narrative of corruption and power. She had come to believe that most people were motivated by self-interest rather than acting for honourable or unselfish reasons. This story explained why some of them were now serving at Stormont at the

Northern Ireland Assembly and others, who had fought in the troubles with them side by side were now dealing drugs or running extortion rackets. It was no excuse, but it explained an awful lot.

A name that kept coming up was Jon Jo Callaghan, an ex-IRA brigade commander. This man was a high-profile IRA Brigade Commander who had not made the comfort letter list. Lynsey was intrigued by what had blotted his copybook so badly that he had been left out in the cold. Instead of making the transition to respectability he had built a criminal empire that now controlled most of the illegal activity across Ireland and had connections in Europe. Lynsey realised that powerful people were aware of what she was doing when her feature for one of the Sunday broadsheets naming Callaghan and his associates, Seamus Meehan and Dessie McFee had been pulled by the Editor with no explanation offered.

After that, every approach she made turned into a dead end. She had tried for weeks to gain some traction but had been met with a wall of silence. Then, just as she was on the brink of moving on to something else, out of the blue she was contacted by Dessie McFee himself.

She thought it was a hoax to begin with. He said he would grant her an exclusive interview, but he wanted her help in return. It took her less than ten seconds to weigh up how prudent it was to owe a real-life hitman a favour. She ignored the internal voice of caution and agreed.

Dessie wouldn't meet face to face, so they set up a video call. That call lasted just eight minutes, and he was very clear about what he wanted. He wanted out, with a new identity, safe passage out of Ireland and help to relocate a woman who was a victim of the gang he was working for. If she could help him with that then he would make sure she got the exclusive. He knew she couldn't give him what he asked for, but told her to take his offer directly to a man called Daniel Grant, Director General of the British Secret Service. She didn't have a clue how to get hold of him, but she was confident that she would find a way.

Dessie said he could deliver key people operating one of the biggest and most dangerous European crime syndicates. He had dates, times, and places about specific crimes and details about how the business worked. He had personally witnessed the trafficking of sex workers, drugs, and money laundering. At great risk to himself and in exchange for immunity he was willing to provide the public prosecutor with enough evidence to dismantle the whole operation. The system would incarcerate vicious criminals, and she would get the exclusive. This was dynamite!

In less than twenty-four hours, and to her great surprise, Lynsey had been able to contact Daniel Grant. It had been far easier than she thought. His contact details were on a government website, and although she felt sure he didn't read all his emails personally, he had telephoned her back! She told him about her conversation with a senior ex-IRA 'soldier' who was seeking a deal, and his conditions, adding in her own role in reporting the exclusive. It was only after she had put the phone down that she realised it was Grant who had referred to Dessie by name. She hadn't used any names over the telephone or in her email.

The wheels were now in motion. Lynsey knew as soon as the approach was made, Dessie was risking his life by turning informant, they would have to act fast to lift him before anyone found out what he was about to do, and she was intrigued about whom the woman was, and why would he risk everything for her?

She contacted Dessie at the agreed time to report back on her conversation. She passed on the secure telephone number and email address Grant had given her and said the rest was up to him. He had sounded agitated. He was clear that he expected her to find somewhere safe for the woman he now referred to as Tatum. He wanted them to meet so that she could get the girl to safety; it could not wait!

Lynsey had an inner conflict about this man. She had no doubt that as an IRA man, he would have been involved in killing, torturing, and maybe even bombing civilians. Others she had spoken with had justified their actions as freedom fighters fighting the injustice of living in an occupied land. They had been governed by a foreign power that had shown no respect or concern for their ways, their religion, or the prosperity of their people.

She had a sketchy picture of Dessie's history. He had been a young man when his sweetheart Theresa had been killed. That had fuelled his hatred of the British, and he was implicated in some major IRA attacks. Now, here he was, giving up everything he had ever believed in to protect a young woman.

Lynsey wondered what had bought about such a monumental shift in his beliefs. Did he love this woman? His description of her made Lynsey think she was very young. Could it really be love that was making him turn his back on everything, betraying the cause that had been everything to him? Her journalist senses were tingling. This could be a human-interest story like no other. Maybe a Pulitzer was the next reward!

Chapter 7:

Saturday 20th July 2019 11.00am
Cork Racecourse

Cork was a modern racecourse and on this July morning it was absolutely packed! The warm day had brought racegoers out in droves and although there had been an early morning mist hanging over the track, that had now cleared leaving the going 'good to firm'.

The racegoers who were there for the craic were ensconced indoors watching proceedings on large screens, drinking, laughing, and swapping the hottest race tips. Hardened aficionados who made their living this way were in smaller groups outside next to the track, poring over the race card, studying form.

Seamus looked around at the melee. None of his family had been into the horses, better things to spend their money on. He was amused by the sight of these people, mainly the women, kitted out in weird and wonderful outfits with outrageous, rented hats, impossible heels, and minuscule handbags. It seemed like they were trying to outdo each other, the more outlandish the colour scheme the better!

He walked out onto the concourse where the bookies boards advertised the race odds. They stood under rainbow-coloured umbrellas, tic-tac men waving their arms about like demented windmills. He knew this is where he would find Tommy Regan, the regular gambler.

Although they'd never met, Seamus knew what Tommy looked like, as he was an excellent self-publicist. The billboards advertising his second-hand car sales business had his picture plastered across them. He occupied the three biggest advertising spots in his hometown. One was on the road into town, one as you were leaving town and the one by the side of the flyover. You really couldn't miss them!

Seamus scanned the scene, he needed to get this right. Mr. Callaghan could be very generous when you pleased him and extraordinarily mean when you didn't. JJ's inventiveness worried Seamus. At the school of hard knocks where Seamus had done his training, a regular beating or kneecapping was usually enough to get the job done but Jon-Jo Callaghan went out of his way to be creative with his punishments.

Having set the bar high, Seamus decided that extracting information from Tommy needed the same creative flair. His plan was to use electricity to loosen his tongue so that he would give up Dessie's whereabouts.

A southern contact had offered Seamus a disused workshop and garage for the purpose. It was only a short drive up the road. His plan was to kidnap him from the race meet then force him to drive to the garage in Seamus's car. He would work on him until he gave up Dessie's location then he would then finish him off. It was important not to leave witnesses.

Seamus spotted him. He had just completed a transaction and was about to head back into the main building. Seamus moved quickly. He thrust his hand into his pocket and closed it around his pistol grip. The QSZ-92 is a semi-automatic pistol favoured by the Chinese army as their service weapon of choice. His had been a gift from Dessie when Seamus first got involved with the darker side of the business. In fact, he had witnessed his first three hits where Dessie had used the gun to great effect. So, it had real sentimental value.

Seamus headed Tommy off before he could reach the building. He grabbed him by the arm and pushed the nose of the gun into his side. "Greetings from Mr. Callaghan, Tommy. He just needs a quick word with you, so come with me quietly, and I will have you back in time for the two o'clock handicap!"

The mention of JJ's name had the desired effect. Real fear registered and Tommy became as compliant as a working sheepdog. The sheer numbers of people excitedly watching the main race of the morning made it easy to leave the meeting without drawing attention to themselves.

Tommy drove in silence while Seamus held the gun on him. He gave clear directions and Tommy pulled the car into the deserted yard just ten minutes later. Seamus had been there earlier in the morning to get everything ready. They got out of the car and walked through the open roller shutter door into the workshop. Seamus pulled on a rope and the roller door noisily closed behind them.

It was a cavernous space with a corrugated tin roof and one small window at the far end. Despite the warmth of the day, inside it was cold and dank. There were puddles of stagnant water mixed with oil and grease that scattered iridescent patterns across the floor. The metallic smell was almost overpowering. A tubular steel chair with thin arms stood in the middle of the space and Seamus used the pistol to motion Tommy to sit.

"What's this all about? I'm up-to-date with my payments to Mr. Callaghan. If one of my lads has been skimming off the top, tell me who it is, and I'll deal with them!"

Tommy had a thin sheen of perspiration on his forehead. He licked his lips nervously.

Seamus took some large cable ties from the battery trolley that stood behind them. At gunpoint, he made Tommy secure his own ankles to the legs of the chair then Seamus fixed Tommy's wrists to the metal arms of the chair

"Where's Mr. Callaghan?" Tommy's voice climbing an octave as his fear grew.

"He doesn't need to be here in person. I'm his right-hand man. You can call me Seamus. Now we just need to know where your nephew Dessie McFee is."

Tommy relaxed slightly. He hadn't seen Dessie so he couldn't help. He felt some of his salesman bravado start to seep back.

"I know who you are, but I don't know where Dessie is. I haven't seen him in months. We were never very close at the best of times."

Seamus put the gun down, put on thick black rubber gloves then started to unravel some electric cables that were clearly attached to a large truck battery on the bottom of the trolley. "We know he was looking for you on Tuesday at the parade and in a small town it's hard to believe he didn't find you. He was looking for you to help him to disappear. Where did you send him?"

Seamus pulled open Tommy's jacket, roughly yanking his tie from underneath his collar, and ripped at the shirt buttons to expose bare chest. Next he picked up the cables and briefly struck the exposed ends together creating a shower of sparks and a loud crackling noise.

"Let's try that again shall we Tommy, where is Dessie McFee?".

A wet patch slowly appeared on Tommy's trousers. "Honest, I don't know. I never saw him last week; I was in Spain on holiday with the wife. I only came back on Wednesday."

He eyed the jump leads nervously. Seamus touched them together again for effect and the increased fear registered in Tommy's face. Seamus definitely had his attention.

"Please don't, I've got a pacemaker. I can't even stand next to a microwave that's switched on. You could kill me with those things!" He strained against the ties holding his wrists. "Please, I really don't know where he is". Panic was seeping into his voice.

Seamus felt a quiver of excitement. Tommy was not going to give Dessie up easily. "Do I look like an eejit?"

"You don't even look like a Seamus!" Tommy took a breath to calm himself. " Honest, you can check. We came back Ryanair on Wednesday night. I haven't seen him." Tommy fleetingly wondered why he was trying to be humorous when he was obviously dealing with a psychopath.

Seamus took a step towards him; he stood on the rubber mat placed there for this specific purpose. He gave Tommy's chest the lightest of touches with the cable ends. There were sparks and a sizzling sound. A red mark slowly appeared on Tommy's skin and there was a smell of burnt hair. Tommy jerked in the chair kicking up dirty water spray from the floor. One of the cable ties snapped, and his right leg thrashed about in a macabre Irish jig.

"Please" he gasped in a scratchy voice "I don't know where he is."

Seamus touched his chest with the metal leads again. This time, Tommy emitted a high-pitched screech then fell silent. He continued to twitch violently in the chair for a second or two then he slumped forward. Seamus disconnected the cables from the battery and hung them across the trolley. He walked over to Tommy and pulled his head back by his wispy hair. There was nothing. No breathing, no sound at all. Seamus removed his right glove and felt for a heartbeat with, but there was none, He examined his chest more closely and there by Tommy's left shoulder was the tell-tale bump of a small device under the skin, Shit, he wasn't kidding! He really did have a pacemaker!

The consequences of what had just happened started to dawn on Seamus, Tommy was the only lead they had to finding Dessie, and he had literally, just fried it!

Mr. Callaghan was not going to be best pleased. No location, no live lead, and no idea how to find Dessie. It was then that Seamus began to sweat…

Chapter 8:

Saturday 20th July 2019
Stormont (Northern Ireland Assembly)

In the Government building in Stormont, Colm Devey answered the vibrating mobile phone on his desk. The screen announced 'Sinead'.

"Hello Colm. You were right. Callaghan is looking for him, and he sent the village idiot Seamus to track him down. That will give us a bit more time at least. It was bad enough when we thought he was just talking to the 'Journo' but now we think he might have contacted the spooks. If he has, they will probably try to get him out over the weekend. Our inside contact will let us know the route as soon as it's confirmed."

Colm was feeling very anxious, this could blow up in his face if it wasn't contained. She sounded wired and confident; not the best combination for her. "Does Callaghan know for certain that McFee is speaking to security services?"

"It doesn't look like it yet, we only know because of what our contact has told us. He will confirm soon enough though."

"OK Sinead, if there's anything you need from my end just let me know." He knew she was able to apply pressure in the right quarters to find out the details of any escape route, but it would leave a trail. Better that a trail should lead to someone in the security services rather than to him. As a serving member of the Northern Ireland Executive he needed to remain above suspicion. In the current climate any hint of involvement would not be prudent. Particularly if the end result was that the first Supergrass in a decade ended up dead! He couldn't be tied to this in any way.

Colm's history was entwined with Dessie since January 1972, when Bloody Sunday happened. Dessie McFee's father had been one of the dead. He left a wife, two sons and three daughters. Dessie was the youngest at just three years old. After that fateful day, local IRA brigades grew in numbers and funds came rolling in from Irish descendants living a prosperous life in the USA. These funds made it easier to organise and train IRA brigades and increase their activities, making hostilities much worse.

Colm had often reflected on how the movement had grown in strength in a relatively short time. He was just seventeen, but he concluded that when young impressionable people spend their formative years having their heads filled with stories of the brave fighting for freedom from oppression it colours their view of the world. That definitely applied to Sinead and Dessie, himself to a lesser degree. They had been young and fuelled by the need for revenge. They lived by a strict code of family, respect for the church and their elders in general but a hatred for British soldiers.

He couldn't pinpoint the time when that had turned into direct action, although he did remember being on patrol on the Shankhill Road one day and coming across a small British Army unit. Something in his head had clicked and for the first time the soldiers were no longer human, not worthy of any respect. In fact, they were deserving of the beatings, even death to even up the score. Callaghan had fed those feelings of hatred into his soldiers, firstly Dessie and later Sinead. Before Colm realised what was happening to her, it was too late. She saw things in such a black and white way that he couldn't reason with her the way he used to. Callaghan cultivated the notion of rough justice and Sinead and Dessie fell for it.

Colm remembered when JJ ordered him to kill for the first time, he had told him, "Colm, killing a man is not something you can learn to do. It takes a special trait in a person, one that is created by injustice. The sort of injustice your Da and me always fought against. It allows those that have it to kill an enemy and carry on with life afterwards. I can see that trait in you Colm. I want you at my side where your Da used to be. I want us to unite Ireland together and drive the British out, forever." Colm silently disagreed.

When he was a teenager, Colm had happily obliged and had set a car bomb that had killed a young, off-duty soldier. They had been the same age, just 19. That was when he realised that Jon Jo was a manipulator. It was difficult to carry on with normal life when you had blood on your hands. You couldn't un-know what you had done, and the consequences were something you had to live with. Confession didn't help either. Colm felt he was carrying an indelible stain that might be forgiven by a higher power but was something he could never forgive himself for. From that time onwards he could clearly see the Svengali type influence Callaghan had over the young.

In 1983 Jon Jo had been implicated in a Derry bombing where three civilians were killed. Dessie had been seen travelling in the van that was used. They were captured and convicted. Jon Jo spent nearly a decade in Long Kesh, also known as The Maze Prison, but due to his age, Dessie been sent to Hyde Bank Young Offenders Institution. He got three years; he was just sixteen.

Colm had taken over running the brigade while JJ served his sentence. JJ had used their network to smuggle a letter to Dessie while he was in prison encouraging him to keep his morale up. He urged the young man to keep true to the cause. On his release, Dessie was welcomed home as a hero. Colm took him under his wing but noted how bitter and angry he had become. Time inside had hardened him, making him so much more dangerous.

Colm really struggled to control Dessie's outbursts until everything changed when he was in his early twenties. He met the love of his life, Theresa Farrell. She was a good catholic girl who fell for Dessie's 'Che Guevara' image. She had shared his passion for independence from British rule and was deeply in love with him. She gave him a glimpse of a different future, but just three months after JJ was released Theresa had been killed. Sinead was responsible for that mess. Colm had risked exposure himself, but the end result was the right one. The official story was that Colm had interrogated her, shot her, and left her burnt, disfigured corpse on wasteland as a warning to others. She was just twenty-one years old.

Things were never the same again for Dessie, he raged against the world. He couldn't believe he had been deceived by Theresa or that Colm, a man he considered almost family had killed the love of his life. To calm the volatile situation down, JJ removed Colm from active duty and sent him to work for Sinn Féin as a party activist.

The details of what really happened on the night of Theresa's death had never been discussed. It was always the elephant in the middle of the room. Colm was sure that they had to make an example of the girl who betrayed the cause for his own credibility if nothing else. Dessie was blinded by anger and refused to see why Colm had made no attempt to show her mercy. They were no longer friends.

Mad with grief, Dessie was determined that the British would pay for Theresa's death. JJ had resumed the retaliatory attacks at Dessie's urging. Targets were selected and Dessie produced the plan, date, time, and method. The targets were occupiers or traitors. Some were shot. Others died in car bombs. The order always came from JJ and was never questioned. They understood that they were fighting for home rule. JJ was the most dangerous brigade commander as nothing was too extreme in the name of the cause. With Dessie's cold rage they were a dangerous and widely feared duo.

Colm was thankful that he had made the move when he had. The seminal moment came with the Omagh bombing. It was an unsanctioned hit that left eighteen innocent civilians dead and thirty-one seriously injured. It was carried out by a splinter group, but that didn't matter. It was the moment when public support for the cause ended. People on all sides were horrified at the carnage and brutality of the event. That was when the fissure opened between the inner circle at the top of the IRA and senior figures in Sinn Féin.

They had already begun to explore a political solution to end the troubles, but the public outcry was so big they knew it was probably the last attempt they would get. The hierarchy began to distance themselves from the active brigades and although it was not proven that Callaghan was responsible for Omagh they assumed it was the case anyway. It was exactly the sort of crazy stunt he would pull. He refused to see the writing on the wall. While his brigade was hell-bent on creating as much carnage as possible, they were completely oblivious to the fact that people living through the troubles were more worried about the quality of their housing or their employment prospects than the great fight for an independent Irish Republic. Colm could see that Dessie was a lost soul and JJ was a loose cannon. There was no coming back from this for either of them.

Colm had already taken steps to ensure that he was on the winning side and positioned himself as one of the architects of a political solution, a lasting peace.

The telephone on his desk rang and shook him back into the present. The caller display told him it was an internal call from someone in the building.

"Colm Devey speaking." He shifted position in his chair and began to focus on what the man was saying. "OK, keep me posted, I need to know the moment you have some news. Has our contact from Special Branch not come up with anything?" He was beginning to wonder what he was paying the man €20,000 for.

"Well, if he doesn't produce the goods soon you can tell him that we may be asking for a refund." Colm replaced the receiver and gazed at the commemorative signed copy of the Good Friday Agreement that hung on the wall opposite him.

It had been signed to signal that the 'war' was over. The brigades had been systematically dismantled, the IRA had declared a total ceasefire, and they had eventually decommissioned their weapons in 2005. The Irish people had become weary of death and saw the political solution as the one that would bring the peace they longed for.

Colm and his counterparts made the transition and gained a veneer of respectability from the establishment. It was this choice that differentiated him from Dessie. Had things been different it could have been Colm running and hiding and Dessie sitting in this plush office attending policy committees and photo opportunities. He gave a little shudder. That didn't bear thinking about. This was shaping up to be a very long weekend.

Chapter 9:

Sunday 21st July 2019
Stormont

Had he even been home? It certainly didn't feel like it. Yesterday's activities had turned up very little and time was running out. If they hadn't located Dessie by lunchtime their window would have closed, and the security services would have succeeded in lifting him.

Colm was eating a very lackluster sandwich of wilted lettuce on something resembling soda bread with a smear of tuna mayonnaise so thin you could see the olive oil spread through it. He should have been at home enjoying a full Irish with white pudding and fried potatoes. He pushed what passed for breakfast away and reached for his espresso instead. He was not used to working on a Sunday, thank God the coffee was good.

He hadn't stopped since he got to the office at 7.30am this morning, he had missed Mass, and by the look of it was going to miss his Sunday lunch too. His wife would have given him grief a few years ago but not now. He wondered if she would even notice.

He was struggling to identify a single task he had completed. Two days had been wasted, and he was beginning to feel a little jumpy. His to-do list stared back at him accusingly, but how could he concentrate, with everything that was going on? He felt the presence of Dessie McFee like a spectre at a wedding. The degree of protection Colm's position afforded him should have calmed some of his concerns. The current UK Government were keen to preserve the GFA at any cost. In a strangely unified gesture both sides of the executive were distancing themselves from their historical allegiances just in case Dessie implicated one of them, but they needed to pressure Westminster about the undertakings made when the agreement was drawn up.

Colm had taken a lead in hammering out the fine detail. They had been very clear that there would be political implications if they tried to use anything to bring about the historical prosecution of anyone apart from Callaghan. And they meant it.

They all hoped Dessie would focus on Callaghan's involvement with the Eastern European sex trafficking and the extortion rackets. The difficulty they had was that his turning had come out of the blue, so no one really knew what he was intending to say or what deal he had cut. Not even Colm and his network of informants was privy to that information.

Colm had suspected for some time that some of the Albanian gang's money, laundered before it left Ireland, made its way to support terrorism but nothing had been confirmed.

Dessie had been on the inside track for a long while and literally knew where the bodies were buried. Him turning 'tout' had created some very powerful enemies; the Albanians wanted him, Callaghan wanted him, and the security services wanted him. They would extract him and question him to build their case, but there would be a lengthy timespan before he would be ready to testify, so they would need to keep him at a safe location. All Sinead's contact had to do was find out where that was, and his team would do the rest. Colm hoped they hadn't lost their edge in the intervening years of peace.

There was a knock at the door,

"Come in" he called out.

An older man in a security uniform popped his head around the door

"Special delivery Mr. Devey. I know you don't normally get post on a Sunday, but it was handed in at the desk and I knew you were in today, so I thought I would stretch my legs."

Colm waved him into the office, “Joe, that’s very kind of you. How is the lovely Elsie and your girls?”

Joe placed an orange A4 envelope on Colm’s’ desk, “I’m a lucky man Mr. Devey. My Elsie dresses to kill, unfortunately she cooks the same way. The girls are fine.” He laughed at his own joke and left to return to the quiet of a Sunday shift.

Colm ran his thumb under the flap and reached into the envelope pulling out a single sheet of paper. The details were handwritten. Extraction point Dublin Zoo. Out to the mainland via Dublin Airport directly to London. Safe house location as yet unknown.

He cursed under his breath. His contact had come through with the goods, unfortunately it was too little and much too late!

Chapter 10:

Sunday 21st July 2019 9.00AM

The Snatch, Dublin

Mitch Bennett picked up the file from the makeshift table in the aircraft hangar where they'd set up a transitional base. He flipped through it for the umpteenth time. This was the first major operation in his new role, and he didn't want anything to go wrong. Dessie McFee was the real thing! A ruthless IRA hitman and a key member of the Cartel jointly run by Callaghan and a psychopath called Kadir Yilmaz. A journalist acting as a go-between had made the initial contact saying Dessie wanted out. Daniel had handled it personally, which reflected how sensitive this whole situation was.

Dessie had been on their watch list since the GFA had been signed but had become less interesting as IRA activity had diminished. There was a political agenda at play that meant there was little desire to capture and prosecute IRA men for old crimes. New crimes, however, were another thing entirely.

The Callaghan gang had reappeared on their radar in the last few years because of the company they were keeping. Yilmaz owned a chain of barber's shops across Ireland. They were in reality, thinly disguised money laundering operations. Some of the money they processed had been tracked as far as the Middle East and was suspected of funding terrorist attacks across Europe. Any information they got from Dessie that helped MI5 dismantle the operation was high value.

Earlier, Mitch and Daniel had explored what a realistic deal with Dessie might look like. Mitch had to put his own feelings to one side. He struggled with the idea that a known killer was being considered for an amnesty, but Daniel had reasoned that this was no different to the comfort letters already handed out to some of the current politicians sitting in Stormont.

When the offer to Dessie was made they left him under no illusions; if he didn't deliver the goods, there would be a significant prison term. Mitch had relished explaining to him that any jail sentence would be served in an English prison and that he would be a target. Irish republicans still had connections in jail who were loyal to the cause and who were handy with a shiv in a prison shower block.

Mitch had driven home the clear message that Dessie would only go into witness protection if his information resulted in prosecutions. Despite that he still seemed keen to share what he knew about the current activities of the Callaghan gang and their links to organised crime.

Mitch hoped the information would provide vital intelligence about the network of Eastern Europeans for hire. These criminals made full use of the open borders across Europe and were responsible for the increase in trafficked weapons, drugs, and sex workers.

Dessie could certainly help with names and locations and had the potential to be a high-value asset for them, but he needed to play ball and not drag this out.

A couple of Mitch's agents were about to pick 'Ragair' up in the Dublin City Zoo and transport him back to London for the initial debrief. Mitch had chosen the code name 'Ragair' as it was Gaelic for 'a late-night rambler' which is what Mitch hoped he would become once they had him in custody. He could feel the anticipation growing. Handled in the right way, the information Dessie could deliver should provide them with the means to significantly damage the gang's activities, maybe take them down completely. He stood and began to pace the concrete floor creating echoes in the voluminous space.

How he dealt with Dessie McFee was essential to the success of the plan. He looked at his watch, they should have him by now if nothing had gone wrong.

It had all the predictability of a classic pick-up point; a public place with multiple escape routes in case things went wrong. Dessie arrived early and scanned the Zoo entrance for faces that he knew. He wanted to be sure that the arrangements hadn't been leaked and that a different welcoming party wasn't waiting with loaded guns to sabotage the plan. Waiting to pay for admission were a couple with backpacks, obviously dressed for a day of sightseeing, and a young woman with a twin pushchair containing a baby about six months old and a toddler about three. The baby was sleeping, but the toddler was beaming from ear to ear, clutching a toy meerkat by the name of Sergei.

He watched as they paid their fees and were handed guides to help them navigate their way around the Zoo. He could feel the tension building. He made his way to the turnstile and paid his money to the disinterested girl who had pink hair and who was noisily chewing gum. He accepted the receipt and a guide and moved through the entrance and onto the marked path. He watched as the couple took an alternative route that hugged the edge of the lake towards the centre of the

Zoo. The mother with the pushchair was headed along the path that would take her past the meerkat enclosure.

They were due to pick him up from the Wolf enclosure on the exit path, it was a good choice. It was a clear route to the exit and one that afforded excellent views if an attack took place. At 9.30am on Sunday morning, there was hardly anyone around. It didn't get really busy until eleven, when visitors could watch keepers feeding some of the more spectacular species. The air was filled with animal calls and the breeze carried a strange mixture of fried bacon smells mixed with a heady aroma of elephant house. If he took the lakeside path, it would bring him out directly opposite the wolf enclosure and the collection point. He arrived at 9.20am, ten minutes to kill. This part of the zoo was deserted this early in the day. He would be able to spot their approach and if anything didn't seem right he could disappear into the bushes and make his escape. He felt the back of his neck prickle with tension. It wasn't too late to change his mind but what other options did he really have?

Dessie had made a carefully calculated decision about turning informant. He had reasoned that with the passage of time, the activities of the IRA in the eighties and nineties would seem tame in comparison to what was happening now. Currently, the focus was on preventing major terrorist attacks in UK cities, so their view of his historic activities would almost certainly be diminished.

He knew their priority would be to get rid of Yilmaz and break up the cartel. Yilmaz was the most dangerous man Dessie knew and that was saying something. It would also be payback for Tatum and that also meant something.

The irony of his current situation was not lost on him. In the old days he would have been the one relentlessly hunting down, capturing, torturing, then killing the tout. That was because informants were not just betraying their brothers in arms, they were betraying the 'cause'.

Dessie was very clear however that this was entirely different. The cause was no longer in play and Jon Jo was not the freedom fighter he once was. Greed had turned him into a common thug making money from organised crime and working with people who were totally devoid of morals. Dessie knew Callaghan would be incandescent with rage when he found out. In fact, he would almost certainly know by now what he had done. Callaghan's power and influence were on the wane, but there were still some people who shook at the mention of his name. Mainly the petty criminals that were way down in the food chain.

Jon Jo had traded on his old reputation to cling onto turf that was slowly being taken over by a new breed of criminal. A violent and dangerous breed. They used exploitation to build their power, and drugs and sex trafficking to grow their wealth. There was no honour among these thieves. Dessie felt no guilt at all about helping to take these animals off his streets. In fact, it felt like a public service.

His overriding concern was if the Albanian had got wind of his 'defection' they would do anything to take him out of the game before he could talk. His watch said 9.30 exactly and on cue, a man approached the enclosure from the direction of the exit. Although he wore a casual jacket, he was clearly 'service'. His physique and the way he carried himself suggested menace. Dessie heard the crack of a twig behind him and turned to see a second man approaching his position. He held his arms away from his body as he had been instructed to do, and the agent quickly frisked him for weapons, pocketing the gun Dessie had been carrying in the back of his trouser waistband.

"I need you to do exactly as I tell you to get you out as quickly as possible, do you understand?"

Dessie nodded his head in compliance. The agent broke cover, guiding Dessie towards the other agent, gripping his elbow firmly. They made a strange sight as they walked along, three heavily built men moving purposely along the path not stopping to look in any of the enclosures, but single-mindedly focused on an SUV with tinted windows parked conspicuously by the gate. Dessie felt his heart rate increase as he realised his current vulnerability; he had no weapon and was being taken into the custody of the British Secret Service. If they were lucky, Yilmaz hadn't followed him, but you could never be too sure.

His 'bodyguards' unceremoniously bundled him into the rear of the vehicle and before the doors had closed were moving swiftly away from the kerb.

Dessie sat in the back of the black Mercedes flanked by his two 'protectors', adrenaline coursing through his veins. On closer examination their casual attire still constituted a visible uniform, which he found inexplicably amusing. Their dark jackets covered white shirts and dark ties. With hindsight, they were unlikely to have been mistaken for tourists. Dessie noticed the driver glancing in the rearview mirror,

"I think we might have company lads".

Both men turned to look out of the rear window.

"Got him. Dark blue Audi with Dublin plates?" The driver tensed and sat up in his seat. He spoke into an invisible receiver built somewhere into the car's interior.

"Control, we have a tail, please advise on nearest backup."

A few seconds elapsed, and a crackly response came through. "There's a decoy waiting at the junction of Ratoath Road and Cappagh Road". The irony of the road name, Rat-oath, was not lost on Dessie. The disembodied voice continued,

"Pull into the slip road behind the hedge and let them take it from there".

The driver obeyed the instructions. He put his foot down and accelerated up to the bend in the road, swerving at the last second into the slip road, coming to a halt behind a tall hawthorn hedge. Dessie saw the tail lights of an identical vehicle to the one he was travelling in accelerate out of the lay by and speed off.

There was a minute of radio silence then the crackle broke again. "Confirming. It was a tail. They have taken the bait. Go directly to the airport. Security will open the perimeter gate on the R108. You are cleared onto the tarmac straight through to the City-jet Hanger. Transport is fuelled and waiting." The three men on the back seat relaxed in unison.

The tall blond-haired agent looked at Dessie. "The Albanians are obviously missing you already. Perhaps they just wanted to wave goodbye." Dessie felt the knot of anxiety in the pit of his stomach loosen a little. He would feel better once they were in the air.

The plane was a Gulfstream G450, with room enough for eight passengers, although this flight contained just four people. Mitch sat opposite Dessie with two agents: one behind Dessie and the other across the aisle from him. There was no air steward dishing out peanuts and drinks just bottles of Evian water on the tables.

The pilot's voice came across the tannoy, staccato and tinny *"Would passengers fasten their seatbelts please and ensure your electronic devices are turned off until we are airborne, and the seatbelt sign has been extinguished."* Dessie shifted nervously smoothing his fastened seat belt across his lap.

"Not a fan of flying then?" Mitch was watching his reactions; how he moved, trying to assess his emotional state.

"I haven't done that much of it. How long will it take to get there?"

"The flight is only 50 minutes so not that long. Water?" He offered Dessie a chilled bottle from the holder in his armrest.

He reached across and took it, his eyes not leaving Mitch's face. He unscrewed the plastic top taking a long drink, almost emptying the bottle.

"You obviously needed that."

The tension was evident, and an awkward silence grew until Mitch spoke up.

"Why are you doing this Dessie. You are turning your back on everything you know, everything you have fought for. Either something terrible has happened to make you think twice or you were never really that passionate about the cause in the first place. Which is it?"

Dessie shot him a look full of hate. "You wouldn't understand. Our history speaks for itself; occupied by the British for hundreds of years, exploited, persecuted for our beliefs, and murdered. What do you know about struggle for freedom and independence? Colonialism didn't just happen in the Empire; it was happening on your doorstep, and nobody gave a toss!"

"So, if it means that much why come to us now? What has the cause done to make you turn at this point in the game? It might be said that your goals are genuinely in sight. This is the closest Ireland has ever been to reunification. Why risk that?"

He sneered at Mitch as he spoke. "It's only a risk if you believe the bullshit! We have puppets in Stormont. Yes, they brokered the deal, and some of them got a very cushy living and a clean slate out of it. Has Ireland changed that much in last 20 years? Tokenism is what we've got. Stormont doesn't function like a parliament should. Our elected leaders have just moved the game on to a different pitch. They throw their toys out of the pram at every opportunity and for what? Political point scoring instead of direct action, and politicians are only interested in growing their own wealth while the very people they are supposed to serve still suffer. It has just watered down the fight. The Good Friday Agreement is the equivalent of a stray dog being neutered. They have our bollocks in a bag!" He took another swig from his bottle.

Mitch could see he was struggling to keep calm, but he wanted Dessie to keep talking. "So how does selling out your mentor help the cause?"

Dessie swirled the remaining water around the bottle. "I worked with Callaghan for years. Our commanders were happy when we were carrying out their orders. Collateral damage was not just accepted it was actively encouraged. No one ever told us to take it easy on a mark. All targets were selected to inflict as much damage as we could. It suited their PR campaign, kept recruitment high and American money flowing into our coffers. The Liverpool bombing changed all of that. Women were sick of losing their men, scraping to make ends meet while more money was spent on Semtex and bullets. The tide began to turn, and Sinn Féin sold out. We were left out in the cold; an embarrassment, the equivalent of a pervy uncle at a family party. They didn't want to be associated with the fight any more, so no comfort letters for us. We were sold out, so they could become the establishment. How were we supposed to live? We had sacrificed everything. We were still the wanted men; no amnesty for us, no loved ones waiting for us in a nice little three bed semi, no lucrative income from a proper day job on the hill. We were sold down the river.

Callaghan set about paying his wage bill however he could. No IRA funds, so he had no choice but to turn to crime. There were plenty of people just waiting to come in and trade on the misery of others when the bombs stopped going off. Prostitution, protection, drugs, fags, alcohol, we did it all. But the more you roll around with pigs the dirtier you get. The Eastern Europeans have seen much the same in their recent history, and we had some things in common, but their fighting was different. Their experiences left them desensitised to violence and exploitation in a way that made me feel uncomfortable, so it must have been bad! The sex trafficking was the worst. I realised that we were guilty of doing to those young girls and boys what we'd been fighting against for years. The ones with the power using the ones who had none for their own gain. I just couldn't stomach it anymore."

He suddenly looked tired and slumped back into his seat toying with the now empty bottle between his large hands.

Once again, the pilot's voice came over the tannoy and announced that they were beginning their descent into RAF Northolt.

"Please fasten your seatbelts and remain seated until the aircraft comes to a complete stop."

Mitch complied. Something that Dessie said had triggered a strange emotion in him. Empathy was too strong a word, but he certainly felt that he understood him a little more. He hadn't considered that it might be Dessie that felt betrayed and that's why he had taken his decision. Mitch's selective bias meant he had taken his experience of the troubles and placed the British on the right side of the fight, with the IRA firmly on the wrong side. Was it ever that simple? He could feel the conflict in Dessie and knew that he may have to reassess his starting point for the debrief, if he was going to get what they needed from this man. It was not as black and white as he had first thought, that was for sure.

Dessie didn't speak for the rest of the journey. They landed and disembarked from the plane into an unmarked saloon. He didn't say a word as they drove through country lanes with their discreet escort, or when they arrived at the holding pen in Enfield. Three hours after his escape, Dessie found himself alone in an interrogation suite in the bowels of a nondescript building on the outskirts of Greater London. The adrenaline now dissipated, his hands shook, he felt hot and hungry enough to eat a horse. He had always been careful during the troubles not to get caught and end up in a place like this. It felt decidedly odd that he was here voluntarily.

Chapter 11:

Sunday 21st July 2019. 3.30pm

Safe House Enfield

The interrogation room, no more than fifteen feet square was lit with naked fluorescent tubes, one had developed an annoying flicker. The room was furnished with a single grey metal table bolted to the floor, three metal framed chairs arranged around the table, in a two-one configuration and a large mirror set on the wall directly opposite the door.

On the table sat state-of-the-art audio equipment, a camera was set high up on the wall in the corner, recording all three occupants of the chairs below. Handcuffs attached to a chain passing through a metal loop in the middle of the table sat unused but served as a warning that freedom could be taken away in a moment.

The walls and ceiling were clad in grimy beige acoustic panels and the air had a distinct metallic quality, only achieved through poorly maintained air conditioning. Dessie assumed that the mirror was two-way, and observers on the other side were keenly noting his actions. He nodded and smiled at the mirror.

The door opened and Mitch and a striking woman walked in. He carried a tray with three mugs of coffee, the woman carried a thick dog-eared manilla folder. She took the seat directly opposite him putting her folder on the table.

Mitch handed a mug to him. “Black with three sugars wasn’t it?” He sat down next to the woman.

Dessie took the mug and nodded. He could smell the rich aroma. Just inhaling it revived him a little now that the adrenaline hit from the extraction had dissipated.

“Well Dessie, that went well. As you know, and for the record, I am Mitchell Bennett, and my colleague here is Dr. Marina Kinskey. I hope you feel rested after the journey?”

He grunted and shrugged, his eyes not leaving the woman. Dessie took a sip of the hot drink. He felt an intense gratitude that it was decent filter coffee. He felt sure he would be drinking a lot of it, and he couldn’t stomach instant.

“So how will this go?” he asked.

"We will do the preliminary debriefing here over the next couple of days, then you will be moved to a more permanent safe location. Somewhere a little more comfortable than here. We will complete the questioning there, and then the law will take over, and we will look at building a case with the information you give us. Your final destination is dependent on how helpful you end up being."

Dessie was still staring at the woman. She was very tall, just a shade shorter than Bennett. She was slim and angular with a shock of shoulder-length curly hair that was the colour of a rusty bucket. She had vivid green eyes that were magnified by a large pair of tortoiseshell spectacles. Dessie wondered what sort of doctor she was. She looked up from the folder.

"So a doctor eh? Are you here to give me a physical then?" He smirked at her.

Marina continued to stare at him. She had a wide full mouth and spoke with a soft Scottish accent. "I'm not that kind of doctor."

Dessie stared back but said nothing. The ball was in their court now. He was interested to see how this process would go. What would the first question be he wondered.

Mitch spoke, and the recording machine responded to his command. "Commencing interview of 'Ragair' Desmond Patrick McFee on July 21st, 2019. Present Mitch Bennett Head of Ops', Dr. Marina

Kinskey Intelligence Officer, and Dessie McFee. Time; fifteen, twenty-seven hours."

Dessie waited. He was reluctant to be the first to speak. He had made his decision to cooperate, and he knew his reasons were valid, but that didn't mean he wanted to make it easy for them. He won; Bennett spoke first.

"So Dessie, we need to make it absolutely clear that in exchange for information on the operations of the Callaghan Gang and the Cartel, the crown prosecution service will be made aware of your assistance and that will influence your eventual destination. We will ensure that your identity is protected, you will get a fresh start, somewhere to live and enough money to keep the wolf from the door. Do you understand?"

Dessie smiled at Bennett. "That's always saying that I live long enough to testify."

Marina took a sip of her coffee and leafed through her folder. "OK Dessie, let's start with your relationship with Jon Jo Callaghan."

Dessie began slowly, introducing them to the key people in the relationship, but only giving them what he knew they would already have. He took a deep breath and focused on a point on the ceiling before making eye contact first with Mitch and then with Marina.

"After the GFA, Callaghan and I met with the Albanian Yilmaz and some of his thugs one evening in Dublin in March 2016 to discuss a joint business arrangement that would give them a foothold in Ireland and give Callaghan links to the 'European Market'.

Right away I could see that Yilmaz was not dealing from a full deck, if you know what I mean, he was a dangerous psycho, ruthless and a bit unhinged. He'd been on the scene for a while, but we had all kept our distance. I didn't want to get involved with him and I told Callaghan as much, but he needed money after the GFA had left him out on a limb, no friends or influence in high places, and Callaghan had enemies. A link-up with Yilmaz would keep his competition at bay, as the Albanians played by different rules. They tended to shoot first and ask questions later, so Callaghan made a deal with the devil as it were.

Dessie continued, warming to his narrative, "At this time I was Callaghan's hired security, doing the heavy-lifting and some of the 'scare-tactics' when people needed to be bought into line, but that was the limit of my involvement in the rough stuff. Yilmaz ordered his own hits and doled out his own brand of swift justice as he saw fit. Look, I knew Yilmaz was not the full shilling, so I began to distance myself from him taking my instructions only from Callaghan directly".

Marina nodded slowly and said, "even so, why did you decide that you wanted out"?

"Ah, the straw that broke the camel's back. Yes, I was getting very concerned about the direction Callaghan's association with the Albanians and the Turks was going in. The drugs, extortion, and sex workers were bad enough but what really did it was when Jon Jo OK'ed people trafficking from Eastern Bloc countries". Dessie sighed deeply and looked down at the table. "These were young, impressionable girls taken from poor villages with a promise of jobs, good money, and a new life. They were shipped across Europe in the backs of lorries to Belfast, Birmingham, and Liverpool. Those girls suffered terribly on those horrendous journeys. When they arrived, they were hungry, thirsty, weak and in poor condition. They were taken to squalid accommodation, subjected to initiation rapes that degraded and subjugated them before they were 'put to work' for their new owners".

Dessie paused, his jaw clenched, he looked angry. "I knew these girls and boys were not the enemy. They were victims. They were at the mercy of men who used them to further their own ends. It was this that finally made me realise the lengths and depths Callaghan would go to through his involvement in this vile trade. He and Yilmaz were recreating a different version of the subjugation and enslavement that we had fought against for a hundred years or more".

He looked into Marinas' eyes and said, "That was the turning point for me. I had to find a way out, to build a new life that was more honest before it was too late. I know I can't wipe away my history, but I can make a different future."

Marina flicked a glance at Mitch and then turned her gaze back to Dessie who was slowly regaining his composure.

"Yes, I knew it was a dangerous decision. But I also realised that Callaghan was no longer the principled man I thought he was. Years of fighting and criminal activity had changed him. He enjoyed the fear he created in others and I knew he would never stop. He was bitter about being left out in the cold by his old IRA comrades. His bitterness became an all-consuming hatred, and it changed him. It was a creeping change that took years. It was only when I stopped and looked at what he was getting into that I realised I couldn't do it any more. I knew I was burning my bridges and my life wouldn't be worth much when they found out what I had done, but I had to do it anyway."

Marina looked up from her note pad and said, "so you came to us to stop Callaghan and Yilmaz?"

"Yes, the only way to stop Yilmaz and Callaghan is to break up the cartel and put them away for a long time. I couldn't carry on seeing the violence and exploitation any more. There are others with equally long memories who are afraid of what I know and what I might say, but my main reason is to stop what is going on regardless of the risk to me. I really have had enough!"

The information was complex, dates, times, places, and names. So far Dessie had given them the details behind the main routes that traffickers took and the main distribution hub for the drugs that were bought into Ireland. He had also given them details of two executions that had been ordered by JJ and carried out by his resident nutcase and hitman, Seamus Mehan. Both targets had been gang leaders who had refused to give up their territories and work for Callaghan.

Dessie had struggled with this more than he thought he would. It was necessary to halt JJ's megalomaniac activities, but he didn't see himself as a 'tout'. He found the term offensive. He knew he could justify why he was doing it, but you couldn't just wipe away decades of history that easily. He talked for four hours, they were feeling the effects, they were tired and getting irritable.

They had eaten a meal of pizza and fries and the filter coffee was flowing, but even that amount of caffeine could not stem the exhaustion.

Mitch began to clear the paper plates away and Marina said, "Let's call it a day for now. Interview terminated at nineteen forty hours. Stop recording." The machine's red standby light came on.

Dessie stretched in the chair and yawned. "Where am I sleeping tonight then? I hope the night porter at the Ritz is expecting me."

Mitch looked at him, "We have a room prepared for you here tonight. Security is good, and it saves us taking any unnecessary risks. You should be comfortable enough. Tomorrow or Tuesday you will be moved to the safe house where you'll be until we have made arrests."

Dessie looked nonplussed, "I'll remember to leave my review on Trip Advisor."

They resumed the debriefing the following morning. Dr. Kinskey strode confidently into the room. She was wearing a charcoal grey pants suit, an acid green shirt and sensible shoes, no heels. Dessie noted that she carried her significant height well. He wondered if the choice of flat shoes was just practical rather than a self-conscious act.

Bennett was in the same suit as yesterday but with an open neck striped shirt, no tie. Dessie studied him closely. He was a solid man, taut, with a pent-up energy and physically imposing. Dessie was particularly wary of him. He could tell he'd been around the block and was hard to fool. His instinct also told him that this was a man who had taken a life.

That act leaves its mark. Imperceptible by most, but not to someone who shares the experience. Like being members of some exclusive club, but there was no membership card or loyalty bonus, just a stain on the conscience that could never be erased.

They both looked rested which was more than Dessie could say about how he felt. "I want to complain about the accommodation. The bed was hard, and the shower didn't work properly. I got toast and marmalade for breakfast instead of bacon and eggs. I thought you would be trying a bit harder than this."

Marina smiled at him, "Sorry Dessie, I know it's not ideal. Things will improve when we can move you to the safe house. In the meantime, we must all make sacrifices."

"And what sacrifices have you made Doctor?" Dessie looked at her crossly.

"I had to have white toast with my salmon and scrambled egg this morning, they had run out of whole meal." She offered him a wide smile then looked down at her notes. She commanded the machine to begin recording and stated the date and time. Then she sat back in her seat. It was obviously Bennett's turn to question him today.

"I want you to tell us everything you know about Kadir Yilmaz and the money trail."

Chapter 12:

Monday 22nd July 2019
Devey's Office Stormont

Sinead was clearly irritated. Colm watched her pace the room making rapid hand gestures as she spoke, her thin frame taut with nervous energy.

"They got him out through the airport and straight across to London. No holding him in Dublin like they've done in the past with the others. They knew there would be an attempt to get to him. Word is that the Albanians took a contract out on him, but the spooks lifted him before they got a shot off. Our contact inside the Counterterrorism Branch has not been able to find out where they are holding him yet, but I am hopeful, it's just a matter of time."

Colm sat working through a pile of parliamentary papers that were precariously balanced on the edge of his desk. He understood her frustration, but he knew that they had to be patient. They had more than one option when it came to information from insiders.

"We need to calm down and take a breath Sinead. They will not be interested in the historical stuff because they can't risk the Agreement. They will concentrate on JJ's links with the Albanians and the trafficking stuff. There is no way they will be allowed to turn over stones from the eighties and nineties, it would be too risky."

"I'm sorry Col, but I am not as sure about that as you are. That bastard tout will say anything to protect his own skin. He's sold us out, betrayed the cause! How can you expect him to keep his mouth shut?"

Colm felt a wave of despondency wash over him. "I don't know how many times I have to say this. Even if he talks, they will not act on historical incidents because they are under orders to protect the agreement at all costs! Your paranoia isn't helping. I told you; I've got this, we'll be fine.

"No, they'll keep digging till they find something. Don't tell me that if they get a hint of who killed the FRU soldier they won't follow it up. It was twenty years ago, but they have never forgotten. It was probably the most pain we inflicted on them in a decade. They will not pass up that opportunity, and it's my neck on the line."

The FRU, the Force Research Unit, had been a covert military intelligence unit of the British Army, part of the intelligence services. It was established in the eighties at the height of the troubles and was intended to penetrate the IRA and splinter organisations with agents and informants. The reality was much more sinister and FRU members had colluded with paramilitaries to murder civilians to protect their cover.

Colm's brigade had discovered one of them operating in their midst in 1997. The soldier had posed as a disgruntled second-generation Irishman with links to the American funders. He had been passing information back to the security services for ten months before he was suspected. Obviously he had to be dealt with, but the mission went wrong and turned very messy. His abduction was caught on camera by a young journalist working on a local story. There was a campaign in the media to get him back before anything could happen to him. They used the footage to paint a story of mistaken identity to try to locate him and get him back safely. What they ended up with was his half naked, tortured body dumped on waste ground just off The Shankill Road. He had been executed, a shot through the head and one in the back.

Colm, the Brigade leader at the time, needed to interrogate the spy to find out the truth, so he had dispatched a team including Sinead to bring him in and find out exactly what he had told his spymasters. Sinead was responsible for bringing the FRU soldier in, during which he had attempted to escape, and she had shot him in the back as he was running away, before finishing him off with a shot to the back of his head. They had underestimated the storm that it would create. The backlash was massive. The British were incensed at the murder and the Prime Minister had taken his death personally. She ordered a no-holds barred manhunt to bring his killers to justice. Colm had lost four of his top brigade men in the aftermath, JJ lost another three. Colm had been able to keep Sinead's involvement secret, but it was a heavy toll on their relationship, one that they had never really recovered from.

He had always resented her lack of self-control and the mess it left behind, and here she was again, causing havoc. He was losing his patience. "Look, if we play our cards right, we may be able to lay that at Callaghan's door too."

Sinead looked thoughtful "Do you think so? We'll need to find out where they are holding him first."

"I am confident our contact will come through with the information, we still have time, we just have to keep a cool head and not panic."

Sinead took a deep breath; she walked back across the panelled office for the umpteenth time and flopped into the chair opposite her brother. "You are not seriously thinking of telling him what really happened with Theresa Farrell are you?" asked Sinead.

"If it provides us with a scapegoat for the FRU death, it might be worth it."

"Dessie wouldn't believe that Callaghan ordered her death, he would think you were lying for your own ends." She shook her head, but she was churning the options over in her mind. Colm continued. "It would have to be me that tells him. I have enough details to convince him that it's true. He wouldn't believe anyone else, that's for sure! But I haven't spoken to him since that night, so it would be a difficult conversation."

Sinead was warming to the idea. "I could certainly help by making sure the police records supported Callaghan's direct involvement in the FRU kidnapping. The best place to hide a lie is among a bunch of similar truths. It happened on his patch after all, no one but us knows that I had strayed into his territory. It would be easy to make it seem like a situation that escalated out of control. We wouldn't need to name an individual; we could suggest that he died at the hands of an angry mob. Most of those foot soldiers are no longer around to argue about the details anyway."

She looked down at the floor and shrugged then back at her brother. "All of this is academic unless we can get to Dessie."

Colm watched his sister carefully; he recognised that look. She was piecing together a plan. She said, "I am not that far away from being able to make the official police records reflect our 'truth' of Callaghan's part in it all. If I move too quickly and change too many records at once it will draw attention. I can redact quite a lot of the detail around the MI5 operation that might lead back to us. Luckily, they are still among the paper files waiting to be scanned for electronic filing. It's tricky though because I need to leave enough behind for them to arrive at Callaghan as the main suspect."

Colm relaxed a little. "OK, see what you can do. I'll have a word with our contact and see how we can get a message to Dessie to try to get him to play ball. If he is going to give Callaghan up anyway we may be able to get him to implicate him in a couple of other things just to make sure."

Sinead picked up her tote bag and left the office. He knew Sinead better than she knew herself and he could not shake the feeling that there was something else going on with her just now. She was too aggressive, too scared by all of this. It was like there was another secret she was hiding, but what could be worse than the death of the FRU soldier?

PART 2

Chapter 13:

Tuesday 23rd July 2019
Shady Fields

Beattie Malone sat alone in the Shady Fields' library. This room was her favourite. She loved the smell, the comfort, the muffled quality of the sound as the soft furnishings absorbed the noises of life in the building. She harboured a suspicion that Hilary was a fellow book addict as she often found her in here enjoying the solitude. Hilary would regularly bring her morning coffee here and peruse the shelves for something interesting. Beattie was intrigued about how such a young woman came to be running a place like Shady Fields. She observed an ordinary, slim, well-dressed woman in her mid-thirties, who carried an air of detachment everywhere she went. Beattie wondered if she had any family, she never spoke of them if she did. She thought next time they were chatting she would make a point of asking.

Dr. Arnot had just left Beattie, after their weekly catch up. He was quite good-looking and very pleasant for a doctor. She asked him about the memory problems she had noticed recently, the strange places she had been putting things, sometimes not being able to recognise whether it was morning or nighttime. He had explained they were symptoms of her vascular dementia.

"But doesn't everyone get a little forgetful at my age, Dr. Arnot?" she had asked.

He had agreed and tried to ease her mind a little. "Beattie, we have it under control. Since you started the new medication the deterioration of your condition has slowed significantly. That is really positive."

She took a little comfort from that, but desperately hoped that she would not be aware of what was happening to her when it did start to get worse. She had seen how it affected some of the others here. Many were younger than her, and it was frightening how quickly they went downhill.

In her youth she had done so many things that women of her generation had only dreamed of. In the fifties she had bought a second-hand motorbike to get her to and from her job at the local Town Hall. She had worn trousers and smoked. Her father thought it scandalous!

He just wanted to know when she was going to settle down and have a family.

Beattie had been a strikingly good-looking young woman. She was never short of a date to the pictures or the Saturday dance. She had plenty of male friends although nothing very serious. But she sought to better herself and had settled into a supervisor's role with the GPO in Birmingham. She was initially assigned to a specialist telecommunications division in 1963 which shortly afterwards had been acquired by MI5. Her hard work and diligence were rewarded with several promotions, resulting in her becoming a Section Head in charge of more than fifty staff. She loved her life and really didn't miss having a family until it was too late.

She met the love of her life when she was least expecting it. John Malone was nearly ten years younger than her. They met at a Renaissance exhibition at the Barbour Institute and hit it off immediately. They began seeing each other regularly, and she became quite the centre of attention when office gossip revealed in the fact that Beattie had a toy boy. It was not a mad passionate fling; it began as a deep friendship, one that blossomed into the need to be together to feel whole.

They married just nine months later. A simple registry office ceremony with two witnesses; John's brother and Beattie's best friend. Their wedding breakfast was at the Midland Hotel in New Street and their honeymoon was a week in Brighton. They settled into a happy and quiet life together in a lovely pre-war detached house in Bourneville, the Quaker built estate next to the famous chocolate factory in the leafy Birmingham suburb.

Their circle of friends was small, but their social life was filled with the pursuit of the arts. They would frequently go to the theatre, to concerts and the ballet. John became the youngest managing director Hartlebury Jams and Conserves had ever had, and although he worked long hours he paid very careful attention to her when they were together. It was something people today referred to as 'quality time'.

They shared a love of travel and culture and their holidays consisted of exploring museums and art galleries around the world. The many cruises they took in later years gave them a circle of acquaintances from all over the globe. This made their Christmas card list significant and allowed them to enjoy many friendships vicariously through the postal service.

John passed away seven years ago with pancreatic cancer. A vile disease that robbed him first of his good looks, then his zest for life. The last insult was when it robbed him of his ability to recognise her. That final degradation had hurt the most. She had rattled around in their home, losing interest in almost everything. Nothing was the same without John.

She had been faced with spending the rest of her life on her own, and then the diagnosis of vascular dementia came. She was worried about becoming the batty old lady who wandered up and down the main road in the early hours, wearing a housecoat and slippers, carrying a toilet brush, like Mrs. Thomas from number 22 had. Beattie decided she needed options.

After a telephone call to her previous employers' HR department, she realised that they had the same concerns she had about some of the national secrets she had been party to, and offered her a place at Shady Fields. She was sceptical at first, she felt she was too well to live in a home, but her first visit had changed her mind. It was a gentile place with nice people. The staff didn't dress like nurses or orderlies, except on the third floor, and the apartments were light and airy with no funny smells and the food didn't remind you of the worst school dinners, in fact, it was restaurant quality.

She had been here for a couple of months now and apart from some of the odd comings and goings, she had settled in very quickly. She felt safe. No, it was more than that, she felt visible here, people took notice of you. They listened and asked your opinion on things. You felt important, as though you really mattered.

"Good morning Beattie" She gave a start, snatched from her thoughts by Layla Strong the manager. "I'm sorry, I didn't mean to make you jump. How are you today?"

Beattie looked up at her, "I am feeling very well thank you".

Layla was a lovely girl. She was petite, about 5'3", slim with green eyes and short dark hair. She was a real people-person, someone who took time with you because she wanted to, not just because it was her job.

She had been very kind to Beattie helping her to settle in and feel at home. Nothing ever seemed too much trouble for her.

She sat down in the armchair next to Beattie and asked, "Is there anything I can help you with today?"

Beattie smiled. "I am struggling a bit. Talking to Dr. Arnot makes my dementia feel too real. Don't get me wrong, he is lovely, but his news was still disappointing." Beattie sat up straight in the chair and gave a little shrug "But, do you know Layla, I came through a war? I've lived through rationing and the swinging 60s! I dare say I can deal with this too."

Layla smiled and looked out of the bay windows, "The roses really are lovely, aren't they?" It was true, the flower borders that ran along the driveway were heavily in bloom and their fragrance wafted in through the open windows, whilst the ornate concrete planters that framed the windows were filled with pink geraniums and white fuchsias.

The front of the building was shaded from the morning sun, so the library was a cool place on what promised to be a very warm day.

Layla stood up to leave and said, "I have to go and prepare a suite. We have a new lady coming to us today. Her name is Ada, and she comes from Derbyshire. A little place called Ingleby."

Beattie fished for a memory that the name had conjured. "I knew an Ada once, a long time ago now. I worked at the GPO, and she worked in the next department to me. She was a real laugh, always making jokes. A neat little woman, very stylish. I seem to remember that she was a bit of a rogue; liked a drink and a smoke."

Beattie smiled as she warmed to the memory. "She was quite outspoken too. No one took her on in an argument as I remember. Now what was her last name?"

Something in her description made Layla think "It wasn't Hale was it, Ada Hale?"

"Yes! Yes, it was" said Beattie excitedly. "It isn't the same Ada surely?"

Layla smiled, "Her name is Ada Hale, and she did work in Birmingham for a while. What a small world! When she's settled in, you might want to pay her a visit. I could arrange afternoon tea for you both in here one day next week if you like. Some of chef's homemade scones and jam might be nice. I imagine you would like to talk about the old times?"

"Oh Layla that would be lovely. Ada had a wicked sense of humour, but she was such a lovely person too. She was one of the seniors, but in a different department to me. It was rumoured that it was something to do with surveillance of important people, but I never listened to gossip. She worked her way up from the bottom but always treated people the same. What you saw was what you got!"

Layla stood up to leave. "When she has settled in, I will ask if she feels up to having a visitor. It would be nice for you to catch up, and I am sure she would welcome a familiar face. Friends and acquaintances are so important, aren't they?" Layla made a mental note to talk to Ada about Beattie. She may not want to reconnect after such a long time, but it might be the support they would both need, given their circumstances.

Ada arrived at Shady Fields at 4.00pm by private ambulance. As they followed the winding driveway through the trees she caught sight of the house once more. It was a beautifully extended, three story, Georgian building with warm stone lintels and trellis supporting vigorous growths of Virginia Creeper and Wisteria. It was even more beautiful than she remembered from her first visit. She had been here a couple of years ago to recover from her first operation and radiotherapy.

The vehicle came to a stop, and in a flash the driver was out and opening the door for her. He presented a wheelchair that one of the staff had bought out for her. She waved it away preferring to walk in under her own steam. So instead, he offered her a steadying hand to help her up the steps, returning to retrieve her bags from the boot of the car. Her luggage was simple; one medium suitcase and a vanity case.

Layla appeared at the door. "Hello Ada, welcome back. Don't worry about your bags, I'll get Alan to take them to your room."

Ada wore a soft, heather-coloured dress with matching coat and stylish black suede shoes with a low Cuban heel. "Hello again Layla, that is so kind of you."

Alan, the orderly, nodded to the driver then picked up the bags. He went back into the entrance hall calling over his shoulder "Room eighteen isn't it boss?"

"Yes, that's right" replied Layla, and turning to Ada she said, "There are just a few formalities, papers to be signed etc. Would you like to do that over a cup of tea in the library or do you want to go straight up to your room?"

Ada gathered herself before attempting the last two stone steps up to the entrance doors. She took the arm offered by Layla. "It's been a long journey. I think I would like to go up to my room first. Can we complete the paperwork up there?"

"Yes, of course" said Layla. "Do you remember Dr. Arnot, our GP? You met him during your last visit here. He's going to pop by later. He wants to check your medication and ensure the best pain relief programme for you. Is that OK?" They reached the doors, and she noted that Ada was a little breathless.

"You seem to have thought of everything Layla."

"We try our best" said Layla. She held the door open for the old lady as she entered the building. They stood in the entrance hall and Ada gestured towards the sweeping staircase. Alan was mounting the stairs two at a time with Ada's bags.

"Why does he call you boss?" It was a rhetorical question really. Layla exuded confidence and authority and Ada suspected that she engendered great loyalty from her staff.

Layla laughed. "Don't mind Alan. He's an ex-policeman who got fed up locking the bad guys up."

Ada smiled "So his career change means he only locks the good guys up now."

"It could be worse, when he first arrived, he used to call me Guv!" She gave a theatrical shudder and guided Ada towards the lift in the corner.

They stepped out of the lift on the second floor, room eighteen was directly opposite. Layla reached the door before her and opened it using a key card. Ada followed her in and saw that her cases were already on the luggage stand.

Her pain was manageable but sitting for long periods was not comfortable, so she walked around the room for a moment before taking a seat by the window. The room was spacious and sunny, the high ceiling decorated with ornate plaster work. The walls were pale cream and a soft gold carpet covered the floor. There was no hint of hospital about this room. There was a heady fragrance of old-fashioned roses coming from a bowl of flowers on the table opposite the bed. Layla took the chair opposite Ada.

They had been followed into the room by a small dark-haired woman carrying a tea tray with homemade biscuits.

"Earl Grey for two with some lemon shortcakes freshly made by chef this morning. Is there anything else I can get you?". Her voice had a soft Irish lilt to it.

"No, thanks Mary, that's fine." Layla said as they watched her leave, closing the door behind her.

Layla opened a green folder she had taken from the long seat at the bottom of the bed and held it out to Ada. "Can I ask you to sign here and here please?". She indicated two pencil crosses on the completed forms. Ada took the folder and with a shaky hand proceeded to sign them.

Layla offered a cup of tea and the plate of biscuits to Ada. Ada shook her head,

"No biscuits for me thanks, and can I have lemon rather than milk"?

Layla poured another cup omitting the milk and handed it across to Ada. "You know that many of our residents have early onset dementia. You may find that you have the same conversation numerous times, but they really are a nice bunch and I think we have a lady living here that you may already know. Beattie Malone believes she may have worked with you at the GPO in Birmingham in the early seventies. She was a Section Head in communications, I think. Do you remember her?"

Ada recalled Beattie immediately. "Oh yes I remember Beattie. A lovely woman. She married quite late in life I seem to remember. Is she here for palliative care too?"

"No" said Layla. "Beattie is a resident. She hasn't been here very long and she's still settling in but does tend to be a bit quiet and reserved. I wondered if you'd like to have tea with her one afternoon. We could set something up in the library or the garden room if you like?"

Ada smiled, "I would really like that, but perhaps I could rest a little now? Would it be possible to have dinner in my room tonight rather than downstairs?"

Layla stood to leave. "Alan can bring up a tray around 6.30pm if you like".

"That would be lovely" said Ada, "but only for tonight. I'm keen to meet my fellow inmates". The twinkle in her eye reassured Layla that Ada would be just fine!

She took her time to unpack her things taking short breaks when breathlessness overtook her. They really did think of everything here. Cabinet drawers all closed softly with very little pressure and the wardrobe rails were in easy reach of shorter people that couldn't stretch the way they used to. She lay on the bed for a moment, just to catch her breath, and was awoken by soft knocking on the door. Ada looked at the travel clock on the bedside table. It was 5.50pm and Dr. Arnot had arrived to give her a brief examination.

When he had finished, she sat on the upright chair by the dressing table, rolling her sleeve down. Dr. Arnot was making notes.

"We normally get blood results back within twenty-four hours, but it will probably be Thursday now. I will let you know if we need to make any changes to your medication." Dr. Arnot closed the folder and then sat on the edge of the bed, opposite Ada. "We can continue with your current pain relief, but I've made a note that Oramorph is available, as and when you need something more powerful. Do you have any questions for me?"

Ada shifted slightly. "You have my instructions Dr. Arnot. My niece Hilary has lasting power of attorney for me. So when the time comes, when I have lost mental capacity because of the pain or the drugs, she knows my wishes."

"I have to say Ada, you've thought it all through very carefully. We want to keep you as comfortable and pain free as possible, so please let any of the staff know if we can do anything for you. So our Hilary is your niece then?"

"Yes" said Ada. "We are very close. I did have a few concerns about coming here, about how others might view that, but Daniel assured me it would be fine. Of course, it will give us a chance to see each other while I am here."

Dr. Arnot smiled at her. "You know Daniel too?"

"Yes, he did some training with my section when he joined the service, although I didn't realise he would reach the dizzying heights of Director General back then."

Dr. Arnot nodded and smiled, "Yes, it's good to have friends in high places. Now I think you need some rest. Recharge your batteries! I don't want you partying into the night on your first evening here."

Chapter 14:

Tuesday 23rd July 2019 11.00pm
Shady Fields

The small convoy of SUVs moved silently along the now deserted roads. The first car was running point and contained a small security detail of two armed plain clothes officers. The second car held their precious cargo; Dessie McFee, accompanied by Marina Kinskey and a driver, also armed. In the rear-guard vehicle there was a driver, another agent and Mitch Bennett, all equipped with weapons. The agents in all three vehicles were in constant communication with each other by means of wireless earpieces.

The only conversation taking place was in the middle car, with Dessie acting like a petulant 5-year-old.

"Where are we going? Are we nearly there yet?"

Marina, seated next to him, showed less irritation than she felt. "Do you honestly think we will get there any quicker if you keep asking inane questions?" She was an experienced profiler with the security services and was fascinated by the ruthless killer that sat next to her at this moment. "I would have thought you would need more patience in your line of work. It must take time and silence to stalk someone you are about to kill in cold blood."

Dessie shrugged. "It depends on who it is. Sometimes, if it's a soldier that's killed one of yours you might need stealth to ambush them, but if it's someone that has information you need, I find that noise and speed creates enough fear to achieve the desired effect."

Unfazed, she looked out of the window into blackness and said quietly "Interesting, I will need to remember that Dessie."

The vehicles turned off the main road onto a narrow lane that wound upwards through dense trees. Imposing gates loomed in the headlights of the cars, the lead driver leaned out of the window, swiped a key card against a security panel and entered a code on the adjacent keypad. Slowly the gates opened, and the convoy swept through the archway and on up the winding drive. Dessie leaned into the centre of the car so that he could see between the seats and through the windscreen. They rounded a final bend and Shady Fields came into view. Floodlights illuminated the exterior of the house highlighting its splendour. The cream stonework bathed in pools of light, its architecture, impressive during the day, looked taller and even more grand at night.

Dessie let out a low whistle "Now this is more like it, have you commandeered a hotel just for me?"

Marina smiled, "Not quite Dessie, this is a place that affords you total anonymity and security. Welcome to Shady Fields, your home for the foreseeable future. It's actually a residential home for old people. She struggled to keep the humour of his situation out of her voice.

"Very funny. Where am I really?"

"I'm serious Dessie, your fellow residents have an average age of 75, their diet is mostly puréed vegetables, and the TV lounge plays Last of the Summer Wine on a constant loop."

The look of shock on his face was a picture, and to keep him at a disadvantage Marina was out of the car almost before it had stopped moving. The two guards from the lead car were out and up the entrance steps posting themselves either side of the front door.

Mitch joined Marina at the passenger door. "All OK? How was the journey?"

Marina shrugged "Not quite the scintillating conversation I am used to but OK. I just broke the news of where he is, he seems quite surprised. I'll get him settled in then join you downstairs in about thirty minutes, OK?"

Mitch nodded. "I'll do a quick sweep of the area with the team and set up a perimeter guard. Hilary has assigned a couple of rooms for the team to use for sleeping and meals next to Dessie, so he will have plenty of company. You OK with settling him in?"

Marina nodded, she was aware that Dessie was trying to get out of the car but couldn't open the door; the catch clicked a dozen times or more. She reached out and opened the door for him "Sorry Dessie, must have forgotten to switch the child lock off."

He climbed out of the car and followed their driver up the steps "This place better not smell of piss and boiled cabbage." He said crossly.

She rolled her eyes at Mitch "Charming! See you in a bit." Then followed them into the building.

Marina moved the small group swiftly across the entrance hall and towards the lift in the corner. She couldn't see any residents about, probably all in bed she thought. The lift door opened and the three of them got in, Marina pressing the button for the third floor. As the doors opened another agent was waiting for them. He simply nodded and ushered them towards a heavy looking, cream panelled door in the corner. Marina watched Dessie; he looked around him trying to take in his surroundings. Although it was more luxurious than he had experienced recently he obviously felt uncomfortable, as if he were being watched.

Marina opened the door to enter the room and Dessie followed. They were in one of the large corner suites in the building. It comprised a sizeable living room with doors off to a spacious bathroom and a bedroom containing a queen size bed. A drinks station stood between the two doors and there was a small refrigerator underneath the walnut counter.

A hold-all stood open on the luggage stand at the foot of the bed and Marina pointed to it. "In there is a change of clothes for you, some nightwear and a toiletry bag with a razor and toothbrush. You should be fine for the basics. We will be back in the morning to see how you have settled in. There will be a guard outside your room 24-7, if you need anything, go through me or Mitch, or at a push ask the guard, but only if it's an emergency. Gavin is on duty tonight. There is tea and coffee on tap and your meals will be served in here. The fewer people that know where you are the safer you will be. Any questions?"

"A bottle of Jameson's would be nice." He said hopefully.

"Yes it would, but not possible I'm afraid. Those sorts of perks depend on how helpful you are." Marina turned and left the room nodding to Gavin as she went, he was just settling down on a hardback chair, and he grunted a goodbye.

Downstairs in the library, Mitch was waiting with a glass of scotch for her. She took it from him and flopped into an armchair. "Well, phase one completed. We got him here without any major mishap, let's hope it stays like that."

Mitch took a sip of his drink "They are sending one of the tech lads in tomorrow to set up the recording equipment then we can get started with his testimony. The stuff he gave us in London is being checked now, but it looks good so far. The intel backs up the fact that Callaghan and Yilmaz are running the largest trafficking ring in the UK and just stopping that would be worth the steps we have gone to, but honestly, I think there's a lot more to come. The money trail is looking promising with links to the terrorist attacks in Liverpool and Birmingham. Daniel was hoping it may even solve the lone-wolf attack on the underground that he's been working on."

Marina crossed her long legs awkwardly. She was too tall to fit comfortably into the leather wing back chair, but she was too tired to swap seats. She hadn't really slept much in the last couple of days. This was her first real outing with Mitch, and she wanted to get everything right.

"I'll stay here tonight, just to make sure everything is OK. Hilary has said I can use the guest room on the second floor for now. You can get back to London if you like, I dare say Daniel will want an update."

Mitch downed the remains of his drink "Thanks Marina, a couple of hours sleep in my own bed would be great. All updates go directly to Daniel, he wants as few people as possible in this loop. Can I bring you anything back?"

"No, thanks, I have an overnight bag with me, it's in the boot of the car. I'm going to turn in myself as soon as you go. We have to be on our toes for the debrief. I don't trust him at all. I just can't believe that someone that has been so devoted to a cause all of his adult life can be so pragmatic about how things have turned out. He's up to something. I'm just not sure what, but I believe there's an agenda we know nothing about yet."

Mitch walked towards the door "Get some sleep and let's worry about that tomorrow. I need to be in London for a couple of days, so Daniel is loaning us an agent from the CIA to help with the debrief. His name is Phil Santos, and he's good, as Americans go. He was in Colombia until recently. A couple of their military personnel were killed in an explosion that killed the President, and he has been helping with the investigation. While he's in London, he is going to lend us a hand."

"Oh, and what will the CIA bring to the party then?"

Mitch smiled. "He's got more than twenty years' experience, he is a decorated agent, a skilled profiler and interrogator, and Daniel has worked with him before. Phil was a US-Irish specialist in the agency for more than a decade and was involved, although I am not quite sure in what capacity, in the American contribution to the Good Friday Agreement, but I'm sure that's just a coincidence."

Marina smiled "You do know that a coincidence is simply a pattern that you haven't identified yet, don't you?"

He laughed. "And just because you are paranoid doesn't mean that people aren't out to get you."

Chapter 15:

Wednesday 24th July 2019

Shady Fields

The following morning Ada awoke to hustle and bustle. It was quiet living on her own in the cottage. The only noise she was used to in the mornings was birdsong. She found it surprisingly comforting to hear muffled chat. There were distant sounds as breakfast was prepared and the gentle hum of the lift as people made their way downstairs.

Hers was one of the larger suites at the front of the building. The queen-sized bed was very comfortable and beautifully coordinated with the rest of the room. She had not noticed the pale oyster wallpaper embossed with exotic birds and foliage yesterday when she arrived, but the morning sun seemed to bring it to life. Satin cushions in various shades of turquoise adorned the two fireside chairs that flanked an ornate white marble fireplace. There were worse places to end your days.

She scolded herself for being maudlin. Mornings were always difficult for Ada, as she needed to allow her medication time to take effect. Bathing and dressing could be uncomfortable, but this morning however, the ultra-modern and well-equipped bathroom had made things much more straightforward. Indeed, when one of the personal assistants had knocked on the door to help Ada, she was already sitting at her dressing table, bathed, dressed, and brushing her chemo-thinned hair.

A plump, fussy woman in her mid-thirties, had bustled in. She was chatty and had a kindness that exuded like toothpaste from a tube.

"Good morning Ada, my name is Jilly, and I came to see if you needed any help dressing, but I can see that you have beaten me to it! You will be doing me out of a job." She smiled, "Let me show you down to the breakfast room." Jilly had already called the lift, and they descended to the ground floor. "Layla asked me to make sure you were OK on your first morning and to ask what sort of assistance you require. Any help with personal care, dressing etcetera, just let me know."

The restaurant was a beautiful room, the large bay windows bathed the tables in warm, dappled light which made their linen coverings look even whiter. She spotted Beattie Malone at a small window table set for two. It had been many years since she had seen her, but Beattie was instantly recognisable. Yes, a little older, but still the same inquisitive look and reserved smile.

Ada walked across the room. “Can I join you Beattie?”

Beattie looked up and beamed. “Oh it is you Ada! I couldn’t believe it when Layla told me about you yesterday. It must be nearly forty years since we last saw each other. You haven’t changed a bit!”

“I sincerely hope I didn’t look like this then!” said Ada with a laugh. “It's good to see you too Beattie. Now let me order breakfast then you can tell me what you have been up to for the last few decades.”

They ate and chatted as easily as if they had seen each other a week ago. “So, what do you think about the place?” Beattie looked eager, her small dark eyes glinting like glass beads.

“Well, the first time I came here was after the war when they used it as a rehabilitation centre for ex-services. It was much more rough and ready then; it's quite luxurious now by comparison.” Ada was enjoying her toast and bitter marmalade; it was the first time in ages she had tasted anything properly, and she was savouring it.

“Really, so what were you doing here?” Beattie’s interest was piqued.

“I was a military nurse, and they sent me here to complete my training, but I think they struggled to get people to volunteer. Some of the patients were in a bad way with burns and amputations. It never bothered me, but some of the girls found it really upsetting. Then I came a couple of years ago when it first opened, it was after my surgery and radio therapy, and I needed to recuperate. Everyone was so good and in no time I was able to go home. Do you like it here Beattie?"

"Oh yes. The people are lovely, and it was just what I needed. I was really lost after John died. It was a difficult time and I struggled to cope for a few years, but when I came here, they gave me support and understanding. I realised I didn't want to live on my own any more and now that I have dementia I know I will need more support in the future."

"So who are our fellow inmates then?" asked Ada with a conspiratorial smile.

Beattie's chest puffed a little with importance, she looked around the dining room deciding whom to start with. She pointed out an elderly, distinguished, and still good-looking man sitting on his own, reading the Times.

"That is Charlie Bingham. He was a diplomat in South Africa until there was some sort of health scare, and he came here. He is very nice but a terrible name-dropper. He talks about the days he lived in London back in the sixties; dinner with David Niven, gambling with Ian Fleming, and he was supposed to be great friends with Graham Hill the racing driver. Someone told me that he is really Lord Lucan, but I think they were pulling my leg, so far-fetched."

Ada examined the old man's face "Yes I seem to remember him from when I was last here."

Just then a younger woman entered the room and took the table to the right of the doorway facing the rest of the diners with her back against the wall. She looked to be in her late forties. She was tall, very slim, with shoulder-length, dark curly hair that was peppered with grey, there was a distinctive, haunted quality about her. She was wearing a long-sleeved dress which Ada thought was odd on such a warm day, until she noticed the burn scars on her hands. The woman's eyes flitted around the room but never engaged with anyone directly.

"And that is Jackie Kelly" said Beattie sadly. "No one seems to know her history, and she never really talks to anyone. I heard she was on a mission that went wrong when she was caught behind enemy lines and interrogated. People here say that the Russians were quite vicious with spies they caught."

Ada watched the woman carefully, there was something disconcerting about her. She did indeed display the signs of someone broken by torture; there was a look of emotional detachment in her vacant expression and yet, the nervous tension was also there. It seemed to ripple under her skin as if she were waiting for the moment she could make a break for it and run away. "Was it definitely the Russians? They tended not to leave spies alive after they had finished questioning them."

"I'm not sure, all I do know is that I can't remember ever seeing anyone so sad and lost, poor girl." Beattie poured herself a top-up from the teapot.

"Now, that lady over there, is '*THE*' Vanessa Telford. Do you remember, the socialite linked with royalty for a while?" Ada vaguely remembered a stick-thin brunette with heavy eye makeup who seemed to live on the front pages of the tabloids in the late seventies. It was not uncommon for public figures to be recruited by the service as agents, particularly in the seventies. "Didn't she end up marrying one of the Beatles or a Rolling Stone?"

"No" said Beattie. "She was a Bond girl with Roger Moore, then married a minor royal I think, but you don't hear her going on about it!" Her eyes flicked back to Charlie who was studying the shares page now.

The table in the centre of the dining room had three men seated together deep in conversation.

"Over there are Bill and Ben, we call them The Dynamite Men, aka Bill Tandy and Ben Faulkner. They were in the army together, bomb disposal, I think. Bill is the shorter one, he says it was special ops, but Ben, the stocky chap, doesn't say much at all.

They left the army in the late 80s and set up in business together, they had a big demolition company and worked all over the world. Bill was the technical brains and Ben was the business head. They did a lot of government contracts here and overseas. They decided to sell their business when Bill was diagnosed with Alzheimer's, and they came here. They are never apart. The man with them is Douglas Phipps. He never uses his first name, and keeps himself to himself, I think he has memory problems too. He came here just after me, but no one seems to know much about him either. Bill and Ben are the only ones he regularly socialises with, someone said he was SAS, that's how he knows the dynamite men."

Almost as if he sensed he was the topic of conversation he turned to look at them, and Ada noted the ugly red scar that ran from his right temple, down the side of his face across his cheek and disappeared under his jawline. It was jagged, raised, and shiny red. Most people would struggle not to stare.

"Phipps seems young to be having memory problems, He only looks to be mid-50s?"

"I know. I thought you had to be our age, but apparently not. Dr. Arnot said all sorts of things can trigger it, poor diet, drink, heavy smoking, PTSD, and high blood pressure. They ought to call it the Secret Service disease."

A diner on the far side of the room rose. He reached for a stick that had been propped against the back of a chair and hobbled out of the dining room.

"Now that is Brooke Ward. He's probably the youngest one here. Early 40s, very brooding. Here to recuperate. He had a bad accident and broke his leg in three places. He's been here for nearly three weeks, but at least he is walking under his own steam now. He spends most of his time in the gym, mind you, no one else uses it. And that's about it. Those are the regulars, the ones that come and use the communal facilities."

Ada spotted an older lady sitting alone at a table near the door to the kitchens, "Who's that" she asked, pointing at the woman, who was engrossed in a seed catalogue.

Beattie laughed, "Oh, that's Jennie, she's the wife of Ken, our resident gardener". She hosts our weekly 'knit and natter' sessions, or as her hubby calls them, 'stitch and bitch'.

"Poor dear, has she got dementia too"

"Good gracious no! She is as sharp as a pin; she just comes in for breakfast. She's addicted to chef's Croissants"

Ada gave a little chuckle "Well Beattie, you haven't changed a bit. Five minutes in here, and you have the skinny on everyone. Not bad for someone who dislikes gossip as you do." She smiled warmly at her long-lost colleague.

Beattie smiled back "I don't know what you mean." She continued unabashed. "There are a few others, but their dementia is advanced, and they tend to stick to the top floor. We also get the occasional guest who comes for end-of-life care, but they don't stay long." Beattie suddenly realised what she had said and flushed deeply. "Oh Ada I'm so sorry, I didn't mean….".

Ada reached across and gave her arm a reassuring rub. "It's OK Beattie don't be daft. I'm very much aware of why I'm here; I just didn't think it would be common knowledge this quickly. This is my choice. It gives me the control I want over this final stage of my life. I've had a wonderful life with no regrets. How many people can say that? I have one more thing I must do for Hilary, and then I can rest knowing everything has been reconciled. Now unless you have emptied it, can I have another cup from the teapot you have been hogging?"

Jackie Kelly watched the new arrival chatting with Beattie Malone. They had glanced briefly over at her but were now focused on others in the room. There was no mistake, it was her. Jackie was sure that the newcomer hadn't recognised her, hardly surprising after the changes she had been through, but she definitely recognised Ada Hale. She was older, but the line of the nose and shape of her head were unmistakable.

Jackie felt her body tense in that dreadfully familiar way, her flashbacks always started with the same signals. There was the familiar smell, then the pain would start in her hands and arms and roll down her back. Next, the fear would overwhelm her, rushing through her body in an intense wave. It felt as if she were straddling a timeline, with her past trying to pull her back to the event, and her present trying to keep her in the here and now, where it was safe. Sometimes, although not so often these days the images flashed into her head, and the noises would follow, all so terribly real. Her heart would race, and if it were a particularly bad episode, she may even black out.

Jackie concentrated, she used the exercises her therapist had taught her to control her breathing and bring her heart rate back to something approaching normal. She had also been taught to focus on a memory from around the same time, when she felt in control and powerful, and to relive that, to substitute the negative emotions for positive ones.

She visualized a younger version of Ada Hale showing them how to strip down a small handgun, clean it, reassemble it, then load it ready for action. Ada had made it look so easy. She had drilled them all until they could do it blindfolded, literally. The skills she had taught them had kept some of them alive, and Jackie was in no doubt that if it wasn't for that unassuming, white-haired old lady she would not be sitting here now.

Chapter 16:

Wednesday 24th July 10.30am

Shady Fields

Hilary was juggling ten things at once, again. Their mysterious guest was settling in after a late arrival the night before. Two armed guards were stationed on the third floor, three rooms were being used by the security team, and no one else besides the normal nursing staff that worked with the two residents currently living on that floor were allowed access. A complicated relay system had been organised to arrange food deliveries to them and a very nice American chap had turned up this morning with a security clearance well above her pay grade, to work with Marina.

If that wasn't enough to keep her occupied, some of the other residents had not missed the tell-tale signs of a break in the routine and were speculating amongst themselves about what might be happening on the third floor. Definitely not, a normal day.

Hilary looked out at the lovely view of the gardens through the long bedroom window. Her Aunt Ada was sitting in one of the fireside armchairs, a cannula projecting from the back of her hand fed liquid pain relief into the thin, pale arm that lay on a cushion. Hilary was checking on her after Dr. Arnot's visit.

It really hadn't occurred to her until recently that her aunt might have led an eventful life. When Hilary was growing up, if the conversation got around to Ada's early life, she would make some vague references, then subtly change the subject back to Hilary. The effect of this was to make Hilary feel like the most important thing in the world to Ada, she never saw it as a diversionary tactic.

It all seemed so fantastical, her aunt working for MI5, and yet there was a part of her that was not surprised at all with the benefit of hindsight. Ada had always been a formidable woman and the idea that a life filled with jam making and libraries being all there was to her was so obviously wrong. Hilary was also intrigued to find out how her aunt knew Daniel Grant. She started the conversation simply by asking

"So how did you meet Daniel? I know nothing of your time in the service. Can you tell me anything?"

Ada plumped the cushion to give her arm a little more support. "I trained as a military nurse and worked abroad in the early days. It was a great life. I went to places and met people I would never have dreamed of. A man, who I thought was a British Diplomat, recruited me to MI6 to do a bit of fact finding when I was in the Middle East, and I discovered that I had a talent for it. I served mainly in the conflicts in Dhofar and Oman. I was there during the campaign against the British Forces in Aden. They were some terrible times. A children's party was bombed. It killed and maimed British children stationed there with their families. There were street riots in retaliation. The police were in a state of mutiny. It was a different world then. A blend of the savage and the fanatical, but it was exotic too. I came back down to earth with a bump when I returned to England. They gave me a job working for the GPO, which, I thought, was going to be quite boring until I realised that I would be helping to fight the Cold War by listening to spies and saboteurs."

Hilary processed what that meant. "You mean you bugged people's telephones? Wasn't that illegal?"

Ada smiled "It was much more of a grey area in those days. The Cold War was in full swing, and everyone was doing it."

Hilary pulled a face and Ada laughed, "I really did too good a job with you Hils. MI6 were up to their necks in Russians and International relations were complicated. The USA had very publicly lost the Vietnamese War, the world's richest nation had lost to one of the world's poorest, the drive of socialism, the Khmer Rouge, Pol Pot, and the killing fields. The world order was shifting and governments needed to know what other Countries' leaders were thinking. MI5 were fighting on a domestic front with the Irish troubles. We did what we had to do to keep our Country safe."

Ada shifted position again, wincing with discomfort. "By 1980 I was head of the department, and we liaised with MI5 to set up a special surveillance service at RAF Menwith Hill. They were recruiting heavily from Oxbridge universities and the military elite, and I was given a rising star as part of my team. His name was Daniel Grant." Ada watched as the penny dropped with Hilary.

"So that's how you know him?"

Ada smiled "I taught him everything he knows! Well, almost everything."

Hilary blinked "You never said anything…". She paused as the truth dawned "I didn't know because I never asked. I never once asked about your life. I had no idea about your past!" Hilary felt stunned, this little, frail woman in front of her had played such an important part in her life, yet she knew so very little about her.

Ada waved her away with a scrawny hand "I couldn't have said anything if you'd asked me. Official Secrets Act. I can only tell you now because you are one of us." Hilary shook her head, she still struggled to consider herself to be anything other than a civil servant.

Ada continued "I worked with a special squad of fearless young women who went undercover in Ireland to gather intelligence on what the IRA were doing. I taught them trade craft and Daniel worked with them and the bomb disposal team, teaching them about firearms and explosives."

Hilary felt embarrassed. "You never said a word when I was banging on about making a difference and wanting to give something back to society through my work. You must have thought me very naive."

Ada smiled fondly at her. "I was pleased you wanted to make a difference, but it was essential that you made your own mark, not just copied someone else's. When your mother had you, she was faced with a decision; giving up her career and being a single mother, which was still very difficult in the eighties or providing you with a life of opportunity. While you were very small, it was easier to manage with an au pair, but as you got older, she needed a more permanent solution. So when I stepped back from the service in 1990, I became a special advisor. That allowed me to spend time with you during the holidays and become more of a permanent fixture in your life."

Hilary cast her mind back to her youth. "I loved our holidays; they were the things that made boarding school OK. I didn't mind being shipped off because I can't remember spending any real time with mother, but the time spent at the cottage with you was different; so many memories."

Ada suddenly became very serious. "Hils, I will always be grateful to your mother and you for those times. I watched you grow into an independent and intelligent woman. But as I face the end of my life I only have one regret; I will not live to see you living a fulfilled life. Don't make the same mistake that I did and give up everything for your work. It doesn't matter how important it is, you also have a duty to yourself to live your life to the full, with all that it entails. What about love, family, and companionship? A life is only half a life if it's spent alone. I need to know that you will be OK when I'm not here. So, tell me Hils, what do you want from life?"

Hilary shifted uncomfortably in her seat and fiddled with a stray thread on her sleeve. "I haven't really thought about it, relationships, or a family. I've been too busy! I still want to make a difference and be important to people. If I don't do that by having a family I need to do that through my work. Listening to what you have done in your life makes me realise how small my own has been up to now. If I'm honest, I don't think I've ever made a real effort to have a private life. Working here, the people, Daniel, well, it's the first time I've felt that what I do really matters." Hilary felt like a light bulb had been switched on. She instinctively knew that this job was the right one for her. "Aunt Ada, what if I am exactly where I want to be, and this is my way to matter and make a difference?"

Ada took a deep breath and as she exhaled, there was a distinct rattle in her chest. "You have been through major upheaval recently. You have lost your mother; you are worried about me, and you have had a significant change in your career. You need to find a holding pattern to let things settle down before you make more life decisions. There's no doubt that for the people who live here, Shady Fields provides a real home. When people have been involved in sensitive work like ours, they may not have the support of close family. As we age and the unlucky ones succumb to dementia the State can't have us spilling national secrets all over the place" her eyes flashed. "That's why I'm here. The work I was involved may have been decades ago, but it's still sensitive and the drugs that manage my pain might remove my inhibitions, and with them my ability to keep those secrets safe! The fact that you get it and are here with me is great, but all of this is no substitute for a personal life Hils. Don't make the people that live here a family substitute. Promise me that you will think about what I have said."

Hilary brushed away a stray tear before it had a chance to track down her cheek. "I will, I promise" She glanced at her watch "Oh my goodness, I'm late for my next meeting." She bent to kiss Ada's cheek. She straightened up, the mask now firmly back in place, she left the room and made her way down the staircase.

Her head was a jumble with everything Ada had said. As she passed the almost deserted lounge she noticed a lone figure seated by the window. Brian was a strange sight. He was sitting bolt upright in his wheelchair with a purple towel wrapped loosely around his head. He had been in a wheelchair for more than thirty years, left paralysed by the bomb that had gone off in a Brighton Hotel, intended for Mrs. Thatcher. He had never been able to return to active duty with MI5 and had recently been diagnosed with Lewy Bodies, a distinct type of dementia. The tell-tale tremor was always present in his right arm and the hallucinations were getting more outlandish and vivid recently.

Hilary decided to check if everything was OK. "Hi Brian, what is the towel for?"

He blinked at her and said, in a matter-of-fact way, "It's to keep the kangaroos away."

Hilary didn't miss a beat "and how's that working out for you?"

Brian gave a knowing smile "Well I haven't seen one yet today so, great, thanks."

Chapter 17:

Wednesday 24th July 2019 2.30pm

Shady Fields

Marina had spent several years working for the Centre for Disease Control (CDC) and had enjoyed the challenges it bought, but she always felt it was a little pedestrian. Her involvement in the poisoning of a resident here at Shady Fields last year had given her a taste for field work, so as soon as the opportunity came up, her sense of adventure kicked in, and she applied for a transfer. Mitch was a great boss. He didn't wrap her in cotton wool, he expected her to perform, but he was approachable, and he encouraged her when she asked questions. He had given her this debriefing as her first real test.

It was clear that he was struggling with the idea of working with Dessie McFee. Mitch needed her to extract as much intelligence from Dessie as possible, and he was worried that his unspoken history with the troubles made him problematic as a sole interrogator, he had told her as much when they discussed the job. His manner and careful wording of the task told her that he was wrestling with the privileges that Supergrass status afforded Dessie. She was surprised at how powerful her profiling training had been. The insights came thick and fast from her observations, both friend, and foe.

Marina knew little of Mitch's history in Northern Ireland as most of it was still classified, but she could sense the anger that rippled just below the surface when Mitch was in Dessie's company, it was tangible. When she saw flashes of dislike flit across his face and heard some of the barbed comments that crept into the conversation, she understood the reason for him distancing himself from the situation.

She glanced at her watch; she was expecting Agent Santos to arrive shortly. She wondered what his take on the operation would be. The Americans definitely had a different perspective on the troubles and on the now infamous peace agreement.

A small anteroom had been allocated for them to use as an office. It was just down the corridor from Dessie's suite and was a glorified broom cupboard, but beggars couldn't be choosers.

The walkie-talkie vibrated on her desk, she picked it up pressing the speak button, it crackled into life. “Agent Santos has just passed through security and is on his way up; over.”

“Roger, out.” That still felt a little ‘boy's own adventure like’ when she said it. She smiled to herself, who was she kidding? She was working in a place where PMT was trumped every time by TMT, Too Much Testosterone! The culture of any organisation was shaped by the worst behaviour it was willing to tolerate and in the security services that bar was set very low indeed. She wondered if the same were true of the CIA? Marina stuck her head out into the corridor in the direction of the lift. She could hear the motor whirring as the car ascended. The doors opened and out stepped Agent Santos who caught sight of her and walked directly towards her.

He was about 5’10” and a little shorter than her, but then, most people were. He was quite nondescript really until he got closer, then you noticed his eyes. They were hazel with long blond lashes and a twinkle that conveyed intelligence, humour, and magnetism. Marina’s profiling and observation skills kicked in to top gear, ‘a man who could master blending into his surroundings and who only becomes visible when he wants to.’ Immediately she liked him.

“Good morning Dr. Kinskey.” He reached out a well-manicured hand. “I am Special Agent Phil Santos, here to lend a hand if you need one.”

Marina felt quite stupid as she began to blush. "Agent Santos, please call me Marina, I only use Doctor with civil servants, politicians, and traffic wardens" she shook his warm dry hand and ushered him into her makeshift office.

"Thanks Marina, call me Phil." He stood, politely waiting for an invitation to be seated on the conference chair she had set out for him.

"Can we just go over a few things before I take you down to meet our special guest."

She realised after just a few minutes of conversation with him that she really didn't need to 'get him up to speed'. He was already familiar with whatever information Mitch had provided to him and knew everything that she knew about the operation.

"Sorry, I didn't mean to teach my grandmother to suck eggs."

He smiled at the colloquialism, raising a quizzical eyebrow. "That's OK, I've never sucked an egg before, but I am happy to share the stuff I know if it will add a bit of context, although it will be from the American perspective." His accent was soft and from somewhere Midwest she guessed.

"Whereabouts in America are you from?" she asked.

"I'm from Kentucky, Lexington actually, do you know it?"

"No, sorry, the extent of my American travel is New York and Los Angeles, both work conferences.

They had difficulty understanding my accent on both occasions."

He smiled tilting his head slightly, "Let me guess, Scottish, maybe Edinburgh?"

She was surprised on two counts, firstly, he was right, and secondly he pronounced Edinburgh correctly! She noted the warm, genuine smile that danced around his eyes making them twinkle even more.

"It's a bit of a party trick for me. I was posted to Scotland for a few years and I got to know the difference between Glasgow and Edinburgh accents. I wouldn't have a clue if you had an English accent, there are so many of them."

She realised she was staring and chastised herself, for God's sake Marina, pull yourself together! She cleared her throat and picked up the folder on her desk. "Shall we go?"

She spoke as they walked. "When the Good Friday Agreement legislation was passed, ostensibly to deal with the emotional and practical aftermath of the conflict, the Historical Investigations Unit (HIU) took over the caseload of those deaths reviewed by the Police Service of Northern Ireland (PSNI) that might require further investigation. Under normal circumstances they would be dealing with Dessie, but due to his connections to organised crime and possible funding of domestic terrorism MI5 are taking the lead. Although he is co-operating, he hasn't given up all the names of people linked to Callaghan yet. We need to act with caution, it is possible that he may implicate serving members of the Northern Ireland Executive in Stormont. That is a potential powder keg politically, so we must tread carefully."

Phil nodded in understanding "I know the comfort letters were viewed by many as a thinly disguised amnesty for IRA killers. Many were released from prison and returned home to resume their lives. That must have been very difficult for those that had lost loved ones in the conflict, on both sides."

Marina stopped walking and looked at him "The reality was that prisoners were only released on licence and the so-called letters of comfort made it clear that there could still be prosecutions should new evidence be found. British soldiers, on the other hand, have been actively pursued and questioned about their actions during the troubles with many of them now in their seventies and eighties facing prosecution for what they would see as following orders in the line of duty. It is still a god damn mess!"

He held his hands up in submission "Sorry I didn't mean to offend you. I understand feelings still run high with some people." He blinked then asked her directly "Did you lose someone in the troubles?"

"Yes, I lost my uncle and a young cousin. They were in Liverpool shopping for my aunt's Mother's Day gift when they were caught up in a car bomb. My cousin Billy was killed immediately, and my uncle, who was a retired army officer, died two weeks later. Billy was just fourteen."

Phil lowered his head slightly and said softly "I am sorry for your loss."

"I can't believe I have just told you that. I hardly know you. I'm sorry, that was unprofessional."

"Grief doesn't have a code of conduct." He brushed her arm gently. "Let's go and see how helpful Mr. McFee really wants to be."

As they entered the room, Dessie was standing by the window. The bars were painted cream, so they would be inconspicuous from the outside of the building. The sash window was open allowing a warm breeze to circulate and bring the heady fragrances from the garden indoors.

"Good afternoon, Dessie, this is Special Agent Santos, he will be with us for a few weeks. Are you ready to begin today's session?"

He shrugged and wandered over to the table that held the makeshift recording station that the tech team had set up. They joined him and Marina leaned across and pressed the record button. "Interview commenced at 1.35pm 24th July 2019. Present, Desmond McFee, Special Agent Phil Santos, and Dr. Marina Kinskey."

As they sat, Phil reached a hand across the table to shake Dessie's. "Hi Dessie, don't mind if I call you that do you?"

Dessie's hands remained firmly in his lap. "You're a Yank." He glared at Marina. "What's a Yank doing here?"

"I have been seconded as an extra pair of hands and also because I worked in Ireland some years ago. I'm here supporting Dr. Kinskey today. It's her operation, I am simply here to do her bidding."

Dessie shrugged. "Makes no difference to me. So, when you were in Ireland, who were you working for?"

Marina sat up straight in her chair, ignoring the question. "Right Dessie, shall we pick up where we left off? How far back does Callaghan's association with Yilmaz go?"

Dessie was still looking at Phil Santos. "Was it CIA? Not all Yanks were sympathetic to the cause."

Phil gave a disinterested yawn "If you must know I was a cultural attaché accompanying President Clinton's official visit in 1995."

Dessie scoffed. "You must have been very proud. That turned into a real shit storm! The only US president that managed to piss off both sides equally. He was so impressive; his visit triggered a mainland bombing campaign."

Marina leaned forward in her chair "I enjoy a trip down memory lane as well as the next person Dessie, but this is not why we are here. Now tell us about Yilmaz." Her tone left the two men with no illusions, it was time for the conversation to get serious.

Dessie stretched his legs out under the table "OK sweetie, keep your hair on! Just making small talk with the Yankee spook. Yilmaz came to Belfast in 1998/99. He left Albania the year before. He moved in dangerous circles and was a key player in the Gradasevic Drug Cartel. He controlled the opium supply direct from Afghanistan and into Eastern Europe for processing. He knew the size of the market in the UK and wanted to exploit Belfast as a gateway."

Marina felt her pulse quicken. The Gradasevic Drug Cartel was exactly who they needed to bring down, but this was the first concrete connection they had been able to make. She controlled her breathing and let Dessie continue.

"It took a few years, but by 2004 they had a smooth operation. At that time Callaghan was only responsible for the Irish link in the chain. He was never the top of the pyramid but was working increasingly with Yilmaz. Callaghan had the connections, was familiar with the terrain and had years of experience hiding weapons caches from the military. Moving drugs was easy by comparison.

At that time, we were still fighting the cause, but the money was drying up. A political war is never as lucrative as a drugs war. The writing was on the wall even then. We knew that when the Agreement was signed we would be left out in the cold. Even though I never had anything to do with that side of his business Callaghan had crossed a line, and we were all being frozen out because of it. Others got protection, we didn't. The Devey's' had done all the stuff we had done and worse, but they were taken on the journey. They were part of the inner circle, so Colm and that psycho sister of his were given a clean bill of health. They left us to fend for ourselves. We never had a say in it, it was a done deal." The bitterness was evident in Dessie's tone.

"When did the business expand to include other things rather than just drugs?" Marina was keen to get a full picture of their dealings.

"That came much later. The political shenanigans kept the Garda's eye off the ball, and it was only when they looked back a decade later that they realised the extent of the people trafficking and sex workers. I suppose 2014 saw the real problem start. I was freelancing security by then. Callaghan had me on a retainer but not enough to keep the wolf from the door. I was there to put the frighteners on people and bring them back into line. Low-level intimidation stuff really. Yilmaz needed a permanent route to get people in and moved onto the mainland quickly, so he was extending his reach. Callaghan sorted the accommodation and I would help with transport from time to time. I never agreed with what they were doing. These were youngsters, late teens and early twenties who had been promised jobs, a place to live and money they could send back to their families. What they got was a crack habit and a life of sex work. Any money they made was snorted up their noses or taken to pay for the ratholes they lived in." Dessie's distaste was obvious.

"So, what happened to make you change your mind? Six years is a long time to decide that you disagreed with their business model." Phil's face was set. Marina noticed the sparkle in his eye had been replaced with a steely glare. There was a hardness emanating from him that had extinguished his natural warmth.

"The last shipment changed my mind. These were kids, you understand, no papers, so I couldn't be certain, but I would be surprised if any of them were over eighteen. Girls with no English, no belongings, only the clothes they stood up in. Some of them had been knocked about a bit and some of them were beyond reach. They just sat around in a daze. Lifeless eyes staring into nothing. They had to be prompted to eat and drink anything, yet Yilmaz's attack dogs made sure they had their fix to keep them compliant. The last shipment I had any dealings with included a kid called Tatum. Hardly a scrap of meat on her. Dark circles under her eyes and her skin looked transparent, you could see the veins in her neck and her forehead. She had obviously been in transit for a while before I came across her at the ferry staging post just outside Dublin. I used to oversee the loading at the port and made sure they all had warm clothes, food, and water on their journey. When I went to load them onto the lorry I saw her shivering in the corner. She had bare feet and was wearing a thin slip; the sort schoolgirls wear under a uniform and nothing else. She was obviously under the influence of something 'cos she was barely conscious. As I moved towards her, she lifted the hem of the slip to attract my attention. I reached out to cover her up and she flinched away as if I were going to strike her. I felt sick. She was a kid doing what she had been taught to do. It's a long time since I felt that angry. I took a blanket from inside the cab of the truck and wrapped her in it. I told the driver she was sick and to go without her then I carried her up to one of the bedrooms in the house. I found some warm soup and tried to get her to eat. She took little sips from the spoon and swallowed automatically not tasting it at all. I left her to sleep with a nightlight on. I watched the door all night to make sure she was not disturbed."

Marina was fascinated by the story that Dessie was telling. Even though she had heard many tales like this before, Dessie's account seemed much more harrowing. Here was a man who was no stranger to killing, showing such compassion for a girl he didn't know. Her plight had obviously touched him deeply. "What happened next?" She prompted gently.

"The following morning, she was more alert. The effects of whatever she had been given had worn off, and she was just terrified. She cowered under the bed covers making whimpering noises. There was no more food in the house, so I went to a McDonald's down the road and bought her a breakfast bun and a coffee. If I am honest I half expected her to have gone when I came back, but she was exactly where she was when I left her. I offered her the takeaway bag, and she shrank away from me shielding her face and body, begging me not to hurt her.

If Yilmaz had been there that morning I would have killed the bastard with my bare hands." Dessie took a steadying breath and continued. "I managed to get her to eat something and talked very quietly to her, not making any sudden movements. I remembered watching one of those programmes about the people that rescue abused animals. They said they had to gain their trust before they could get them somewhere safe, and I thought it might help if I tried the same thing. She did understand some English 'though I think she struggled with my accent. She told me that her uncle had taken her from her village telling her parents he was taking her to England for a better life. They had been very grateful and had given him their life savings to pay for her passage and school fees. She was a bright kid and realised when they got to a remote border in Germany what was really happening. There was a disagreement about money with two men at the border crossing that turned nasty. Her Uncle was stabbed and left at the side of the road. The €15000 he had pocketed disappeared, and she became one of a group of young girls with no papers, exploited by brutal men that saw them as cargo." He shook his head. "These traffickers are scumbags of the worst order. If you want to know why I decided to expose Callaghan and his dealings, Tatum is why."

Marina poured herself a glass of water from a jug on the table. "What happened to her Dessie?"

"I knew there would be a backlash for sending the shipment without her, so I decided to move her to a house in Belfast I sometimes used. I had a contact that wouldn't ask questions and I thought I could keep her hidden until I figured out what I was going to do. I had to try to help her. There was a journo, Lynsey Parry who had been putting out the feelers, trying to get in contact with me about some documentary she was making. I wondered if I could make a deal with her. I thought she might be able to help Tatum. The kid was terrified. She couldn't go home; said she would bring dishonour on her family if they found out the truth. She couldn't stay with me because they would find her eventually, and then we would both be in trouble. Parry was desperate to do an interview with me, so I agreed, on the condition that she could arrange for Tatum to be got off the street and into some sort of protection; a refuge or something. I thought I was doing the right thing. I thought she would be safe with Parry ...." His shoulders slumped and he became absolutely still. Phil sat up in his chair "Jeez, never mind coffee, is there any bourbon in this place? I think we could all do with a drink!"

Chapter 18:

Wednesday 24th July 2019 3.00pm

The Garden Room Shady Fields

Douglas Phipps was staring at the backgammon board. He knew he used to enjoy this game and that he was quite good at it, but for the life of him he could not remember how to play at this moment. The 'chips' were laid out on the board and the dice were in the cup, but he had no idea how to start the game.

Sitting in the garden room on a beautiful summer afternoon he thought it would be nice to play again, kill an hour or two. Something else his damn brain was robbing him of.

It was ridiculous! He remembered being taught by young Sapper Cooper, playing for hours as they sat in the observation room of the stakeout. That must have been 1996, or was it 97? He did remember that there were many rules and strategy you had to learn, and you needed luck too. He was surprised that a young man in his early twenties was such a seasoned player.

People always assumed that intelligence gathering was all fast cars and James Bond. What they didn't realise was that often, it meant long periods of doing nothing but watching a 'mark' dig their allotment or watching the door of a house that hardly anyone ever visited.

They were the FRU, covert military intelligence for the British Army. They gathered intel about republican activities ran agents from the local population, and sometimes deep cover military personnel to infiltrate IRA cells. They were considered the most dangerous missions. Life expectancy for those who went undercover was generally less than twelve months.

Sapper Cooper or 'Coop' as he was known, was one of those. He had begun as an army engineer, building bridges, fortifications, or sometimes blowing them up to sabotage the enemy. Commanding officers soon realised that his skills would be attractive to a live IRA unit. Coop had done his intelligence training with Douglas. As the more senior officer he had taken him under his wing, he was a bright lad and a quick study. He was 24 when he went undercover, he never reached 25.

The FRU had sent him to infiltrate a rogue IRA cell. It was during the early negotiations for the Good Friday Agreement. For a whole rake of reasons the UK Government and Sinn Féin were trying to broker a political solution to end the troubles. The cell commander had distanced himself from their activities and was now one of the negotiation team, but his sister still called the shots. The renegade he had left in charge had ignored the ceasefires, carried on with the bombing campaign and dished out punishment beatings for those who dared to disagree with the violent struggle for freedom.

Coop had been rumbled by a cell member who had seen him enter a pub with known British Military links. Before they could extract him, he had been kidnapped and murdered. Douglas had to identify his body. Coop left behind a young wife who had just given birth to their second child. Douglas had never really dealt with the anger he had felt.

With hindsight all the signs had been there. They should have pulled him out earlier. They should have communicated better with Special Branch and vice versa. No amount of going over the details could bring the young soldier back. Coop had died on his watch. Even though it had happened a long time ago Douglas still felt the sting of guilt.

The injustice of dementia was that it didn't take the painful memories and leave you with the good ones, it was a spiteful disease.

"Hiya Phipsy, how's it hanging?" Bill Tandy breezed into the room and threw himself down into the bucket chair opposite, scraping the wooden feet along the tiled floor.

"Where's Ben?" asked Douglas, looking up from the board.

"How do I know? We're not joined at the hip you know."

Douglas smiled. "Yes, you are. You are the original Buy One, Get One Free offer."

"The bar's open, do you fancy a swift pint, or I could challenge you to a game?"

"Neither thanks. I think I might take a wander outside. Layla has organized something called restorative yoga in the sunken garden. I thought it might be worth a look." Douglas stood and stretched out. "My God I'm getting so creaky just lately, it might loosen me up a bit."

"I feel a bit stiff today too, I could come with you if you like, will Vanessa be there?"

Douglas shook his head "I don't think yoga will help that sort of stiffness."

Two sets of large French windows that led onto a wide terrace which overlooked beautifully manicured lawns were already open. To the right was the walled kitchen gardens where chef instructed Ken the head gardener on what varieties to plant, and Ken as usual, ignored him and planted what he knew would grow better in these conditions.

To the left was the woodland walk that took you past the sunken garden and onto the ornamental pond. It was there by accident rather than design. The Dynamite men had 'helped' Ken last year by removing a particularly stubborn tree root. Fed up with how long it was taking, Bill had mixed up a little explosive cocktail from household chemicals. Suddenly, there was a crater, that with a bit of tidying up made a large and fairly deep fish-pond. Of course the explosion had also removed an old shed and three enormous rhododendron bushes, but the overall effect was quite pleasing. Bill had been banned from the store cupboards and the workshops from that day onwards, though.

The men walked across the terrace towards the shallow steps at the end. A pair of elderly ladies sat under a parasol drinking tea and eating biscuits. Bill stopped to say hello making a little bow towards them.

"Hello Bill" said Beattie, "I'm not sure if you've met Ada yet? She has just joined us. Ada Hale, this is Bill Tandy and Mr. Phipps"

Douglas Phipps gave a gruff reply, "Ladies" and carried on, walking down the steps.

"Forgive my friend, his manners are atrocious. How are you settling in Ada?"

"Fine thanks, I came here expecting to be on my own and discovered that Beattie and I worked together some years ago." Although she was sitting in the shade,

Ada still squinted at Bill because the sun was directly behind him. "So you are one half of the Dynamite Men then?"

"Ah, notoriety is a terrible thing. Guilty as charged, though I have hung up my explosives and am content to live a quieter life now."

"I am sure the neighbours will be pleased" said Ada smiling.

"Well must be off, going to join in a little yoga in the garden. Stretch out on a mat and clear my chakra's."

Beattie took a sip of tea "You will be in good company I saw Vanessa heading down there with the instructor to set things up."

"Well, I must get going then ladies, I need to practice my downward dog." He almost skipped away.

Ada smiled "Not bad for someone who bats for the other side" she said.

Beattie topped up their cups from the teapot "I thought he said yoga, not cricket?"

Chapter 19:

Wednesday 24th July 2019 7.00pm

Shady Fields

The day had gone by in a flash. One of those when you didn't have a minute to yourself yet struggled to identify a single task you had managed to finish. Now Hilary was late for her last meeting of the day with Daniel. They had arranged a catch-up over dinner, so she dragged a brush through her hair, applied some lipstick and made her way down to the dining room.

Daniel had changed from his trademark suit into dark trousers, a lightweight grey turtleneck sweater and a dark jacket.

He greeted her and there was a real warmth in his eyes. "Good evening Hilary." She took her seat at a table set with crisp white linen, where a large gin-and-tonic was already waiting for her. "I thought you might need that."

"You must be psychic". She took a sip from the long glass, the ice chinked as she set it back down on the table.

Daniel picked up his single malt and took a swallow. "I take it she's told you about the full extent of her condition now?"

"She has told me a lot of things. I know this sounds strange, but I had no idea about her service history or about the fact that you two knew each other."

Daniel smiled "Ada and I go back a long way. She was one of the first training officers I had, she was one tough cookie back then and still is today. She was never an active field agent, always in a support role, but people knew that if Ada had your back you were relatively safe. Her attention to detail was second to none. She could read a situation like no one else. She could tell if a cover was about to be blown, and she would work to extract the agent before they were caught. Intuition like that can't be taught. I worked with her on the Irish desk when she was training '14 INT' operatives. My God, they were heroes.

Women in their early twenties who put some of their male counterparts in the shade in terms of bottle. Our agents were mostly drawn from the army and infiltrated some of the IRA brigades. They were some of the bravest people I have ever worked with. The Irish commanders were merciless if they caught a soldier working undercover and were barbaric with some of the punishments they doled out. The women came off worst. Ada saved more than one skin when she worked there."

"That's why all of this is such a shock, she never said a word. I know she couldn't go into detail, she never even hinted about what she did!" Hilary looked sad "She had to keep it all to herself, no one she could confide in. I don't know how she did it all those years."

"I have never known Ada make a bad decision or do anything without consideration for others as a motive. What you see as isolation she sees as her duty. She understands that the reason we live double lives is to protect those that mean the most to us."

Daniel picked up the menu and handed it to Hilary "She couldn't tell you what she did without breaking her oath to her country. In our line of work that's an incredibly difficult judgement call and so easy to get wrong. Too much disclosure and you put your loved ones at risk, too little, and you keep them at arm's length, never let them in and remain alone all your life. It's a balance I have struggled with and got wrong on a couple of occasions."

He made his selection and waited for Hilary to give her order to the waiter. "I have no close family, most of my friends are in the service and I go abroad for my holidays, so I am not reminded of what I might be missing at Christmas and the New Year." He smiled but there was more than a hint of regret in his words.

Her life had taken a turn for the surreal; she was sitting in a building run by the Secret Service, her aunt was dying in a beautiful room upstairs, and she was eating dinner with a suave and attractive man who could probably kill a person with a teaspoon. What made it even worse was that this was the nearest thing she had had to a date in three years, how sad did that make her?

Hilary took another sip from her glass.

"The simple truth is that I trust Ada completely, even at this stage of her illness." She paused and swirled the ice in her glass around. "She is worried that I'm not happy. But this job's the best thing that has ever happened to me. I know how important it is. The people here have sacrificed their private lives in service for this country, and now they are vulnerable. We offer them a place of safety that gives them the care they need with the dignity they deserve. It's essential work, we really do make a difference. I think that's enough for me at the moment. I am not sure that I have time for a private life."

The waiter arrived carrying two beautifully dressed plates which he presented to them and then took an enormous pepper mill from a side table with a theatrical flourish, offering to season their food. They waved him away, and he left as silently as he had arrived. As they ate Hilary took the opportunity to deliver her monthly report about the residents and of course, their special guest. It did occur to her that this could have been done in an email, and she wasn't quite sure why Daniel had suggested doing it over dinner. He listened, never interrupting until he was sure she had finished.

Then, out of the blue he said "Ada really is a force of nature. If she's worried about you, you should probably listen to what she has to say. Working for the service requires some adjustment. Although you are not an active agent, you can see the toll that being one has taken on some of the residents here. All she is saying is think carefully before you cut yourself off from life. She gave me the same advice twenty years ago, and I didn't listen. Working in the security services is a very intense environment, there's a tendency to priorities your work over other things, particularly when it's all new. Early in my career I tended to take few vacations, and it took me a while to figure out how to create a sustainable work-life balance. I missed friend's weddings and other really important celebrations and if you don't participate in the important milestones, they stop asking you to the mundane stuff as well."

He gave a deep sigh. "I did manage to cobble together a bit of a routine and create a few weekends for enjoyment, but that was mainly because I couldn't physically take work home with me. I often found myself in amazing places where it would have been great to be a regular tourist. Catching those glimpses and making plans to return one day made me want to connect more deeply with people who might want to share in the trip, but the risks were too great. Ada wants more for you, and you can't blame her."

"We were discussing her funeral arrangements earlier. She asked me to organise a humourist service, I queried it, do you mean a humanist service? She just gave me one of her looks that said I know what I mean! She was looking very tired when I left her tonight, said she was going to rest and not to call in on her until the morning, but I will go and sit with her later. The truth is I really don't know what I am going to do without her."

Daniel looked at her with a kindness that made her eyes fill up. "She really doesn't have much time now, you know that don't you Hilary?"

"I've always been a realist, she told me she has days rather than weeks, so I accept that, but I also know how strong her will is. It wouldn't surprise me if she stares the grim reaper in the face and sends him packing."

It was clear that Hilary was trying to convince herself; she realised that her appetite had deserted her, and she returned her knife and fork back to the plate, pushing it away. She looked around the room, they were the only diners left. Daniel poured her a glass of wine and to change the subject said, "I have just finished reading your white paper on the state of residential care that you did a couple of years ago. Was the funding shortfall really £20billion over the next couple of years?"

Hilary nodded. "I bet that made you about as popular as a Jimmy Carr Tax Return with the treasury!"

Hilary laughed out loud "If I am being honest I came here just in time. You don't survive long in a government department when you tell it like it is. I decided to go before I was pushed."

The waiter returned with a cheese board and Hilary realised that she hadn't noticed him clearing the plates away. They ate for a while in companionable silence, Hilary just picking at the grapes and celery before she asked, "How are you getting on in your new job?"

Daniel looked serious for a moment before he answered, "It's big, complex, and infuriatingly political. In the Cold War you knew who the enemy was. When we were dealing with the troubles in Northern Ireland, the players were clearly identified even if some of them were untouchable. Missions from those days still cast long shadows, but 9/11 changed all of that. We don't know what our enemies look like any more. So many are home-grown and that leads people into dangerous assumptions. People rely on stereotypes to give them a little advantage.

We end up watching a broad group of people that share some common characteristics. It's the classic misnomer—not all Muslims are terrorists, but all terrorists are Muslims. That thinking breeds distrust and discrimination, it's an imperfect system. People naturally take sides, and before you know it, views are polarized, and every extremist is on a mission. We can't eradicate that, no country's security services have that power, so we enter into the biggest cat and mouse game in history to try to neutralize the worst incidents and learn from those that slip through the net. All the time we encourage people to go about their business and not let it affect what they do or where they go. And so far I think we are doing an OK job at that. My days of being on the front line are over but so much can be accomplished in other ways, Shady Fields for example, plays its part in the bigger picture."

Hilary wanted to see how far she might push him "I must say I am more than a little curious about our special guest. Can you really tell me nothing about who it is?"

"I'm afraid not. All I can say is that it's an extremely sensitive situation and if people discover his identity and his location, then more than one person would be in danger."

They finished their meal and took coffee in the library. Hilary looked at her watch it was 10.00pm. Over coffee, she talked more about her life with Ada. It felt good to talk about her in happier times and remember the fun they had shared. Daniel talked about being an army child, Sandhurst, then his Army commission and how he had been approached to join the service. As Hilary listened she realised he had perfected the art of telling a story in broad generalisations, devoid of any real detail at all. She wondered if that was a natural talent or was that part of his training.

At 11.00pm she excused herself. “Thank you for suggesting dinner, I probably wouldn’t have bothered if I was alone. Are you back to London this evening?”

“I am, but I’ll do a final check on our guest before I leave. I haven’t had a chance to deliver the welcome basket.”

Chapter 20:

Wednesday 24th July 2019 8.00pm

Belfast

There was a knock on the door and Callaghan called "Come in". The door opened and a large, red-faced man in a Garda uniform filled the door frame. "Hello Ian, thanks for coming, have a seat." He gestured towards the chair on the opposite side of the desk.

"Thanks, Mr. Callaghan"

He reached into the desk drawer at his side and pulled out a thick manilla envelope. He slid it across the polished mahogany desk and tapping it said "there's a little extra in it this month. I appreciate your help with our current problem."

The man took the envelope and shoved it unopened into the inside pocket of his uniform jacket. "I am still digging, but it now looks as though they suspected we have an insider and planted false info to throw us all off the trail. For sure, we are not the only ones looking for McFee."

"No, I appreciate that, but it's a worry if they suspect an insider. I am receiving real pressure from our Eastern European friend to find and deal with him. I promised I would, and I can't let him down, there is too much at stake. It might be helpful if I knew who else was interested in Dessie."

"Let me see what I can do. There have been requests for information sharing from Stormont. The politicians are getting a bit jumpy in case he blots their copybooks with inconvenient truths, but I can confirm that MI5 are responsible for the whole operation, and they are keeping it all under wraps."

Callaghan nodded thoughtfully "How about that other little job? Any news of Lynsey Parry?"

"No, she seems to have gone to ground. I think she was shaken up by the death of the kid. It was unfortunate that she was able to ID Seamus…." He paused, as if making a decision about whether it would be prudent to say more. "It's none of my business Mr. Callaghan, but Yilmaz made a lot of enemies over that girl. I am just saying that people on the ground are less willing to help us now."

He looked at the guard with narrowed eyes. "You are right, it is none of your business and I suggest you keep your opinions to yourself. Understood?"

The man looked distinctly uncomfortable. "Yes of course, sorry Mr. Callaghan. Well, I'll be off then." The Garda made a hasty retreat.

Callaghan had warned Yilmaz to let it go. The girl was of no consequence, and yet, he had taken Dessie's interference very personally. As far as Yilmaz was concerned she was his property and he had lost income when Dessie had taken her. He had instructed Callaghan to kill Dessie to send a message to others who might want to ignore orders in the future. It had put him in a very difficult position. They went back a long way and Dessie had always been loyal to the cause and to him personally. But this was business and unless Callaghan acted he could be seen as going soft. In this game, weakness made you ripe for takeover. No nice golden handshake waited for you when your time came to retire. A bullet in the back of the head and one through the heart was more like it.

He felt stuck between a rock and a hard place. He didn't want to kill Dessie at the instruction of the Albanian thug but if what he was hearing was true, Dessie had turned tout anyway. He knew enough to put him and lots of others away for the rest of their lives. If he could only speak to Dessie to find out what was really going on, but he needed to know where they were keeping him to do that. It truly was a god-awful mess.

Callaghan really couldn't understand what had happened to make Dessie flip. He used to be totally trustworthy, and they'd been through so much together. When money for brigade activities got scarcer, and it was clear they needed a new source of income, Devey had carved a very comfortable little niche for himself as a gofer for the negotiation team, leaving that sister of his in charge. For a while timing had been on JJ's side, and his personal wealth grew along with the number of foot soldiers he had, even though many of them were not interested in the cause at all. Some of them were not even Irish! But his coffers were full, and the cause was everything! He thought all he had to do was hold out for his comfort letter, and then he could retire permanently. The problem was: It never came. Instead, they had found his offshore account and seized his assets. He was €8 million lighter. That had been his pension scheme.

He felt very angry at this level of betrayal. His brigade had been one of the most successful. Under his command the unit had produced some of the best media coverage for the cause with its operations. They had always raised their fair share and more of the fighting fund to keep the cause going. Not to be included in the inner circle makeover was unthinkable. JJ became more enraged by the very public snub. Previous associates began to distance themselves from him. He had to take risks that exposed his organisation to the authorities. On one occasion he'd sacrificed a couple of his own foot soldiers and put them in the frame for prosecution by the Garda just to keep his own slate clean.

It was a dangerous game he was playing and as a result, he had underestimated the brutality and the personal threat that came from doing business with Yilmaz. It looked like the only way to get out of this with any degree of a positive outcome was to deliver Dessie up on a platter to Yilmaz.

Chapter 21:

Thursday 25th July 2019 11.00am

Shady Fields

Ada was alone and sunning herself on the terrace. It was a warm morning but looking at the forecast it promised to be a sultry afternoon with maybe even the possibility of thunder. It had felt a bit oppressive yesterday, but she was unsure if that had been the weather or the atmosphere generally.

There was someone being kept here on the third floor. She had gleaned that much from snippets of conversations she'd overheard. Hilary had been quite guarded and there seemed to be quite a lot of comings and goings.

Ada relaxed into the wicker chair, closed her eyes, and breathed in the fragrant summer air. The July heat radiated through her dress warming her tired skin. She could feel muscles that had been tense with pain begin to relax. She was unsure if it was the sunshine or the drugs that were having the soporific effect and decided it really didn't matter. For once, none of it was her responsibility. She was heading towards the end of her life and she had no regrets. But it had been one hell of a ride, she had done things and seen things that many couldn't even begin to imagine. Just because she had not worked in the field didn't mean she hadn't had her share of intrigue. She had worked with brave men and women, people who had made sacrifices for their country, some had given their lives. She really had got off light.

Lazily, she opened her eyes and noticed a movement way across the lawn by the edge of the trees. A large cedar spread its distinctive limbs creating shade, the garden designer had situated an ornate wrought iron lover's seat directly underneath the canopy it created. She squinted a little and saw that it was the woman Beattie had pointed out to her the other morning at breakfast. Jackie Kelly was sitting bolt upright looking directly at Ada. There was something vaguely familiar about her, although she couldn't put her finger on what it was just at the moment.

They watched each other for almost a minute, then Jackie slowly got to her feet and began to walk towards

Ada. She got to the flight of shallow stone steps before she hesitated.

Ada called out to her "Morning, Jackie, isn't it? What a lovely day again."

The woman was silent, as if she were wrestling with her next action, decision made, she quickly mounted to the steps and came over to where Ada was sitting.

"Good morning, can I join you?"

It seemed to Ada that her sentence had taken a herculean effort to utter. "Please have a seat."

She looked at the woman more closely. She was prematurely grey for her years, the lines on her face made her look care worn, but it was her posture that troubled Ada. She held herself stiffly with a straight back but rounded shoulders, she couldn't possibly be comfortable like that. It seemed that every muscle in her body was taut with suppressed tension. Her hands were clasped tightly together, the backs were white, shining with scar tissue, and even as she sat the woman's right foot tapped out a constant beat. Jackie rested one hand on her knee to quiet the involuntary movement. The feeling of familiarity became amplified for Ada.

"I was asking Mr. Grant about you. You're Ada Hale, aren't you?"

"Yes, I am. Have we met before?" Ada was puzzled. Normally, she was so good with faces.

"He said you were very ill, that you might die here."

Ada looked directly at the woman, and suddenly it hit her. "Oh my goodness, you are 'Jackie Kelly!' No wonder I didn't recognise you. I had no idea if you were still in the country. The penny didn't drop the other morning at breakfast, but it's good to see you after all this time." What a stupid thing to say, Ada scolded herself.

Jackie blinked at Ada. "I never had a chance to thank you. When they got me back home, I was in hospital for a while, and then I was moved for my own protection. They told me that it was you who raised the alarm. They would have killed me; I wouldn't be here if it weren't for you. No one here knows about me except Mr. Grant and I would like to keep it like that. He offered me a chance to move somewhere else, but I have settled here, so I decided to stay. I just had to say something though, so I waited until I was sure you were alone; I am in your debt."

Ada reached across and covered a scarred, trembling hand with her own. "My dear, I am just so pleased that you are OK. I realised that you had been 'made' so I made a call to Daniel. He did the rest."

Jackie arm went rigid as Ada's hand touched hers. "I am sorry I still suffer with my nerves; I don't like to be touched,"

Ada respectfully removed her hand and smiled at Jackie. "That's perfectly understandable. I was really concerned when I heard what had happened. I kept thinking if only we had got you out the day before. Hindsight's a wonderful thing isn't it."

"I have never told anyone the full story about what happened. My therapist thinks it would help, but it is so hard. The physical scars healed quickly, but the mental ones didn't. I keep myself to myself and I manage. When I came here, I was in a bit of a state. Drink, drugs, you know, anything to try to forget really. Then I realised that I could never forget; that I had to learn to live with it. My therapist taught me Emotional Freedom Techniques and as a result, I can function now. It's only taken twenty years." She laughed half-heartedly at her own joke.

Ada felt the woman's distress radiating from her in waves. If this was learning to live with it, God knows how bad she was when it happened. "If I can help in any way, you only have to ask."

"That's kind of you, but just acknowledging you today has helped tremendously. It feels like I have taken a step back towards living again. Thank you." She leaned across and kissed Ada softly on the cheek. She rose and wandered off into the house through the French windows leaving Ada with some very disturbing images floating around in her head.

It all seemed a million miles away from this beautiful place in the leafy countryside.

Back in the day Ada had assisted in the recruitment and training of women operatives into an elite force called 14 Company, also known as The DET. They were considered the equivalent of UK Special Forces. They trained candidates to infiltrate and work as deep cover operatives with IRA cells. Her operatives were highly intelligent, confident, and self-reliant. Their missions were incredibly dangerous, and often they would be in place for a long time before they were activated in a bid to build a believable legend.

Ada remembered the training she had led with something bordering on pride. In weaponry, she had taught them to handle guns, they had favoured the relatively small Walther PPK as it suited female operatives with smaller hands. It had a magazine of eight .22 rounds, and although it lacked the stopping power of larger handguns its size made it easier to conceal under female clothing. Ada had also been a surprisingly good shot.

She taught advanced driving skills, high-speed pursuit, how to use a vehicle as a weapon, controlled crashes, and anti-ambush skills. Those were the days! Jackie had been an excellent recruit, one of her brightest. She studied hard and learned very quickly.

Her forte had been covert surveillance, particularly nighttime Infra-red photography. She hid all sorts of equipment in clothing, household objects and cars. The demanding discipline of surveillance in Northern Ireland meant she might be concealed for hours in a roadside ditch or an attic, or she may have to follow someone on foot through residential streets without detection.

Jackie's most successful mission was when she managed to conceal a camera and listening device inside an IRA weapons cache and record the planning of a mainland bombing. It was her intelligence that foiled that attack. The bombers had been arrested before the device could go off, potentially saving dozens of civilian lives. Ada knew that Jackie had received the Military Cross for her service, but her infamy came from an entirely different incident. She had been the last recorded tar-and-feathering in modern history. No wonder she was suffering from PTSD!

Chapter 22:

Thursday 25th July 2019. 4.00pm

Shady Fields

They had been at it most of the day. Marina and Phil going over and over the same details until Dessie became short-tempered and tired. It was a known technique to test if the informants' story changed at all after numerous repetitions. So far Dessie's testament was surprisingly consistent.

Marina was pleased with how things were going. Working with Phil Santos at such close quarters gave her an opportunity to learn his methods. His reputation for being a skilled profiler and interrogator preceded him and his performance today more than justified the billing. He had mentioned to her this morning that at some point during the day he wanted to go 'off-piste', to ask Dessie about a historical incident he needed information on. She trusted that it must be important so decided to let him run with it. They agreed that she would take notes, allowing Phil to observe Dessie's micro-expressions and body language at close quarters. If the truth were told she was intrigued about what it would produce.

"So, Dessie, let's talk about something completely different. Tell us what you know about Colm Devey."

There was a tumbleweed moment and Dessie's eyes narrowed as he stared directly at the American. "Nothing to tell. We knew each other a long time ago, fought for the cause side by side until our paths went in different directions."

The answer was loaded with emotion. Marina studied Dessie closely during every session they had with him. She had observed distinct 'tells', autonomic indications that were evident when he was under pressure and when he was lying or just omitting the truth. When he was feeling stressed his salivation rate decreased, and he drank more water, in small sips from the bottle. When he was concealing something his mannerisms became much more exaggerated.

"What sort of person is he Dessie. Is he like you?" Phil waited for the eruption that he knew would come.

"We are nothing alike!" Dessie shouted. "He is a turncoat, a liar, and cheat. He was never interested in the cause only the power that he could get from it. His father would be ashamed to see what he has become. I hate him!" he spat the final part of the sentence out and reached for his water bottle.

"But surely you were the three musketeers, weren't you? You, Devey and Callaghan?"

"We fought for justice in the early days, me, and Callaghan. Devey always had an angle. He was a slimy bastard even then. He knew exactly when to get out, when to pass the baton to someone else. When to kill someone to save his own skin. My mother used to say that if he fell in the river, he would come out wearing a mackintosh. The only one he has ever protected apart from himself is Sinead and that's because she has a screw loose."

Marina noticed that Phil became more alert at the mention of the sister, he leaned forward in his seat. "But you all grew up together, fought against injustice of your occupiers. You had to trust each other with your lives surely?"

"You Yanks think you know everything don't you. You stand next to a pint of Guinness at the St. Patrick's Day parade and claim your Irish roots! Let me set a few things straight for you. The British never acknowledged that we were at war with them. They simply referred to it as "the troubles". They called the street fighting a 'theatre'. But let me tell you that my brothers and sisters were not actors and the injustices and oppression we had to endure were not scenes from a play. When they were shot by occupying British soldiers they didn't get up at the end of the act and come back for the matinée performance. But by far the worst betrayal was that it wasn't the British we had to worry about. It was people like Devey who sold us down the river for a Stormont office and government pension. Trust! You couldn't trust the Devey's if your life depended on it." Dessie's voice had reduced in pitch and volume. He stood up and paced around the room in an unconscious attempt to calm down.

"He killed the only woman I ever loved." He said so quietly Marina nearly missed it.

"Ah yes, the beautiful Theresa Farrell."

Dessie looked quickly at Phil "What do you know about her?"

"I know you met and fell in love when you were in your twenties. She supported the cause, encouraged you, even took an active part in civil unrest. The Irish version of Bonnie and Clyde until she was outed as a British spy. Then I know that the IRA tortured and murdered her." Phil, still watching Dessie like a hawk.

"It wasn't true! We knew there was a tout, and she was the scapegoat. He took her and got her to confess before killing her, then it turned out the tout was an undercover soldier. Devey was not above framing somebody to take the fall if it protected the brigade. She was a kid, an idealist who hated the injustice of what the British were doing to us. Callaghan didn't trust me to question her, said I was too close so Devey volunteered. He took her off the street, him, and that evil bitch sister. They killed her then burned her body on waste ground where it would be found to act as an example to others. I never believed it. My sweet Theresa was no spy. I never spoke to him again from that day on."

"Is that why you killed the FRU man, as revenge for Theresa?"

"I never killed him, Sinead did, but I carried the can for it. Like Colm said, people would believe it was me, it could have been me, but in the end it wasn't."

"Why did Colm say it was you if it wasn't?"

"There was already bad blood between us because of Theresa. He did it to keep that mad bitch out of it, and I was the obvious mug. Callaghan recommended him for a cell commander, his own brigade. I think he knew we would have ended up killing each other if we had to work together after that. He kept us separated so that our missions didn't cross.

When it became clear a political agreement was going to be done, Colm Devey underwent a Damascus moment. He converted to politics and had his previous sins washed away. The ceasefire and decommissioning of arms were a critical part of the agreement and while we were all stripped of our defences, him and Callaghan managed to hide a significant cache of guns and Semtex that were never included in the IRA's inventory. When Devey was drawing up the lists, Callaghan's name wasn't included. He had forgotten what JJ had done for him."

Dessie sat back down in his chair, vigorously scratching his chin and along his jaw. "I never knew where they stashed the weapons and explosives, they could still be out there for all I know."

Phil nodded. "But if you did know, you wouldn't tell us, would you? The thing is Dessie, we have reason to believe that Semtex from that stash was used in a device that killed the President of Colombia and three of our military personnel. There is some forensic evidence that we are still checking, but there's no doubt that it was Irish Semtex. If we could recover the remainder of that cache we could make the connection we need. Devey would be worried too. He wouldn't want to be associated with this regardless of how long ago it happened. It could seriously damage his political aspirations."

"I don't know anything about a bomb in Colombia but I can't believe Callaghan would be involved in something like that. I didn't stash the stuff so I can't help you." But Dessie didn't sound too sure.

Chapter 23:

Thursday 25th July 2019 8.00pm

Shady Fields

Ben took a long pull from the full beer glass in front of him, "Real ale my arse!" he said dismissively. "I think they refer to them as session beers. Weak as maids' water and strained through a miner's sock. It's meant to give us the illusion we can still drink. The irony is none of us hold liquor like we did when we were younger, so in a strange way, it works."

Bill screwed up his face as he placed his glass on the beer mat in front of him. "Changing the subject, I thought I would start a sweepstake on who the guest is on the third floor, are you in?" Bill looked at his lifelong friend. He waited for the predictable eye roll, and there it was.

"Bugger off, I'm fed up with losing my shirt to you. I think you only start a book when you already know the outcome so cut to the chase. Who is it?"

Bill gave a sneaky smile "Well I'm working on a process of elimination. It's definitely an informant rather than a terrorist because they would be in Bellmarsh. It's unlikely to be someone with an ISIS link because they would be held in one of the operational safe houses so that any intel extracted could be checked immediately." He paused to check his friend's agreement with his analysis.

"Go on I'm listening".

"It's unlikely to be a Russian, things are quiet on that front since Salisbury, so I'm going for domestic. Either linked with an internal cover up of some description or maybe Irish. There are still a few people with scores to settle after the GFA, perhaps they have someone who knows what really happened when the negotiations took place."

"We have a lot to be grateful to the Irish for". Ben said. "They gave us our trademark, the 'Dynamite Men'. Belfast was tough, but there were good times too. Without it, we wouldn't be here today, literally!" The men nodded in silent agreement. "It was our strategy for dealing with car bombs that was the game changer. Our tech identified bomb components, so they could be traced to their source. It's still being used today. They never paid us for that you know. The difference with us Bill was that we thought like bomb makers." Bill rubbed his chin considering his friend's earlier suggestion. Ben continued "But would whoever it is, really be a valuable source after all this time, though. There doesn't seem to be much of an appetite to bring those old terrorists to justice, the agreement made that go away, didn't it?"

Bill was getting into his stride now. "Unless you were a Tommy that is. You remember what that was like, backing down The Shankill Road with a rifle in your hands, knowing there could be a sniper lining you up. Bugger me! The best laxative known to man! It was bad enough then, but it's not the officers who gave the orders that are facing court now it's us poor sods that were following their orders. Where's the justice in that?"

Ben shook his head. "I know, they did their bit for Queen and country and were then hung out to dry by politicians whose definition of risk is eating sushi from Tesco Express on the day it expires. It's a terrible thought, but that could be me facing prosecution for something that happened more than twenty years ago."

Bill gave an involuntary shudder. "I've just had a worse thought. It could be me!"

Phipps and Ward joined them "I have managed to convince Brooke to join us for a night of fun and laughter, but I guess I got that wrong." He nodded at the dynamite men. "Who pissed on your cornflakes?"

Bill plastered the roguish smile back on his face

"Hiya both now what can I get you to drink?"

Phipps smiled "I'll have a bottle of Guinness please; they can't water that down."

"Make that two." Said Ward. Bill went to the bar leaving the trio behind.

"Well, we don't see you down here very often. How's the leg coming along?" Ben took a half-hearted sip from his drink.

"It's OK, thanks. I'll be here another week, ten days if Arnot gets his way."

Phipps took the opportunity to quiz him a little more. "What do you do exactly?"

"I am a P.T. instructor, so until I get the all-clear I will be on light duties behind a desk." He pulled a face to show he wasn't impressed.

Phipps nodded and smiled. "Special Ops training?"

"Friggin' hell, is it that obvious?"

Phipps smiled. "No, just takes one to know one. Did a stint myself; training snipers, 06 to 2011." He turned to Ben and said more quietly "How's he doing?" gesturing towards Bill.

Ben looked cheerful "Not bad at the moment. Sawbones says they have slowed the effects with the latest drugs, so he's with it most of the time. He's got a few memory problems and the odd flashback but nothing we can't handle. We were just talking about the guest on the third floor, Bill is taking bets."

"Oh, it's an old IRA hitman." Phipps mentioned in a nonchalant manner.

"How the bloody hell do you know that?"

"My place is directly under the room next to where they are holding him. I pick up bits of conversations between the blokes guarding him through the vent in the wall, it must be open, and I can hear stuff. I know it's a man, they call him Ragair, a code name I would guess, whatever that means, and he is being debriefed by us and the Americans."

Ben shook his head "For a bloke who doesn't talk much you certainly know how to stop others in their tracks!"

Bill rejoined them at the table and placed a bottle and glass in front of the two men. He looked at Ben "I didn't bring you one, is that OK?"

"That's fine, but I have decided to take you up on the bet, I'll have a hundred quid on our guest upstairs. I think it might be a blast from the past, no pun intended. I think our guest might be Dessie McFee!"

Bill openly scoffed "Don't be ridiculous, he's dead, isn't he?"

"I don't think you are taking me seriously; I think it is McFee"

Bill shook his head. "We aren't drunk enough yet to take you seriously."

Ben continued "Hear me out a minute. People were shocked that the IRA's' most notorious hitman didn't make the cut when they were handing get out of jail free cards to everyone else. It would probably have been too controversial to add him to the list. Ruthless doesn't even begin to describe him, everyone was scared of him. He sorted out the big stuff, not really involved in the bombings, but he did the hatchet jobs, disappeared people and handled the ones they needed to be left alive as a lesson to the others."

He looked across at Phipps expecting to see amusement at his sleight of hand with Bill but what he saw was pure, unadulterated anger. No, it was more than that, there was real hatred on his face.

"Are you OK Phipsey?"

"Do you know it's him for certain?"

"Well, I don't know for sure. It's a process of elimination really. He's the only high-value mark that isn't dead or given amnesty. He didn't go into politics, he quickly dropped out of view, but we heard he had gone into business for himself, hired muscle for syndicates and stuff. He would still be in the frame for several high-profile hits though, so it would be worth his while to turn informant and cut a deal for himself."

Ben noticed Phipps was gripping the arms of his chair, his knuckles shone white. "Are you OK, what's wrong?"

"McFee's the bastard that killed Coop. When I was working undercover with the FRU, we put Dave Cooper into a brigade, McFee's brigade. He'd been with them nearly a year before they found out who he was. They kidnapped and tortured him for two days, but he never broke. They killed him as he was trying to escape. McFee shot him and left his body on wasteland like a piece of rubbish. I had to break the news to his family. Nearly finished his wife off, he was only twenty-four. It was an almighty cock up. Special branch had been tipped the wink that his cover may have been blown, but it was Friday evening and by the time they passed the information to us on Sunday night he had already been taken."

Bill lent forward in his chair reaching out for Phipps' arm, but he shied away, sitting bolt upright in the seat. "He was the only one I ever lost on my watch. I tried to keep in touch, but his wife remarried. His kids had to grow up without knowing him, my fault of course."

Ben did place a hand on his arm "I know why you might feel like that, but it isn't true. We all knew the risks of doing what we did. Circumstances change the run of play in your favour or sometimes against you. Shit happens Phipsey. You can't be held responsible for that. I know what it's like to lose someone on your watch. I wondered about the what-ifs, the road not taken, but in the end a commander must focus on the what-is. That's the price of leading soldiers."

Phipps stood up to leave, "Thanks for the drink, but I think I'll turn in early, I seem to have lost my taste for Guinness." He began to walk towards the door but hesitated and turned to look over his shoulder. "A true soldier fights because he loves what is behind him not because he hates what's in front of him. I should have had Coops' back and I didn't. Nothing can change that. A man like McFee hates what's in front of him. It is the only thing that explains what he did." He turned and left the bar.

Bill looked at the others, stunned by the outburst. "We should confirm if it is him. If it is, he won't leave it Ben. He'll do something. I've seen it before. The opportunity for payback is too great to pass up."

"You're right. I've never seen him like that, normally he is so together. We need to let Hilary know about their history so that she can keep an eye on the situation." A glimmer of mischief spread across Bill's face. "Or we could do a bit of digging on our own, just to confirm it's really him."

"Then what?" Ben didn't like the way this conversation was going. "We don't know if it is him. We don't know for definite that he was the one who killed Coop. We don't know why he's being kept here or to what end. And we don't know what Phipps intends to do if it is him. We should take this to someone then leave well alone."

Bill was warming to the situation playing out in front of them. "You know our approach when diffusing a bomb; if there are sixty minutes on the timer, we spend fifty-five of them working out the problem. The solution will come in the last five minutes. All I am saying is let's spend some time contemplating the issue. It will be good exercise for the brain." He tapped the side of his head with a stubby finger. "We don't have to act until we've worked out what to do. We could go to Hilary then."

"Bill, you forget how well I know you. When have you ever identified a problem without trying to solve it yourself?"

"Oh, come on, where's your sense of adventure? It's as quiet as a grave around here. It could do with livening up a bit. Let's just turn over a few stones and see what we find. What could possibly go wrong?"

"The last time you said that a shed disappeared and was replaced with a deep ornamental water feature."

"There you go then, we added to the value of this place!"

Ben could feel his resolve slipping. He found it almost impossible to say no to Bill, but he would be lying to himself if he didn't acknowledge how uneasy he was feeling.

"OK, but as soon as we confirm it's him, we go to Hilary."

Bill was already heading back towards the reception area and the lift to the third floor.

Chapter 24:

Thursday 25th July 2019

Crossnacreevy, Northern Ireland

Callaghan was driving along the Ballygowan Road towards Crossnacreevy. The meeting place had been chosen for its isolation and its neutrality. Seamus sat in the passenger seat sulking. Callaghan was still cross with him, although the anger was fading a little. Seamus really was incompetent at times, yes he was compliant and never questioned the messy jobs he gave him to do, but he had failed to get to Dessie before he'd been moved to the mainland, and he had taken his punishment for that. His eye was swollen, turning black. The cut made by Callaghan's pistol grip had been glued rather than stitched. The scar wouldn't be that noticeable. His sulk would wear off in a bit.

Callaghan couldn't quite believe it had been nearly a decade since he had last seen Colm Devey face to face and that meeting hadn't ended well. If he was honest, he was surprised that Colm had agreed to meet him at all. He must be just as worried as he was about the developments around Dessie. He was hoping they would be able to put aside their history and work together to find and neutralise their common enemy. It pained him to refer to Dessie in that way, but that's what he was, a tout.

He slowed the Jaguar XJ6 to a crawl as he passed the Dog's Charity building looking for the service entrance to the industrial unit where they were meeting. He spotted the opening and turned sharp left, looking for the warehouse, the cars' suspension handled the bumps and ruts on the uneven concrete driveway without complaint. He had asked Colm to come alone and hoped he would keep to his word.

Their last meeting had ended acrimoniously when he and Colm had crossed swords and the old bitterness about the lack of a comfort letter had come tumbling out. This situation was not ideal, but if he could enlist Colm's help, with his assembly connections they may be able to salvage something from the mess.

Callaghan entered the warehouse through a metal door next to the huge metal shutters. It looked deserted. Seamus had his instructions; wait in the car and keep his head low until Devey arrived, and only come in if he wasn't alone. Even Seamus couldn't get that wrong.

His eyes adjusted to the dim light, Devey was already here. His government issued saloon was parked in the shadows inside the cavernous space, and he was leaning against the passenger door, waiting.

"Hello JJ, it's been a long time."

Callaghan stopped about ten feet away, he nodded towards the driver seated at the wheel behind tinted glass.

"Are we OK to talk?"

"Yes, John's been with me for years, luckily he's hard of hearing. So what's all this about? I don't hear from you in years then suddenly you want a reunion. What do you want JJ?"

Callaghan was uncertain about starting this conversation but took the plunge anyway. "If Dessie talks it's not just me at risk Colm, you must know that. Damage limitation is the order of the day. If you know where he is I could take care of our problem."

There was no flicker of emotion on Devey's face. "I don't know what you mean, I don't have a problem. The agreement protects us from what happened during the troubles. For anyone who has kept a clean sheet since, there really is nothing to be concerned about. I agreed to this meeting out of respect for what we fought for back then. If I'm honest JJ, I don't recognise who you are any more."

"I am who you made me Colm!" Callaghan's jaw was taut as his teeth began to grind. "I did what I had to do to survive when you all sold me down the river. I could have retired somewhere out of the way when the deals were being done, but for a reason, I've never been able to fathom I was betrayed by my own so that they could reinvent themselves a new future. They left the ones that took all the risks behind. It was every man for himself."

"If this is going to be a rehash of our last conversation JJ I can't see the point. I can't turn the clock back. The decision wasn't mine to make, I fought your corner, but it was never going to happen. You'd already taken things too far and had become a liability in the eyes of the leadership. The company you keep now is your choice, no one else's. My guess is: They want those crooks taken down, and Dessie is willing to help. Have you considered doing your own deal? There might be something to salvage, reduced jail time, nice open prison, might be worth a thought."

Callaghan's rage suddenly surfaced. "You insolent pup! You say that to me when you know what we went through, what we fought for! I would rather die than sell out to the British, unlike some. My heritage still means something to me, your father must be spinning in his grave!"

Devey stood up straight and took a step towards Callaghan. "My father might be, but my mother isn't. She was the one that had to keep everything on track. She kept our family together despite the filthy housing, the menial jobs, and low wages. She was the real hero along with thousands of others just like her. They didn't fight for an ideal they just wanted to be treated like everyone else. A home that wasn't damp or condemned, education for their kids, opportunities just like everyone else had. A bit of respect and a chance to live without hatred and fear. You may not agree with how we achieved it, but we did, and we didn't need to become gangsters to do it either!"

Callaghan threw his head back and laughed. "Who are you kidding? You are all gangsters! Gangsters play by their own rules, and you made your own rule book when you sold out. You became milksops. Gangsters because you got your own way on the backs of others, but weak all the same."

Devey shook his head. "I knew this was a waste of time. I agreed to meet as a gesture of kindness to you JJ. Don't mistake that for weakness. Trust me, you will not remember me for my weakness. As I see it you have two choices; Dessie is already on the mainland singing like a bird. Either you give up Yilmaz and his network in exchange for a deal, or you start checking out places without an extradition treaty and make sure you have the necessary jabs. Self-justification is a treacherous defence." He turned and opened the car door. There was a click and the large roller door began to open with a loud metallic grinding noise.

"You may have reinvented yourself Devey and think you are safe, but I wonder if the same is true for Sinead?" A sly smile was spreading across Callaghan's face. "I have proof that it was Sinead who shot the RFU man, and that she was the one that delivered Theresa Farrell to you immediately before she was killed. I wonder if the amnesty covers her with the same blanket protection. I've been tailing the journo Parry that kicked all of this off. She would be very interested in a tell-all exclusive with me. I could watch the fallout from a Venezuelan beach somewhere without batting an eyelid. That wouldn't do much for your political ambitions, would it? They would drop you like a hot potato. All I want is the location where they're holding him, that's all. That shouldn't be difficult for a man with your connections. There's no love lost between you and Dessie; he has never forgiven you for Theresa's death. I could do us both a favour."

The driver started the engine, Devey was obviously calculating the odds. "Give me a couple of days and I will see what I can do."

"I might not have days. I'll give you twenty-four hours before I contact Parry with my information, that's the best I can do."

Devey slammed the car door, and they drove off leaving the acrid smell of diesel fumes in their wake. Callaghan needed him to come through with a location. Yilmaz was not a patient man. Dessie had crossed him on several occasions, and if he gave up the syndicate, there would be no place for any of them to hide. These people made JJ look like a light-fingered priest. They had turned revenge into an art form. In the old days he had people that were willing to die for him, some were willing to kill for him. It never made him feel any luckier. A location was all he needed to make it all go away, Yilmaz would handle the rest.

Seamus stood on the concrete apron in front of the warehouse. “Everything OK Mr. Callaghan?”

“What a feckin’ stupid question Seamus! I trust we still know the whereabouts of Ms. Parry?”

“Yes Mr. Callaghan, she went back to London yesterday, and we have a contact keeping tabs on her movements.”

“Well, that’s something I suppose. You know Seamus if stupidity burned calories you could live on chocolate cake for the rest of your life without gaining an ounce.”

Chapter 25:

Thursday 25th July 2019 4.00pm

Shady Fields

Charlie Bingham was the product of a bye-gone era. His demeanour was that of an elderly gentleman with aristocratic lineage and a military bearing that meant he carried his eighty-five years very well. When he spoke it was with a hint of a South African accent. He had a full head of snow-white hair and a neatly trimmed beard that matched, but his bushy eyebrows had remained stubbornly dark. His eyes were still a clear blue, and he could hold a listener enthralled during a conversation. He would frequently regale his fellow retirees with tales of his youth; a member of the original jet-set, rubbing shoulders with the rich and famous in London in the swinging 60s. Those that knew him believed him, those that didn't put it down to his dementia.

Charlie had enjoyed a low-key but significant career in the diplomatic service, in his case a synonym for Secret Service, spending many years in Johannesburg. That posting was the result of a family scandal that threatened to make headline news. It had deprived him of his wife, any relationship with his children and grandchildren, and forced him to the other side of the world losing touch with his friends and the life he loved. But Charlie was nothing if not pragmatic. He considered that he had served his country well and made up for the mistakes he had made in his early years. The service obviously valued his contribution since he was one of the original residents at Shady Fields when it was opened two years ago. Until last year he had enjoyed his life here but the events he had witnessed; the death of a friend and a member of staff had left a mark on him.

Charlie had decided that life was too fleeting to allow grudges to go unchecked. There was no scar too old to be healed, it just took someone brave enough to make the first move.

He tried to reconnect with his children but discovered very quickly that his son was still angry and wanted nothing to do with him. One of his daughters now lived in Australia and the other had already passed away, but she had left a feisty granddaughter behind who had wanted to meet him.

He wasn't sure of her motivation, whether it was just curiosity or a long-held grudge but if it meant he got to meet her it would be worth it.

He had followed her career closely, he knew that she was an award-winning journalist, but when they first met, her appearance was not what he had been expecting. Her mother had prized her designer wardrobe and even at a young age had cultivated her own look based on her innate sense of style rather than fashion. Lynsey however, dressed without finesse and her lifestyle generally left a lot to be desired. What he saw was a woman who was confident in who she was and really didn't worry about what she looked like. He loved her immediately.

It had been six months since their first meeting, and they had already developed a deep bond. She had appreciated his candor and the fact that he had filled in some of the blanks about events forty years ago that her mother would never talk about. She had listened to his side of the story and did not judge him. She had been very unsentimental about the whole thing, like she said, it all happened before she was born.

As they got to know each other better he could see why she made such a good journalist. She had a talent for critical analysis, a thirst for the truth and a nose for a good story, in fact, the perfect combination.

She walked across the entrance hall past the double doors to the library and on towards the back of the building, she knew exactly where he would be. The garden room was his favourite place to sit on summer afternoons. She found him sitting in one of the cane armchairs chuntering to himself. He stopped when he saw her and rose steadily to greet her with a kiss on both cheeks.

She put her arm around him and felt the shape of his boney shoulders through his summer jacket. She wondered if he had lost a little weight.

"Hello Charlie, you are looking well. Were you talking to yourself?"

"Of course, sometimes I need an expert opinion. Are you eating properly? You look thinner since we last met."

She sat in the seat opposite him and smiled warmly. "I'm fine, thanks. I've been very busy though so the local takeaway has been my best friend. I'm looking forward to a nice tea though, what have you ordered for us?"

"Today we are having a selection of summer wraps, whatever they are, with smoked salmon, ham, and duck egg and chef's selection of fancies with scones, clotted cream and fresh strawberries from the garden."

"Honestly, I don't know how you do this every day, I would be the size of a house! So, what's the gossip?"

"Nothing much ever goes on around here. They have started yoga classes but to be honest, it's not my sort of thing."

He smiled at Layla as she arrived with their tea.

"Hello Lynsey, how are you? It must feel good to be out of the London traffic"

Lynsey acknowledged the manager. She always thought how 'hands on' Layla Strong was. No sitting in an office somewhere issuing orders. She was an active member of the staff, turning her hand to all sorts. She knew her grandfather had a soft spot for her too. Layla had been a great support to him when he had lost his good friend William last year, he was very grateful to her for that. "I haven't been in London much to be honest Layla. I've been working on a story in Ireland, so I've spent a lot of time on the Emerald Isle, but it's nice to be back in a dryer climate though."

She began pouring tea for Charlie, and they chatted inconsequentially as they tucked into their wonderful spread. Charlie watched her closely and realised how much like her mother she was. She even had the same mannerism of rubbing her right earlobe when she was thinking.

"I was looking at some old photographs yesterday and found some lovely ones of your mother when she was a little girl. I think they were taken on the beach at Sainte-Maxime, it was so much nicer than Saint-Tropez. I think it was the year we stayed with the Minelli's. Sadly Judy was a faded beauty by then, but she took a bit of a shine to your mother if my memory serves me right."

"Are you seriously telling me you holidayed with the Minnellis' Charlie?"

"I think that's a bit strong, we went for drinks a couple of times and stayed overnight after the odd cocktail party."

Lynsey smiled "I never know whether you are teasing me or not. I am going to have to write your biography one day, the great expose of Charlie Bingham!"

His faced suddenly took on a very serious look. "You couldn't get it published if you did, Everything I know is still covered by the official secrets act." He changed the subject deftly. "I left the photo album upstairs, but you could borrow it if you like, have a good look through it. Shall we go up and get it?"

"Am I allowed? I've never seen your apartment."

He laughed. "Of course you are, this is where I live not a 1960s boarding house, I am allowed guests in my apartment, but my knee is playing up a little, so we will need to use the lift if that's OK?"

They finished their afternoon tea, left the pleasant view of the gardens behind, and walked towards the front of the building. She followed as Charlie took a sharp left and headed down a corridor. They heard the lift doors open and Charlie picked up his pace a little. Two men in dark suits came out of the lift, joking with each other. They looked decidedly out of place on a warm summer afternoon. Their suits did not disguise their toned physiques and as they passed she noticed the telltale cord of an earpiece.

As they stood in the lift she asked "Charlie, who were those two men?"

"No idea. They must be visiting someone on the top floor." He shuffled his feet impatiently.

"And who might be on the top floor being visited by bodyguards? Do you have someone famous here?"

He was out of the lift and heading down the corridor before the doors had fully opened. Briefly touching his key card against the electronic panel, he opened the door and stood to one side, ushering her into his apartment. "Me casa Su casa," he said smiling at her. "Have a seat and I will fetch the album for you." He disappeared into the bedroom.

Her eyes travelled around the room taking in the details. It was a lovely sunny sitting room decorated in a restful pale green. The furniture was not the same period as the room but didn't look out of place. A cream damask settee and matching winged club chair stood in the centre of the room and a large mahogany pedestal desk stood against the side wall. Two large widows provided a lovely view out into the gardens. Everywhere was neat and tidy, uncluttered, except for the top of the desk where a myriad of framed photos stood clustered together. Most of the frames were old and silver and looked quite valuable. There must have been a dozen or more. She wandered over to them, intrigued to see if she would see familiar family members. Immediately she recognised some of the faces, but they were not her family.

There was one of Charlie as a young man standing between Graham Hill the racing driver and Ian Fleming the renowned author and some said, spy. As she studied some of the others she spotted an older version of her grandfather with Nelson and Winnie Mandela and another with Desmond Tutu. All this time she had thought his stories were widely exaggerated, but here was a record of a truly influential diplomat who really had played his part in the making of modern history.

He came back into the room with the album and watched her as she scanned his little collection. “Ah, I see you have found my rogues' gallery.”

“Charlie I didn’t realise you moved in such important circles.” She was finding it difficult to tear herself away from the images.

“A typical diplomats’ legacy Lynsey. The only things you are left with after your service are the memories of your glory days.”

Charlie walked over to her and picked up the picture of Desmond Tutu. “Now, he was a funny man! We used to have long discussions about apartheid and racism. He once told me that it was “just a pigment of my imagination.” He gave a wistful smile and put the picture back in its place. “We did make a difference you know, although sometimes I am not sure what that was. I used to sit in meetings where reclassification figures were reviewed. People actually choosing to be classified as 'coloured' so they could remain legally married." He shook his head "Can you imagine having to do that now? We started that process of changing attitudes, and I am immensely grateful that I was able to do something worthwhile with my life after such a shaky start."

"We've seen so much change in our lifetimes Charlie, not all of it good either. This really was pivotal stuff. The problem is that history is written by the victors and is only ever a partial record. The story I have been working on about the Good Friday Agreement is a classic case in point. There are families who will probably never get the justice they deserve for their loved ones, the victims of the Birmingham Pub bombings for example."

Charlie could hear the passion in her words.

She continued, "It isn't hard to argue that stopping the troubles was a positive change and moving on to a non-violent solution was the only way forward, but there were still casualties on both sides of that conflict. Men and women were left out in the cold, cut off from a cause they'd been born into. No wonder some of them went off the rails. I suppose that's where I see the value of what I do. I force the victors to be transparent about the fall-out of their victories. They should acknowledge the costs of their actions as well as the prize."

Charlie stared at her for a moment, clearly internally debating whether to continue this conversation. He decided to engage her. "The idea that transparency is not an opponent, but an inevitable component of national security is a naive view my dear. It creates a massive conflict of interest between those that protect national security and the media. To protect human rights, it may be necessary to keep certain information secret to protect legitimate national security interests. Striking the right balance is made even more challenging when the stock phrase of the media is 'but it's in the public interest'. I have seen the consequences of such transparency when serving agents actively trying to protect us have lost their lives in the name of an exposé'."

Lynsey turned sharply towards him obviously ready to defend her profession and its values.

"But Charlie, you can't trust that governments will not use that defence simply to cover their tracks, to cover up some massive incompetence or conceal illegal activities. There must be some tension in the system. What if we discovered that the whole process of negotiating peace in Northern Ireland was done just to provide an escape route for terrorists. They knew they were losing the fight, and they wanted to come out of it with some protection against prosecution for their crimes? That makes the government morally questionable, doesn't it?"

"Surely the question is: Would that be a price worth paying if the bombings and killings stopped and the people of Northern Ireland no longer had to live in a war zone? War is a dirty business, but it's probably one of those circumstances where most of the time the end really does justify the means."

Lynsey realised that not only was there a huge generation gap between them, but he was also a man from a different world not just another era. He may have served in a diplomatic role, but she knew how the system worked. His talk of agents made her realise there would have been shady links to the security services. This newly discovered grandfather had hidden depths and secrets she could not even begin to guess at.

Chapter 26:

Thursday 24th July 2019 8.00pm

Belfast

Callaghan had just finished his perfectly cooked steak. He replaced the fork and sharply serrated knife back on his plate and dabbed at the corners of his mouth with a linen napkin. He settled back in the plush chair and stretched his legs out under the table to give his girth a little more space. He drained the last remnants of the rich, fruity Malbec that had been a perfect accompaniment to his meal, leaving a rose tint clinging to the inside of the glass.

He approved of the refurbishment that the owner of the Taphouse Bar and Restaurant had recently completed. The staff were turned out in crisp white shirts and black bartender aprons. There was a cocktail menu for the more exotic weekend punter, and they were turning over a very healthy profit. Perhaps it was time to review his protection fee?

He looked across to the door where Seamus had suddenly appeared, looking furtive.

My God, what now he wondered. It had recently occurred to him that at some point he would have to tackle the Seamus question. He was loyal and obedient and never questioned orders, but he was truly as thick as a brick. He screwed up on a regular basis and while he was willing to overlook some of his more idiotic actions, Yilmaz would not. Perhaps it was time for a parting of ways.

Seamus pulled the chair out opposite Callaghan and sat down. The waiter appeared out of nowhere to take his order but his boss intervened. "He won't have anything to drink thank you, he isn't staying."

Seamus took the hint. "I've just heard from our bloke tailing the journo. She left London and went to visit a big country house. She was there all afternoon, then left and went home. She got back about an hour ago, I thought you'd like to know."

"Could it be the safe house where they are keeping Dessie?"

Seamus breathed in, his mouth begin to water and his stomach rumble. He hadn't eaten since breakfast. He focused his attention on his employer. "No, it's a posh retirement home, and she was visiting some old man. It doesn't look like she knows what they've done with him. We would have found something by now." His eyes were drawn to the remaining chips on the plate in front of Callaghan.

"Seamus, you can't make assumptions like that when dealing with MI5. They have safe houses in the oddest places. Besides, she is a journalist, and she will keep tabs on her exclusive source if she can. He owes her, and she won't let the opportunity of an exclusive story slip through her fingers. She will certainly have a way of getting in touch with him or at the very least will know someone that can contact him. That's all I need to know. You need to get on the next flight to London to go and pay her a visit. I want to know exactly what she knows. I don't want her killed until we have Dessie's whereabouts, do you understand? She might still be useful to us with Devey. The last thing he wants is a journo sniffing around."

Seamus left the restaurant and hailed a cab. If he got a move on he would just make the evening flight.

Just his luck! No onboard catering. That would mean just a cold stale sandwich and bottle of water. One day, he would be the one calling the shots and eating steak dinners while everyone else did his bidding. He boarded the busy flight, found his seat, and buckled his safety belt. An attractive young stewardess was doing the safety briefing. She was slim but curvy in all the right places. Seamus had texted his contact as he'd waited to board, now would be a good time to check his messages.

"Sir, can you please turn off your phone until we are in the air and the signs have been extinguished, thank you?"

Seamus looked up at a smiling face with large eyes, full lashes and a perfectly formed mouth. Great, perhaps this flight wouldn't be a washout after all. He smiled back "No problem. Perhaps you could remind me later."

"Of course sir" and the stewardess turned and sauntered off down the narrow aisle in response to a flashing passenger light. She knew full well she was being appraised as she went.

Seamus's contact was waiting to collect him at the arrivals' terminus in the drop-off and collection zone. They drove directly to Parry's apartment block and parked in an underground car park next to her building. The men got out of their car, took a small sports bag from the boot, and made their way to the building's entrance doors. A bank of numbered buzzers sat on the wall to the right of the double glass doors.

Seamus pressed a buzzer at random, and almost immediately it was answered by an exasperated voice

"Where the hell have you been, you're an hour late!" The electronic lock released, and they entered the vestibule.

The two men looked at each other, pleasantly surprised.

"Well, that was easy, I had a spiel prepared and everything. Perhaps it's a sign that this won't take long."

It was a nice building in an up-and-coming area but not flash enough to have CCTV in the corridors or on the staircases. They climbed the stairs to the second floor and found number 26, it was 11.30pm exactly.

A straightforward Yale lock gave Seamus fifteen seconds of trouble before it yielded and the door opened. They walked quietly along an empty hall. Music was playing softly from a room on the right and the door was ajar. Seamus needed to locate the woman, so he carefully scanned the softly lit room from the doorway before entering. He could see several takeaway boxes piled on a low coffee table. A bottle of whiskey and an empty tumbler sat next to them. Then he saw the shape of a slightly built woman lying on the sofa covered with a throw. Her breathing was slow and rhythmic, she was asleep.

Seamus nodded to his accomplice, and they entered the room, the other man walking around the back of the sofa. He reached over and put his gloved hand firmly over the woman's mouth. Lynsey's eyes opened immediately and let out a muffled scream.

Seamus was standing in front of her with his finger raised to his lips, "Shush, don't make a sound, and you won't get hurt."

She swung her legs onto the floor and sat upright, but that was as far as she got. The silent man had her shoulder in a vice-like grip pinning her to the back of the couch.

Seamus slid the takeaway boxes off the coffee table on onto the floor then sat facing her. He poured a shot of whiskey into her glass and downed it in one. "If my friend lets go you must not make a sound. We just want a little information from you that's all. Do you understand?" She nodded her head, but there was terror in her eyes.

The man relaxed his hand but kept it at the side of her face ready to silence her again if needed. "Now, we have a mutual acquaintance, Dessie McFee. I want to know where he is. We know you helped him contact the authorities, and we are keen to get him home to his loved ones. All you have to do is tell us where they're holding him, and we will leave you in peace."

Lynsey's mind was racing. This man was mad if he honestly thought they would have told a journalist where they were holding a Supergrass!

"I have no idea where he is. They are hardly going to take me into their confidence are they?" Her voice sounded strangely calm and steady which was the direct opposite of what her heart was doing at that moment.

The man who was speaking to her looked vaguely familiar. She rifled through her mental card index, and she retrieved a name. "It's Seamus, isn't it? Seamus

Mehan? Look Seamus, I really can't help you. I don't know where he is."

He struck her hard across the face with the back of his tattooed hand. She slammed into the back of the sofa; her ears were ringing, and a white-hot pain shot through her teeth and into her jaw. It took her breath away.

"Now please let's not make this any harder than it has to be. They must have promised you something, an exclusive interview or story about him. You wouldn't have let them take him without some guarantee of contact with him. Who did you visit today when you went to the residential home?" He flexed his fingers in anticipation.

For a moment, she looked confused. "What? What has that got to do with anything? I was visiting my grandfather, he lives there." Seamus would store that bit of information and relish that he could tell Mr. Callaghan that he'd been right, she was just visiting an old man. His earlier assumption was now a confirmed fact.

"So how do you get in touch with Dessie then? Is there a burner phone or a contact you have?" He reached across to the chair where her open bag was thrown. He rummaged through the contents until he found her phone and a small voice recorder. He switched the phone on, but it requested her thumbprint for identification to unlock the screen. Seamus grabbed her roughly by the wrist, his large fingers crushing her bones together, making a wave of nausea rise from her stomach into the back of her throat. She cried out. He hit her again and roughly held her right thumb to the button until the screen came to life. As she struggled, she heard a crack, a shooting pain that ran up her wrist and into her arm like an electric shock. She screamed too quickly for the man to silence her with his gloved hand.

Seamus was indifferent, he was more interested in scanning her call log. It showed the phone number for Shady Fields. "So, your dear old grandad was OK, was he? I would guess that if he's knocking on a bit, he probably needs to be careful and not have too many shocks. He won't react well to hearing that his granddaughter has been hurt. Look. All I want to know is who your contact is, the one who knows where he's being held. We'll leave you in peace and grandad doesn't have a stroke."

Lynsey began to feel the effects of shock setting in. Her skin was cold and clammy and her heartbeat was racing, she took a deep breath. "This is going to sound crazy, but I called a number I found on the internet and someone called me back. I don't have their number, they contact me." Her voice was becoming thin and raspy. "Check it, you'll see the withheld numbers are the times we have spoken." Her head felt light, and she began to lose focus. "I have to wait for them to make contact, I'm telling you the truth."

Desperation was creeping into her voice now. That last blow had cut the inside of her cheek and she could taste blood on her tongue; warm and metallic.

Suddenly, the doorbell rang, immediately followed by a knock on the door, a muffled voice called out,

"Lynsey, are you OK? Are you alright in there?"

Seamus tensed and nodded to his accomplice as he stood. He picked up the whiskey bottle from the table. "We'll be leaving now and if you have any sense, you will say nothing." He smashed the bottle on the side of Lynsey's head, and it shattered sending shards of glass and whiskey everywhere. Lynsey slumped unconscious across the cushions; blood began to flow freely from a gaping wound.

The accomplice looked urgently toward the hallway. "We should be going Seamus." The noise at the front door was becoming more urgent. Seamus pocketed the voice recorder and headed towards the back door and the fire escape that his accomplice had already confirmed was there in case they needed a quick getaway. Callaghan was wrong about him; he did think ahead.

Chapter 27:

Friday 26th July 2019 11.00am
Belfast

They were back here again, sitting in the Taphouse Lounge. Twice in as many days was becoming worrying for the owner. He was resigned to the protection payments he had to make to Callaghan, but he was reluctant to become the gangsters' Belfast Headquarters. He signalled to his waiter to take the tray of coffee across to where Callaghan was sitting with his henchman Seamus. Who knew that owing a trendy bar and restaurant in Belfast city centre would be classed as a dangerous occupation that required your own stress counsellor.

JJ sipped the strong filter coffee and stared at Seamus. "Tell me what happened."

Seamus added four sugar lumps to his small cup of strong coffee and stirred it carefully.

"We surprised her at the flat and asked her for a name or a number that would put us in touch with Dessie. She said she hadn't got one and that the security services contacted her directly when they needed to. We roughed her up a bit, but her story stayed the same. Turns out she was only visiting her grandad, just as I thought. Then her neighbour came and knocked on the door to see what the noise was all about, so we left by the back entrance and down the fire escape. She was alive when we left. Leon took some photos while he was tailing her and is going to email them to you today. That's about it Mr. Callaghan. Sorry but it looks like another dead end."

Callaghan took a deep breath and looked directly at Seamus. It was a cold stare filled with controlled anger and impatience. "So let me get this right. You break into her flat, genuinely believing that she will give you the personal contact details of the head of the security services who you can then call up and ask where they are holding their first Supergrass in two decades. Is that about the size of it?"

"Well, I thought we might be able to get to her contact and extract a location out of him." Seamus was sounding more doubtful by the minute.

Callaghan slammed his fist down on the table sending the cups flying in different directions. Several people enjoying their brunch turned to see what the commotion was about. He sent a warning look to the waiter not to approach them, the waiter returned to the bar and began speaking in hushed tones to the owner, who was now a sickly shade of pale.

"Seamus, did it not occur to you that by leaving a trail of casualties across London you might be drawing attention to us? If she didn't have a direct contact number for him, then he has been taken out of circulation and our chance to speak to him has been lost."

Just then his phone pinged, and he picked it up to read the text. He concentrated on the file of images attached, opening each one and scanning them carefully.

They were long-range shots taken with a powerful telephoto lens and the quality was not brilliant, but after a few seconds he let out a low whistle.

"Well, well, what have we got here? I recognise these men". He let the images catch up with his memories and then gallop to a conclusion.

"Feck me! They ARE using this place as a safe house. No residential home has spook bodyguards at the front door and has Bill and Ben the feckin' Dynamite Men as guests!" He poked at the screen with his index finger. "Once again you have been saved by your own unique brand of stupidity Seamus. Quite by accident you have discovered where they are almost certainly holding him. It is too much like a coincidence for her to be visiting some old codger in a high security nursing home, where two of the most notorious ex-members of an elite bomb squad have been spotted. I have a good feeling about this Seamus. I need to call Yilmaz and put the ball in his court."

Seamus felt despondent, he could never seem to get it right. He would treat himself to an all-day breakfast at the café down the road. There was certainly nothing here for him

.

PART 3

Chapter 28:

Friday 26th July 2019 11.00am

Shady Fields

Bill was conducting a surveillance operation from the comfort of a leather sofa in the entrance hall, watching the movements of visitors and staff to the third floor. Ben was not at all happy with him. He thought they should mention what they knew to Hilary, but Bill had disagreed. “She would just dismiss us out of hand. The ramblings of two old blokes with too much time on their hands. Let’s just see if we are right, then we can take her something substantial.”

“I don’t like it Bill, Phipsy could do something rash. You saw how badly he was affected. Anger like that, stored up for years, it’s dangerous. It makes him unpredictable and reckless.”

Bill could sense his friend was torn between his argument and doing the right thing. But he was feeling sharper and more alert than he had in months. His brain was working on solving this problem, and he felt alive! His old skill set was kicking in. He promised himself that he would enjoy himself for a day or two, and then they would take their concerns to Hilary.

Bill already knew the times of the guard changes and their shift patterns. It was well concealed amongst the comings and goings of the place, but there were clear patterns if you knew what you were looking for. The next quiet time would be around 3pm this afternoon. He decided that he would do a physical recce of the holding suite then. There would be fewer people milling around generally, and it was one of the scheduled rest breaks for the guards. With any luck, he might hear something that would confirm who it was. He would be in and out in five minutes.

He was pretending to read a copy of Country House magazine when Jonny, one of the home's personal assistants came hurrying along carrying a yellow waste bag.

"I never had you down as an interior designer Bill." He laughed at his witticism but carried on walking. He would have to go past the staircase Bill wanted to use. He decided to give him a couple of minutes before following in the same direction. He stood and dropped the magazine onto the cushion of the seat. He had made a schoolboy error, drawing attention to himself by the choice of his reading material. Nothing should ever draw attention to you on a stakeout. Nothing should make people remember that you were there. He really was out of practice.

He checked the passageway one last time before ascending the stairs. He was slightly short of breath when he reached the third floor but quickly recovered. He moved stealthily along the corridor and heard the sounds of banter coming from a room on the right. No guards were visible, so he moved quickly along to the suite at the far end of the corridor. He knocked softly and tried the doorknob. It wasn't locked, the door opened onto an empty room. He quickly slipped inside, unseen. It was set out in a similar fashion to all the other rooms in this place, but he noted the additions of a debriefing table with service issue recording equipment and discrete window bars.

Bars at the window were not uncommon on the third floor, but he wondered whether these were meant to keep people out rather than keep them in.

The bathroom was empty apart from a used towel draped over the edge of the bath. On the shelf above the sink he saw a razor, toothbrush, and shaving foam, definitely a man then. The bedroom door was closed. He listened carefully but could hear nothing. He opened the door a little and let his eyes adjust to the darkness. There was a shape in the bed. Bill stood dead still. He decided to check it out and was not the least bit surprised when he found the old pillow decoy. You tend to get a sense of life when standing that close to a sleeping person, and he had felt nothing. So where was he then?

The guards certainly thought he was still there; otherwise there would have been alarms going off already. They hadn't taken him somewhere else for questioning otherwise the equipment wouldn't still be here. It was a puzzle.

Ben returned to the sitting room and looked around. It had all the hallmarks of a safe house. Generic possessions like clothes, toiletries, magazines and reading materials were dotted around. Nothing gave any indication of identity or even personal ownership. There was no iPad, phone or watch to be seen. He began scanning for any paperwork that might give something away.

A notepad lay on the table with some scribbling made with a blunt pencil. They were hard to read, a few dates and the odd name. The name 'Gradasevic' was heavily circled. Bill searched his memories for a familiar reference. He knew it was organized crime, but that was as far as his recall could be pushed. Perhaps they had been wrong about an IRA connection, but Phipps had been so sure about what he had overheard.

He flipped through the rest of the pad just in case, and sure enough spotted some more writing in the same hand hidden about a third of the way into the unused pages. Jackpot! There was a roughly drawn table with names places and dates listed, almost as if the writer was trying to arrange things in a chronological order.

Bill reached for his phone and pulled up the camera app. He took pictures of both pages before checking the time. He'd been here long enough; he should go back downstairs.

He moved towards the door checking for noise in the corridor and slipped out quietly, heading for the stairs again. He had almost reached the top of the staircase when he heard a door close.

"Bill, what are you doing up here, you know this part of the building is restricted."

He turned slowly rubbing his forehead. "Er hello, er, Jimmy, isn't it? He sounded frail and confused.

"It's Jonny, mate. What's wrong, how did you get up here?"

Bill looked at him vacantly. "I'm not sure. I was trying to find my way down to breakfast. Have I taken a wrong turn?"

"Bit confused today are you, Bill? I thought that magazine I saw you with downstairs was not like you. How about if I take you down, and we'll see if we can find Ben? Come on, let's see what he's up to."

Bill physically brightened up "Thanks very much, I haven't seen him in ages, is he here too?"

Jonny took him by the elbow and guided him gently towards the lift. "Let's go down this way, it's quicker."

"Thanks very much son, I seem to have lost me bearings. What I need is a nice cuppa."

The well-groomed head of one of the security contingent popped out of the mess room door, Jonny acknowledged it "Just got a wanderer, I am taking him downstairs, sorry to have disturbed you."

The head shook in a patronizing manner "Poor bugger, I hope they shoot me if ever I get like that."

He didn't hear Bill say "Happy to oblige" under his breath as they prepared to enter the lift.

As the two men stepped out of the lift on the ground floor they could see Ben looking around the hall. Jonny smiled "Here he is Ben, I found him wandering on the third floor. Is he having a bad day?"

Ben looked sceptical "What have you been up to now?" He smiled at Jonny who seemed quite happy to hand his charge over and return to what he was doing before.

"Jimmy here has been helping me. He said we can have some tea in a bit."

They walked down the main corridor towards the bar, a smile growing on both their faces. "Well, you look chipper enough to me. What did you find out?"

Bill's pace quickened. "There was no one there, I think he may have gone walkabout. The guards have no idea that he's not in his room. He's obviously here voluntarily, which means he hasn't escaped. Maybe he wants to shake them up a bit. There was nothing with a name or personal details, typical safe house set up."

Ben looked mildly disappointed. "So a bit of a waste of time then really?"

"I wouldn't say that. I love a bit of larceny in the afternoon. I took a couple of pictures of some notes he'd been making. Let's see if they tell us anything over an afternoon snifter shall we?" The sparkle was back in his eye and there was a definite spring in his step.

The bar was deserted, Ben took a couple of cans from the fridge behind the bar and expertly poured them into beer glasses, achieving a foamy head. Two club chairs were separated by a small circular polished table and Bill slumped into one of these, fiddling with his phone as he did. He pulled up the photos he had taken and began to study them.

As Ben returned to the table his friend was obviously excited by his find. "I didn't have a chance to read it properly when I was upstairs, but I think this is interesting. The dates go back to the 80s and 90s. All the big hitters are here; JJ Callaghan, Colm, and Sinead Devey but no mention of Dessie McFee."

He sounded disappointed. "So obviously it's not him then?"

Bill looked at him in disbelief "Do you know, for a clever bloke, you can be surprisingly dim sometimes. It proves it's him!"

Ben looked puzzled. His friend felt quite exasperated now, so he spelled it out for him. "He would have no reason to write his own name down, would he?"

Realisation dawned on Ben's face. "It is a significant list isn't it. Remembering our run-ins with Callaghan still give me sleepless nights. Cat and mouse games with car bombs and IEDs. Do you remember those bowling ball devices we rigged up under the Q cars? A flash bang dispenser triggered by a foot switch that released a shed load of stun grenades. Flew out in all directions before detonating. They saved us from a few IRA roadblocks, but we seriously pissed Callaghan and his gang off."

"Yes, you had to get up early in the morning to get one over on us. I wonder if this is really about the rumours of an agent close to Callaghan. What if it was Dessie McFee Bill?"

Bill took a long draught of beer. "There was a legend, wasn't there? Someone very close to the top. I never really believed it, though. I'm sure it would have come to light when the agreement went through wouldn't it?"

It was Ben's turn to look sceptical. "I'm not so sure about that. Can you imagine how much shit would have hit that fan, if they found out that the people they were negotiating with from Her Majesty's Government were the handlers of the traitor sat at their table? They would never have got the Agreement through if it had been common knowledge. It would have wrecked everything. I think it was probably misinformation planted to generate suspicion and divide the ranks."

Bill was turning it all over in his head. "I can't believe if Dessie was a plant that he would have stayed in place all these years. Someone would have tumbled to it?" he said slowly.

Ben cocked his head on one side "Where are you going with this?"

"Just thinking aloud really. If there was someone still in play, he would have the inside track on Callaghan's organised crime activities. Callaghan would be cornered, his links to organised crime would mean that they could lock him up and throw away the key and take down a major crime outfit to boot. If it was Dessie McFee, then why wait 'till now? What would trigger him leaving? Did Callaghan find out somehow? Did someone blow his cover? No wonder they would want to bury him out in a place like this where no one would think of looking. It sort of makes sense, doesn't it?"

Ben suddenly became very serious. "I hope you are wrong Bill. You know how resourceful Callaghan was. If Dessie is about to offer him up he won't let that go. He'll be doing everything to try to track him down and if he finds him, he will come for him. We could find ourselves facing an old adversary." He shivered and not because he was cold.

Chapter 29:

Friday 26th July 2019 pm

St. Guy's Hospital London

She was having the same horrible dream. Like an observer of her own life, she watched the woman and the young girl as they walked along Corry Road in Belfast en route to meet with the social worker that could help Tatum. Her confident stride was shadowed by the smaller nervous steps of the young girl at her side. They were almost at the rendezvous point. Just around the corner lay safety. Suddenly, from out of nowhere, they pounced from a large black transit van with side sliding doors and tinted windows. There were four of them, big, menacing, and rough; the first man pushed Lynsey to the ground, the second and third men picked Tatum up and threw her into the van. She had looked terrified.

As Lynsey tried to get to her feet, the fourth man said in a thick Irish accent "Stay on the floor if you don't want to get hurt". He showed her the gun he was grasping under his jacket. That was the first time she had seen Seamus Mehan up close and personal. He got back into the van which sped off before the door had even closed. That was the last time she had seen Tatum alive. The promise she had made to Dessie to keep the girl safe had failed.

Images of the young girl's dead body swam in and out of focus. She had been the one to identify her; tiny and pale, lying on the gurney behind the glass viewing window at the mortuary. She had failed her. The promise she made to Tatum and Dessie was broken. She wondered if the guilt would always be with her as sharply as she felt it now.

The images were distorting into feelings and sounds. There was a strange bleeping noise, Lynsey struggled to open her eyes. She swam in and out of that unfathomable blackness. Her body felt leaden, and she knew instinctively that it would hurt if she moved. She concentrated, and gradually the bleeping became steady and rhythmic. She was unsure how long she'd been in this state, but she willed herself to open her eyes. The light was blinding and created a pain in her head that seared through her whole body. She squinted as several blurred shapes came closer and leaned over her. She could make out a voice, soft but with a trace of urgency.

“Lynsey, can you hear me? You are in St. Guy's Hospital and you are safe.” The voice sounded familiar, but she couldn’t place it. It spoke again but this time not to her. “She’s coming round Doctor; will she be OK?” More mumbling. Why couldn’t they leave her alone, she just wanted to sleep.

The voice tried again. “Lynsey, can you hear me? You are safe now. Your neighbour raised the alarm, and they brought you here. I need to ask you a few important questions.”

Lynsey felt panic rising in her, she had an image of the men in her flat. They had hurt her. They wanted information from her, but she didn’t know anything. She opened her eyes again and tried to focus. Her right eye opened, but something was preventing her left one from opening, there was just a slit of light. She channelled all her efforts on focusing on the blurry features. It was a man’s face. He looked kind and full of concern.

“Lynsey, my name is Daniel Grant and I need to ask you a few questions if you’re up to it. We want to catch whoever did this to you, but we need you to tell us anything you can remember to help us do that.”

He spoke quietly and in a controlled way, like he was speaking to a child. He was holding her left hand very gently.

She tried to speak, but her voice was croaky and the sound that came out didn’t sound like her at all. She realised that her face was bandaged, a tight dressing covered her chin and ran up each side of her head. "What happened? Why am I here?" She struggled to shape the words correctly, it all sounded so jumbled.

The man sat down next to her so that he was at eye level with her. "We know that two men were in your apartment last night Lynsey. They were looking for something, and they hurt you to find it. Your neighbour heard noises and came to see if you were OK. We think he must have scared them away. He called an ambulance and they bought you here. Can you remember who did this to you?" He sat patiently waiting for her response.

The events of the previous night were jumbled but as she listened to him two things came to mind. "Seamus Mehan." She croaked, and "Water."

Daniel reached for the beaker with the straw on her bedside table and offered it to her. She gingerly took a sip, swallowed, and continued, "He works for a gangster called Callaghan. I'm a journalist, he was linked to a story I was working on. He took a young girl, she was killed." The effort to speak was painful, she closed her eyes and tried to focus on the events that had taken place in her flat.

Daniel smiled in encouragement. "You are doing great Lynsey, well done. Did you recognise the other man? Anything you can remember, anything at all?"

She tried to shake her head, but that set off a wave of nausea. She waited a moment "No, he was behind me." She took another sip of water. "They were looking for Dessie McFee, but I don't know where he is." She was breathless and felt exhausted.

Daniel smiled at her "That's really very helpful. Now, I want you to get some rest, we will take care of everything else."

As he stood to leave, she squeezed his hand and mumbled something. He lent down closer to her so that he could hear what she said. She whispered "I'm worried about my grandfather. They must have been following me because they knew him and where he lives."

Suddenly, the man wasn't smiling any more. He turned and quickly strode out into the corridor. Daniel addressed the security guard stationed outside her room. "No one goes in or out without you checking ID, and make sure you get a staff roster from the nurses' station before every shift change. I don't want them trying to finish the job off while she's in here." The guard nodded in response.

Daniel turned to the Doctor who had treated her when she was bought into A&E, he was hovering close by with a flip chart of results. "Her attackers made a bit of a mess I gather?"

The doctor referred to his notes "She had multiple fractures, jaw, eye socket, ulna, radius in her right forearm and a broken thumb on the right hand. She also sustained a hairline skull fracture and had a bleed on the brain when she came in. We managed to treat that successfully, but she was very lucky. Being found so quickly probably saved her life."

The sense of urgency that Daniel felt was very real. They had to track Mehan down as soon as possible, though he was probably back in Belfast by now. They would issue a warrant for his arrest; it would be done through his department; they couldn't be sure that the local plod hadn't been compromised where Callaghan's gang was concerned. He didn't want anyone getting skittish and making a bolt for it before they had their arrest strategy in place. A great deal of planning and effort had gone into this operation and it was one of the few joint missions between MI5 & 6 that seemed to be working well. He didn't want it to blow up in their faces.

Chapter 30:

Friday 26th July 2019. 3.00pm

Shady Fields

Dessie knew from the noise levels that there would be far fewer people milling around in the afternoon. He guessed that the residents would mostly be resting after their lunch, after all, that's what old people did, sleep most of the day, waking up to be fed and watered. There was a shift change due soon and Dessie knew that Tweedledum and Tweedledumber, his nickname for his debriefing team, would not start another questioning session until 4.30pm at the earliest.

He had complained of feeling a bit off after his lunch. He said it was something to do with the prawn salad. At about 2.30pm he told his guards he wanted to sleep and not to disturb him. He went to his room, closing the curtains, shrouding it in a dim light despite the bright sunshine outside. He was going stir crazy and needed to see something other than the suits and the inside of this room. He arranged pillows under his duvet to mimic his sleeping form and prepared himself for a little jaunt in the gardens. What harm could it do? It might shake these guys up a bit too.

He listened at the door, there was no sound coming from his sitting room. He opened it a little and waited. He stepped into the room. Through the dividing wall he heard muffled laughter coming from next door. That must be where his bodyguards were.

This was his chance. He just wanted a walk in the grounds, and he would be back before they even noticed that he was gone. He felt he would go crazy if he stayed couped up in here one minute longer.

Dessie sensed the familiar increase in his pulse triggered by an adrenaline hit. It heightened his awareness rather than create anxiety. He knew that the guards would be sure to investigate any noise from the lift, so he picked up a key card that one of the guards had carelessly left on the table, slipped into the corridor, and headed quietly in the opposite direction, towards the sign for the stairs.

Once in the stairwell he checked for movement, but there was no one on the stairs. He hugged the open banister on his left as he moved down to the next floor.

That afforded him a clear view if anyone was coming up the stairs from below. He reached the ground floor without meeting a soul, crossed the hall and slowly edged open the large wooden door. It led into a passageway at the back of the building. He could just see the back of a female member of staff hurrying to her next task. He waited for her to disappear before he began his 'escape'.

He moved swiftly towards the back of the house and out through the conservatory doors that opened onto well-manicured lawns and the tree line beyond. His luck was in, there was no one in the conservatory to see him go and no one on the wide terrace either. He made for the steps at the end of the terrace, quickly descending, heading for the protective cover of the trees and large shrubs. It felt so good to be out in the fresh air on his own, and not being watched or controlled. He closed his eyes and took a deep breath in. The birdsong, the warm summer air that filled his lungs, for a moment, he could forget where he was and feel completely free.

A tingling sensation in his scalp pulled him back to reality. He sensed a movement somewhere off to his left. He began scanning the grounds. He was right, there was someone sitting on a bench underneath the canopy of a cedar tree. Dressed in muted colours and partially concealed in the dappled shade, the figure had been virtually invisible. There was something strangely familiar about this figure, though. For a moment he felt completely back footed, the hairs on the back of his neck were standing up and there was a distinct fluttering in his chest. If this was a heart attack, then why was there no pain?

He remained rooted to the spot for what seemed like an eternity. He didn't want to attract any attention to his presence, but the figure looked directly at him, and in that instant his whole world exploded. Was it his imagination or was he seeing a ghost?

Theresa Farrell was sitting there right in front of him, not moving, apart from the shimmering effect of the heat haze. He blinked to see if the vision would disappear, but she was still there. They stared at each other for maybe ten seconds, then she got to her feet and quickly moved off into the trees.

He tried to call out after her, but no words came. He ran across the lawn to where she had been, following the path she'd taken through the trees and into the shady undergrowth. The loamy smell of the earth filled his nostrils, he stopped and listened for sounds of movement. There was a rustle of branches away to his right. He set off again following the direction of the sound and found himself in a clearing with a large ornamental pond and a viewing platform at one end. The woman he sought was standing on the wooden deck griping the handrail tightly with badly disfigured hands. She was completely still, looking down into the water, almost frozen in time.

He made his way around the edge of the pond, not daring to call out to her in case she took off again. He was terrified that if this was a vision, any sudden move or noise would break the spell, and she would simply disappear into thin air. As he moved closer, he drank in her image. She was older, but her face was unforgettable, and she was still as beautiful as he remembered her. Her distinctive features, her full mouth, the tilt of her head. Was he going mad?

Only when he was almost within touching distance did he speak. "Theresa. Is it really you?"

She turned to look at him, her face was still, no trace of emotion. The merest hint of movement played around her lips. "Hello Dessie."

The sound of her voice turned his whole world on its axis. "This can't be. You're dead. Colm Devey killed you. I was the only one at your funeral."

She watched the entire gamut of human emotion dance across his face, like clouds scudding across a winter sky, anger, confusion, relief, hurt, disbelief. He steadied himself against the rail, wanting answers but unsure which question to ask first.

She took a step back "People had to think I was dead; otherwise they would have hunted me down and killed me for real. My team got me out, but they had to make people believe that I was dead. It would have been too dangerous for the others left behind."

Dessie was trying to take it all in. "You let me think you were dead! All these years grieving, feeling guilty, feeling angry. You put me through hell!" Emotion rolled off him in waves.

She reached out placing her hand lightly on his arm. "Dessie I'm so sorry, but I needed to disappear permanently. It wasn't my choice; it was my job."

That seemed to hit home and his eyes flashed angrily. "So, it was true, you were a plant. My God, you were bloody good. And I fell for it, didn't I? You must have been laughing up your sleeve at having fooled the great Dessie McFee. I loved you; I was willing to give up everything for you." He was shaking.

She faced him full on and with scarred hands, grasped his muscular arms. "Dessie, all I can say is that it started as a mission, but then I really fell in love with you, and that compromised everything. Sinead always disliked me and had begun to suspect me. She was so jealous of us. She saw me leaving a meeting and decided to exact her revenge. She nearly killed me."

Her head dropped, and almost in a whisper she said, "She tarred and feathered me herself, and when I could take no more, she took me to Colm. We both thought he would finish me off and deal with my body, but he saved me. I think he felt sorry for what she had done to me and helped me escape. He was the only one who knew the truth, and he kept my secret all these years."

Dessie felt numb "I've hated him for your death, I never forgave him. I couldn't bear to look at him because of what I thought he'd done to you. We always suspected the Brits of getting someone close to the top, but I had no idea it was you. Why didn't you sell me out? There must have been plenty of opportunities to hand me over, what stopped you?"

For the first time, she smiled at him. "I know this is hard to believe, but I never lied about my feelings for you. I wouldn't give you up. I acted as though it was part of the mission, but I really loved you. I was naive to think that I could keep it up, and when Sinead came after me and MI5 had to protect their remaining assets, I was sacrificed to make that happen. I was given a new identity and a new life. Much good it did me. My nerves were shot and all I could think about was what I'd lost."

"But I saw your body. It was damaged and burned, but I was sure it was you."

She nodded. "You thought you saw me because it's what you expected to see. It's called motivated reasoning. We come to conclusions that we are predisposed to believe are true. Fifteen years of therapy taught me that. In short, we see what we want to see. You didn't want to acknowledge that what they were saying about me was true, so it was easier to believe that I had died. Once you'd accepted that, you were able to blame the one person you thought was responsible. The body you saw was similar in physical appearance to me, but it was a student who had died from a drug overdose the week before. No family to speak of, they used her as the decoy to stop people looking for me. But Dessie, what are you doing here?"

Dessie was struggling to process it all. He had a thousand questions, and yet he couldn't think of one to ask her. "It's a long story, and I am not sure that I'm up to telling it now. You've completely taken the wind out of my sails. I have to get back before they realise I'm not there. Do you live here or are you visiting someone?"

"I live here. Everyone here knows me by my real name, Jackie Kelly. I'm truly sorry for any pain I caused you Dessie, that was never my intention." She reached up and kissed him tenderly on his cheek. Then turned and walked briskly past him, disappearing back into the cover of the trees.

He had no idea how long he stood there. His whole world and everything he had believed had just fallen apart, and he really had no idea what he was going to do next.

If his luck was still good, he could get back without them realising he had been out at all. He needed time to take all this in.

Chapter 31:

Friday 26th July 2019 6.00pm

Stormont

Sinead looked at the email her contact had copied her into. She felt the familiar rise of anger like a rash spreading up through her body. Why were they requesting files on the FRU soldier now? She had warned Colm that this could happen. Dessie had only been gone a few days and this was too much of a coincidence.

She picked the phone up and dialled his number, he answered after the first ring.

"I feckin' told you this would happen. I'm looking at an email from the security services requesting files on the FRU killing. We need to act now Colm."

"Calm down Sinead, we need to think before we act. Tell me what it actually says?"

She scrolled down, so she could see the request in its entirety. "It is requesting the police investigation file that was done when the body was found and the autopsy report too. It also says they have requested the military files on the investigation and the physical evidence that was gathered when they took over. He's told them Colm; Dessie has told them it was me."

Colm realised that she was probably right, it was too much of a coincidence.

"At the end of the day Sinead, it's his word against ours. He's going to shift the blame as much as he can. But he has no proof other than what Callaghan told him. There is nothing to tie you to the killing other than his account, and he is notoriously unreliable because of his record. You have a letter; they can't do anything. You've got to stay calm and keep your head. Don't do anything that could draw attention to yourself. Do you understand?"

Her voice had become louder and gone up an octave too.

"Of course I feckin' understand. He's about to sell me down the river to cement his new relationship with them by giving them new information Colm. They would love a test case to try to break the power of those letters. What have I possibly got to be worried about?"

The adrenaline was pumping through her body, raising her blood pressure, causing a pounding in her eardrums.

"For Christ's sake Sinead get a grip of yourself. Who made the request?"

She paused while reading "It comes from someone called Santos, Phil Santos. I've never heard of him, have you?"

"No I don't think so, but we can't just go blundering around asking for him by name without setting alarm bells going. Leave it with me and I will see what I can find out. In the meantime, keep your head down and shelve what you are doing for party members now. Aren't you due some holiday? Take a break, put some distance between you and this. I'll call you when I have something. And Sinead, promise me you will not do anything reckless."

It was the first time he had ever heard anything approaching fear in her voice.

"That's the problem Colm, there is absolutely nothing that I can do." Her voice turned steely "I'm a sitting duck but let me be clear, I will not go down without taking others with me!" The phone went dead.

Chapter 32:

Saturday 27th July 2019 1.00am

Shady Fields

Hilary crossed the hall to the ornate staircase. She reached the first-floor landing and approached Ada's door. She took a deep breath before quietly entering the room.

The nurse stood and came over to Hilary.

"She's sleeping just now; we are administering pain relief through her drip. If you need anything just press the buzzer." With that, the nurse left them alone in the room.

She settled herself into the armchair by the bed, her head awash with jumbled thoughts. She felt sure she wouldn't sleep tonight, but the silent, flashing lights of the monitors proved too mesmerising to resist.

Hilary was suddenly awake. She looked at her watch, it was 3.30am. The nurse was standing next to her checking the equipment monitoring Ada's vital signs.

Ada was awake, her back was supported with pillows, but she was lying on her side. She looked tiny. The ravages of her cancer were written all over her face and although the nurse assured Hilary she was not in pain; she was in no doubt that there was very little time left. She took Ada's hand. It was delicate with long manicured nails, a map of veins traced under paper thin skin. Hilary looked at the flashing numbers that told her Ada's heartbeat was weaker than it had been. She was just conscious, her eyes fluttered open and looked at Hilary

"Hello darling girl, you nearly missed me" Ada gave a weak smile.

"I'm here now, that's what matters" she replied lightly, but she felt tears start to form and blinked them back. "Ada, you need to rest, don't talk now."

Ada opened her eyes wider "Now is exactly when I have to talk. When I'm gone it will be too late. The grey case you bought from the cottage, it's for you. It contains some important papers, and things I have cherished from my secret life. I would have told you if I could, but I was always good at keeping secrets. I want you to have my key."

Ada reached for the familiar golden key that she always wore on a chain around her neck, she struggled to take it off, so Hilary unclasped the fine gold chain for her. Ada reached out and folded Hilary's fingers around the precious gift. The act had used her energy reserves, and she caught her breath.

"Pass me my Guinness." Hilary noticed a small glass on the bedside table containing the distinct black and cream liquid. She added a straw then held it to Ada's lips for her to take a sip. She took a long drink, almost emptying the glass, a look of satisfaction came over her face, "I needed that." she whispered as she visibly rallied.

"Hils, I want you to live a bigger life. No more shutting yourself off from the world, promise me…" The effort of talking was clearly taking a strain and Ada closed her eyes. She never spoke again. Hilary was unsure whether she was sleep or if she had slipped into a coma, but she felt sure that she would still hear her, so in a soft voice, she began to sing to her.

"Are you lonesome tonight,
do you miss me tonight?
are you sorry we drifted apart…"

(Roy Turk and Lou Handman – 1926)

It was one of the songs they used to sing together. They had been the backing singers to all their favourite tracks and as Hilary sang, a peaceful smile formed on Ada's face. She passed away barely ten minutes later. The monitor gave a low continuous bleep and the nurse, who had been standing at a discreet distance came to the side of the bed and felt for Ada's pulse. She listened for a heartbeat, and when she could not detect either, she turned the machine off, and recorded the time of death in her notes.

Hilary felt the deep pain of loss tear through her chest and her tears flowed freely. Her best friend was gone.

The nurse brushed her arm with her hand

"I'll notify Dr. Arnot, it will take him about thirty minutes to get here." She disconnected the monitors and wheeled them out into the corridor, softly closing the door behind her.

Hilary was absolutely still. She watched Ada who looked as if she was sleeping peacefully, and held her hand tightly. Neither of them had been particularly religious, and at a fairly early point in her adulthood they had both agreed that they preferred to live by a moral code rather than a spiritual doctrine. Strangely, Hilary felt she needed to mark Ada's passing in some way, she recalled one of Ada's favourite poems, by Emily Dickinson and spoke quietly.

Because I could not stop for Death –
He kindly stopped for me –
The Carriage held but just Ourselves –
And Immortality.
We slowly drove – He knew no haste
And I had put away

My labour and my leisure too,
For His Civility –

She bent down and kissed Ada's forehead. When she stood again the familiar coping mechanism had asserted itself. She walked over to the chest of drawers, selected Ada's white Broderie Anglaise pyjamas and white satin slippers, laid them on the end of the bed, bid her loving aunt a final farewell, turned and left the room.

Hilary went back to her office in a dreamlike state. She had buried her mother less than two weeks earlier and had lost her dearest friend today. She was now truly alone in the world, and she felt exhausted. She needed sleep. The leather couch in her office would have to do. She curled up into a fetal position and began to sob into a cushion. She thought she would never stop. She lay there until the first light of dawn crept through the windows; the clock blinked 5.45am.

A soft knock on her door was accompanied by Daniel's voice,

"Hilary, I have tea, or I can get you something stronger if you prefer." She struggled off the coach and opened the door, he stood in the hallway holding a tray containing two mugs of strong, hot tea. Judging by his appearance he hadn't slept much either, she ushered him inside.

"The tea is most welcome, I'm not sure about the something stronger though." Hilary caught sight of her reflection in the windowpane, "I look like the Wreck of the Hesperus! What a fright" she attempted to smooth her hair down, but it had other ideas.

He handed Hilary one of the mugs, "Would you like some company or shall I leave?"

Hilary was surprised at how much she wanted him to stay. It seemed strange that he had known a version of Ada that she knew little about. It was a different aspect of her life and an important one that Hilary wanted to know everything about. "Please stay, have your tea. I will have to let Layla know that I've left the things I want Ada cremated in laid out on her bed."

"She was a remarkable woman wasn't she." Daniel looked subdued.

Hilary smiled, "Yes, she was. I'm going to miss her so much. She has been the True North in my life and when I had a decision to make, I would go to her because she always saw things differently to me. When she reframed something it was like you were seeing it for the first time. Suddenly the right answer always seemed so obvious. That's a rare skill!

"She ran interference between my mother and me. When I got angry because of her latest irrational demand, I would go to Ada complaining about her. She would just look at me and ask one or two questions, which made me realise how unreasonable I was being. She probably did the same thing with mother. We were both too stubborn to listen to what she was telling us."

"And what was that?" sipping his tea.

"Ada was an expert in tuppenny philosophy. She did a healthy trade in those life quotes that are either banal or profound depending on whether you are ready to listen or not. One of her favourite's was that 'life's too short to stuff a mushroom' and she was right. We get caught up in life and waste so much time on the tiny details that we think are important, but often miss the big stuff as a result. The time spent with her was some of the happiest in my life and I should've spent more of it enjoying her company rather than complaining about my mother!"

"Don't beat yourself up too much, Ada would have told you if you were becoming self-absorbed, she told me that on a couple of occasions." He drained his cup and stood up to leave.

"Ada mentioned the case I bought up from the cottage." She reached down the side of the sofa, pulled the case out and placed it on the low coffee table. She reached into her pocket and drew out the gold key on a chain.

"Are you sure you want to do that now?"

Now he was doing it, asking the right questions. She realised she couldn't face the contents. "No, you're right, it can wait, at least until I've taken a shower."

He reached over and laid his hand gently on her shoulder. "Take as much time as you need, no one expects you to be at work at the moment." He left her to get ready for the day ahead.

She took her toiletry bag into the guest suite next door to her office, undressed and climbed into the spacious shower. The hot water beat down on the top of her head, running in rivulets down the full length of her body. She massaged shampoo into her hair and watched the suds disappear into the gurgling plughole. She must have stood like that for ten minutes, letting the water erase her tears and the tensions of the last couple of days. She stepped out of the shower and wrapped herself in a large towelling robe from the hook on the back of the door. She walked into the bedroom, sat at the dressing table, and began to dry her hair.

There was a knock at the door and a disembodied voice called "Breakfast."

She opened the door and Eileen bustled in setting a breakfast tray down on the table.

"If you need anything else Hilary just call down. I am so sorry for your loss." The sound of her soft Irish accent felt comforting. She turned to leave and then stopped, "I didn't know her well, but your aunt seemed like a lovely woman." She left, closing the door quietly behind her.

Hilary sat in the chair feeling the sadness return, tears formed in her eyes and ran down her cheeks again. She finished drying her hair and dressed in the navy tulip dress she kept in the office for emergencies. Her only accessory was Ada's gold key on a chain. She ran her fingers across it lovingly and looked over at the case.

It was an odd shape for a case, thought Hilary. It was square rather than oblong and as she lifted it, she admired the quality grey kid leather. Gold tooling proclaimed, 'Bahrain International Travel Bureau' and what she took to be the Arab translation in script underneath. On closer inspection, it was a Louis Vuitton creation with the distinct monogram embossed into the leather and the trademark padlock that accompanied every piece of luggage they made. The locks and keys were unique to each piece. Hilary placed it on the bed, inserted the little golden key into the lock and turned it to the left. She popped the clasp and opened the lid. Ada's familiar scent rose like a subtle cloud.

The case contained a bundle of photographs that all appeared to have been taken in other countries judging from the architecture. The top picture showed Ada and a very young Daniel. There was a manilla folder containing letters and legal documents, the deeds to the cottage, a guardianship document for Hilary and a long narrow envelope clearly marked 'Ada Hale: Last Will and Testament'.

A slim, well-worn jewellery case covered in battered black leather, with the initials ***RRC 2nd*** in silver tooling in the centre of the lid was partially concealed beneath the documents. Hilary opened it and discovered inside, a silver and red enamelled cross with a gold edge, suspended from a red and blue medal ribbon.

A telegram on tissue-thin paper was folded into the lid of the box informing Ada that she had been awarded the Royal Red Cross Medal 2nd Class, for the bravery she had shown when the British Embassy in Aiden was bombed. The date was December 1964. It was the first real evidence Hilary had ever seen of Ada's distinguished but clandestine career. She set it aside on the table and began to examine the rest of the contents.

There were three leather-bound diaries and a collection of objects wrapped in tissue paper within a drawstring linen bag. Hilary carefully unwrapped each of them in turn. There was a green jade Buddha figure about four inches tall, a small, footed, blue and white enamelled bowl and a beautiful gold-figured locket, with a rare, faded picture of her mother and Hilary as a little girl on one side, and on the other, a picture of a handsome man in his thirties. Hilary didn't recognise him.

At the bottom of the case was a letter in Ada's familiar hand addressed to Hilary, she opened it and began to read.

Dearest Hilary,

I want you know I how terribly proud I am of you, who you have become, and all that you have achieved. These belongings represent the hidden part of my life and I want you to have them. No doubt you will have questions, and perhaps Daniel may be able to answer some of those. The jade Buddha was a gift from David Cornwall (you would know him by his pen name) and the bowl was given to me by the Sultan of Dhofar. My time with the service was wonderful. I saw the world and really experienced life. My only regrets are that I didn't marry the man I loved (he gave me the locket) and didn't have children of my own.

We met on assignment in Baghdad, he was much younger than me and was already married. They also had a family, so when his assignment came to an end we decided our relationship should end too. I loved him desperately, but it was not meant to be. A few years later I read that he had taken his own life, strange, but I never thought Robert capable of that.

When you were seven, your mother asked me to act as your guardian, it was the most precious gift she ever gave me. The best times of my life were the times we spent together.

Loneliness is no way to live, so here is my last advice for you. Find someone to share your life with. You deserve the love of a person who appreciates all your gifts.

Learn to have fun and laugh more. You do know how, remember the green felt hat!

You can't carry a tune in a bucket, but don't let that stop you singing.

You are my sole heir, and it is my last wish that you spend more of your time and most of my money on yourself and LIVE A LITTLE.

Forever yours my darling girl
Aunt Ada xx

Tears blotted the paper as they fell.

Daniel was pleased that he'd changed his plans so that he could work from Shady Fields for the next couple of days. He felt decidedly uncomfortable now that Callaghan knew where Charlie Bingham lived. His henchmen had used that information to try to coerce Lynsey into giving Dessie up, but the irony was that she had no idea he was here in Shady Fields. He was also certain that if they put two-and-two together, they would definitely try to get to Dessie and that would put his other residents in danger.

Daniel knew he had a serious problem. It would be difficult to move Dessie at short notice, the arrangements needed to keep a high-value asset safe were complex and costly. They also took time that he may no longer have.

There was another reality that he was also reluctant to acknowledge, he wanted to be around for Hilary. When he called on her this morning he couldn't remember seeing anyone that lost in grief for a long time. It took him back to when he'd lost Martine. It had been a long time before he could think of her without that familiar pain and longing, but as it always does, time had healed that wound.

Hilary was different though; in a strange way she was stronger than him. He knew she would still function despite how she was feeling. She had the ability to suspend her emotions at will and carry on as if nothing had happened, but it was written all over her that she had lost a major touchstone in her life. Daniel knew exactly how that felt. He had convinced himself that he wanted to be there for her as a supportive boss and refused to admit that there was anything more to it than that.

Chapter 33:

Saturday 27th July 2019 9.00am

Shady Fields

Mitch couldn't shake the feeling of unease gnawing at him as he drove towards Shady Fields early that Saturday morning. Something was not sitting right, but he couldn't put his finger on what it was. Dessie had been demanding to talk to the 'person in charge' of his case. Marina and Phil had fobbed him off so far, but he was becoming more truculent by the hour. Mitch had reluctantly agreed to talk to him, but he wasn't sure what good it would do.

Daniel had been clear about him keeping his distance from Dessie. Mitch was in complete charge of this mission, but any direct contact could complicate things, and he was already aware of the tightrope they were all treading. It was a common ploy by an informant to make demands like this mid-way through a debrief. It made them feel as though they had some control over what was happening. It was an illusion, of course. Mitch knew where the power sat, and it wasn't with Dessie. He had chosen this course of action and would be owned by the security services for the rest of his life. But it was not beyond reason to consider giving him gainful employment and putting him on the payroll. After all he had a singular skill set that might come in useful somewhere.

Mitch had been in the game a long time and what troubled him was not the Irish Supergrass but the American interest in him. What had seemed like a genuine offer of help was turning out to be a bit of a pain. There was clearly another agenda in play that the Americans had forgotten to mention. Santos's boss Bruno Gomes had placed him at Mitch's disposal in the interests of inter-agency cooperation. Not traditionally something the CIA was well known for, and he had received yet another request for an update on the status of the debrief from the Northern Ireland Assembly via Special Branch. Although bringing down the syndicate would be a significant scalp, it seemed like small potatoes to the Americans. The syndicate's main base of operations was Europe, so why would the Americans be interested in that? They barely knew where Europe was!

Mitch had received a message saying that Dessie was not going to give them anything else until he could speak to him in person. The runt was threatening them that unless they arranged a meeting, his information would dry up, permanently. Mitch was beyond irritated, who did this treacherous little shit think he was? The details of his deal had been explained quite clearly. He gives up the syndicate leaders and brings down Callaghan's operations, and he gets a new identity and a fresh start. It was far more than he deserved. If it was up to Mitch they would lock him up and throw away the key for his part in the troubles. He was certainly not at Dessie's beck and call, and he would make sure that Dessie knew that.

He arrived at Shady Fields and made his way directly up to the third floor, to the suite where they were holding Dessie. Phil and Marina were seated at the table but Dessie was lounging in one of the armchairs by the fireplace. He looked up as Mitch entered the room.

"About feckin time".

Mitch glanced at the two agents but was getting nothing from them.

"Wish I could say it was nice to see you too Dessie. This is my day off, and I am wasting it here with you. What's this all about?"

Dessie stretched his legs out in front of him. "It's simple really. I want to know who bought Theresa Farrell here and why?"

Mitch looked puzzled for a second, "Dessie, what are you talking about? Who the hell is Theresa Farrell and what makes you think that she's here?" He could feel his anger grow.

Dessie smiled, "Theresa Farrell was the woman I loved who later turned out to be an undercover MI5 agent. I thought she'd been shot and killed, but it turns out you lot faked her death and she was bought back to the mainland. I know she's here; I've seen her!"

Mitch's thoughts tumbled over each other trying to find an order that made any sense. "Probably mistaken identity. Did you see her through the window? It may have been someone visiting that you thought you recognised."

"I didn't just see her; I spoke with her. It's definitely Theresa."

"What do you mean, you spoke with her?" Mitch shot a glance at Marina. "Has he been having bloody visitors?"

Marina shifted uncomfortably in her chair,

"Of course he hasn't had visitors, security has been watertight since we arrived".

Dessie laughed, "Yes, so tight I took myself off on Friday afternoon for a walk in the gardens and bumped into her down by the pond. It was her alright. I spoke to her, and now I want some answers from you. Who was running her back in Belfast and why did Colm Devey take the blame for killing her?"

Mitch struggled to keep it together. “Marina, Santos, next door NOW!”

He stormed out of the room and down the corridor into their mess room. He waited for the two agents to follow him in and closed the door behind them before he let rip.

“What the fuck has been going on here? We have the most valuable asset we’ve had in two decades, someone who is going to help us bring down the biggest organized crime syndicate in Europe and take the Irish Al Capone with them, and you two are letting him wander around the grounds contacting God knows who. He got away from under your noses. He could have been spotted and the whole operation compromised. Words fail me!”

The two agents looked stunned at his outburst but decided it would be wiser to say nothing until he had finished. Mitch took a deep breath to calm his racing pulse and continued in a more controlled manner.

“There has clearly been a major breach of security protocol. He’s used a weakness in our system to wander freely around the building and the grounds, and although he is an informant, you seem to have missed the fact that he is also a seasoned killer to boot. Your complacency has put the entire operation in jeopardy and the safety of the residents here at risk too. I want a full report of how this happened in two hours, do you understand? I could understand this from you Marina, but you Santos, you’re an experienced agent, have you been sleeping on the job?

The head of the security detail needs checking out too. He's either bent or incompetent. Either way, he's looking at a disciplinary for this. Arses need to be kicked; do I make myself clear?"

Marina squared her shoulders.

"Crystal clear Mitch. Let's meet back here at 11.30am with the answers you need. I am sorry, but I will do what it takes to get a lid back on this."

Mitch breathed deeply again, it wasn't helping much, but in a more measured tone he said, "You'd better, there's a lot riding on this for all of us."

He looked directly at the American agent whose still face gave nothing away. Mitch needed to shake him up too.

"Bruno is keen that I keep him updated on your progress Phil. I'll hold off until I review your findings, but I don't need to tell you what's at stake here. This collaboration may be about to come to an abrupt end. Whatever the real intention was behind his generosity in loaning you to us, he may find the door firmly shut and information permanently on hold. Do I make myself clear?" Phil nodded but maintained eye contact with Mitch.

Marina watched the exchange between the two men. She had fallen at the first fence and put this operation at risk. Mitch had trusted her, and she had let him down, and potentially, her career as an active agent was now hanging by a thread. Phil seemed unapologetic in the face of this revelation. She was positive that they would find out what happened and report back, but she had not missed Mitch's barbed comment about the real reason the American was here. Maybe Phil wasn't as trustworthy as she believed him to be.

Chapter 34:

Saturday 27th July 2019 11.00am

Shady Fields

Daniel was looking out of the window. When this had been his office, it had been a sterile environment devoid of any personality, just the way he liked it. Hilary had definitely made her mark on the place now that it was hers. There were subtle touches; Scottish water colours on the walls, a contemporary coffee set on the side table, even a throw and some cushions on the leather settee. He thought that was probably a practical move to make an all-nighter more comfortable if it was needed.

Mitch had already briefed him about Dessie's walkabout and his unexpected and potentially explosive meeting with Theresa Farrell. He cursed himself for not considering an obvious risk. When they had decided to use Shady Fields as a safe house, he hadn't thought about the possibility of them meeting. Why would he? That was what security protocols were there for.

His greater concern now though, was that Callaghan knew where Lynsey's grandfather lived. It was possible that they had already infiltrated the grounds and carried out surveillance on the comings and goings. It was also possible although unlikely that they had seen Dessie or Theresa. If that were the case they would be coming for them, Yilmaz would see to that. This whole operation could come crashing down around him, and he wasn't the sort of man to let that happen. If it became common knowledge that Theresa Farrell was still alive, Colm Devey also risked exposure and that would really set a cat among the pigeons.

Dessie was nobody's fool, and it wouldn't take him long to work out the truth, that they had sacrificed Theresa to keep Colm in play and that the judgement call they had made, was the right one. The IRA had stopped looking for a spy and celebrated the fact they had uncovered the MI5 source. If the truth came out now the consequences could be catastrophic.

Contrary to popular belief the Good Friday Agreement was not as safe as politicians would have people believe. There were still factions who thought a return to violence to achieve a united Ireland was a price worth paying. If it was known that an insider to the original negotiations was really an MI5 informer, then it would be all the excuse they needed to kick off all over again.

What was strange though was the timing of all of this. He had received a coded contact request from Colm at midnight, demanding a call on a secure line at 1pm today. There was no way he could have known about Dessie being here. They had done everything to keep that information limited to a small, select group. So what did he want to talk to him about?

The investigation into Dessie's impromptu walkabout was scheduled for noon. Security would be reviewed, and a tighter plan put in place. He wanted to be in full possession of all the facts before he spoke to Colm. Daniel recognised that Colm had been an excellent asset all these years, but he was also a costly one that was producing less and less useful intelligence. Maybe their arrangement had run its course, and it was time for a parting of the ways. Colm certainly didn't need MI5's money any more. With his Stormont pension, he could afford to retire and live very comfortably. Daniel wondered if this was the call that turned out to be an exit interview.

A knock on the door disturbed his thinking. "Come in" he called and was surprised to see Phil Santos enter the room. "Hi Phil, what can I do for you?"

Santos closed the door and walked over to the desk. He was obviously trying hard to phrase what he wanted to say and hoping that Daniel might make it easy for him. Daniel's stonewall persona made it clear that that wasn't about to happen.

He was angry that an experienced CIA agent was part of this gigantic screw up. In counter-intelligence old habits die hard, so any opportunity to remind the CIA that they had gone to sleep on the job would not be wasted.

The American shifted uncomfortably under Daniel's gaze.

"I have just gotten off the phone with Bruno, and he's given me clearance to share some highly confidential information with you about why I'm really here." He waited to be invited to sit.

Daniel didn't oblige. "So what's this really about then Phil? We've known each other a long time so let's just be straight, why did you really come here?" Reluctantly, he gestured towards the seat opposite him and Santos took it.

"You're aware of the Colombian assassination and the subsequent identification of the explosives used in the attack; Irish Semtex?" Daniel nodded, "Well we need to find who's responsible because we lost American citizens, and we can't let that go unchallenged. Bruno put me in charge of the investigation, and I've identified three people of interest, one of them has a clear Irish link. Bruno thought that if you had an IRA Supergrass on ice, then there may be something he could tell us about the explosives and where they came from. I was briefed to come and support you and try to get close to whoever you were holding; maybe do some interrogation of my own if possible. The more time that passes the colder the trail gets Daniel. We really need to know if he knows anything."

"So why didn't Bruno come to me with this in the first place? We've collaborated before, why the secrecy?" Daniel was intensely irritated by this blatant subterfuge. There was no need for it, and it made him less likely to want to share information with them now.

Phil hesitated, he was obviously torn between honesty and loyalty.

"Come on Phil, it's a bit late to go all coy on me now. Just tell me or get out, but don't waste my time."

"One of the people we need to speak to has been identified as someone with a link to a senior member of the Irish assembly. We wanted to question her before they could close ranks around her. Bruno was worried that we wouldn't get any information if we asked directly. It wasn't personal, he's being pressured from above for a result."

Daniel listened with mixed emotions. He understood what it felt like not to hold all the cards, but there was a code around international collaboration and Bruno had overstepped the mark. There was something else, though. A nagging feeling in the back of his mind that he knew where this was going, and he didn't like it one bit. "Well give me some names and I will see what I can do."

"Bruno said I can only share names with you if you give us an undertaking that we will be allowed to speak to these people before they can disappear."

"I don't think you're in any position to negotiate, but as a gesture of cooperation I will ensure that IF an opportunity presents itself, you will be given the chance to speak with them, when we've finished with them. Now who have you identified?"

Phil shifted uncomfortably in his seat.

"Two weeks ago I was going through old footage from Bogotá Airport and I identified two men and a woman being met off an international flight by General Raúl Hernandez. He was the Presidents' deputy, and we suspect, the architect of the attack. Running them through our database we identified the two men as members of the Gradasevic Cartel, but that didn't make any sense. Why would international drug dealers be interested in supplying explosives for a military coup or an assassination in Colombia?

The third person was Sinead Devey, sister of the Deputy Minister in the Irish Assembly Colm Devey. I met her years ago at one of the meetings Clinton had when he went to Ireland in the late nineties. We think she has accessed a cache of weapons that were never disclosed by the Agreement and is using their sale to fund something, but we're not sure what."

Daniel felt his anger rising, "So let me get this straight. You've identified someone with known criminal connections who has access to weaponry on UK soil. A person who is known to us and with a history of terrorist activity, potentially raising funds from the sale of explosives to do God knows what, and you decided to keep this information to yourselves?" He shook his head in disbelief. "In the spirit of international cooperation, I should tell Bruno to go screw himself, but there's a bigger game at stake here, one that you are about to trample all over. So let me tell you what's going to happen. You can stay on the team, but you report directly to me and I will brief Bruno. I'm offering this as the only option because of the respect I have for you Phil, but I expect you to play by my rules from here on in. I'll tell Bruno that if he has any plans to complete an extraordinary rendition on this suspect I will not sanction it. The service may have been compliant with that sort of thing in the past, but I am not my predecessor, and if Bruno wants to speak with Sinead Devey, we do this my way or not at all. Do I make myself clear?"

Santos looked Daniel directly in the eye "Yes, and I'm sorry, Daniel. If it's any consolation, I did advise the direct route, but we are under terrific pressure to get quick results. Do you want me to contact Bruno and relay your offer? It's my guess he will accept, there's too much at stake for egos to get in the way of this."

"No, I think this requires my personal attention. I will speak to Bruno myself."

There was a sharp knock on the door Daniel barked impatiently "Come in."

The door opened and Marina Kinskey entered followed by the extremely worried-looking Head of the security detail. Phil took this as an opportunity to make his exit, but as he passed Marina he whispered to her, "Do you need me to stay?"

Marina shook her head "No, thanks, I've got this." And she really hoped that she had.

Daniel listened patiently to the results of their investigation and resisted the temptation to sack the head of security on the spot. He couldn't believe that trained agents had been so lax, irresponsible, or so gullible. Marina had accepted full responsibility for the breach, but he was quite clear where the blame lay. If the fallout wasn't so serious, he would find the whole debacle funny, something worthy of the Russians but not MI5.

Mitch had inherited a security service that had been poorly led and deficient in so many ways. Daniel had no doubt that he would remedy that. Already he was sending a hand-picked team up from central to replace this detail.

Marina had made three recommendations. They were preparing a different safe location to move Dessie to as soon as possible, but it wouldn't be ready for 24 hours, in the meantime a 24-hour armed guard would be posted at his door and manned patrols would be reconnoitering the grounds to spot any intruders.

Daniel was impressed with her performance so far. This sort of problem on a first assignment in charge could be career limiting if not handled properly. She had identified the weaknesses and produced solutions without throwing any of the team under the bus. He'd been right about her appointment, Marina Kinskey was definitely one to watch. On the other hand, the Head of Security was toast, he would find himself on filing duty in the basement of Thames House before the end of the day and probably for a long time to come.

He checked his watch and picked up the receiver, keying the code for his secure line. It had barely rung before he heard Colm's voice.

"What's all this crap about the dead FRU officer being dredged up for?"

"And hello to you too" said Daniel sarcastically.

"I haven't time for niceties, what's McFee doing dragging up old stuff. And please don't insult me by denying that you have him, and that he's giving you this stuff! I thought you would have him lining up Yilmaz and his gang, not putting the GFA at risk. Everyone knows he killed the FRU tout, whatever he's telling you, he's playing you for an easier ride."

"Calm down Colm, it was part of a wider discussion, and you know what we are like for dotting the I's and crossing the t's." Daniel detected real concern in Colm's voice. Having read the initial transcripts he knew there was truth in them. Sinead must have been involved, if not totally responsible for the young soldier's death; otherwise he wouldn't be having this conversation. What he didn't know, was who had requested the files? He certainly hadn't and Mitch hadn't mentioned it to him either, because of the softly-softly approach they had adopted for historical stuff. He would track the request down without delay but right now, he needed to get to Sinead before the Americans did. "How is your sister? She seems to have gone quiet for a while now?"

"What's he been saying?" There was an urgency to his tone.

"I really can't discuss an ongoing investigation. Has Sinead been on any nice holidays recently, to South America for example?" Daniel listened for a response.

"What the feck are you talking about" Colm said crossly "I can't even get her to take a long weekend in Dublin. She's been on a couple of European trade missions recently, that's about it. Anyway, why all the interest in Sinead suddenly?"

At that point Daniel became very interested. If the Americans had footage of her in Bogotá and Colm genuinely knew nothing about it then he smelled a rat.

Colm's voice sounded in his ear "What is going on Danny?"

Daniel decided that a calculated risk was in order. "The Americans have been working with the Colombians to run democratic elections and safeguard them from a military coup. They also think it will give them the inside track on drug routes. An American contractor that makes and calibrates electronic voting machines was servicing them for the forthcoming elections when the President and about thirty others were taken out by a bomb a couple of weeks ago. Five of them were US contractors."

"Yes, I heard about that on the news, but what the hell has that got to do with anything?" Colm was irritated by the cryptic conversation.

Daniel paused until he was sure he had Colm's full attention. "It was old IRA Semtex that caused the explosion. A woman answering Sinead's description was spotted at Bogotá airport a few months ago meeting with the Colombian General, the one that just got a new job."

Colm was silent while this information sank in. "Are you sure?" he managed after a considerable silence.

"Yes Colm, there is no mistake. Obviously, we can't overlook this. We need to question her to see what the reality is. We think she was there with two of Yilmaz's crew. Did you know she had been working with Callaghan?"

Colm was struggling with this revelation. "If Sinead was involved in this then she was under duress to do it." But even as he spoke the words he knew he didn't sound convincing. She had lost the plot and was getting into something that was way over her head. Colm continued "She's not working with Callaghan; I'm sure of that. If she's got into something with Yilmaz, then she's in real danger, that guy's a lunatic. She will need some protection. Whatever she's involved in, I know nothing about it Danny, you have to believe me."

"I can't promise anything Colm, the Americans are involved and if I'm honest, I'm surprised they haven't resorted to rendition and taken her already. American civilians died. You know what they're like. It would be better for her if we got to her first, you know that don't you?"

The Irishman was mentally processing possible outcomes with lightning speed. Reluctantly he said "Let me speak with her, I will see what I can come up with. I need to know that she'll be OK, you will treat her OK won't you Danny?"

"She stands a better chance with us than with the CIA, I can promise you that. Was that all?"

Colm suddenly sounded very weary. "No, there was something else. The arrest warrants have thrown everything into confusion here and the gang is scattering, but I think Callaghan knows where you're keeping Dessie. He and Yilmaz took a charter boat to the mainland in the early hours this morning in case you were watching the airports. They are coming for him Danny, and they don't care about the collateral damage." The line suddenly went dead.

Today was one of those days when it felt like his telephone was a natural extension of his ear. Daniel got through to Mitch on his mobile.

"Hi Daniel, the new detail should be with you in the next couple of hours and I will do the briefing as soon as I get back to HQ."

"Mitch, I need that detail now! I think they know we have him here, and they are coming to kill him. I am staying up here in case they do show up, but I've got another job for you, and it's urgent, your ears only. I need an extraction done but made to look like something else. I need you to locate Sinead Devey, an analyst in the Irish Assembly in Stormont, and coincidentally, Colm Devey's sister. I need you to bring her in, completely off the grid. I want her in London by the end of today and no one any the wiser. Who have you got in the vicinity that you can trust?"

Mitch was unphased by the request. "I have three of the extraction team that pulled 'Ragair' and if it's that important, I can be on the ground in person."

Daniel felt some of the tension ease. "Yes, let's do that. Whatever you need to get this done cleanly is yours. I don't need to stress the importance of this, we could be upsetting the biggest apple cart in history, but we have no other option at this stage. The arrest warrants for Yilmaz and his gang have already been issued and that seems to be keeping special branch and the police busy, so they won't be watching what we are doing that closely."

Daniel didn't like planning on the run, but time was of the essence if they were to pick Sinead up before she went to ground. A few choice words from her and a protection net would draw around her making her untouchable. Right now, the element of surprise was theirs, and they had to take advantage of it. Satisfied that wheels were in motion, he decided to see how Hilary was doing, then find an alternative safe house for Dessie.

The door opened and Hilary walked in, Daniel could see she was troubled. “Are you OK?”

“Not really Daniel. I think your little secret is out. Our guest it seems, is an ex-IRA hitman called Dessie McFee who has not been held as securely as you might have hoped. I’ve just had a conversation with Bill and Ben, who told me that Dessie may have been wandering the building. They were concerned enough to seek me out because apparently, he has an old enemy under our roof. Phipps lost one of his team when serving in Belfast during the troubles, and he seems to think it was McFee that killed him. They are extremely worried that he might take things into his own hands.”

Daniel shook his head “And I thought today couldn’t get any worse.”

Chapter 35:

Saturday 27th July 2.30pm

Shady Fields

Daniel had bought Hilary up to speed with the current situation. He was aware that it was a lot to take in so recently after the loss of Ada, but she seemed to welcome the distraction.

He took a mouthful of the strong black coffee she had given him and felt the effect immediately.

"It is a real mess, but we've got to get Dessie out of here and protect the other residents. If Yilmaz is with Callaghan he will shoot first and ask questions later. The extra security Mitch is sending may not get here before they do, so it would be better if Callaghan thinks he's been given the wrong information. The easiest way to do that is to remove all obvious signs of security; no guards stationed at the front door or black SUVs in the car park. The real difficulty I have is where to put Dessie?"

Hilary had been mulling an idea over in her head, she drained her mug and placed it on the coaster on the desk. "This might sound a bit impulsive, but how about taking him to Ada's cottage in Derbyshire. It's empty, remote, and unknown to anyone in the service. It's at the end of a private lane with a quarry wall at the rear of the property. Ideal for knowing exactly who is coming at you, I should imagine, and it should buy you some time until you can set up a more permanent solution."

Daniel considered the proposal. He was impressed, it was an excellent tactical response to an impending threat. "We would need to keep it between us to ensure secrecy. I could take him myself, but that would leave Shady Fields vulnerable."

Hillary was watching him closely for any sign of agreement. "Then why don't I take him? From what you've told me he's an unlikely flight risk as he knows it is safer under our protection than anywhere else. They don't know me or my car. We wouldn't draw attention because we wouldn't have an escort. We could be there in three hours."

Daniel was suddenly uncomfortable with her involvement. "No Hilary, I can't put you at risk like that, you have no field experience, no combat or firearms training, and you are far too vulnerable. You must remember that regardless of his cooperation or motivation now, Dessie McFee is a very dangerous man."

"Then let Marina come with us. She's had the training, and she's been working with him, so they know each other, and that would leave you free to handle the situation here with Callaghan. You know it makes sense Daniel." She really hoped she sounded convincing.

He rose and paced the room, quickly mulling over the risks and consequences of this hastily cobbled together plan. It shouldn't do, but it did make sense. Everything Hilary had said was true. It was a solid way to protect Dessie and to take the attention away from Shady Fields.

"It's not ideal but it could work. I want you to drive, take Marina's car, and she can babysit Dessie in the back. You can't trust him or anything he says. Don't stop for anything. Take what you need from the kitchen here so that you don't have to get provisions or stop on the way.

He reached for the phone and called Marina's extension "Marina, it's Daniel, I'm with Hilary in her office. We have a plan but it requires immediate execution. You are taking Dessie on a little road trip, oh, and bring your black bag with you."

He watched as they packed the essentials into the boot of the car and saw a handcuffed Dessie being bundled into the back seat by a very determined Marina. It was clear that she hadn't appreciated his deception or the way he'd made her look as a field agent. Daniel had no doubt that it was a lesson quickly learned and Dessie would not be able to fool her again. Initially he'd kicked off about being moved without seeing Theresa again, but when Marina explained that Yilmaz and Callaghan might be on the way, he became surprisingly agreeable.

Daniel was faced with an unexpected opportunity. With Dessie gone and the hit squad on the way, he could turn this situation to his advantage by capturing Callaghan and Yilmaz. He had limited resources, but he had pulled off more daring missions with far less. But to make things work, he needed to enlist the help of some of the residents.

The Dynamite Men were held in high esteem by Daniel. In their long and distinguished careers they had served their country with courage and guile. Their sense of duty and their expertise had exposed them to situations where they had seen things no one should have had to see, but through it all they had forged an unbreakable bond that was more than just friendship. In their early careers their service records were not without incident, and Bill's sense of humour had resulted in disciplinary action on many occasions, but these were men that you could trust with your life. It was true they were not as physically fit as they once were, and their memories were not as sharp as they used to be, but they still had a skill set that was ideal for the situation they were about to face, and he was glad they were on his side. He called them all together in the third-floor apartment that had housed McFee to enlist their help, Bill, Ben, Brooke-Ward and Phipps. He just hoped he was not placing unrealistic expectations on them.

The four men filed into the room that was now devoid of agents or any sign that Dessie had ever been held here. The recording equipment had gone and the table it had stood on was back against the wall sporting a vase of flowers. "Come in guys, I want a word please." The men sat down waiting to be told why they were here at all.

Phipps spoke first, looking at Daniel then at the others. "Where is he, the murdering bastard?"

"If you are referring to Dessie McFee Douglas, he has gone."

Phipps thumped the arm of his chair "I knew it, I knew it was him. I suppose you've moved him to protect him yet again." He spat out the words with real venom.

"Allow me to explain something to you all. Dessie McFee was an IRA assassin, and he was guilty of a lot of things, but I can categorically assure you that he did not kill the FRU soldier Sapper Cooper. He took responsibility for that to protect the young woman who did kill him."

Phipps looked confused. "No, no, he's just saying that. He would say anything to push the blame onto someone else. He virtually admitted it himself at the time. It put him on our most wanted list."

Daniel sat in the chair directly opposite Phipps, he waited to make direct eye contact with the man to ensure that he had his full attention. "What I am about to tell you is still classified, but you need to hear the truth. Sapper Cooper was picked up for questioning by an IRA cell that was linked to Dessie McFee, but he was not part of the incident. He wasn't even in Belfast at the time. The cell captured the soldier and interrogated him and for two days, he gave them nothing. They were not a very organized group and Cooper attempted to break free. They discovered the escape and shot him in the back as he was getting away. It's likely that the other stuff was window dressing to disguise the fact that it was the woman that had shot him. Her brother was a brigade commander who later worked with Sinn Féin on the GFA. Essentially, they closed ranks to protect her. Dessie was ordered to take the blame by a senior level operative, maybe even Callaghan himself. We know it wasn't Dessie that killed Cooper, do you understand that Douglas?"

He stared back at Daniel with moist eyes "It doesn't change the fact he died on my watch."

Daniel nodded in agreement "No it doesn't, but had the right hand known what the left hand was doing, there would not have been the confusion there was between special branch and the FRU. We had an opportunity to get him out before they took him and we ballsed it up. If we are being accurate Douglas, the service was responsible because of poor communication.

But gentlemen, we have a far more pressing problem at the moment. I have a unit on their way here from London to secure these premises because we believe that the people who want Dessie dead believe he is here. They are not the sort of people to ask questions first before shooting, so I want to see if we can apprehend them when they come for him. My concern is that they might arrive before our backup does, and we need to avoid a full-scale assault that puts everyone here at risk."

Brooke-Ward spoke for the first time. "My guess is that you have no weapons here, just a few blokes with historic training and a kamikaze desire to taste adrenaline one more time. I'm the one with the current skill set and experience, and I am dragging a leg with two plates and four metal pins in it. We are about to be hit by a team of experienced killers who have absolutely nothing to lose, probably armed to the teeth and filled with a desire to find and kill the tout who betrayed them. How am I doing so far?",

Daniel nodded, "That's about the size of it, although we do have the element of surprise and our dearly departed friend William Wright may have left us a few 'toys' we could use to our advantage"

Ward shook his head. "You have no plan. Do you even know the 'tenable' and 'fatal' grounds of this place? At least if we knew that, we could occupy the first and attack on the second."

While Ward had been talking, Daniel had removed the flower vase from the table and spread a blueprint of the house and grounds out for them to study. "And that is exactly why I asked you to come Ward. We need your tactical brain."

Ward made a quick study of the plans, first checking the grounds and any vulnerabilities, then the house itself; exit and entry points. "The key thing is to control the ground. We want them to go where we want them to go, not let them go running around all over the place. If we drive them in this direction from the main approach then we can predict that they will enter the house from the front door or the conservatory at the back. Two points where we can have a reception committee waiting. Although looking at our numbers, probably not at the same time. So that's the house sorted, now what about the grounds? What equipment does the gardener have?"

Daniel scratched his head. "Well, he's got a vintage Massey Ferguson tractor with lots of accessories, a sit-on-mower, the usual garden tools, a pushbike and I think he has a mini-digger thingy."

"Excellent, and I am hoping he still has some of the bales of hay he harvested from the fields out the back at the beginning of the month. We can do quite a bit with them." Ward was warming to his challenge.

Bill looked at Ben with a twinkle in his eye. "And what exactly can we do to help?"

Chapter 36:

Saturday 27th July 2019 8pm

Belfast

Mitch had taken a private flight to oversee Sinead's extraction in person. He had landed in Belfast thirty minutes ago, but she seemed to have gone to ground already. Their last sighting was of her leaving Stormont and heading back into the city, but then the trail went cold. Her mobile phone was switched off, so there was no way to locate her using GPS tracking until she switched it back on.

Mitch's team were trying to access her phone records to see if she had called anyone for help, but that would take time and Mitch was worried that time was something they had a limited supply of.

Peter King was the Services' best information analyst. His department was probably one of the most technically advanced in the world. Their edge was not just the gadgetry they had access to, but his uncanny ability to root out a connection between seemingly unrelated facts or people. Peter had an eidetic memory and could sniff out a problem like a scent-trained spaniel. He sat feverishly tapping away on a well-used keyboard in front of a bank of monitors, each showing different spreadsheets, websites, and analytical modelling algorithms.

Mitch didn't think it was possible to get this quantity of electronics into a long wheelbase transit van.

"Are you enjoying your weekend escape then Peter? It must be a while since you did some real work in the field."

He was concentrating on the streams of data dancing across the screens.

"Cheeky sod, this is a favour to Daniel. I was supposed to be at a symposium in Brussels this week, on 'How the rise of the machines means we will never be anonymous again'. Do you know that there are now vehicles that can identify your gender? Unless you live in a concrete bunker with only a landline for communication, your every move, desire, and action can be recorded and viewed. Anonymity is dead, and the internet is holding the smoking gun!"

Mitch pulled a face. "It's being so cheerful that keeps you going Peter. Do we have any intel on where Sinead is yet?"

"I've pulled footage from the cameras that cover the exits of the Stormont building. She left by the north door at 18.20hrs on Friday evening. We picked her up again on Saturday afternoon in Woodvale Park, off The Shankill Road. She met two men, they looked like heavies, but the images were too poor for positive identification, they spoke briefly, exchanged packets, and then left. We lost her for another couple of hours then picked her up again entering her apartment building at 16.55hrs. Nothing since, but she isn't in her apartment now, we've checked. The team is trawling through footage from the rear of her building, but coverage is patchy and the camera covering the car park has been out of action for nearly a week. Her regular phone has not been switched on, but it's highly likely she has obtained a burner by now. We're trying to locate burner signals around her flat, but that's like searching through a haystack looking for a particular strand of hay."

Mitch never failed to be impressed that so much information was available at the touch of a few keys if you knew how to use the system. "Well, you seem to have everything covered. I know you will do your best."

"There is one 'unorthodox measure' I could try, but it may require me to break at least a dozen data protection laws and against a foreign power too, so I am not confirming that I am going down that route. All I can say at this point is that somewhere in the city the Americans definitely have a live extraction team as we speak."

Mitch looked shocked. “Shit! Game over then.”

Peter shook his head and gave a wry smile. “Oh, ye of little faith. If they are operational, it means they haven’t found her yet either. We might find it useful to tail them closely just in case they catch a break before we do. I only have ears on them, but that should be enough.”

“I never heard any of that.” said Mitch, silently thanking King for his geekiness. He had to avoid a skirmish between the US and UK security services on the streets of Belfast. What he really needed was a genuine break, but this whole debacle made him feel that lady luck had sent her apologies and was being courted by someone else right now. He was willing to admit he might have been hasty, when King suddenly exclaimed “I think we’ve got something!”

Colm checked his messages for the umpteenth time today. His wife had taken the grandchildren down to their cottage in Dunfanaghy, Donegal. He’d bought the place years ago to give her somewhere to take their daughters for the school holidays. But now they were grown up, married, with children of their own it seemed to be even more popular. She still enjoyed the seaside and her absence gave him the freedom he needed to work. She had left a message to say they had arrived safely and would be eating out, so not to bother with a call tonight. She used to call him every day when she was away and have proper conversations about what they had been doing, but recently a text sufficed. The arguments and pressure for him to retire had fizzled out, and they seemed to speak less and less now, but in his defence, he did have a lot on his plate.

The Irish Assembly was a mire of petty point scoring, that was when it sat at all. He wondered what had changed in Northern Ireland apart from the cessation of the fighting. The reality was they were no closer to a united Ireland today than they were when the agreement was signed. There were other demands on his time too. Sinead was hard work, and he spent too much time managing her outbursts. She was his sister, but he honestly wondered whether there was something seriously wrong with her. She had never thought or acted like anyone else he knew since she was little. He hadn't heard from her since Friday afternoon, and he needed to speak to her to get her side of what Daniel had told him. If it was true, and she had sold Semtex to the Colombians she was about to bring a world of hurt down on her own head, and he would not escape the fallout. What was she thinking, crossing Yilmaz like this? He hoped that just this once she had taken his advice and decided to go on holiday somewhere to lie low. He didn't really believe that. He had left more than a dozen texts and messages without a single response. It was unnerving when she went silent. Her last threat was still ringing in his ears, *'I will not go down without taking others with me'*. She was a difficult woman to deal with, but she was family, and he knew what the Americans would do to her if Daniels' information turned out to be true. If they got to her first he doubted he would ever see her alive again.

Sinead was scared. Her life had been dedicated to the greater good, a United Ireland. Everything she had done was done in the name of the cause, but it was all starting to unravel. The death of the soldier all those years ago had been justified, he was the enemy and had been killed in action, not at all like the murder of civilians carried out by the British. He had been a young soldier that had lied and cheated to infiltrate their cell, so when he was discovered, he had to die. He was shot while trying to escape, and she had done it. He was her first kill, although not her last. Even now, she was surprised at how calm she had been when she pulled the trigger. She had taken a life and felt nothing, no regret, no guilt, nothing. Well, not exactly nothing. She felt vindicated that she had ridded her compatriots of another enemy. She hadn't considered his age or whether he had a family, she just hated him because of the uniform he wore. But anxiety was building in her insides. She couldn't understand why they were going back to all this old stuff now. The Agreement had given her a clean record, she couldn't be held responsible for what happened back then, they were at war and her actions had been justified.

She looked down at the coffee cooling in the corrugated cup. The tannoy announcing the train arrivals and departures was barely audible, but she could see the overhead display from where she sat, and her train was on time. In half an hour she would be speeding her way towards Donegal and Colm's holiday cottage. It occurred to her this morning that it would be a brilliant place to lie low for a few weeks, at least until the heat died down. She had just switched her phone on for a minute to check messages. Colm had been calling and leaving texts asking her to get back to him, but they might be tapping his phone, so she didn't respond. She knew the cottage had been empty for weeks. Colm never took time off to take Gloria and the girls away.

Slowly, she felt herself begin to relax. No one knew her down there, and it would put distance between her and Yilmaz's men. It had been a short but lucrative partnership for the three of them but it was over. They had made the connections they wanted with a drug supplier in Colombia and she had a very tidy war chest to reignite the fight for freedom. She smiled to herself as she assessed the odds. Hers were excellent in achieving her goal but theirs were not so good. Once Yilmaz got wind of two of his men setting up as independents and opening their own supply route she figured they would only have days to live.

She didn't take betrayal well but Yilmaz made her look like Mother Theresa. The simile amused her. It was strange how many people believed nuns were gentle, forgiving, and caring women of God. In her experience they were judgmental and creatively sadistic. Yes, she had learned from the very best.

She had been shocked and wounded by Dessie's betrayal, she thought he was better than that. He would have been fine if he hadn't got involved with the cartel. He'd gone soft and tried to save that young kid. She shook her head in disbelief. Fancy crossing a man like Yilmaz over a slip of a skirt who was destined for a short life anyway. She, like so many others were disposable, that was the trade.

Sinead thought about Dessie as a youth; his strong, handsome features. She was sad that they had not turned out to be a 'thing'. They could have been happy. He was never a yes-man; it was one of the things she had first admired about him. In her mind they could have been the IRA's Bonnie and Clyde, at least until Theresa Farrell had come along. Dessie was smitten with her. Not just her flowing jet-black hair and quiet confidence, but her challenging spirit. He once told Sinead that she made him think about what he was doing, about the consequences of his actions. Sinead felt her anger rising. He might have been taken in by Theresa but she hadn't been, she never liked her. She hated the influence and control she seemed to have over Dessie, it wasn't right. Without Theresa's influence he would never have turned against anyone in the cause, least of all her. Things should have been different; they should have been together.

The regret she felt festered away at her insides. She was glad that Colm had finished Theresa off, it saved her a job, although she would have taken pleasure in doing it herself. The irony was that she was now going into hiding because Dessie had given her up. The thought of his betrayal rose as bile in the back of her throat. If she ever got the opportunity, she would make sure he paid with his life. That would be justice.

Glancing at her watch, she realised she needed to make her way to the platform. She had reserved a seat and paid cash for her ticket. Even so, they had still asked her for personal details, so she gave a false name and address.

She moved purposefully along the concourse dragging her small, wheeled, overnight bag pushing against the flow of passengers arriving from off another train. Although it was Sunday evening the station was busy. It was holiday season and people were also coming into the city ready for work tomorrow morning. She saw a young man and woman walking up the platform towards her. They were dressed in jeans and cowboy boots, both had party streamers hanging around their necks. Glittery badges stating 'Bride' and 'Groom' were pinned to their denim shirts. They were holding hands and chatting, but they were not looking at each other. She wondered if she should step to the right or the left to pass them, then they looked directly at her, separated, and grabbed her by the arms. She didn't even have time to cry out before she felt the prick of a syringe in her arm and suddenly the crowd and the platform began to swim in front of her eyes. Her legs buckled and she slipped to the floor between them.

She felt them hoist her up, and suspended between them, they carried her back up the concourse towards the entrance. Her head lolled to one side like a rag doll, she was gabbling, unable to form a coherent sentence. A concerned guard came to see if they needed help, but the woman explained with some embarrassment that this was her mother who had drunk too much at their engagement celebrations. They were taking her straight home to sleep it off. Sinead registered the look of disapproval on the guard's face and that was the last thing she saw before slipping into oblivion.

Chapter 37:

Saturday 27th July 5.00pm

Shady Fields, The Plan

Ward reviewed their progress.

"They are most likely to come this evening so that gives us a few hours' preparation time. Ben, are you clear about what you need and where to find it?" Both dynamite men nodded, they looked sharp and attentive.

Daniel hardened his gaze. "We only need to delay them until the armed unit arrive. I want this kept under the radar; no local plod involved. It has to be quick and quiet, minimal contact with these guys is my preference. They will be well armed and I don't want anyone taking any unnecessary risks." He looked directly at Bill. "Is that understood?"

Bill grinned. “Of course. We can rig up a few devices to alert us when they get into the grounds. Nothing fatal but enough to disorient them and noisy enough to get our attention. If they bring vehicles into the grounds we can disable them to stop them escaping. I know you want the two ringleaders alive so that you can talk to them. So stopping them, not killing them is the priority, right boss?”

Daniel looked unconvinced. He knew old habits die hard and their ability to follow orders could be easily outweighed by their enthusiasm for their craft. “I mean it you two. If we escalate the level of force, it puts all our other residents at risk if any of Callaghan’s team gain entrance into the house.” He turned to Phipps. “Are you clear about your role in this?”

Phipps nodded making notes at the same time

“Yes, I can find the drugs and syringes I need to make some crude knockout darts. All I need is the gardener’s air gun to deliver them. They will only work over short distances but if they get to the house, then it will all be close-quarter stuff anyway.”

Daniel was keen that they bought enough time for reinforcements to arrive. “Bill, before you start making your toys, make sure Phipps has what he needs from the workshop will you? Did you check William's old locker?”

Bill dropped what looked like miniature hearing aids on the desk. “These are wireless earpieces that have a range of about 500 yards from what we can tell. They should keep us in touch with each other."

Bill looked across at Phipps. "There's plenty of flex, cable, a few timers, and other electrical bits that might prove useful. Come over with me after the briefing and I'll show you where everything is."

Ward was listening but processing other information at the same time. Multitasking was part of his training and he was very, very good at it. He was poring over the map of the grounds.

"So Ken is digging trenches across some of the forest access roads as we speak, that should kettle them up towards the house to the two key entry points. Presumably you've already slipped Dessie out on the disused track along the eastern boundary?"

Daniel nodded. "It's quite overgrown now, but they were in Marina's SUV so it shouldn't have been a problem. They left about forty minutes ago, they should be well on their way by now."

Ward turned his attention back to the plan, ringing a couple of tactical positions at the front and rear of the building. "Bill and Ben, I need you to put your devices here and here." He pointed to marked areas on the plans. "You need to discourage them from getting into the house, but we would rather there were no fatalities. I believe that a front of house assault will be their first action followed by a rear entry assault across the lawn into the conservatory. The expanse of glass makes that a weak spot, particularly if they are heavily armed. Locking all the French windows apart from this set, he again pointed to the plan, means they will be in clear sight with little cover. If they do gain entry we can contain them on the ground floor relatively easily and keep the residents and care staff safe on the second and third floors, thereby removing some of the risk. I presume you want to brief the staff personally Daniel?"

His eyes caught a faint detail on the map. "Oh, that's interesting, what is this?"

Daniel leaned across the desk to see what Ward was pointing to.

"That's the old connecting tunnel from the cellars to the outbuildings; the garage and the workshop. It's no longer in use, I think the exit was sealed up when we took over this place."

Ward perked up considerably "Bill, first job. Check it out and unseal that exit. If they do get into the house, we could use it to double back on them and give them a surprise."

Bill was pleased with the allocation of his first real task. "Ben, tackle the other end, that tunnel could be really valuable." Ben nodded.

"So, are we all clear about what we are doing?" Ward looked around waiting for acknowledgement. "We only have one chance at this and they have nothing to lose. They are likely to shoot on sight, so no heroics, we need every one of you if this is going to work. I want everyone in their positions in an hour. With any luck, we'll only have to hold them off for fifteen to twenty minutes. If you have to communicate with each other use the radio earpieces but keep contact to a minimum. We can't be sure that they won't be able to hear us."

He was clearly in charge of the operation, his authority immediately accepted by agents about to go into active service for the first time in decades. The dynamite men were already heading towards the door.

Bill led Phipps out through the main door, around the side of the house and towards the workshop. "We can gather the stuff we need then maybe you can help me locate the trap door for that passageway. I can't say I've ever noticed one before but if we can open it up I can clear the tunnel back up to the house and meet Ben at the other end.

Phipps nodded in agreement. The workshop was very well-equipped and organized with precision. Nothing was out of place. He couldn't understand why he had not been in here before. He knew it existed, but he had no real interest in it before.

The shelves and storage racks were meticulously labelled. He picked up a tray, moving from bin to bin, filling it with the components on the mental list he had made. Bill was doing the same, but filling a large black hold all with cable reels and an assortment of tools from their hooks on the pin boards. They worked silently until Bill zipped his bag shut. "Got everything you need?"

Phipps nodded. "Yes, I think so. So where do you think this tunnel entrance is then?"

Bill walked to the back of the workshop and scoured the floor looking for any tell-tale signs of a hatch or trapdoor, but there was nothing. "There's nothing here. This is where it should be if the map is right."

Phipps stood back and examined the racking that covered the back wall. He spotted something. "Give me a hand to shift this rack."

The two men grabbed the racking and levered it away from the wall, swinging it into the room so that the wall behind was exposed. There was a flat, grey metal door without handles or keyholes embedded into the brickwork.

"Well spotted Phipps, but how do we get it open without explosives?"

Phipps grabbed two crowbars from their hooks and threw the larger one to Bill. "Will these do the trick?"

Both men set about finding a weakness in the edge of the door, and in a few short minutes were faced with an entrance to a metal staircase that led downwards into complete darkness.

"There are a couple of hand torches over there."

Phipps unhooked a torch from its wall-mounted charger and accurately threw it to an eager Bill, who was already making his way through the opening to the top of the steps.

"Will you be OK from here? I'm keen to get back to the dispensary and start making up my sleeping cocktails."

"Yes, you go ahead." But that sentence was an echoey, disembodied voice drifting up to an absent audience.

Having gathered some cleaning supplies from the house and three small bags of fertilizer from the shed, Ben made his way to the utility room next to the kitchen of the main house. It was clear from the map that the tunnel entrance originated here.

He dumped his loot unceremoniously in the corner and turned his attention to a metal, circular manhole cover sunk into the floor. It looked very solid and clearly hadn't been disturbed in decades. There were two discrete holes in the top of the cover where manhole keys would fit, but there was no sign of them anywhere. Ben cast his gaze around the room for anything he could use as a makeshift key.

Above his head was an old-fashioned pulley arial dryer, suspended by thick cords which were tethered to a cast metal cleat secured to the wall. He untied the cords lowering the rack to the floor. He unscrewed the weighty cable cleat from the wall, cut a length of cord from the contraption, and tied it to the centre of the metal fitting, then with a little manoeuvring and a lot of brute force, he forced the cleat into one of the holes in the manhole cover, turning it horizontally to secure it in place. Before taking up the slack in the cords, he planted his feet firmly, either side of the edge of the cover. Then pulled hard on the cords. The cover groaned but did not move.

"Come on you bugger," Ben mumbled more to himself than the obstinate disk. He adjusted his grip, took a huge breath, and launched himself upwards in a monumental effort to shift the lid. It came out of the hole cleanly, landing on the edge of the hole with a clang. He dragged the heavy cover to the side of the opening, completely exposing the manhole shaft and was pleasantly surprised by Bills' grinning face looking back up at him.

"Knock, knock."

Ben gave the automatic response, "Who's there?"

"Keith",

"Keith who?"

"Keith me Hardy Keith me!"

Ben leant down to help his friend wriggle his way out of the concrete shaft.

"Too many afternoon teas mate. This won't be a quick getaway for you without 5 lbs. of butter to grease you up a bit!"

He laughed as Bill struggled to a standing position. "Cheeky bugger, these things were built for beanpoles like you!" He brushed the dust from his head and face. "Did you take Ken's squirrel gun upstairs for Phipps?"

"Yes, although I had to solemnly promise him that he would get it back in one piece. I left him camouflaging a very neat and well disguised trench. If they come in that way by vehicle they won't get far."

Bill had placed a large, galvanized bucket into the Belfast sink on the far wall. "Now, pass me the fertilizer and those plastic containers. We have enough stuff for a half a dozen devices, I hope that will be enough."

In the dispensary, Phipps worked quickly and diligently. His task was somewhat more delicate than Bills', now he was surveying the results of his handiwork. Six hastily fashioned tranquillizer darts had been constructed from hypodermic syringes that now contained a powerful pharmaceutical mix that would render a small pony groggy for several hours. The effects on an adult male would be far quicker, and the unlucky recipient would probably be unconscious for several hours. He hoped there would be no permanent damage, but if he was honest, he really couldn't be certain. Anaesthesia wasn't an exact science. He had also discovered a medical vaccination injection gun and the compressed air cylinder to power it in Dr Arnot's office, the relic of a field kit he still carried. If the six darts he'd made didn't do the trick and it came to close quarter combat, he had enough left to deliver a couple of similar doses manually.

This was the part Phipps hated, the waiting. He had been mulling over the earlier conversation with Daniel. He remembered how difficult communication was back in the day. Agencies didn't really work together then and the transfer of information was hit-and-miss at best. It was difficult because you couldn't tell who was working for whom. If MI5 had people infiltrating IRA cells, then he thought it stood to reason that there were also Irish loyal to the cause that could have infiltrated our security services. He was left wondering whether it was conspiracy or cock up that had resulted in Coopers murder. Had the information transfer been bungled or had there been a leak that enabled the IRA to pick him up before his handlers could get him out? After all this time he supposed it didn't really matter, but it did to him. Courage, discipline, and loyalty had been their watch words. The company had fought to protect civilians in Northern Ireland and on the mainland. Sapper Cooper had placed his personal priorities below those of protecting the nation, putting himself in the path of danger, only to be betrayed by someone with less integrity. That was the nature of modern warfare. Most of the time it was difficult to tell friend from foe.

Chapter 38:

Saturday 27th July 2019 8.00pm

Shady Fields (The Assault)

The three-car convoy travelled quickly along the main road towards Shady Fields, quickly, but not fast enough to attract unwanted attention. Like so many British rural roads, the dwindling numbers of village policemen had seen a corresponding growth in speed cameras; silent but effective. There were lots of myths about these electronic sentinels; they were rarely active, if you travelled fast enough they didn't record you, but it was all bunkum. No one wanted to take the risk of being captured on camera so they were carefully observing the speed limits.

Yilmaz had come mob handed. There were three other men in his Range Rover and another four men in an Audi estate following closely behind, all armed with semi-automatic pistols. Each car carried an assault rifle and a skilled marksman to use it.

Callaghan had Michael and Padraig with him in a silver BMW. Men who had been with him for nearly three decades and who he could trust with his life. Both were armed with IRA handguns from their glory days. They were tout-hunting.

The hastily developed plan was simple enough, Callaghan would enter the estate from an old service road that began along the Eastern perimeter of the grounds, skirting the woods and making directly for the car park at the back of the main house, that was if their map was to be trusted. He would then go in through the front door. Security would be tight if Dessie was here, so he would need a distraction.

Yilmaz would enter via the rear of the building after taking out any security personnel in the gatehouse. It was a brute-force approach but one that Yilmaz and his team were well versed in.

The four men in the black Audi would gain entry to the estate from the West using old forestry maintenance tracks, rendezvousing with the others at the side and rear of the house.

It was the most effective way to assault the house with a small number of men, their goal was to capture Dessie alive and find out exactly what he had told MI5.

The reality was that once they'd interrogated him, he wouldn't make it out of there alive.

Callaghan knew they had the element of surprise on their side; however he expected a low-key security service presence, one that wouldn't attract too much attention, but they would almost certainly be combat trained.

Yilmaz had warned everyone not to take anything for granted. He watched the Audi peel off from the middle of the convoy and disappear into a rough entrance at the start of the property's west boundary wall. Five hundred yards further on, his grey Range Rover swung into the main entrance and raced up the well-maintained drive. Callaghan's BMW continued on to the East service road access. In a couple of minutes, their coordinated assault would begin.

The Audi bumped along a rough track cut through a dense canopy of trees and scrub. After a couple of minutes, they exited the trees and stopped at the edge of a clearing; it resembled something like a firebreak. A clear stretch of land about twenty feet deep that extended to their left and right as far as the contours of the ground would allow them to see. Running across the middle of the clearing and blocking their progress, stood an imposing chain-link fence supported by ten-foot-tall steel posts set about twenty feet apart. This was the first line of Shady Field's perimeter defences, designed to keep out trespassers, lost hikers and the plain curious, but the fence was no match for professionals with the right kit.

Two men got out from the rear of the car, taking equipment from the trunk. One picked up a black attaché case and quickly carried it over to the fence. He saw that the wire-link mesh stood proud of the metal posts by several inches, separated from them by non-conductive isolators, the sort they used on old overhead power lines. So clearly the fence was electrified. He also spotted a Wi-Fi aerial on the top of the nearest post, meaning that it was being monitored as well. He opened the case and chose a multi-meter. He plugged two cables with probes into the device, clipping one of the probes to the fence. The other he pushed into the ground by his foot. The needle immediately swung to the right. Yes, it was electrified, at approximately 2000 volts. Not lethal, because of the low current, but enough to give a stray animal or a wayward hiker a nasty shock. He returned the meter to his case and picked up a small black box, switching it on and pointing it in the direction of the Wi-Fi antennae, he picked up the Wi-Fi signal, pressed two more buttons on the box and nodded to the second man who had donned a pair of thick rubber gloves, and set about cutting through the fence with a pair of powerful hydraulic cutters. In seconds, he had made an opening wide enough to drive the car through. They stowed their equipment and got back into the car. The driver guided the Audi through the opening and across the open ground, picking up the trail again under the cover of the tree line.

The car was making slow progress over the deep ruts and undulations that crossed the track. It bottomed-out several times, each time, a deep metallic thud vibrated up through the thickly padded seats, shaking the occupants who complained bitterly.

The track improved a little, it was nowhere near as rough as it had been, and the route between the trees now seemed clearer too. Obviously, this part of the track was used more regularly to maintain the estate. His three passengers were scanning the undergrowth for any signs of movement as they approached two piles of straw bales that channelled the car into the centre of the track.

The driver's sixth sense, developed over years of staying alive told him something was wrong, and instinctively stabbed for the brake pedal, he was a second too late.

The car pitched forward into a well camouflaged trench cut into the mossy track floor launching all four occupants violently forward in their seats. Unfortunately, the two men in the rear had not put their seat belts back on after disabling the perimeter fence. The driver felt the impact and heard the sickening crunch as their heads made contact with the backs of the seats in front of them.

A spray of bright red blood shot from the nose of the 'cutter' spattering his t-shirt. The other man sustained a deep cut across his left eyebrow from which blood poured profusely. The engine was still running, but the car would be going nowhere today. The driver turned off the engine and cursed loudly as he tried to open his door only to find it blocked by the side of the trench. No four-wheel drive meant no escape for this vehicle. He lowered his window fully and squirmed out onto the ground next to the imprisoned car. The two men in the back were able to exit via the rear doors, whilst the man in the front chose to exit via the sunroof. He looked at the position the car now occupied, the nose was buried two-feet-deep in a carefully prepared trap, obviously they had been expected.

They would have to proceed with greater caution from now on. He popped the tailgate and took out an automatic rifle fitted with telescopic sights. They would make their way to the house on foot. The two men from the rear of the car were attending to their injuries. The driver instructed them to fan out and follow at a distance. He and the third man would make for their agreed positions at the side of the house. He didn't want to annoy his boss by not being there as expected. Yilmaz never accepted excuses, regardless of how genuine they were.

With their guns ready, but concealed from view, the Range Rover stopped next to an entry keypad and screen fixed to a metal post in front of an imposing archway barred by a sturdy metal gate. A brick-built gatehouse stood off to the right, it was deserted. Only the winking red light of a solitary surveillance camera monitored the entrance from the top of one of the tall brick pillars above the imposing gateway.

“There’s no one here, the place looks deserted” the driver said.

“Ram the gate” Yilmaz barked.

The driver reversed the car back some thirty or forty feet, engaged drive and floored the accelerator.

The cars twenty-two-inch town-and-country tyres screamed and ripped at the tarmac as he aimed three and a half tons of rapidly accelerating metal directly at the middle of the gates. The Range Rover smashed into the obstacle with an irresistible force. The impact of the collision destroyed the gates, flinging them several yards away from the entrance. The driver kept his foot firmly planted on the gas, guiding the car through the wreckage and on up the winding drive. He slowed to a crawl as they approached the impressive building, still no one was visible as they passed the front of the house. The place looked deserted.

Yilmaz had briefed his men that they could take out anyone they encountered, but they were to leave McFee alive so that he could interrogate him and then kill him. He wanted to send a message to anyone who even thought of crossing him. There were no lengths he wouldn’t go to, and nothing he considered to be a reasonable exception. The message must be clear; if you crossed him then the price was your life.

He signalled two of his men to cover the side of the house. The only exit was a solitary fire door that opened on to the car park, but it only opened from inside, however it was possible that McFee would try to escape this way. He signalled to his driver with the semi-automatic rifle and to one other, to follow him. He told the last man to stay put and watch the fire exit.

They slowly edged around the corner of the building until Yilmaz could see the full expanse of the conservatory. Again there was no one about, and both sets of double doors were closed. He thought that was an unusual thing on such a warm night.

As Callaghan approached the front of the building two loud explosions somewhere in the woods on the far side of the building detonated in quick succession. Yilmaz had bought weaponry but no explosives, so whoever or whatever was responsible for that noise did not belong to them. He realised that they'd walked into a trap, which meant his hunch was right and Dessie was here!

It stood to reason that they would be keeping him on one of the upper floors, so he was going to have to improvise. These old buildings were all the same. There would be a big wooden staircase off the entrance hall, that's where he would head. His two minders would draw fire, to give him cover while he went searching for Dessie. The building wasn't that big so it shouldn't take him long.

He stood in the frame of the main entrance doorway looking into the reception area, it was deserted. The thickly carpeted staircase off to his left swept upwards and out of sight as he had surmised.

Padraig walked cautiously into the middle of the hallway, eyes darting around to detect any sign of movement. A loud popping sound resonated in the open space and he stood stock still for a second, surprise etched on his face, as his fingers clutched at a dart embedded in his neck. He didn't have enough time to pull it out before he slumped to the floor, unconscious.

Callaghan had to take a calculated risk; he wasn't sure where the shot had come from, but if there was a shooter at the top of the stairs he needed another way to get up there. He saw a door beyond the stairs slowly closing and reasoned that this would take him to the back of the building and maybe to a service lift or stairs.

If he stayed close to the right perimeter of the hall, he could make it to the exit door without offering the shooter a clear shot. He may have to sacrifice Michael in the process, but that was acceptable, all that mattered now, was getting to Dessie.

He moved quickly and passed through the door just as a flurry of shots rang out. He hoped briefly that Michael had not been on the receiving end of one of those, but his attention was now on searching an unfamiliar building, seeking a man who he had treated like a son and who had betrayed him. His hate propelled him through the corridors.

Yilmaz heard the two explosions and also realised that their arrival had been anticipated. He peered through the conservatory windows into the room beyond and tried the first set of doors, but they were locked. He signalled his driver to follow him as he ducked below the window line, making for the far set of doors. He tested the handle; the door was unlocked. He opened it and pushed the driver into the long conservatory using him as a human shield. For a few seconds nothing happened, then a loud 'pop' echoed around the room. A projectile embedded into his driver's neck. There was a look of surprise on the man's' face as he dropped his gun and fell to the floor, eyes rolling back in his head, his limbs twitching.

Yilmaz crouched low behind one of the large cane armchairs. It was an ambush. He knew it was a mistake to trust Callaghan to handle the details. The old man was not up to it any more. He had tolerated him while they were setting up their operation but he was no longer needed. When this was settled he would deal with him personally.

He extended his left arm and fired his handgun around the side of the chair, sending four shots in the direction the dart had come from. Noise didn't matter now; they knew he was in the building so he would just carry-on shooting.

Daniel moved down the staircase, his handgun pointed at the first man's body, slumped on the bottom three steps. Phipps still had a good eye and the drug cocktail had rendered the assailant unconscious in seconds. He took the gun out of his hand, slipping it into his jacket pocket, noting that the man would be in no condition to use it for several hours. He wasn't a young man and he had proved no match for their training and marksmanship. The second man lay groaning on the floor, blood pooling under his shattered knee. He was about to lose consciousness and his gun lay out of reach where he'd dropped it when he fell. Daniel picked it up and tucked it into the back of his trouser waistband. He scanned the hall, but there was no one else here. Either they were incredibly amateurish, believing that two middle-aged men could storm a safe house or more of them were already in the building. Four gunshots caught his attention. Yes, they were definitely in the building. He moved cautiously towards the sound, checking for more intruders, before passing into the hallway. The gunfire was coming from the conservatory. Phipps only had tranquillizer darts, so the shots must be from the attackers. He had to get to Phipps fast. He moved quickly along the corridor and could see into the conservatory; Phipps was hunched behind an upturned table. Periodically a shot came whistling in from an unseen gunman or maybe there was more than one? He kept low and zigzagged towards the crouching figure, using furniture to shield him from sight.

Phipps whispered "I'm pinned down here. I got one of them, but the other one is fast. I only have two darts left and I can't get a clean shot."

Daniel thought quickly, "If you can draw his fire by heading for the corridor. I'll try to get him from here, and Callaghan is somewhere in the building. I need you to find him, save one of those darts for him, I need to talk to him."

Phipps made a sudden move across the room, bent double, holding the modified air rifle above his head but not firing. Yilmaz saw movement and lent forward to take aim, he wasn't aware that he had presented Daniel with a clear target. The bullet hit his right shoulder shattering the bone, before exiting through his chest. He collapsed to the floor as the pain rendered him useless. His limp hand was still holding his weapon, but he was completely unable to raise or fire it.

Daniel walked over to him, relieving him of his firearm, taking in his swarthy features. "Mr. Yilmaz I presume. So nice of you to drop in. How many more of your men are there?"

"Go fuck yourself". Yilmaz spat in his thick accent, a trace of blood smearing his lips.

"Please yourself. Your friend here will be out for a good while and I can either leave you to bleed-out here or get you some help, your choice, of course. How many more?"

Yilmaz realised that this man was serious and he had no choice if he wanted to live.

"Four with me and two with Callaghan." He was having difficulty breathing now and the distinct gurgling told Daniel that he had a punctured lung. He grabbed a scatter cushion from one of the upturned chairs and pressed it against the exit wound. "Hold that in place while I get you some help."

Dr. Arnot would not thank him for the custom, it was a long time since he had treated gunshot wounds.

Another explosion out in the grounds focused his attention. Thank God for the dynamite men! If they were on their 'A' game, they might all get out of this in one piece. He looked at his watch, where was that backup unit? They should have been here by now. He looked again at the prostrate figure of Yilmaz and headed for the stairs at the other end of the building.

The dynamite men moved silently through the trees, surprised at how easily their old skills had come back to them. That last explosion had been a trip wire between two saplings which no longer existed. Instead, there was a crater with two sets of legs sticking out of it. They were moving, but not very much. The IED's Bill had set were there to disorientate not to kill, but they must have been virtually on top of them when they went off. There would be shrapnel wounds for sure but hopefully nothing life-threatening. Bill signalled to him and pointed off to the right. Two men were moving through the undergrowth and up towards the house. They would miss the last booby trap if they continued in that direction which meant they would have to be taken out manually.

Their well-practised sign language was as clear as if they were discussing cricket scores over a pint. Ben would circle around and cut them off before they got to the house and Bill would come at them from behind. The retired agents began to close in. They were on familiar ground so knew exactly where their best cover was. Bill was close to the back of one of the men and even though it was now quite dark under the thick canopy of trees he could tell by the way the man moved that he was carrying a weapon. He picked up a hefty branch and edged forwards, swinging the makeshift club swiftly, hitting the man solidly across the back of his head.

He dropped his gun, but the blow hadn't felled him if anything it just seemed to make him angry. He spun around to face his attacker and pulled out a knife. Bill could see it was no ordinary blade, it was a WASP injector, a serious killer's weapon.

The man lunged towards him, but in that split second, he had made a fatal miscalculation. What he saw was an older, shorter man that carried a bit of weight and had grey in his hair. What he encountered was a well-trained hand-to-hand combat fighter who knew how to use his speed and body weight to deflect the attack. The assailant didn't even feel his own knife entering his gut, he just heard the click as the injector deployed.

Bill stood back and watched as the tiny canister of CO2 gas concealed in the handle, expelled 850psi of pressure into the man's abdomen, effectively freezing his organs. Not a pleasant death. "I have just got to get me one of those" he said and set off in Ben's direction in case he needed a bit of help.

Ben crouched in the cover of dense rhododendron bushes, the remnants of their flower heads, brown and crisp. He listened for movement, any rustle or branch snapping. Then he heard it, the crack of a twig underfoot. It was slightly off to his left, but he required more than that to locate the intruder accurately. He listened again and decided to change position for a better view.

What most people don't realise about the mechanics and art of sniper fire, is that it isn't just about lining the target up in your sights and pulling the trigger. You have to take into consideration wind-speed and velocity, even the rotation of the earth. A bullet travels in an arc determined by gravity before it comes down towards the target. That calculation is made even more difficult if the target is on the move, as you need to predict their movements and compensate accordingly. Then you have to manage the adrenalin spike which can affect the fine motor skills required to squeeze the trigger.

All those calculations were taking place automatically as the sniper centred Ben in the crosshairs of his telescopic sight. He had a perfect side view and a clear shot directly into his temple. Unfortunately that level of concentration and focus also meant that he was completely unaware of Bill standing behind him wielding a hefty garden fork that Ken, had usefully left leaning against a tree. He swung the heavy metal prongs down hard, aiming just above the snipers left ear, connecting with a sickening thud. The shooter fell forwards; the gun went off as it fell from his grip. He landed on top of it, unconscious and bleeding from a wound that had incapacitated him but probably not killed him. Bill rolled him over to retrieve the weapon and used a couple of heavy-duty cable ties he'd shoved into his pocket as an afterthought, to secure the gunman's hands behind his back. The downed man groaned but remained still. By his calculations they had neutralized the threat in the grounds, so now they needed to move up to the house to check in with the others.

He called out to Ben, but there was no reply. Bill had a sense of foreboding, he called out again, but there was nothing. He tried the micro radio-transmitter in his ear, still nothing. He knew Ben should have been in earshot so the only reason he didn't reply was because he couldn't.

Bill began to pick up speed, running towards the position the shooter was aiming at, the place Ben was most likely to be. He called again but was still met with silence. A chilling shudder shook Bill's body. Scanning the area was becoming more difficult in the fading light, but his trained eyes picked out a dark shape crumpled on the ground a little way off to his right. He charged towards the body, not daring to think of what ifs until he could see for himself. He reached his friend and could clearly make out the twisted body, lying face down in the undergrowth.

Bill knelt down and rolled him over so that he could see his face. There was a jagged tear across Ben's forehead that disappeared up into his hairline. He held his ear close to Ben's mouth, he wasn't breathing! Years of experience told him that head wounds like this often looked much worse than they were. They bled profusely and left a scar but were seldom fatal, so why was Ben not breathing? Was it shock? Had his heart given out? Had the bullet penetrated his skull? He tried to feel for a pulse, but fingers like a bunch of bananas made that almost impossible in his current state of anxiety.

Bill lifted the lifeless form of his best friend in the world and clutched him tightly to his chest. "You silly bugger, what did you have to go and get shot for?" Tears began to fill his eyes. "We've been mates forever." the words choked in his throat.

"Oh Ben, you can't leave me now? What am I going to do on my own? You and me, we're the dynamite men. You're a part of my life, I'm a part of yours. I can't do this without you Rocky."

Tears now flooded freely down Bill's face. Ben's unmoving body hanging limply in his friend's strong arms. They were locked in a final embrace, time meant nothing to Bill now.

"Well it's a frigging good job he was such a crap shot then wasn't it!" Ben mumbled.

Bill released his grip and Ben fell unceremoniously to the floor. As he rolled over he winked at Bill who didn't know whether to laugh or punch him, instead he breathed a sigh of relief. "You tosser! I thought he'd killed you. It's a good job he didn't hit you somewhere important. If ever I want to get rid of you, I'll remember not to shoot you in the head."

Bill quickly checked Ben for other injuries, but there were none.

"Come on then, we still have a villain to catch." He took a large handkerchief from his trouser pocket and swirled it into a bandana which he roughly wrapped around his friend's head. "Are you really OK?"

"Ouch," Ben winced as he tied it tightly. "Of course I'm not OK, I've just been shot in the head!" He sounded cross but was obviously groggy from his injury. He gingerly felt his wound. "Did you get him though Bill?"

A smile spread across his friend's face "Oh yes, and he'll have a headache to rival yours in the morning. We need to get you up to the house and get 'sawbones' to take a look at that gash. Can you stand up? Bill didn't wait for a reply, he pulled Ben's arm around his neck and hoisted him to his feet. Adrenaline fuelled strength was an awesome thing.

They made their way up to the house; Bill was carrying most of Ben's weight, but it didn't hamper his vigilance in case they had miscalculated and there was still someone lurking in the grounds. They reached the front steps of the building; the big doors were open, and the interior was silent.

He sat his friend down carefully on the top step with his back leaning against the wall. "Wait here, let me check if it's safe, I don't want you getting one on the other side for a matching pair."

Ben grabbed his friend's arm "Thanks, but I am telling you this is the last time we do crazy shit like this. This is no job for old men with dodgy hips who take beta blockers!"

Bill grinned back at his friend and cautiously entered the building, only to discover that they had obviously missed a lot of the action, judging from the two prone bodies and a copious amount of blood on the carpet. Hilary wouldn't be pleased about that.

Chapter 39:

Saturday 27th July 2019 8:30pm

Shady Fields (The Escape)

Callaghan had used the service staircase at the back of the house to gain access to the first floor and was moving silently along the carpeted corridor, listening intently for any sound, it was eerily quiet. They would surely have raised the alarm by now and help would be on the way. If he didn't find Dessie soon he would have to leave. This would be a god damn failure; no Dessie, no information, men down and for nothing.

Suddenly the hairs on the back of his neck bristled. A door to his immediate right began to open; deliberately and slowly. He pressed back against the wall. Someone was checking to see if the passage was clear. He hugged the wall tighter and a head emerged, he made a lunge for it. To his surprise it was a young woman. Shorter than him by at least a foot, she had very short dark hair and was slight in build. He easily overpowered her clamping his left arm across her body, pulling her tight to his chest. His hand was across her mouth, the muzzle of his gun connecting with her rib cage. He whispered menacingly into her ear,

"Where are they holding Dessie McFee?"

He felt the women shake her head under his grip and mumble something. He took a calculated risk

"Don't scream, just tell me where he is." He removed his hand from her mouth but maintained his grip on her body.

She nodded. "If it's the man I think you mean, he's gone. They took him an hour ago, took him away in a big car. I just look after the residents here; I don't know anything about him."

He noted a slight accent to her voice.

"Where did they take him?"

"I have no idea; I didn't even know he was here until this morning." Her voice was surprisingly steady.

Callaghan didn't have time for this. He moved the gun to the side of the woman's head so that she could see it from the corner of her eye.

"There's no point keeping you alive then, is there?"

The door she had emerged from was flung wide open and a second woman stepped out into the passage.

She was older, and there was something strangely familiar about her. Callaghan tensed and pushed the gun into his captives' temple

"Don't come any closer if you want her to live."

The woman was staring at him intensely, looking into his eyes.

"Hello Jon-Jo, it's been a while." She took a step back almost inviting him to take a closer look, willing him to recognise her.

She watched as the colour drained from his face.

"It can't be…. You're dead!"

She nodded her head

"That is exactly what they wanted you to think but it really is me, Theresa Farrell."

Callaghan felt all the air leave his lungs. His grip relaxed and Layla took the opportunity to wriggle from his hold and stand next to Theresa.

"But how is this possible?" He stammered.

"I gave the order and Colm carried it out." Theresa could see realization dawning on his face.

"My God. You were with the British all along. Everything Sinead said about you was true."

He looked confused. "How did you pull it off?"

"They made a switch and got me out. It was such a long time ago, but the point is, Dessie has gone. I saw him leave JJ. You are too late."

Callaghan thought quickly. He pointed the gun at both women. "He may have left but I still have to get out of here. Turn round and put your hands on the wall." He gave them a quick pat down to ensure they were not armed. He took a bleep and a mobile phone from Layla. He dropped the bleep and pocketed the phone.

"You're both coming with me to guarantee my safety, then you are going take me to him, to Dessie. I have a score to settle that will not wait any longer." He ushered them along the corridor towards the exit marked stairs. He pushed them roughly through the door and down the service staircase, warning them to be silent; they complied.

He needed to think. If Theresa was there, then this place was definitely run by security services. Someone would be sure to know Dessie's whereabouts and if he played his cards right he could use these two to get to him. He had no idea where Yilmaz was, or even if he was alive or dead but he couldn't concern himself with that now.

Reaching the bottom of the stairs without incident they crossed the hall, following a passageway through a series of turns until they came to a heavy fire door. The reinforced glass door gave access to the rear car park and Callaghan could see the car he had arrived in, but they would have to cross at least twenty-five yards of open ground. He pushed the door release bar and it swung outwards smoothly. Almost immediately an alarm went off somewhere in the building and a shot rang out from behind one of the huge flower urns, hitting the wall near the open door. He had to pick up the pace so he roughly shoved the women out of the door in front of him shepherding them towards the nearest cover.

The gunman who fired the shot recognised Callaghan and stood up, lowering his weapon as he spoke.

"Oh my God, Mr. Callaghan, I'm so sorry, I thought you were McFee"

"I gave orders not to kill him you idiot." Callaghan raised his pistol and shot the man cleanly between the eyes.

He pushed both women towards the car. As they rounded the rear of the Range Rover he saw that the drivers' side front and rear tyres were punctured. Looking through the BMW's window, he could see there was no key in the ignition. They were going nowhere in this. He swore under his breath,

"Feck, what am I going to do now?"

He heard shouting coming from the wooded gardens away to his right. At least one person was there and heading this way. "Back to the house, quickly" he shouted.

They ran through the open fire door and made their way towards the back of the building. He needed another way out.

"What's along here?" he shouted at Layla as they ran past the dining room.

"Just the kitchens, the laundry, and the stores"

Perhaps there would be something in the stores he could use, or maybe a place to hold up, a cellar or something, to give him time to make a plan. They entered the scullery behind the kitchen and Layla almost fell into the open manhole in the floor, leading to the secret passageway that Ben and Bill had uncovered earlier that day.

"What's down there," Callaghan pointed to the opening with his pistol.

"I've no idea, I didn't even know it was here" Layla replied.

"Look JJ, this is no use. There will be a small army of agents crawling all over this place in minutes. Let us go, we'll say nothing" Theresa urged.

"Get down there now, both of you" Callaghan ordered, pushing Layla towards the hole in the floor. "You too, go on". He waved the pistol at Theresa.

Layla lowered herself over the edge of the opening, her feet making contact with the metal rungs set into the wall. She disappeared into the hole and Theresa followed her.

Callaghan took out Layla's mobile phone and turned on the light as he too entered the manhole and began to descend the steps.

Twelve steps down then solid ground, He looked round and could see they were in a tunnel, but the phones light was too dim to light up more than a few feet of the passageway.

"That way" Callaghan pointed with his gun. "I'm right behind you, so don't think about getting clever with me"

The two women began to move along the tunnel.

"Why don't you go first Jon Jo, I can't see a damn thing" Theresa said?

"Oh yeah, and have you bang me on the back of the head? No, thanks. Just keep on going."

Callaghan held the phone higher and the tiny light picked out the side walls of the tunnel heading off in front of them. The tunnel looked quite straight and Layla picked up the pace now that her eyes were becoming accustomed to the dim light. They travelled along the tunnel for a couple of minutes, Callaghan alert, listening for any noises from behind them that would suggest they were being pursued. So far so good he thought.

A faint glow of light in the distance showed them the end of the passage was near. The tunnel ended at a flight of steps, and looking up he could see the outline of a partially opened doorway

"OK hold it. I need to know what's waiting for us on the other side of that door. Where are we?"

Layla said

"I think this must be the garages and workshop. Some of the old boys use it as a place to hang out and talk"

"Right, any sudden movements or noise and I will kill you. Get up there and go through the door, no tricks"

Theresa and Layla entered the workshop and stood unmoving as Callaghan's face peered round the edge of the door taking in the equipment the dynamite twins had been working with earlier. He stepped into the room, scanning the benches for makeshift weapons or something that might aid his escape. He shot a quick glance out of the window and did a double take!

Seamus had arrived in the rear car park just a couple of minutes ago and was considering what he needed to do next. The exterior lights came on illuminating the tarmac as he slowly crawled to a stop. There was a Range Rover with two flat tyres standing on the hardcore next to a BMW, so he parked next to them.

He had used his initiative and followed them in Mr. Callaghan's Jaguar on a ferry earlier this morning. He was never allowed to drive the car unless his boss was in it, but Seamus thought this was an exception. He didn't want to be left behind and thought an extra pair of hands might come in useful. He wasn't sure why Mr. Callaghan had left his car behind, but it had given Seamus the excuse to get involved in the action. His boss would be pleased.

"Change of plan, get out there to that car and get in". He pointed the gun at them to make sure they understood it was an order not a request. They broke cover and ran to the car. Callaghan burst out of the workshop door into the car park and stared at Seamus who was sitting in the driving seat of his Jaguar, looking more than a bit bewildered and lost. JJ had never been so glad to see this useless lump in all his life.

Seamus looked shocked, but he opened the window.

"Jesus Mr. Callaghan, you can hear that feckin alarm going off half-way to London."

"Get in" he commanded and pointed at Theresa with his gun.

Theresa spoke for the first time since they got outside.

"Jon-Jo leave Layla here, she can't help you. It's me that you can trade with, she doesn't know anything."

Callaghan opened the rear door pushing the girl onto the back seat and gestured for Theresa to get into the front next to Seamus.

"You are both coming with me, two hostages are better than one."

Still holding his gun he slid into the back seat and slammed the door behind him.

"Go Seamus, just get us out of here — now! You can tell me why you are here later."

The Jaguar's tires screeched as Seamus flung the heavy car round and headed for the estate entrance.

Daniel heard the roar of the engine as it fled down the driveway. He stood on the top step his gun clenched in his hands; arms braced to steady any shot he might make, but he was too late. The car was fast disappearing down the drive. He knew it was Callaghan, as they already had Yilmaz in custody, albeit now unconscious and in need of urgent medical attention, and there were several other casualties including their own Ben Faulkner, although luckily his was just a flesh wound, but Callaghan had got away.

Daniel took stock. They had managed to keep everyone safe, and the immediate danger had been neutralised. Not an ideal result but one he could live with. He was contemplating what to do next when the phone in his pocket began to vibrate. He looked at the caller display before answering, it was Mitch.

"This had better be good news because your protection unit are still on route, and we've had to fight off Callaghan and Yilmaz with brown paper and sticking plaster!" As he listened to Mitch's update he heard the cavalry arriving in the distance, in a few moments they would come roaring up the drive, too late to be of any use.

Chapter 40:

Saturday 27th July 2019 11.30pm

Shady Fields

Daniel re-entered the main building and saw several people milling around assessing the damage. Doctor Arnot had blood smeared across his white shirt and jacket sleeves where he had administered emergency treatment to two gunshot wounds. He had a serious scowl across his face and he glared at Daniel as he walked across the hallway.

"Well, this turned into a dog's breakfast! Arnot growled. "The ambulance has arrived to take Yilmaz and the knee injury to hospital under guard and you'll need to have a word with Ben, he's kicking up a fuss and won't go to get checked out. I am going to stitch his wound now, but I would feel happier with an x-ray, just to ensure nothing else is going on. Ward will need extra pain relief because of the strain on his pinned leg and Phipps and Bill are in need of a stiff drink, but apart from that everyone is peachy!"

"Thanks Doc. It wouldn't have come to this if the backup unit had arrived in time, but thankfully it's over now. Have you seen Layla? I want her to do a head count and make sure everyone's OK. I thought she would be here." Daniel felt a stirring in his gut. He called across to a couple of staff making their way down the stairs

"Alan, Penny, have either of you seen Layla?"

Both looked blank

"No, not since before it all kicked off."

Penny added "I think I saw her heading towards Jackie's room, but that was a couple of hours ago."

"Can you go and check on them both right away? Alan, check the office, please? I need to know where they both are, now!" Something about the urgency in his voice conveyed concern and the two hurried back up the stairs.

Daniel turned on his heel and went to check the dining room but it was deserted. The next couple of hours would be chaotic with the clean-up and he had to know that everyone was accounted for.

The local police had arrived in response to reports of gunshots and Detective Inspector Bissiter was standing in the hallway looking a bit shell-shocked.

"I am looking for whoever is in charge. DI Bissiter." He held his identification up for Daniel to read even though he was twenty feet away. He could just about make out the photo and the initials CID. He walked across to meet him

"Hello, I'm Daniel Grant, Director General, Security Services. My ID is up in the office if you want to follow me."

The DI looked back unsure if this was a wind up or not. No one had informed him there was an operation going on in his patch and yet, this scale of violence at a residential home definitely suggested something was happening. He decided to play it by ear and follow this man up the stairs.

"What happened then Sir?" He was irritated. Some sort of explanation was needed.

"Sorry I can't tell you that, it's classified and part of an ongoing operation."

Bissiter scoffed, "Of course, you could tell me, but you would have to kill me, right?" Grant just blinked at him.

They walked quickly along the corridor towards Daniel's office. Alan, the orderly, come out of the office.

"Sorry Daniel, they're not here. We've checked all the rooms on this floor including storage and no one on the other floors has seen them either. I did find this outside Jackie's room though." He held up Layla's bleep.

Daniel turned and spoke to Bissiter "Come with me."

He led the way past the general office and entered the security office next door. The room was dark with no windows and was illuminated solely by an iridescent blue glow from a bank of consoles sat atop a wide desk. The only things on it were a keyboard, a mouse, and a telephone. The screens were split into four images each showing various scenes inside and outside the building.

Daniel sat down and pulled the keyboard towards him entering commands quickly. On the central monitor in front of him appeared a single image of the corridor outside. Bissiter felt like a spare part. If there really was something that threatened National Security he didn't want to be on the outside looking in, he wanted to be useful.

He watched as Daniel skillfully navigated the system, isolating the right camera feed, then winding the footage back until he spotted movement. These images were not the grainy shadows that are so poorly defined you struggle to tell if the figures are human, let alone identify someone's face. These were crisp, high definition colour pictures, like watching a TV series or the news. He saw himself and Daniel leave the security room and walk backwards down the hallway. After a few more seconds looking at the picture of an empty corridor he heard Daniel take a sharp breath. He paused the tape and focused on three figures; he could clearly see two women being held at gunpoint by a man.

"That Inspector, is an organized crime boss called Jon-Jo Callaghan and I think he has taken one of my residents and my ops' manager as hostages."

Bissiter was suddenly on the right page. “What can I do to help Sir?”

Chapter 41:

Sunday 28th July 2019 1.30am

Just outside Aldershot

Seamus; "no one's following us so you can pull over when you find somewhere quiet."

Callaghan was mightily pleased they had got away with such ease. For once, Seamus the idiot had done OK. He considered what his next steps might be. It had been a real shock to find Theresa there. He couldn't believe that Dessie had known that she was still alive, he would have acted if he had. This was a typical trick played by the spooks. Plant someone like her in your midst then disappear her when the time was right.

It left Callaghan in a real dilemma. Why had Colm Devey said he had killed her when she was still very much alive? He had believed Devey's report and the identification of the body. The spooks had obviously found her before she died and substituted the body. He needed to understand exactly what had happened, and only one man could tell him that, Colm Devey.

Callaghan felt sure that the British must have used her existence to tempt Dessie across to their side. Dessie had never got over her, there had never been anyone else since Theresa. He felt a strong conviction that Theresa was the key to get to Dessie he just didn't know how that would work at the moment.

They pulled off the road into a deserted lane. Neither of the women had spoken since they left the house. Seamus stopped the car and switched off the engine. There were no street lights along here, but the full moon shone so brightly they could easily see each other's faces.

"I want you to call Dessie and tell him that I want to exchange you for him." He fixed Theresa with an icy stare.

"Jon-Jo, I can't do that, I don't know where he is."

"What about her then?" He gestured to Layla with the muzzle of his gun. "If she ran the place she must know where he is."

"I only run the residential home; I have nothing to do with anything else. I could call my boss and see if she knows anything."

He fished around in his coats' voluminous pocket and pulled out her phone.

"What's his name?"

Layla leant across to take the phone, but he held it out of reach.

"I am not about to have you call for the cavalry and I'm not a patient man so tell me his name." He grabbed her hand and unlocked the phone with her fingerprint.

"Her name is Hilary Geddes."

Callaghan scrolled through her contact list and pressed call. The phone gave the distinct bleep and pre-recorded message that said the person was not available and to leave a message after the tone.

He spoke menacingly. "I have Layla and Theresa Farrell and I want to exchange them for Dessie McFee. Do not waste my time denying that you have him. If you want to see them alive again call me back on this number. You have one hour."

He looked at his fellow passengers "And now, we wait."

Hilary had just made a pot of coffee. Their journey had gone without incident and a sullen Dessie, and a watchful Marina sat on opposite sides of the kitchen table in silence. She moved around the kitchen gathering cups and spoons, her head was a jumble of thoughts as she mulled over the events of the last thirty-six hours. Her bag lay on the counter along with the box of provisions they had bought with them.

"I am not sure if this will help anyone sleep, I'm afraid it is quite strong."

She handed them both coffee-filled mugs and pushed milk and sugar across the table.

Marina smiled, "Thanks but in all honesty, I am not sure any of us will get any sleep tonight."

She put the rest of the food in the empty fridge as the others warmed their hands on the hot mugs. It was summer, and yet they felt a chill from the after-effects of the adrenaline rush, soon the exhaustion would kick in.

Hilary rooted through her bag and found her phone. Daniel had warned them about being tracked so she had switched it off when they left Shady Fields. Marina stopped her before she could switch it on.

"Don't do that. I'll check in with Daniel. Better to be safe than sorry."

She dialled his number and it was answered almost immediately.

"Just to let you know that we have arrived." She waited for a response. Hilary watched the tension increase on her face; something was definitely wrong. "Has anyone heard from them?"

Another silence.

"Hilary, Daniel wants to speak to you." She handed her phone across.

"Hello Daniel, what's happening?"

"They attacked and we captured or incapacitated most of them, but Callaghan escaped, he took Layla and Theresa…sorry, I mean he took Jackie Kelly with him. There is no doubt in my mind that he intends to use them to get to Dessie."

She could hear the concern in his voice, Daniel was worried.

"But he doesn't know where we are, so we're safe for the time being aren't we? What are you going to do?"

"We are on our way to you but I need to get there before they do so I need a delaying tactic. About an hour should do it. We know that Layla has her phone, or to be more accurate, Callaghan has it. He took it from her before they left. The likelihood is they will use it to contact us to set up an exchange. Have you checked your mobile Hilary?"

"No, I was just about to do it when Marina called you, let me check."

Hilary switched her phone on and waited for signal. The familiar notification for a missed call flashed immediately.

"Hang on I have a voicemail."

She switched to speaker and let the message play, holding Marina's phone close enough to the microphone for him to hear.

As the message played from his old mentor, Dessie's anger became palpable.

"The bastard will kill them both whether he has me or not. He never makes idle threats. What are you going to do about it?"

It was a general question to everyone.

Hilary felt a knot tighten in her stomach. It was one thing for her to be here with Dessie, but Layla was not involved in this at all. She had been kidnapped, and her life was in real danger. They had to do something.

"So, what do you want us to do Daniel?"

"You said he left the message ten minutes ago; I'll get someone to locate where he was when he made the call. I'm on my way but we need to buy some time. I want you to call him back and make an excuse. You have to delay giving him your location. Tell him you aren't authorized and must get clearance. He will probably try to get you to a neutral location but we stand a better chance if this happens at the cottage. Do you think you can do that?"

"Yes."

Her reply was strong and steady. Up to that point, she thought she had no aptitude for acting.

"I'll wait another twenty minutes before calling him back. He won't do anything until he has spoken to us."

Daniel was hoping she was right.

"Keep your phone turned off and use Marina's, hers has a higher level of protection on it. And Hilary, please be careful."

Daniel called Peter King. It rang six times before he answered.

"Jesus, it's two in the morning Daniel, this better be important" he said crossly. No one else spoke to the DG in that manner, and normally, Peter would have been more respectful of authority but he was a poor sleeper anyway and extremely grumpy when woken up at such an hour.

Daniel was too worried to pull him up about it.

"Sorry Peter but I need a trace done and I need it now! Long story short, in a bid to get to Dessie McFee, Callaghan has taken Jackie Kelly and the ops' manager from Shady Fields hostage. He's just made contact to arrange a trade and I need to know where he is."

Peter sat bolt upright in bed. "Text me the number you want me to trace, I can do it from the den here. Where is Dessie now?"

"I'd rather not say, but Marina and Hilary are babysitting, without backup."

Without a second thought Peter pulled on his dressing gown and headed downstairs bare-footed.

"I'll call you back when I have something."

Daniel was methodical and sensed risk like an arthritic knee ached when it was about to rain. Callaghan couldn't have been thinking clearly when he escaped from Shady Fields, he had no idea where Dessie was and he took two women hostages not knowing if they would be valuable or not. His first consideration would have been to put distance between him and those who would come after him. With any luck, he could have travelled at least 30 miles in the wrong direction. If that was the case it would give Daniel a fighting chance of getting to the cottage before Callaghan.

He grabbed his car keys from the desk and left the office heading for the stairs. There were still people milling around in the reception area. His own team had taken over the clean-up operations and the blue uniforms were outside on guard duty. Bissiter stood in the hall talking to Dr. Arnot. Daniel briefly considered taking him to ride shotgun but realised he knew nothing about the man or his capability. He might be a real asset or he might be a liability. He didn't know him well enough to make that judgement. He called over the banister to him.

"Bissiter, I need a police escort, two cars with your best drivers, can you sort it?"

Bissiter nodded, "I'm one of the best, and I have another in mind, he's outside. Where are we going?"

As he reached the bottom of the staircase a familiar face appeared at the door.

"What is going on Daniel?"

Daniel pushed his earlier annoyance to the back of his mind. "Phil, do you fancy a road trip? I am on my way to secure Dessie. We moved him because we thought something like this might happen, and he is holed up in a safe house with Marina and Hilary that's about to get a lot less safe!"

At the sound of Marina's name, Phil Santos became tense and more focused.

"Are they in danger?"

"If I am honest, it is a race to see who gets there first. Callaghan's using a couple of hostages to leverage us into giving their location away."

Santos was a quick study. He understood exactly what the play was and how high the stakes were.

"I'll drive, where are we going?"

"M25 then M1 and we can take my car. Just organizing a blues and twos escort to clear the way."

Hilary waited the twenty minutes before making the call, it seemed like the longest twenty minutes of her life. She pressed the call button; it rang once before she heard the deep voice of Callaghan answer.

"About time. So where is he?"

"Hello Mr. Callaghan, this is Hilary Geddes here, I only just got your message and I'm afraid I can't give you our location without clearance from my boss."

Callaghan had a short fuse at the best of times.

"Look girlie I'll make it really simple for you. I have two women that you probably want back in one piece. You have a man that has presumably delivered what he promised, namely me, Yilmaz, and the cartel. His usefulness is over, theirs is not. I'll hand them over if you bring McFee to a place of my choosing. If not, I hope you look good in black."

Hilary took a deep breath and said in a steady voice

"No, that is not how we do things. Firstly, I want proof that they are unharmed. Once I get that I will call my boss and ask for orders on what he wants me to do next. When he has given me those orders, I will call YOU back and tell YOU what will happen. Please understand Mr. Callaghan, this is not me being obstructive. I am a civil servant and we are incapable of working outside of protocols. I just don't have the authority to make those sorts of decisions so if you want

Dessie, let me find the quickest way to make that happen. I will need at least thirty minutes to arrange things. It's still the middle of the night."

Her measured tone was almost hypnotic and was the model of logical thinking. No emotion, just fact.

He listened carefully to what she had said and knew it was true. The British and their procedures and protocols. It was what made them so vulnerable. They didn't know how to wing it, if there wasn't a procedure that told them what to do step-by-step then it didn't get done. It was exactly how the IRA had inflicted such damage on the British Army in the early days. The Brits' followed orders, did everything by the book. All you had to do to catch them out was learn what it said in their book. Their predictability, their discipline, their slavish observation of hierarchy all contributed to their downfall.

"I want to speak to Dessie."

Hilary hesitated.

"First I want proof of life from Layla and Theresa." Marina looked impressed.

Callaghan held the phone up in the middle of the car and signalled to the women to speak.

"Hilary, it's Layla here. We are both fine and unharmed for the moment."

He thrust the phone towards Theresa

"Hilary, we are both fine, they are both armed and Seamus Meh…".

She was cut short by a backhander from Seamus who needed to shut her up. She cried out.

"Well, that was stupid. You may only get one of them back if the traitorous little bitch does that again. Now I want to speak with Dessie." It wasn't a request.

Hilary passed the phone across to an impassive Dessie.

"Hello JJ, It's me.

"I know who it is. I know what betrayal sounds like when I hear it. When I get my hands on you, you'll wish you'd never been born. I was like a father to you and this is how you repay me. You need to know if they don't give you up then Theresa will die by my hand in the most painful way. No rescue this time, no escape, just pain before death. Do you understand?"

Dessie spoke quietly but with real conviction.

"I have never asked you for anything JJ until now. Please leave her out of it. I'll come willingly but she has moved on and has another life now."

Callaghan had heard enough, he sneered sarcastically, "I'm glad she was able to move on and have a nice life. Many of our families never had that opportunity. Hilary, can you hear me? Do what you need to but If I haven't heard from you in thirty minutes you will need someone to recover a body." The phone line went dead.

The three looked at each other in silence, digesting what had just happened.

"He won't hesitate to kill them if he doesn't get his own way." Dessie stated the facts, no emotion or bravado, just the facts.

Marina called Daniel back. They were now hurtling along the M25. It was by no means deserted, but the police escort meant that the few cars that were on the road were moving out of the way. Stop and search at this time in the morning on the busiest orbital road in the UK would normally be a very profitable collar for patrol cars. There were plenty of drivers grateful to move into the slow lane if it meant they wouldn't get caught in possession of recreational drugs they had carelessly stuffed in the glove box or the front armrest.

Normally the journey to Ada's cottage was about three hours in normal traffic, longer if it was a weekday. At their current speed, Daniel estimated they could be there in just under two.

His phone vibrated in his hand. The display showed the initials PK.

"Hi Peter, what have you got for me?"

"He was using the phone a few moments ago, but you know that because you were speaking to him. They are stationary on a side road, West of Aldershot. Can you get them picked up?" There was no trace of irritation, just an eagerness to share what he had found out.

"We can't risk picking them up now. There's not enough time to mobilize armed units and we're not sure what vehicle they are in. Tracking all that takes time we just don't have. The good news is that if they're in Aldershot they did just drive to put distance between themselves and Shady Fields. They will have to get to the M3 before they can get on the orbital, we will have passed that point before them, so hopefully we can be in control of the location when they arrive. That's great Pete. Thanks, you can go back to bed now."

"Won't bother thanks, I'll hang around doing a bit of monitoring if that's OK with you?

As soon as he ended his call with Peter, his phone rang again.

"Hi, have you contacted him yet?"

Marina relayed the conversation, word for word, that she had listened to including the fact that they were dealing with two men, Callaghan and one called Seamus, both armed and not displaying any empathy for their hostages. If the situation was not as dire, he would have smiled at the way Hilary had handled the negotiation. He had never heard of bureaucracy being used as a delaying tactic for a kidnapper. Perhaps they should add it to the training play book.

"OK, this is what I want you to do …"

Chapter 42:

Sunday 28th July 2019 11.05am

MI Northbound Hertfordshire

They sped north along the M1 Motorway following the blue flashing lights (no sirens), both men deep in their own thoughts.

Phil wondered how the hell he'd ended up hurtling towards an English backwater to protect a woman he had only just met, but who had got under his skin to a ridiculous degree. She wasn't even his type. Much taller than him, who was he kidding, taller than most men in the service, with a shock of rich orange-red hair and huge glasses. She had a soft lilting accent and fierce intelligence that offered a glimpse of a passionate woman who cared about her work. His unexpected feelings for her had complicated things. With everything going on in his life at the moment it was almost impossible to consider a relationship. As an active agent, there was no routine year-on-year. Life was governed by assignments and location. You could be gone for weeks or months. Who in their right mind would put up with that?

He had already requested that his next assignment should be one that took him out of direct field work, he was getting too old for it anyway. Bruno understood and had already secured his next posting. Phil would be managing the business relationship with a non-governmental venture capital firm that worked clandestinely with Security Services.

Historically, the CIA and FBI directed government spending as strategic investments in new technologies with start-ups. It was their way of controlling which new technology was developed for the public domain and which could be adopted by the intelligence community. It had been responsible for some of the fast-track developments in missile guidance systems, electronic surveillance, and counter cyberterrorism. The US government may be prohibited from making investments for profit, but it didn't stop them capitalising in a practical way. It would be seen as a cushy assignment, but given his long career, Phil thought it was about time he had cushy. Being shot at for a living was losing its appeal.

Daniel had been rehearsing his speech to the Home Secretary, trying to justify why he was getting involved in an active mission again. How naive he'd been when he accepted the role. He hadn't bargained for the ridiculous amounts of time he would have to spend justifying his department's actions, asking for more resources, and smoothing political feathers. He thought that running the service would give him complete autonomy. The reality was that he'd been able to make more decisions as an active field agent.

His old boss had made it look so easy, but she didn't have his problems. In truth, he held much of the civil service in contempt. He saw it as an out-of-date monolith that served no greater purpose than its own survival and perpetuation. It was filled with career bureaucrats who made decisions that could change someone's life completely but would never extend to include them personally. They were protected by triple locked, index-linked, gold-plated pensions and most of the time were completely oblivious to the real world of people risking their lives on a daily basis.

Active duty was a different world. His mind went back to the high point in his career ten years ago when in just one-week he had worked on four different continents. That week had changed the way he viewed life. He witnessed the worst poverty he had ever seen and by contrast, two days later, had experienced some of the most opulent luxury he had ever encountered. At the end of that week, he had lost his mother and seen his father begin the downward spiral that would lead to his death just months later. No amount of wealth or power could prevent that from happening.

Those memories and contrasts had left a lasting impression and reminded Daniel how fortunate he was to serve and work to make the world a safer place, regardless of circumstance. He struggled to find his purpose in the weeks that followed and turned to his old boss Ada Hale to find some answers. She'd helped him process it all. Hilary was right about her; she was a very wise woman.

He often replayed that conversation; it still helped him to reconcile the current nonsense he presided over. The disagreements over departmental budgets, the eye-rolling between those who were assigned to nice locations doing desk jobs and those who spent their time in the war zones, and consequently held a very different view of the service. He couldn't remember when he became this cynical and took the view that most politicians and civil servants really were a waste of oxygen. In his experience, you occasionally came across the odd one or two with integrity, capability, and principles, but it was a rarity. It was the people who did the job day-in and day-out that were worth something, people like those he was heading towards at this moment.

Shady Fields was the brainchild of his predecessor Celia Browning. She wanted to build something that acknowledged the sacrifice of agents who had given much in the service of their country, often at the cost of a personal life and all that it entailed. In reality, since the Cold War ended, agents seldom died in service. They grew old, retired, and drew their pensions. Sadly, some of them got dementia or Alzheimer's and start to talk, spilling the secrets of their missions. Their deception-filled lives had made it difficult to have a relationship based on falsehoods, so many end up alone. Many harboured real fears of getting close to someone whose very existence could be used as a weapon against them. Their deaths could be caused simply by association. The toughest part of the job was dealing with the guilt that you were still alive when so many of your friends and colleagues didn't make it home.

Brake lights on the patrol car in front of them indicated that they were stopping suddenly. In the distance a myriad of blue, red, and amber flashing lights bought all motorway traffic to a stop, and they had joined the back of a lengthy queue of parked cars. Traffic Police were making their way down the lanes of stationary traffic speaking to drivers through open windows.

Daniel got out of the car and flashed his ID at the approaching officer.

"We are in the middle of an operation, I need you to fast-track us along the hard shoulder, now officer."

"Sorry sir, I can't do that."

"It wasn't a request officer, it was an order, move whatever vehicle is in the way and lead us through."

"Sorry sir, I didn't make myself clear. I can't because the accident up ahead involves a ruptured diesel tanker. It hit a bridge support and thousands of litres of fuel have spilled across all three lanes and the hard shoulder. We have declared a major incident and we are in the process of closing the motorway. I will try to get you moving as quickly as I can, but you will need to go back to the previous exit. I can arrange an escort if you like, but that's the best I can do."

Daniel was seething. The remainder of the journey would be considerably slower, perhaps an extra half-hour or more added to their journey time. On the plus side, Callaghan would have the same problem if he was coming this way. Perhaps the traffic Gods were smiling down on them.

Hilary had been surprised when Callaghan had bought her story. Her excuses about not using a neutral venue had seemed weak even to her and yet, Callaghan seemed so consumed with the idea of getting to Dessie that he'd gone along with it. She hoped she had bought Daniel the time he needed, and it wasn't an exaggeration to say she felt huge relief to know that he was on his way.

Chapter 43:

Sunday 28th July 2019 11.05am

MI5 Interrogation facility London

Sinead hadn't yet opened her eyes and had no idea where she was, but she knew from her headache that something was not right. It was the pounding, bilious pain of the worst sort of hangover. She hadn't touched a drop in over a decade so it wasn't that. Her eyelids were heavy and she would have drifted back to sleep if it weren't for the cold. The hairs on her arms stood to attention and she shivered. She sat up after the third attempt and opened her eyes. She was on a bunk that was simply a metal tray attached to the wall, with nothing but a lumpy mattress to make it slightly more comfortable than sleeping on the concrete floor. There was no pillow, and only a thin hospital-type blanket for warmth.

She swung her leaden legs over the side of the bunk and steadied herself, her hands gripping the metal frame edge. The only fixtures in this tiny room were the bed and a seatless, stainless-steel toilet bowl in the corner, the sort with a hand wash basin built into the lid of the cistern. She was in a cell, but how the hell did she get here? Her memories were cloudy and jumbled as she tried to sift through them. Her eyes registered a bulkhead light positioned above a flush-fitting windowless, steel door. There was no handle on this side of the door, yes it was definitely a cell. Panic started to form in the pit of her stomach. Where was she? It was an important question, but the one that was really freaking her out was, who were her captors?

Mitch had messaged Daniel to say that they'd lifted Sinead successfully, but he understood that Daniel had more pressing matters had to deal with. Phil had gone with Daniel to provide protection for McFee and Hilary, so Mitch was left to conduct the interrogation by himself. Although there were two separate agendas at play here, his focus was clear, MI5 wanted to question Sinead about the murder of Cooper, the FRU soldier. It was a historical event, but a valid investigation now that new information had been provided by McFee.

The American interest was much more puzzling. They had evidence that she was involved with the Colombian bombing. On the face of it she was guilty of conspiracy at the very least. Mitch looked at all the available intel, but there were inconsistencies that didn't add up. If her profile was to be believed she was single-minded to the point of obsession about the fight for Irish unity, so how the hell had she got mixed up with a Colombian assassination plot? And more to the point, with the connections that the Colombians had, why were they going to a non-entity on a different continent to supply them with explosives?

The obvious questions of who was paying her, and what was she using the money for were not straightforward either. She was a woman who spent very little money on herself. She had normal expenses, no fancy car or holidays and a modest savings account. If she had been promoted to an international arms dealer, where was the money? Scanning the list of files that Phil Santos had sent him, he wondered if he should be bothered to go through all this historical stuff, but if Santos thought it was important, then there must be some link here.

He poured himself another coffee and settled down for a lesson in US-Irish relations. He certainly had the time. Considering what the snatch team had given her, she was likely to be out cold for another hour at least.

The first surprise he got when he opened the file was a handwritten note which said,

'Sensitive and from protected sources, no one must know that you have seen this or that I was instrumental in obtaining it. P'

The document was a CIA briefing paper from 2002, which had been prepared for the office of the US President, and although it was partially redacted, enough detail was left for Mitch to get a feel for the American view of the troubles and their part in funding the IRA.
He read the text:

> *The total amount of money contributed by Irish Americans will never be publicly known but it was significant. American funding all but dried up following 9/11 and the IRA had no choice but to put down their arms.*
> *The IRA was an expensive operation to run; paying a stipend to its active service operatives ("volunteers"), supporting the families of IRA members in prison, the widows, and children of those who had been killed in action, purchasing arms and munitions on the international black market, and funding the operations of Sinn Féin.*
>
> *It had two principal sources of revenue:*
> *(a) organized crime, such as armed robberies, kidnapping, smuggling, and counterfeiting, illegal drugs, and protection rackets; and*
> *(b) donations from Irish Americans.*

We also have concerns about links to Eastern Bloc countries and particularly Libya who have supported IRA activities, mainly with arms rather than cash. It is estimated that fundraising from Irish Americans has been the most important of these activities.

The second report Mitch looked at was prepared by Phil Santos himself during President Clinton's visit to Ireland. Santos had uncovered IRA links with Colombia as far back as '96 and Bruno Gomes had been one of the negotiators seeking to influence the Anglo-Irish agreement.

What the report described was a disclosure of how IRA engineers had been sent to train rebel fighters in Colombia with rocket launchers and mortar bomb technology. The enemies they were fighting at the time were American servicemen. The IRA leadership had tried to deny this, but the Americans had evidence, and used it to threaten a complete withdrawal of political and financial support. It seemed to be the straw that broke the camel's back because it heralded the beginning of negotiations for the Good Friday Agreement. The threat of losing more than $1million a year was too much; they announced a significant decommissioning of arms to commence immediately.

Clinton's advisors knew American politicians would see the IRA's relationships with the Colombians and their drug-pedalling reputation as devastating.

The IRA had tried to wait it out, to see if Clinton would pressure the British into a withdrawal, but that was never going to happen. The majority of the American/Irish supporters were as right wing as the extreme IRA were left wing. The relationship was growing cooler, and the IRA were left with little choice.

Mitch was surprised at the level of American involvement and influence they had, in the run-up to the negotiations. And he wondered why Phil had offered him this historical Colombian link if it didn't have something to do with their current investigation.

There was also a series of text messages between Sinead and a contact called Mungo Boser. Santos didn't say how he'd come by these texts, just that he'd had no luck tracing the man. Instinctively he felt that it was a CIA legend, but not an active one. What was clear was that 'he', Mungo, had acted as the go between for the Colombians and Sinead.

Mitch felt like he was knitting fog. He was inundated with information but nothing that explained why Sinead was involved. He thought that he had stalled for long enough, it was time to interview Sinead and see what answers he could get from her.

He was already seated in the interview room when the guards bought her in. She looked tired and drawn, and yet there was a feistiness about her that Mitch had to admire. For someone who had no idea where she was or what this was about, she seemed remarkably cool about it all. The taller of the two guards shoved her roughly into the plastic seat opposite Mitch and stepped back but remained within an arm's length behind her.

Mitch spoke without looking at her. "So, Sinead, did you have a nice rest?"

She stared at him with dark, penetrating eyes but remained silent.

He lifted his head. "I get that you don't want to talk to me. But you should know that I have all the time in the world. No one knows where you are; your brother thinks you have taken a holiday to let the heat die down a bit. And there is no one else to miss you, is there Sinead?"

He let that sink in for a while flicking idly through the folder in front of him.

"Let's be clear about your situation. No one knows you are missing, and no one is looking for you. We could keep you here for weeks, months maybe and no one would turn a hair."

He saw the anger surge in her from across the table.

"Who the feck are you people? What do you want with a researcher from the Irish assembly?"

Mitch gave the briefest of smiles. With her utterance the dance had begun.

"I don't think you get what's happening here. You don't ask questions; you have to answer them. If you fail to do so, then in all likelihood you will not leave here in one piece. Not because we will harm you, we don't play those games; however, we do know people who are very keen that we hand you over to them. They do play those sorts of games. It's your choice really, I'm not bothered one way or the other."

His voice was quiet and measured, which made it seem all the more menacing.

"You haven't got anything on me. I know who you are, you're spooks, British Secret Service. As soon as the Party realise that I have gone, they will ask questions and you will be in deep shite for putting the agreement in danger."

"Yes, you might think so, but there's a major flaw in your reasoning, allow me to explain what that is. Our American friends, you know, the ones who waterboard suspects, well, they want to know when you were last in Bogotá. They have pictures of you at the airport but apparently you didn't stay long. It was just a few weeks before the country's President was blown up and American civilians died. The cause of the explosion was a device made with Irish Semtex, old but still very effective. They are testing the hypothesis that there may be a link.

Irish Semtex and a woman who now works for Sinn Féin in the Irish parliament called Sinead Devey, and who, incidentally, used to be the quartermaster for an active IRA cell back in the day. I can't think why they might have jumped to that conclusion, can you?"

Fear flicked across her face for the first time. Had she got it wrong? She couldn't understand why she was being questioned about this. It was the Americans that had bought her into the Colombian deal, why would they suddenly want to question her about it now?

She tried to remain cool, "I was in Colombia on an international trade mission, I had nothing to do with any explosions or Semtex." Even to her ears, her denial sounded hollow.

Mitch smiled at her and looked directly into her eyes. "If that's the case, why was it not recorded in the official calendar, and why were the tickets not purchased through normal channels? That sounds like someone wanting to stay below the radar to me."

She realised that she had a decision to make, get this cleared up quickly and gain release, or protect her American contact who had offered her no protection in return for the favour she had done him. When push came to shove this was a dangerous game to play and her loyalty was definitely not to any Yank.

"If I co-operate, what do I get out of it?"

"You will get the chance to experience freedom again, at some point, but there's a lot of information we need before that can happen. We need to know how you got involved. Who approached you and how that came about?"

Sinead considered his words for less than a millisecond before making her decision.

"My contact was a man called Mungo Boser. We met back in '96. He worked for American intelligence. We required funds and he needed a contact for the Colombians that couldn't be traced back to the CIA. The Colombians were offering a lot of money for expertise and hardware, so he connected us. Obviously, all that was before the Agreement was negotiated. I thought no more about it, then he called me out of the blue about six months ago, for one last favour, as he put it. He wanted to provide untraceable explosives for the Colombians again and thought I might be able to help. I did go to Bogotá but the quantities they were looking for were beyond me, so I had to refuse."

"Don't treat me like a fool Sinead. We've already identified the explosives used in the Colombian attack as old IRA Semtex, and we can prove you supplied it. What I want to know is why you did it, was it just the money?"

She wanted this to be over, quickly.

"The money was secondary. He pressured me into it. He was going to make my past public in a big way, he's got stuff on me. You lot wouldn't have hesitated to haul me in if he had gone public with it."

"Well, call me cynical if you like but I don't think you scare that easily. I think it's more likely that your contact promised to reactivate US funding to restart a bombing campaign that would bring the Peace Agreement to an end."

Guilt flashed across the woman's face.

"That's ridiculous. Why would I want to break the agreement? I work in the Assembly for the Executive, for God's sake!"

"But you know it's not working don't you Sinead. All the promises that were made and yet, the reality is that you are no nearer a united Ireland than you were thirty years ago. You've got rid of the soldiers, the checkpoints, and the patrols, but you still dance to a Westminster tune. I have never understood the passion to get the British out of Ireland and at the same time engage in slavish support to the EU where Irish Sovereignty will never be recognised."

"That's where you are wrong. We want to be a part of a forward-looking country that works together to break down barriers as opposed to a class-ridden, old school tie network. The British pay lip service to equality, they don't want collaboration, they want to maintain the status quo. Borders keep people in their place. The reality of Irish membership of the EU is that it's our CHOICE, not a hangover of a feudal system where we are still treated as second-class citizens."

"There's a problem with your logic Sinead. Any perceived gain won by violence is only temporary, however the damage it does is permanent. The people of Northern Ireland will not thank you for taking them back into conflict and fighting on the streets."

“Sometimes people don’t know what’s best for them until they see the end result.” She was absolutely defiant and bore the appearance of the indoctrinated freedom fighter. It was a scary thing.

“We are going to have to agree to disagree, as I really don’t have time for this debate now. Tell me about your contact, Mungo Boser? Obviously, a pseudonym, what’s his real name?”

Sinead looked like a sulky teenager.

“How the hell should I know! It’s what I’ve always called him.”

“Why did he want to blow up the President and the American contractors if he was working for the service? Either he was lying, or you are.”

Sinead swallowed hard. She hadn’t realised until he said it out loud, but the spook was right. It didn’t add up, and she could be left high and dry unless she could convince him that she was telling the truth.

“He told me that the explosives were for the Colombian Army to deal with dissident rebels in the north, he never mentioned an assassination. Boser said American interests would be better served if the Colombians had a stronger leader in power, and to ensure that, they had to deal with the rebels who were trying to derail the election. If I got him the Semtex he said he could reactivate some of the old funding streams for us to reignite a revolution of our own. Do you have any idea what will happen to Ireland if the UK leaves the EU? The borders will be put in place again and a United Ireland will be put back decades. We will need to fight it with everything we have, which is not much at the moment."

Mitch decided to take a different tack.

"How did you know he worked for American Intelligence?"

"What do you mean?" she asked, genuinely puzzled.

"Well, I could tell you I worked for the KGB, but you would know I wasn't being truthful, wouldn't you?"

Sinead sat and thought about this for a few minutes.

"He was an American, he had an American accent and he told me he was with the CIA. He knew all about the funding we got, and the US channels it went through. After the first contact he was true to his word and US funding was there. I believed him. Then later, I saw him when Clinton attended secret talks with Sinn Fein and I saw him in the entourage. He would have needed to be Secret Service to get that close to the President surely?"

Mitch was disturbed by her revelation. She was right, if the man she had spoken with had been that close to a US President then his credentials would not be questioned.

"I need to know what he looked like, describe him to me."

Later, Mitch was reviewing the notes he had made when his phone rang, it was Daniel. He answered immediately.

"I think we might have a problem, Daniel. Sinead Devey is saying that her involvement with the Colombians was orchestrated by the CIA, her handler was someone called Mungo Boser. I've checked, but there isn't an active agent with that legend according to our records, and Santos says he has also drawn a blank."

This new development troubled Daniel. There was clearly another agenda playing out that they couldn't fully comprehend yet.

"It does explain why the CIA wanted her so badly. If the assassination was an off-the-books operation, it raises two key questions; Who is running it and why? I am not convinced that if I confront Bruno with this now, I'll get an honest answer. Do you think that's all she has?"

Mitch pondered his response. "Yes, I do, but I think we should keep hold of her for her own safety, at least until we know what's going on."

"Agreed. Bruno's in this up to his ears but I am not clear about the game he's playing, and I am a bit distracted at the moment. We are on our way to Derbyshire to where Hilary and Marina are holding Dessie. I think we've done enough to get there before Callaghan but it's still going to be tricky. I'll call you when it's over."

Daniel thought it was time to put a cat amongst the pigeons so he called Bruno's direct number and left a message.

"Hi Bruno, this is a professional courtesy call to let you know that we have Sinead Devey in custody, and she is helping us with an historical investigation. Until that is concluded, any request you make to speak with her needs to come through formal channels. I will need to know what you want to question her about, with some detail about how it fits into your bigger investigations. Just to let you know, she is being surprisingly helpful."

Chapter 44:

Sunday 28th July 2019

Ada's Cottage Derbyshire

The postcode had been entered into the satnav correctly and showed the general location, but Seamus was having difficulty locating the property. He knew it was around here somewhere but the lanes they were travelling along didn't even register as proper roads. It was just before 5am and it was already getting light.

"Where the bloody hell is this place? It's no wonder they are using it as a safe house. It's so safe no one can find it." Callaghan barked.

Seamus steered the car into a narrow track barely wide enough for the vehicle to pass, if this was wrong, he would have to reverse, he certainly wouldn't be able to turn around. The 'road' was no more than compacted earth with grass growing between the tyre tracks. It made for a bumpy ride for the occupants of the fully laden car.

"Are you sure we're in the right place Seamus?" Callaghan said crossly. "It wouldn't be the first time you lost your bearings after all."

"If it's not here then I don't know where to try next Mr. Callaghan."

They continued slowly along the track, as they rounded a bend the roof of the cottage became visible above the high hedges.

"Stop here Seamus, get out and have look around. I don't want to walk into an ambush."

Jackie noted how apprehensive Callaghan was now that they had arrived. He kept nervously adjusting his grip on the pistol. She knew that this made him more dangerous, as it increased the possibility of him accidentally discharging the gun. They all watched as Seamus approached the gates and took a furtive glance into the driveway. He then skirted the hedges that bordered the side and rear of the property until he was out of sight.

It seemed like an age before he reappeared, making his way make to the car in a low stoop. Seamus was slightly breathless.

"There's a single car in the drive and everywhere is quiet. No visible guards. What do you want to do next Mr. Callaghan?"

He called the number again and Hilary answered.

"Hello."

"I want you to open the front door then raise your hands where I can see them. I will have Theresa with me. The other hostage will stay in the car with my man who is also armed. Any sign of an ambush and he will kill her. Do you understand?"

"Yes." What else could she say? Where the hell was Daniel?

Callaghan readied himself and gave orders to Seamus.

"Tape her up and stick her in the boot then go around to the back of the house. I want an element of surprise."

Seamus popped the boot lid, pulling a struggling Layla around to the back of the vehicle. He grabbed a roll of duct-tape and began binding her hands in front of her. Callaghan used his gun to motion Theresa out of the car.

"Don't do anything stupid or I will shoot you and come back for her, understand?"

She nodded.

Seamus lifted the woman up and dropped her into the boot. She landed heavily on an assortment of ropes, tarpaulin, and various tools. That would hurt he thought as he slammed the lid shut and went back to the driver's door, taking his gun from the side pocket. He slammed that door shut too.

"Jesus Seamus, could you attract any more attention? Why not turn the radio on full, there are people back in Belfast that didn't quite hear you."

He sighed heavily as he watched his boss move towards the front door. He was getting sick of being the butt of Callaghan's frustration. Not everything was his fault. He'd saved Callaghan's hide back at the care home, and all he had got for his trouble was abuse.

Callaghan positioned Theresa in front of him as a shield, gripping her arm tightly. She yelped, but he ignored her and pushed his gun roughly into her ribs. The door opened and a tall, slim, red-headed woman stood there with her hands in the air.

"Hilary?"

She nodded and stood aside to let them enter.

"No, you lead the way."

She turned slowly and moved ahead of them down the wide hall, past a room on the right that was filled with bookshelves and on towards the back of the house. Early morning light was streaming in through windows that overlooked the small rear garden. Callaghan followed, pausing only to kick the front door shut behind them.

They entered the kitchen, sitting at the table with a cup of coffee in front of him was Dessie McFee.

"Where are the others?"

Dessie looked puzzled.

"There are no others. We had to leave in a hurry when you and Yilmaz announced your arrival. She bought me here", he nodded towards the woman,

"There are just the two of us."

Callaghan glared at her.

"So it was a load of bullshit when you said you were trying to find out his location. You were with him all the time. I don't like being lied to."

He cocked the gun, pushing it harder into Theresa's side, making her grimace with pain.

He was clearly angry about the delaying tactic, but then a thought dawned on him.

"If you're waiting for reinforcements don't hold your breath. The motorway is closed due to an accident of some sort. We were diverted before we got caught up in it, but the traffic was backing up even then. If they were in front of us they are cooling their heels waiting for the police to clear the jam. They could be hours yet."

Finally, a smile crossed his face.

The woman spoke, "Is Layla OK?"

"She's in the boot of my car feeling very uncomfortable and no doubt very afraid, and that is where she will stay until I've concluded my business here."

Callaghan roughly shoved Theresa towards the table, Dessie was on his feet in an instant to stop her from stumbling. He caught her in his arms and guided her into the vacant chair next to him.

"Well, look at you two. The big reunion, no tears, no professing undying love? See Dessie, this is what you betrayed us for. A British spy who lied to you from the beginning. She had your card marked, took you in hook, line, and sinker. Told you she loved you and all the time she was selling you and the rest of us down the river."

He spat the last sentence out.

Dessie checked that she was OK before looking up at JJ. "It was so long ago. I know you want me, so let her go."

"Time is irrelevant. It's your heritage she sold out. Or have you forgotten what happened to your Da and the rest of them?"

Dessie's eyes flashed anger and he thumped the table

"Jesus Christ JJ, you don't hear the crap you spout, do you? My Da wanted the best for his family at a time when that wasn't possible. I'm ashamed to think what he would say if he could see me now."

Callaghan shouted, "He would see a god-damn filthy tout who's sold his birthright to his oppressors at a bargain price! Betrayal is worse when it is done by someone you've known and trusted all their lives. Betrayal by your enemies is to be expected, but betrayal by your friends is unforgivable. You're just another in a long line of turncoats. They were willing to set aside years of struggle for a cushy job on the hill and political respectability bestowed on them by those we had sworn to eradicate. I thought you of all people would understand that. What's happened to you? We used to believe in the same things. I never thought you would turn your back on me too Dessie."

Dessie shook his head in disbelief

"Is that honestly what you think? If Da was here now he would be ashamed of us both JJ. Me for being a career killer, a common criminal that fell into this because he mistook another common criminal for an honest leader. But he would be most ashamed of what you've become. I'm nothing like you JJ. I never supported women and kids getting drawn into the fight and punished without question. The gangs who meted out beatings to fifteen-and sixteen-year-olds were twisted. You did it for the fear it generated, and Seamus for the pleasure it gave him. It was never about justice. I turned and looked the other way when it was booze, fags, and even drugs. When you were running brothels in Belfast filled with women on the game who were there as a matter of choice or necessity, I could even stomach that. But when you began trafficking kids that had been kidnapped, I couldn't square that no more."

Dessie glowered at his old mentor. "My Da trusted you to look after me and set me right, not to turn me into a killer with no chance for a future, without a family and without the things he valued. You think you knew him but you didn't. He would have taken the opportunity to stop the violence and build a peaceful solution. How proud would he be to see the company you keep now? That psycho Yilmaz, the kids he buys and sells so that some pervert can get a fix. Is that really how you want to be remembered? Because I don't, it makes me sick, that's why I want out! I want to see if I can live the rest of my life repairing some of the damage I've done. I can never bring people back, but I can stop any more lives being ruined by my hand or yours. Taking Yilmaz out is an act of public service on its own. He doesn't even think like a human being."

Callaghan exploded. "You ungrateful little bastard! I could understand if that tripe came out of Seamus's mouth, he's about as sharp as a marble, but not you. I fought shoulder to shoulder with your Da for the cause. We are the injured parties here, sold out by our own because they didn't want to be associated with the dirty work they gave us to do. We did what was necessary and we did it willingly. They didn't do right by us Dessie, and we had to resort to other measures just to survive. It's their fault I do what I do. Sold out by everyone and left to make a living however I could. I don't understand why you've become so squeamish all of a sudden. We always operated on the wrong side of the law to earn what we needed. When did you suddenly grow a conscience?"

They were so busy shouting at each other, neither of them noticed that Seamus had entered the kitchen by the back door and was listening to the argument as it raged.

Dessie continued, "there's a world of difference in peddling booze and fags or even robbing from those who have everything, for the benefit of those that don't, but Christ JJ, people trafficking. Tatum was fifteen years old, and now she is dead!"

"I didn't kill her, Yilmaz did!"

"But you might as well have. You let him spread his poison right across our country. The very people you talk about fighting for are stuck with kids they don't recognise because they're permanently high. They live in ghettos where brothels filled with KIDS are their neighbours. They get caught up in gangs, stabbings, and shootings at the whim of a man who seeks power to do exactly what he wants, and exploits whoever he needs to get it. I'm just sorry it took me as long as it did to wake up to what's happening and stop you both. It won't be long before Seamus realises that you're doing the same thing to him, gives up his hero worship and sees you for who you really are."

Callaghan let out a laugh. "Do me a favour, Seamus will continue to do exactly what I tell him to because he has no other opinion, he's too stupid to think for himself. Anything that's been done in my name has been carried out by that moron. He'll take the rap for it, which is how I planned it. His mother should have thrown him away and kept the stork. My job here is to finish you both off then escape to somewhere hot and sunny and leave Seamus to carry the can. It's about time I caught a break."

While Callaghan was speaking, McFee was inching towards him. Callaghan raised his gun and aimed it at Theresa. Dessie lunged at JJ, propelling his body-weight at him.

They collided, and all hell broke loose as they began a violent dance of death. Dessie made a grab for Callaghan's gun, smashing his forehead into Callaghan's face. JJ recoiled from the headbutt, his nose streaming blood. He grabbed Dessie by the back of the head, pulling him down and forwards into his body. Dessie had his hands on the gun. They struggled, twisting, turning, shouting, kicking, and firing punches at each other.

A gunshot rang out! Dessie and Callaghan were locked face-to-face staring at each other, as immobile as statues. After a few seconds, Dessie staggered away from Callaghan. His hands were still gripping the barrel of Callaghan's gun, but a vivid red stain was spreading across the middle of his chest. Callaghan recoiled in shock.

"It didn't have to be like this Dessie, you were a good kid, I loved you like a son, it should have never come to this… I only wanted……"

He never got to finish the sentence. Seamus flew at Callaghan like a man possessed. He didn't even notice Dessie hit the floor. His only focus was Callaghan, he screamed profanities at him as he repeatedly smashed the butt of his gun into the side of Callaghan's head. Under the brutal force of the assault, the older man fell to the ground. Seamus was quickly on top of him, beating him with his fists.

Daniel stood in the doorway, gun drawn, Hilary, and Layla were close behind him.

After Callaghan's phone call, Hilary had concealed herself in the library. When she heard him tell Marina where Layla was, she waited for the door to close and slipped out to release her. Daniel and Phil arrived just minutes afterwards. She briefed them and they decided that Daniel and Hilary would go in through the front to try to capture Callaghan and Seamus. Phil would cover the back of the house in case anyone tried to escape. They had not expected the carnage they found.

On hearing the gunshot, Phil sprinted around to the rear of the cottage and burst in through the back door, weapon drawn. Marina was standing over a subdued and weeping Seamus, now in handcuffs, who was staring at his bosses bloodied and battered body and muttering,

"He shouldn't have treated me like that, I did everything for him. I never killed anybody that didn't deserve it."

Phil couldn't believe the relief he felt knowing Marina was unharmed.

Theresa was in the middle of the room cradling Dessie in her arms. It was clear that Dessie was mortally injured. She had grabbed a towel and was applying pressure to stem the bleeding but it was never going to be enough. He looked up at her, a solitary tear trickled from his eye, tracked across his cheek and into his hairline. In a barely audible whisper he said,

"You know there was never anyone else Theresa, it was always you I loved. I made such a mess of things. I should've had the courage to leave and start a new life with you when we talked about it. I'm so sorry."

Theresa tenderly cradled his head in her lap, tears streaming down her face.

"I loved you too Dessie and I missed you every day."

She watched as the light went from his still beautiful brown eyes.

Chapter 45:

Monday 29th July 2019 8.00am

Dealing with the fallout

Daniel needed to clean up this mess before it got out of hand.

"Colm, you should have seen this coming. What have we been paying you for all these years, you didn't even know that the biggest threat to the GFA came from your own bloody sister! Well, I'm telling you, this stops now. Don't you find it ironic that Dessie gave us more useful intel in two days than you've given us in twenty years? We have taken down the cartel, captured Interpol's top two most wanted and left Belfast businesses thousands of Euros better off by smashing Callaghan's protection racket, all thanks to Dessie." "I was never party to Callaghan's dealings Daniel. I tipped you off when something big might be going down, it's not my fault if it never came to anything. All these years I have taken a risk, living a double life so that I could be in the right place when you needed me. At great personal risk I might add."

There was that familiar whinge again that had begun to grate on Daniel.

"It strikes me that the risk was ours, we stood by while your political career flourished. I've watched you win elections one photo opportunity at a time, never having to account for your actions. I've kept you in play at great risk to other assets. Those days are over. This episode has rendered it necessary for me to inform the PM of your history with us. I am sorry Colm, but our arrangement has come to an end. The report I file will have a top secret—eye's only classification, so there's no immediate threat to you, but I suggest you consider your next steps very carefully. There will definitely be fallout from Sinead's activities which will make life awkward for you."

Colm listened and replied, the sound of defeat in his voice. "The Party leadership is not happy about the revelations the Minister shared regarding Sinead and the Colombians. In fact, I have a party executive meeting today in Stormont to discuss the situation. They are all in asshole-protect mode wondering how they can limit the damage when this becomes public knowledge. They will want this buried and demand a press embargo on the whole thing. “Well, you might as well hear this from me, the Americans will go for extradition for her part in the assassination.”

Colm became more animated,

“Daniel, you have to stop it. She won’t survive that.”

“Sorry Colm, it’s out of my hands. They’ve already approached the Foreign Secretary and he is keen to do them a favour before our UK/US trade deal is signed at the end of the year. I hope she likes the taste of prison food because it looks like she is going to get a lot of it.”

Daniel decided to turn the screw a little more.

“And if I were you Colm, I would be putting plan B into operation as soon as you get into the office!”

“But Danny, I don’t have a plan B.”

“Don’t be ridiculous Colm, a strategist like you always has a plan B.”

It was just before 10am when the intercom on his desk flashed, the tinny voice of his PA came from the loudspeaker,

“The Home Secretary is here sir, she is alone, shall I show her in?”

“Get her a coffee, I just need a couple of minutes”

She was early and Daniel thought she must have come directly from briefing the Prime Minister. That wasn’t good. He knew there would have been a damage limitation discussion and talk about how the situation could be spun to give the government the best possible tactical advantage. He would have expected the Minister for Northern Ireland to be with her. Daniel did not like how this was shaping up.

He checked his email inbox before clicking the intercom button, “I am free now Anna-Marie, please send the Home Secretary in.”

The politician swept into the room, the sense of power and entitlement dripping from her. She sat in the padded chair on the opposite side of Daniel’s desk, fuming.

“I don’t like being kept waiting.” she snarled.

“Sorry Minister, I was on a secure call about another operation. Presumably you are here to tell me that we will be recommending Sinead Devey is committed to trial for the murder of Corporal Cooper? Even after all this time I am sure his family will get some closure by seeing his killer bought to justice.” Daniel waited for the excuses to begin.

Her voice was an audible oil slick.

“The PM is not sure that a public prosecution would serve any useful purpose at this stage. His main priority is getting Stormont sitting on a regular basis and dealing with the mounting policy backlog that has built up since the assembly was suspended. The revelation about the agent you were running will also be buried, Sinn Féin leaders would have a field day with that. The Minister for NI will use the Devey case as a lever to get them back around the table and begin the next Assembly session."

"I am not sure how the loyalists will react to that"

"Don't be ridiculous Daniel, they will never know! You still don't seem to appreciate the nuances of political expediency. We want you to offer her a deal, she resigns her job and her office in the Party, draws her pension and drops off the grid. Because of the connection, we need her brother to do the same thing. He will be tainted by association, and we don't want anyone digging into that compost heap, do we? He will make way for a younger and more astute representative; they are sorting a retirement package for him as we speak. The leader of the party will make a big thing of it, thank him for exemplary service blah blah…"

"So even though we have incontrovertible evidence of her committing murder and then supporting some sort of US black op' resulting in the death of a sitting South American President you want her to be given a free pass?"

"No offence Daniel, but you need to grow up! The fallout would damage Anglo-Irish and Anglo-US relationships irreparably if we were to take the moral high ground on this one. This is how the PM wants it. You can always put her on a watch list if that makes you feel better."

Daniel could barely contain his anger.

"No offence meant Minister, but plenty taken. This is not a game. If the Agreement is to have any integrity at all we must hold people to account, otherwise what's the point of it?"

Her eyes flashed at his challenge.

"You need to remember who you are speaking to. You and your lot are appointed into jobs, my colleagues and I are elected by the people to serve in Her Majesty's Government, the same government that employs the security services. We have oversight on what you do, which means I call the shots."

She softened a little, "But there is some good news, I am giving you the green light to go after those orchestrating the black op'. It never hurts to have something to hold over the CIA, does it?"

She rose from her chair in a cloud of self-satisfaction and Chanel N° 5, waving her hand airily at him.

"Let me know the outcome." And she was gone.

Daniel thumped the desk and his computer monitor shook.

"And who has oversight over your decisions and actions minister?"

The day was getting away from him, it was nearly 4.30pm already. A sharp knock preceded Mitch's appearance in the doorway.

"Can I come in? I gather you saw the Home Secretary earlier. Am I OK as I am, or should I be armed?"

Daniel shook his head, "With the best will in the world Mitch I am no diplomat, and this political circus is so frustrating."

He indicated a seat then pressed his intercom again

"Where are Agents Gomes and Santos, Anna-Marie?"

"They are on the way up Daniel, I will send them straight in."

He needed to focus. This would test loyalties and friendships, he just hoped that he had backed the right side.

A knock on the door heralded the arrival of the two Americans who entered the room, both greeting him with "bonhomie' warmth. He indicated to the two seats Mitch had set out and ordered coffee via the intercom. Anna-Marie was also set to play her part.

"Well gentlemen, I met with the Home Secretary this morning and I am afraid it's not good news. The politicians have decided to forego any historic prosecution for Sinead Devey which also means any extradition request will be denied. This is not my preferred solution but it's the one the government has decided on, so we will have to abide by it."

Bruno looked puzzled "Does that mean she gets away with it free and clear because I'm not sure that I like the sound of that."

"The Foreign Secretary is worried about the impact a prosecution would have on the Peace Agreement, and the PM is advising that we put Sinead on a watch list, but she will cease all current activities with immediate effect. I am not happy about it either but there it is."

Bruno's eyebrows tensed and he was obviously choosing his words carefully.

"The Oval Office was quite clear that we identify and bring to justice those behind the assassination, to send a clear message to anyone that might seek to disrupt democratic elections in the future. They also want justice for the American lives that were lost. If I go back with this message Daniel, they won't take it without pushing back."

"No Bruno, I expect they will, but it's a political decision, although there may be some room for manoeuvre if you decide to share what you have about the black op' that set this hare running in the first place."

"What do you mean? There is no black op'"

"It's clear from our initial debrief that Sinead Devey believes she was recruited by the CIA to provide training and hardware to the Colombians in '96 and that the latest transaction was just an extension of that supply relationship. It would make sense because it was the same contact that brokered both operations. The fact that you can't officially locate Mungo Boser suggests you have a rogue agent in your ranks."

"Now hold on a minute, you're taking the word of a known terrorist that any or all of this took place. There is no evidence that the CIA was involved. Our own internal enquiries have drawn a blank Daniel. You need to be careful that she isn't leading you on a wild goose chase."

"Well, someone's leading the goose chase. Let's look at the evidence shall we?

Bruno, you were the one that offered us Agent Santos here as an extra pair of hands when you heard about our Irish Supergrass. You needed to know who it was because if it turned out to be Sinead, everything might come tumbling out. When he reported back that it was Dessie McFee you realised that you had a bit more time, but you still needed to know what he knew in case Sinead had been less than discrete. Then you heard that we had lifted her, and how cooperative she was being."

"That's completely ridiculous! It makes no sense, what would I get out of it?"

The office door opened and Anna-Marie entered with a loaded coffee tray. She deftly slid it onto Daniel's desk, handing him an envelope at the same time.

"Here are the photographs you requested from the US Embassy."

Everyone's attention was suddenly focused on the envelope in Daniel's hand, which bore the US seal. Anna-Marie closed the door behind her.

Daniel continued, "Is it also a coincidence that the rogue agents' legend, Mungo Boser, is an anagram of Bruno Gomes?"

Bruno rallied and replied sarcastically,

"Oh, please. Do you honestly think I would use such a clumsy device if I was running a black op'? Why on earth would I create such an obvious link to myself? I am too experienced to make such a rookie error."

"Unless that's exactly what you wanted us to think. I have a couple of photos that you might find interesting."

He removed the black and white press photographs from the envelope and handed them to Bruno to look at.

"What am I looking at?" he said impatiently.

"They are the official photos taken when Clinton visited Northern Ireland to give the negotiations a helping hand. You should remember them being taken, that is you just behind the President is it not?"

Bruno studied the picture, "Yes, it's me. I was part of his security detail, along with eighteen other agents."

"So, you were in Belfast on the President's visit when Sinead Devey was approached by Mungo Boser for the original Colombian deal. You were the head of the British desk in London when Mungo coincidentally reappears and arranges delivery of old Irish Semtex to a Colombian General, and within months an assassination takes place using said explosives. You head up the investigation into it and when you hear that we are about to debrief an old IRA commander, you orchestrate the loan of one of your agents who reports directly to you, sent to us to find out who it is and what they know. Stop me if I am wrong about any of this."

"Daniel, I know how this looks, but you've got it all wrong. Why would I do any of this?"

"As I understand it Bruno, a lot of your time recently has been briefing the senate oversight committee on why your funding shouldn't be reduced. They seem to think that traditional counter-intelligence is old hat, and that they would be better served investing in new technology and electronic surveillance. Fewer agents would definitely lead to a smaller budget. I can think of several million reasons why you might be prompted to take action."

Daniel turned to Phil Santos who had remained silent throughout the exchange.

"You have been remarkably quiet Agent Santos, does this all fit together for you?"

Santos sat shaking his head in disbelief, thinking carefully before replying,

"I did wonder why the investigation into the assassination seemed to be going so slowly. And the secrecy, and the need for me to report directly to you Bruno, I just can't believe it. I've worked with you for years; I thought you were so trustworthy."

Bruno was now angry, "Don't come over so innocent, it was you that requested the Colombian operation and you that suggested we needed an inside track on the British informant."

"Well, you would say that now Bruno, you can try to shift the blame, but you know the truth."

Santos turned his attention to Daniel.

"As soon as I began to suspect something was not right, I came to you Daniel."

"Yes, that's true Phil, you did come to me, but only because we lifted Sinead before your extraction team could get to her. She was very helpful by the way. We showed her the photos and she recognised Bruno from the first visit."

He took the photo from Bruno and passed it to Santos.

"Just there, behind Clinton, do you see him?"

Santos nodded.

"But if you look more carefully, on the last row, second from the left, that's you, isn't it?"

Phil gave the picture a cursory glance,

"Yes, it is. I was stationed at our London Embassy at the time.

"Oh yes of course, but you became quite the Irish expert while you were there, didn't you?"

"I was very junior at the time." Bruno snorted, "No such thing as a junior CIA agent, and you came as a cultural attaché which is shorthand for agent."

Santos shifted uncomfortably in his seat.

Daniel continued. "So, you were here when Clinton was, and looking at your passport history, you've been a regular visitor to Northern Ireland for the last twenty years. We only have your word that Bruno offered you to us to carry intel back to him. You could have easily suggested it to him, as a trusted agent and he would have listened. It's also strange that a request for files going back to the killing of an FRU soldier came from you Phil. No reason at all why they might be of interest to you, and you would never have got access to them if you hadn't been working with MI5. If it was you leading the black op' it might have amused you to use an anagram of Bruno's name to implicate him. What's really interesting, is that not only did Sinead recognise Bruno from the photos, but she also identified you, as Mungo Boser."

There was silence as Daniel's last statement sank in.

"You're not going to take the word of a terrorist with blood on her hands are you?"

Bruno stared at Santos in disgust. "What was in it for you Phil? I don't understand."

Santos glared at him. "No, you wouldn't. You are weak Bruno; you have always been. You stood by and watched them strip away the layers of national protection that we had built so carefully since 9/11. We currently have more than 200,000 people working in security services at the moment and we are still not winning the war on terror. People think it's all about the Middle East, but we are facing threats much closer to home. South Americans traffick drugs and fill their coffers with impunity. Some of that money funds activities designed to weaken us and make us vulnerable. They want to take away our status as the most powerful country in the world."

We are the guardians of the free world, and without us the world would quickly take on a different look and feel. The only constant we have is the security service. Administrations come and go, they all have their own version of America's role in the world, but ours is the one that keeps us on top, protecting the world from itself. Diplomacy has its place, but in the bigger picture it's too fickle and lacks teeth."

Back in the nineties we were actively encouraged to support the Colombians to eradicate their enemies, insurgents if you prefer. A change of administration, and suddenly the Colombian government are the enemy and those same insurgents are rebranded as freedom fighters wanting a regime change."

We are just expected to toe the line and focus on whoever they tell us the enemy is. We know who our enemies are because we see the threats and where they come from. Technology has its uses, but there's no substitute for the intelligence you gather from working on the ground."

Bruno, you are letting people who know nothing of how intelligence communities work dictate how we should operate. The only way to stop that is to reinforce the value of having people on the ground. If that means creating false flag operations that keep politicians focused on what we want them to see and the funding flowing, then it's a price worth paying."

He eyed them both. "You will struggle to prove anything. I'm an experienced agent with a long and distinguished record of distraction techniques and trade craft."

Gomes was struggling to accept what he was hearing. "Look Phil, I know what you mean, but you can't control everything. What you may not be aware of, is the late Colombian President's temporary replacement has already arrested General Hernandez for his role in the assassination. The military have lost the support of the people and morale is low in the ranks; there's a queue forming to give up the conspirators. We have an eyewitness that can, and will place you at the centre of this whole debacle, and expose the money trail between the Colombians and Sinead Devey that you set up. Honestly, I'm struggling to see how you think you can get away with this."

Santos could see his entire plan unravelling before him. "I thought I'd done enough, but I hadn't factored in Dessie McFee. I knew he and Sinead had been close, served in the same IRA cell back in the day. I couldn't be certain how much she had shared with him. The stupid thing about it, is that if I hadn't made the connection, you wouldn't have either."

Bruno stood and faced his once trusted agent

"Your weapon and badge please Agent Santos."

Phil reached slowly inside his jacket for his service weapon. He removed it from its holster and handed it, handle first to Bruno, quickly followed by his shield. Bruno raised a finger and lightly tapped his earpiece,

"Please come in and secure the prisoner."

Two formidable looking, suited, and booted agents appeared at the door. If he was being honest, Daniel hadn't expected Santos to fold so quickly, or go so quietly, but it was clear that he appreciated how limited his options had become since entering the office.

"Just one thing I don't understand Phil, how long had you been planning this, it can't have been for twenty years, no one has foresight that's that accurate."

"The writing was on the wall when this administration came in; the bleeding-heart liberals who think that world peace is actually possible. Those of us who operate on the dark side of the tracks know what we have to do to keep the world safe. Mungo Boser was put in place at the request of the service, but he was always off the radar. Clinton and others like him know the meaning of plausible deniability. When it became a necessity to acquire non-American explosives quickly, I took advantage of an old contact and an old legend. On reflection, it was an expensive coincidence that I should have thought through more carefully.

Gomes was visibly controlling his anger.

"Years ago, I was diving in the Seychelles, just off Palm Island and when I came to the surface I realised I'd lost the signet ring my father gave me. I dived again and again, searching the seabed for it but never found it. Last year I went back to the same place and went to a seafood restaurant on the beach. I ordered red snapper and when it came it was huge, just lying on my plate. I cut it open and what do you think I found?"

"Your ring?"

"Nothing, I found nothing! That's what I like about coincidence, it doesn't really exist and everything means something."

Daniel watched as the guards led this once respected agent away to face the music. Just as they reached the door, Santos turned to Daniel and said,

"One last favour, please? Tell Marina I'm sorry."

It had been an exceptionally long day, and as he watched the London lights turn on along the embankment he poured himself a decent measure of Laphraoig, something he kept especially for days when he appreciated perversity. Anna-Marie knocked and put her head around the door.

"I'm leaving now Daniel, is there anything else you need before I go?"

He lifted his glass in salute "No, thanks, unless you want to join me?"

She smiled "Sorry I'm afraid I can't, dinner club tonight and I've already missed the starter. You might want to put the news on though, Reuters are reporting that Colm Devey has died from a suspected heart attack in his office today."

The Epilogue:

Thursday 29th August 2019 7.00pm

Belfast

Sinead breathed a sigh of relief as the taxi stopped in front of her apartment building. She stepped out of the cab and onto the pavement, having given the driver a decent tip. She took a long, deep breath. It was a warm, dry evening and she realised there was still at least a month of good weather to enjoy. It's strange the things you appreciate when you think you might not be able to enjoy them for much longer. The news of her brother's death had been a shock but being able to secure her liberty had gone a long way to lessening the blow.

She knew she'd been lucky; it had been a close call. She felt sure Colm had been instrumental in negotiating her release. The Brits and Stormont had not been happy about using the Agreement as a lever, but it would have opened the flood gates if her prosecution had been allowed to play out in a court of law. Her comfort letter had worked after all. Everyone agreed that it was the best outcome. Her part in this was to tender her resignation from the party and announce her retirement. People would assume that she was going because of Colm, and that served her purposes too. It would give her the time she needed to generate grassroots support to get the ball rolling once more.

This time she would be directing the attacks, not carrying them out. She engaged the key in the lock and turned it, there was a satisfying clunk as it opened. It seemed like an age since she'd been home. A night in her own bed would do her a world of good, she would begin planning first thing tomorrow morning.

She stepped into the hall and threw her bag on the floor by the coat stand, kicking the door shut behind her. Making her way into the kitchen she switched on the lights. The LED strips that ran under the wall cupboards threw pools of illumination onto the countertops. She decided that she should toast her big brother who had always had her back. She reached up into the cupboard and from the back of the shelf, retrieved a bottle of Bushmills 10-year-old single malt that she kept for the odd occasion when he called around. It wasn't really falling off the wagon, it was remembering him and everything he had done for her. She set it down, but as she was reaching for a glass she froze.

The distinct metallic click of a gun's safety catch being released was unmistakable. Sinead turned her head slowly to see an elderly man pointing an Obsidian 45 at her. The classic silencer extending the barrel of a nameless gun. It really didn't matter what it was, at this distance, even if he was a poor shot, it would be fatal.

"Don't move."

"I wasn't about to. Who the feck are you? We have never met so I assume someone sent you?"

"A ghost sent me."

"An English accent, so you're here to settle an old score I would guess?"

"You would be right. Please keep your hands away from the drawer, where I can see them."

She pulled her hand away from the unit.

"Which ghost? There are so many."

"You should remember this one, he was a 24-year-old hero who never got to meet his youngest child because you shot him in the back. His name was Corporal David Cooper, and he was posthumously awarded the Conspicuous Gallantry Cross in 1993."

A flash of fear crossed her face.

"The FRU plant? For God's sake, that was decades ago. There was no proof it was me." She watched as the gun's muzzle came up a fraction in line with her heart. "Please, don't do this." Panic entering her voice.

"Is that what he said to you as you tortured him?" The old man's voice was steady, like his hand.
"No... please, we were at war, but that's all over now. I didn't have a choice. What good would it do to kill me?"

"Violence is always a choice, besides, this will be revenge for an honest soldier whose boots you were never fit to clean. He was defending the innocent people you were killing, and you shot him, cowardly bitch that you are."

"We were at war, there were no innocents. He was about to serve us up on a platter, I had to stop him."

She took a step forward and he shot twice, once to the heart and once through the head.

Sinead Devey was dead before she hit the ground.

The old commanding officer slipped a black backgammon chip into the pocket of her crumpled jacket that was already rapidly changing colour.

"I'm sorry that took me so long Coop. Now we can both rest in peace." He closed the front door quietly behind him and walked away into the Belfast night.

ABOUT WENDY CHARLTON

Wendy Charlton was born in Walsall in the West Midlands at the start of the "Swinging Sixties". She describes her childhood as "happy and carefree" and spent most of it exploring books, spending hours in the local library.

She has enjoyed a broad and varied career in the public and private sectors coaching leaders to develop their teams and their businesses. The Personality Profiling aspect of her work has given her unique insights into what motivates and drives people to behave as they do.

Now, Wendy has swapped her "proper job" for one of author and novelist. Working from her home in a beautiful part of rural Staffordshire, she is finally able to pursue her passion for writing. **Hidden Secrets** is her second gripping novel featuring the unlikely duo of ex-Secret Agent **Daniel Grant** and civil servant **Hilary Geddes**

Wendy is currently working on the third novel in the "Secrets Trilogy', State Secrets.

Set deep in the world of espionage, murder and intrigue, State Secrets is sure to grab you by the collar and drag you kicking and screaming to its gripping conclusion.

State Secrets is expected to be available to buy in the 4th quarter of 2023.

To find out more about the world of 'Secrets', receive newsletter updates, enter competitions, buy exclusive merchandising, visit www.wendycharlton.co.uk

Printed in Great Britain
by Amazon

21159068R10253